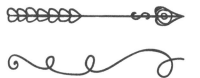

Books by Alina

The Holbrook Cousins
 The Successor
 The Screw-up
 The Scion

The Frost Brothers
 Eating Her Christmas Cookies
 Tasting Her Christmas Cookies

The Svensson Brothers
 After His Peonies
 In Her Candy Jar
 On His Paintbrush
 In Her Pumpkin Patch

Check my website for the latest news:

http://alinajacobs.com/books.html

ON HIS

Paint Brush

A ROMANTIC COMEDY

ON HIS

Paint Brush

ALINA JACOBS

Summary: My career as an artist is a joke. I'm desperately trying to live the #bossbabe life after I couldn't hack it as an artist in New York City and moved back to my small hometown. But hey, suffering is inspirational, right? But then so is Archer. With his model good looks and muscular, tattooed chest, Archer might be the creative, maybe even crazy, idea that I desperately need to save my disaster of a life.

To the next door neighbors who refuse to keep their giant Doberman from barking...it's a miracle I was able to finish this book.

I paint my own reality.

—Frida Kahlo

CHAPTER 1

Hazel

The desire to create is supposed to be the deepest yearning of the human soul. At least that was what one of my professors at my horrifyingly expensive private arts college would tell us. His name was Gustav, and he was from the Netherlands. Gustav also spent most of the class time that we were paying thousands of dollars for screaming at his agent on the phone about why his paintings weren't selling.

I think that might have been when I started to give up on art, if I'm being honest. Unfortunately, back then I ignored the little voice in my head that said, *Switch to accounting. You would do well in accounting.*

No, I told that voice, *I want to be a cool artist.* I had grand visions of owning a chic studio in Brooklyn with all-white walls and glass garage doors. A billionaire art investor would walk in, see my paintings, and buy every single one. It would catapult me into the art-world stratosphere, making me the next Fang Fei. I would be asked to sit on the Art Zurich board. I would travel around, giving talks. My paintings would fetch millions of dollars at auction…

The dream never materialized after I graduated. Did I then listen to the voice in my head telling me to go get a job, for the love of God, *any job*? No. No I did not. For the next three years, I scraped around in New York City. Instead of getting a chic art studio, I interned for free at snooty galleries and worked nights as a chef for pop-up restaurants. I sublet an illegal apartment that was really a windowless walk-in closet. My roommate was a guy named Melvin who had moved to New York City to live his best gay life. That included bringing random men home to the closet. Ironic right? Melvin seemed to think so. He would remind me of this fact loudly at three in the morning. Every. Single. Time. Sometimes this revelation would be accompanied by Melvin and his hookup *du nuit* singing that Alanis Morissette song drunkenly off-key.

My life post art college was sad and lonely. The only *Sex in the City* I got was whatever I experienced vicariously through Melvin. My unpaid internships did nothing to put a dent in the massive student loans I had racked up. I had to face the cold hard truth that, though I may love art, it did not love me back. All it did was make me poor and miserable. So I packed up my paintbrushes and said goodbye to the closet. By that point I was living in it all by myself. Melvin had found a rich guy, adopted a bunch of kids, and moved to Seattle. Meanwhile, I was fast approaching thirty and had nothing to show for myself.

In a delusional fit of third-time's-the-charm, I took out even more debt and bought a historic building on Main Street in my small hometown of Harrogate. I had grand visions, (anyone see a pattern here???) of turning it into the hip Art Café where there would be painting, themed alcoholic drinks, and tasty food. I had the restaurant background and the art background. How could it possibly go wrong?

"*Where did it all go wrong*?" I wailed to my friend Jemma. We were sitting in the Art Café. We were the only ones there. This was a usual occurrence and the reason I had a minor panic attack every time the mail carrier showed up with a stack of late notices. "Why did I buy this building?"

Jemma sipped on her Michelangelo mojito. "It was so cheap! You're lucky you bought it before the Svenssons snapped it up."

"It's not cheap enough to pay the mortgage." I set down my paintbrush and picked at the bowl of Jackson Pollock popcorn. It had truffle butter and parmesan on it. Usually it was one of my favorite snacks I made at the café, but not tonight.

"It was busy yesterday," Jemma consoled me.

"Because Ida brought all of the seniors over after bingo night," I said, wiping my hands then adding touches of light-green oil paint to the eyes of a baby in a vegetable patch I was painting for an Etsy commission.

"Maybe you could cater more toward that demographic," Jemma suggested, grabbing a handful of popcorn.

"I already have the art retreat," I complained. "If I start hosting canasta evening, this place is basically going to be an old folks' home."

"Hey, if they pay!" Jemma said with a laugh.

"I should have quit a long time ago and found a real job," I said. I looked around at my artwork that hung on the café walls. "I know I'm supposed to suffer for my art, but when does it end?"

Jemma gestured to one of the paintings. Instead of the avant-garde paintings we were trained to make in art school, I now made what I considered to be inspiration porn. Paintings of shoes, purses, and women in suits and high heels with quotes like, *I know I changed, darling. That was the point!* and *Slip on the Louboutins and get dat money!* I desperately wanted to be the next It artist, like Fang Fei, and sell my paintings for millions. Instead I was lucky to make a hundred fifty dollars off a painting.

"Your sister could find you a job in the city government," Jemma said.

"Then I'd have to move back home. I'm on the wrong side of twenty-five. I cannot move back into my childhood bedroom."

"You might win that Art Zurich grant," Jemma said, trying to fish a piece of booze-soaked watermelon out of her drink.

"I only win it if Harrogate wins the Art Zurich Biennial Expo," I reminded her. "And to make this place into an international art city would cost more money than what the Harrogate Trust budgeted."

I looked up at the inspiration porn painting in front of me. It was the biggest painting in the café, and the colorful pink-and-gold swirls taunted me with the thought that I simply wasn't trying hard enough.

"Wasn't Fang Fei discovered by a billionaire?" Jemma asked, taking another handful of popcorn.

"She was lucky," I grumbled.

"On the off chance that a famous art investor walks in and discovers you, you should at least put up some of your nicer paintings," Jemma said.

"Collages are very much the style right now," I sniffed. "Fang Fei just sold one similar to this for three million dollars."

"Really?" Jemma asked skeptically. "Fang Fei sold a painting that said, 'May your day be as flawless as your makeup' in pink curly letters over a selection of vintage advertisements?"

"Well, not exactly, but motivational artwork is very popular. I've sold two of these paintings in the last month. Also I get Instagram likes off of it."

"Instagram likes don't pay bills," Jemma said.

"Don't remind me. I had to block the phone calls from the bank."

"At least reglaze that one. I think it's flaking bits of newspaper. You don't want the health department in here," Jemma said, munching more popcorn.

"Fine," I grumbled. "I'm just over here trying to move the art world forward."

Jemma snickered. "You don't even like those paintings. Why don't you put up the cute one of the chunky raccoon?"

"Don't underestimate the power of coffee and a girl with a dream," I quipped, gesturing toward the painting that displayed the quote.

"You don't even drink coffee," Jemma reminded me.

"Don't walk all over my dreams. A billionaire art investor could walk in here right now and see the genius behind this painting of a baby in a vegetable patch," I said, gesturing dramatically to the almost-completed canvas.

"'I treat myself to French manicures because, when I snap my fingers, things happen,'" I quoted.

"Your fingernails are covered in paint," Jemma said, laughing.

"You don't know. I could be famous," I retorted, snapping my fingers. "Just like that!"

The door slammed open, cracking against the opposite wall. Jemma and I screamed and clung to each other.

The warm summer air blew in, followed by a man—a very attractive man. I gaped at him. Tattoos traced up his forearms and around his collar and disappeared into the dress shirt that was unbuttoned one button too many to count as professional. He had expensive-looking sunglasses pushed up on his head. Normally I would consider a guy who wore sunglasses at night to be a grade-A douche, but I would allow the infraction to pass this time.

He tilted his head slightly, and Jemma and I swooned.

"Hazel, I think you have a customer," Jemma whispered after a moment.

"Hi," I said breathlessly. Then I cleared my throat. I couldn't be the groupie of a guy I hadn't even seen before. He was just so attractive. His blond hair had this artfully messy style and hung a little in his face.

"Are you open?" the man asked after a minute of enduring our staring.

"I am very open, wide open; you might say, Spread open. I mean—" I coughed, the nervous sweat starting to bead on my skin. "Yes, my shop is peddling wares."

Jemma threw her straw at me.

"Would you like me to drink? I mean, would you like me to make you a drink?" My voice cracked. I always got tongue-tied around attractive men. Actually, tongue-tied was a generous understatement. I got awkward, weird, and frankly downright creepy around attractive men.

Get it together, Hazel. You're a small business owner—for a little while longer at least.

"I'll drink you, if you're offering," Sexy Sunglasses Man said. He didn't wink or anything, just stared at me like I was on the menu. I blushed from my chest to the roots of my hair. Trying to tell myself it was the summer heat, I ran to the bar.

"We have Monet martinis, Old Fashioned Norman Rockwells," I said, rattling off the list of artist-inspired cocktails. The attractive man seemed confused until he realized I was going through all the cocktails along with their descriptions and ingredients.

"That's quite the cocktail list," he said and jerked his head slightly at the chalkboard menu.

"Right, ha ha! I guess you can read. Sometimes you can't tell with really attractive people if they even bothered to learn or not."

You're blowing it, Hazel.

Jemma choke-laughed into her drink at the table. The man's eyelids lowered slightly, and he made this sort of growl in the back of his throat. Gawd, his voice was so deep! It was like the *Starry Night* painting—I just wanted to fall into it.

"I'll take the Old Fashioned," he said.

"Of course. Would you like to snack on me? Sorry, would you like me to make you a snack?" I gave him a pained smile.

His eyes swept down my form then settled back on my face. "Maybe later."

"We have—" I started to rattle off the bar snack menu.

"I can read it," he said. He was slightly annoyed.

"Of course. You're not that attractive."

Jemma cut off a shriek of laughter.

"You don't think I'm attractive?" he asked, staring at me with intense gray eyes.

"I mean you're not stupid attractive. Just stupidly attractive," I amended. "Feel free to peruse the artwork while you wait." I even did finger guns. *Kill me.*

The hint of a smirk played around his stupidly attractive mouth as the man slowly walked around the small historic building. I didn't have much, okay *any*, money really to decorate. I had done what I could with paint and old furniture I refinished. Sweat dripped down my back as the well-dressed man slowly studied my artwork.

"See anything you like?" I chirped.

His gaze swung back toward me. "Maybe."

"If you don't, I can paint you," I offered then mentally kicked myself.

He looked at me. "Paint me? Like paint on me or paint a painting of me?"

There was a creepy answer and a less creepy answer. Guess which one I went with.

"Paint on you." His eyes widened ever so slightly. "That came out wrong. Whoops! Make a painting of you. I just— you have a proportional face. I didn't mean that as some sort of innuendo. That would be creepy, and besides, I couldn't paint *on* you. You're wearing too many clothes," I finished lamely.

Geez, Hazel, go right for the dial and turn the creep factor up to a hundred, why don't you? I tried to ignore him and hurried to measure out the ingredients for the drink.

"That's easily remedied," he said then turned back to the painting. It was the big collage that Jemma had been teasing me about earlier. I was acutely aware of him studying my artwork. Maybe Jemma was right and I should have hung up something a little more intellectual.

"This is the ugliest painting I've ever seen," the man declared.

I froze. Jemma looked wide-eyed between us.

"It's perfect," the man announced. "How much?"

"Wha—"

"How much for the painting?" he prodded. I gaped at him.

"A thousand dollars," Jemma answered.

"Sold," he said, walking back toward me.

"Seriously?" I sputtered and spilled some of the liquor. "Sorry," I muttered, searching for a rag. Sexy Sunglasses took the glass and slowly licked off the spilled droplets. I swallowed. He put down the drink.

"Nice cocktail," he all but purred.

"You too…"

He almost smiled. "Cock… tail?"

"What I meant was—" I swallowed. My throat was dry. "I'm sure it's very adequate."

"Adequate?"

I nodded then realized what I was doing and shook my head. "I'm sure it's the talk of the town."

"She takes credit cards," Jemma called out. Sweat dripped down under my boobs. I flapped my cropped T-shirt to try and get some air under there. His eyes followed the motion.

"Sorry, you're making me wet," I said then hastily corrected myself. "Like sweaty, not the other kind. That would be weird."

"It is getting a little hot in here," Sunglasses said.

"You're not that hot." I coughed and flapped the shirt.

"You said I was stupidly attractive."

"Obviously you are hot, but this room is not that hot… see I have a condition…"

"A condition," he repeated. "Like a medical condition?"

"Like a sexual condition!" Jemma called out. The man seemed confused yet amused as I floundered.

"You're not helping," I hissed at Jemma. I swallowed again. The sweat dripped down my scalp.

"It's not contagious. I just go a little weird around—" I swallowed again. "Stupidly attractive men." The last bit came out in a rasp. I took a sip of the drink I had just made for Sexy Sunglasses. "Crap. I'll make you another one."

He held up a hand to stop me. "So, attractive men make you wet? I mean sweat?"

Trying to avoid his gaze, I rang up the painting. Or tried anyway. My iPad wouldn't register the finger taps. I wiped my hands. "It's almost as if it doesn't want your business," I joked while silently threatening the iPad with a baseball bat in an empty field. "To think, this is supposed to be a quaint, historic town, and yet here I am, offering my nighttime services," I joked desperately as the app made a frantic beeping noise and told me it couldn't connect to the server.

"This is a brothel?" Sexy Sunglasses asked, confused.

"Lord no! This is an upstanding establishment! I was just trying and failing to be funny. I don't do *that* for payment. I just paint. That's my painting. It's a joke, ha ha." More finger guns. I could feel Jemma cringing. It was like those dreams where I was back in middle school and suddenly I didn't have any clothes on, except this guy was so attractive, I actually wished I sort of didn't have any clothes on.

"I know," he said and smiled. Then he took out a wad of cash and put it on the counter. "For the painting." He took the drink and downed the rest of it. "And that."

I counted the money. "I can't charge you for the drink. Let me get you your change." I knew I didn't have enough cash lying around to give him money back, and I prayed some would magically appear as I opened and shut the drawers on the bar.

"Keep it," Sexy Sunglasses said.

I mentally did the math. "It's a seventy-five-dollar tip."

"I like to support local business," he replied, taking the giant painting off the wall and hefting it easily with one arm. The muscles bulged under his shirt. "I like making art too. I'm a very talented finger painter, you know."

I made a squawk like a dying chicken.

He slipped on the sunglasses and looked over the top of them at me. Jemma shoved a handful of popcorn into her mouth.

"Actually, I think I will take that snack," Sexy Sunglasses said, looking right at me but reaching for the popcorn. "May I?"

"This is mine," Jemma said around the popcorn, holding the bowl to her chest. I grabbed the bowl from her, and we engaged in a brief tug-of-war.

"It's *mine*."

"You said you were on a diet, Jemma," I hissed.

"I lied."

"He paid a lot of money. Give me that popcorn." I wrenched it out of my friend's hands and shoved it at the man. "All yours! You even get the bowl! Come in me anytime! I mean, come back in to see me anytime!" My clothes were drenched in sweat.

The man paused and looked at me. Seeming like he decided something, he slid a black business card across the tabletop. "If you ever want to get creative in a way that doesn't involve selling a painting," he said in that atrociously deep voice, "call me. Ask for Donut Danish."

"I'd like to eat his donut Danish," Jemma muttered under her breath. I kicked her.

My friend and I waved furiously through the window as Sexy Sunglasses walked to a sleek sports car parked across the street. He didn't turn around, just drove off like it was the most normal thing in the world.

"Man," Jemma said a moment after we both managed to calm down. "You really blew that one. It was one for the record books. I was about to have a stroke from secondhand embarrassment."

I took her drink and downed the rest in one go.

"Blue-eyed devil walks into a bar," she said, eating a piece of spilled popcorn off the table.

"Gray," I said automatically. "His eyes are gray."

Jemma looked at me in bemusement. "You noticed."

"I'm a painter. I notice colors," I said, crossing my arms.

"Uh-huh. Well, he did say he was a good finger painter. Maybe you two should compare notes." She waved the black business card.

"I'm not going to call him!" I shrieked. "I can never see him again!"

Jemma left a little while later, and I set about cleaning the café and locking up for the night. Sexy Sunglasses's card was still on the counter. I looked at it. It only had a phone number printed in a shiny ink against the matte black. It was so pretentious it had to be a little tongue-in-cheek.

I'd like his tongue somewhere else...

"Shut up," I said out loud.

But the card beckoned me. I missed out on my true *Sex in the City* New York experience. Maybe I would channel my inner Melvin. Maybe I would call.

CHAPTER 2

I am a creature of the night. When other people are waking up, that's when I'm just going to bed. Work hard, play hard. Of course that lifestyle choice makes more sense for a single billionaire playboy out on the town in Manhattan. It doesn't work so well in a historic small town at the family estate complete with three dozen younger non-drinking-age little brothers.

I had barely fallen asleep when they woke me up. I'd like to say I was using my middle-of-the-night awake time productively. It wasn't like I didn't have work to do for my hotel conglomerate. I needed to come up with a game plan to make my conference center idea profitable and to get my older brother Greg off my case. But instead, all I could think about was the curvy painter in the cute crop top. I sat for hours in front of the painting I had just bought. It was insane—the glitter, the pink, the collage—but I kept studying it, taking in the small hidden sketches layered onto the vintage makeup advertisements accentuated by the subtle shading of pinks. It spoke to more depth than I would normally find in a craft-store inspirational painting.

I should know quality when I see it. I collect art. I put it in my hotels and use it as a secondary investment portfolio along with all the real estate I own. Still, this painting wasn't my normal style. I wasn't even sure why I bought it except that the café owner was so adorably cute in her paint-stained pants, her hair a big poofy ponytail.

She wasn't like any of the women I usually went for, and I went for a lot. My usual women were like photographs printed on canvas—all flash and no substance. Hazel was different.

Stop it, I told myself. I wasn't ready to admit that I was tired of the playboy life. Besides, I had ruined any chance of being with the café owner by simply giving her that card.

The door to my room rattled as several of my younger brothers banged their fists on it.

"Breakfast, Archer!"

"Don't you want breakfast? Josie's cooking."

I hauled myself out of bed and grabbed the bowl of popcorn that was on the nightstand. There were a few handfuls left, and it was just as good the next morning. I hadn't even bothered undressing before collapsing on the bed a few hours ago. Now I was starving.

"I can't say no if Josie's cooking," I said, swinging the bedroom door open. My brothers shrieked. Henry, the youngest, clung to my leg. I picked him up and swung him under my arm as we went down to the large kitchen in the estate house.

My identical twin brother, Mace, was already downstairs. Though we looked alike, he was my polar opposite.

His suit was neatly pressed, his hair combed back. He was concentrating on helping Josie, his girlfriend. She was formerly Mace's assistant. There had been a kerfuffle, and long story short, Josie now lived here.

She was also somehow in charge of making breakfast. Josie ran around the kitchen, hair flying. She knocked into a pan, and Mace caught it before it fell on the floor. I felt a pang of jealousy that I stuffed down. I was happy for my brother. I just couldn't believe that the perfect woman had dropped into his lap.

"Need help?" I asked Josie, setting Henry down.

"Yes," she said. She looked frazzled. Mace lovingly tucked one of the errant curls back in her bun. "But I'm the worst at organizing, and really what I need is a field marshal to get everyone in an assembly line. All the college kids are throwing me off."

My college-aged brothers were back home for summer break. They stood around the kitchen, tall, still a little gangly, and very, very hungry.

"It's double the amount of people," Josie continued.

"I know. This place is like a prison," I said.

Mace frowned at me. "It's nice to have everyone together. You should set a better example." He looked meaningfully at my rumpled appearance.

"I thought you were helping him lighten up," I said to Josie.

"Not right now. I have to go into Manhattan to help your brother, Liam, with his marketing plan. And I had food stockpiled." She glared lovingly at Eli, Tristan, and the rest of the cohort. "But they ate everything!" Josie said as she grabbed a large casserole pan out of the oven. My mouth watered. "It's already gone. All of it!"

I slowly took a bite of the popcorn.

"What are you eating?" Arlo asked, looking up at me with big eyes.

"You guys are like pigeons," I said as several of my younger brothers crowded around me.

"You made popcorn?" Mace asked disapprovingly as I chucked pieces of the snack at my little brothers.

"I got it from a bar."

"I thought you came to Harrogate to work, not go barhopping," an annoyed voice said behind me. There was Greg, the ever-present look of general disapproval affixed firmly to his face. He was followed by Mike, my business partner at Greyson Hotel Group.

"I need to hire someone to play villain music every time Greg walks into a room," I said. "You want a job, Henry?"

"I want a job," Eli said. "You should hire me and Tristan. We're almost done with college."

"Um, no. I'm not a babysitter."

Mace frowned. "I'm taking in several of our younger brothers as interns at Svensson PharmaTech. You need to take a few of them on at Greyson Hotel Group. Family should support each other."

"And look how well that worked with Adrian," I scoffed. Adrian glared at me. "Did you ever get the money back?"

"He made a mistake," Mace insisted.

I snorted.

"You were a mistake," Adrian shot back at me. "Mace should have eaten you in the womb."

"Gross."

Greg turned to Hunter, my older brother, who was handing carafes of coffee to the kids to take into the dining room. "Is this what you allow to go on over here? This place is a zoo."

"Right? I can't believe how disorganized this place is," I said to Greg, knowing it would rile up Hunter. I enjoyed irritating Greg. Sometimes when I felt like really flying close to the edge, I would try and set him and Hunter against each other. Bonus points if I could set Mace off as well and let the three of them spiral into chaos. I snickered to myself. They should call me Loki.

"Maybe if you did more than breeze in here, throw your weight around, and then leave," Hunter growled.

"Are you going to let him talk to you like that, Greg?" I asked, hugging the popcorn bowl to my chest in mock shock.

My older brother's eyes narrowed. "This type of behavior is not inspiring me to invest in your conference center."

"You were supposed to butter him up," I complained to Mike. "You know, make a really nice spreadsheet and show him how much money we're going to make."

"I'm not even sure Harrogate can physically hold a conference of the size you're talking about," Mike said, rolling up his sleeves. "The old Mast Brothers' chocolate factory is huge, yes, but we need hotel space, and the city of Harrogate will not allow us to demolish any of the existing historic brick buildings to build hotels."

"We have enough space. Svensson Investment owns all that land in Harrogate," I said as Mike cut up fruit.

"I will not allow you to build hotels on every single parcel I own," Greg said, setting down his briefcase and jacket on a stool.

"There's the strip mall next door. Buy that," Hunter said.

"We need to talk to the city about it," Mike warned. "I think they own it with the Mast Brothers' chocolate factory site. They may not want to sell it."

"The bigger issue," Hunter said, "is that you don't even have a marketing plan to attract conferences large enough to justify such a large complex of exhibition halls. You need to bring tens of thousands of people here several times a month to make a profit."

"We're like two hours outside of New York City. By car, it takes about as long to drive here for a conference as it does to sit in traffic going into Manhattan," I scoffed. "Besides, I'll pay Josie to do a killer marketing campaign."

"My plate is full," Josie said as she slid another breakfast casserole out of the oven. She motioned to me, and I tossed a piece of popcorn at her. She caught it in her mouth. "That's pretty good."

"It's Jackson Pollock popcorn," I said. Greg looked at me in disgust.

"You know what you could do?" Josie said thoughtfully. "The Harrogate Trust has an art and beautification committee. A few of the girls on the committee are trying to convince the Art Zurich Biennial Expo to choose Harrogate for their big exhibition in a couple years. The Art Zurich Biennial is like the Olympics but for art. There are grants associated with it, and the convention is enormous. But to win the host spot, Harrogate has to show we can handle such a large influx of people. There're a couple more spots on the committee. Maybe you could join up."

"I'm not really a committee person," I said. "I'm a lone wolf."

"Well then, it sounds like you're not really a conference person because that's the only solid plan anyone has put forth for how this conference center isn't going to be an abject failure," Greg snapped.

"You like art. You collect it," Mace cajoled.

I groaned dramatically.

"You need to prove to us Harrogate has a market for large conferences," Hunter warned, "if you want Svensson Investment to give you money for the real estate deal."

Mike looked at Josie. "Do you think Harrogate can win?"

Josie smiled at me. "If Archer's there helping give the entry some pizzazz, I think we might have a good shot. Meetings are at nine in the morning. You should be able to make the one today."

I sighed. "I guess I'll go. I just don't want to get wrapped up in small-town politics."

"Harrogate isn't that small," Mace said. "Besides, it's not the size that counts. It's how you use it." He smirked at Josie.

"Not that anything about you is small," she said, her mouth quirking slightly.

"There are children present, Mace!" I said, clapping my hands dramatically over Henry's ears. He was too interested in the food waiting on the counter to notice.

Josie waved oven mitts at Greg and Hunter and motioned them to each grab a casserole and take it to the dining room.

"Before we worry about the Art Zurich expo," Greg said, "we need to buy the land. The meeting with the city about the factory site is in a couple of days. There won't even be a conference center if Archer blows it."

"I've done hundreds of these types of presentations!" I countered, taking the platter of fruit. "I'm the master of sales pitches."

Greg's phone rang, interrupting my speech. I adjusted the fruit platter, and I helpfully pulled the phone out of his briefcase and glanced at the number.

"It's a Harrogate area code," I told my half brother.

"Put it on speaker. I've been trying to get people to give me more information about the strip mall site since apparently I have to do your work for you now," he said as I followed him into the large dining room. My older brother Remy was already in there, setting out utensils and stacks of plates.

"Hello," Greg called in my direction while he slid the casserole onto the long buffet.

The phone was staticky for a moment, then a woman's voice came on. I recognized her as Hazel, the cute Art Café owner. I tried to keep my expression neutral.

"Hello? I—this is awkward," Hazel said.

"Your name is awkward?" Greg asked, eyes narrowing.

"No, it's Hazel. Uh, you left your card last night?" Mike chortled and clapped a hand over his mouth as Greg took off the oven mitts.

"I'm sorry. Who did you want to speak to?" Greg asked, voice flat. I clapped a hand over my mouth to stop the snickers.

"Um, I'm calling for Donut Danish? Is that you?"

I silently choked on my laughter as a scowl formed on Greg's face.

"This is a private line. I don't appreciate you prank calling me," Greg said in a clipped tone, taking the phone from me.

"I didn't!" she cried. "I mean, you told me to call you last night."

"I wasn't with anyone last night," Greg snarled. "Let me guess. Someone with messy hair, terrible taste, too much money, and not enough sense gave that card to you?"

"Yeah…"

"Well, that would be yet another ill-advised prank by my younger brother Archer, who is childish, immature, and a stain on the Svensson name." Greg glared at me. I rolled my eyes.

"I'm really sorry," Hazel said in a small voice that made me feel ever so slightly guilty.

"Do not call this number anymore." Greg hung up.

Mace glared at me. "You're terrible."

"It was hilarious!" I said, laughing.

"You can't just give out my number, Archer," Greg warned. "You're already on thin ice."

"Greg, lighten up! I'm about to make you even more billions with this conference center."

"We can't even be certain you're going to be able to purchase the property."

"Of course I'm going to!" I said. "Harrington Investment doesn't have the vision I do. Besides, Mayor Barry likes us. He'll be at the pitch meeting."

Hunter didn't look convinced. "I just wish Josie had been able to work on this pitch."

"I am really tapped out," Josie said, coming into the dining room and slumping down in a chair.

"Of course, dear future sister-in-law," I said, cutting a huge piece of the sausage, egg, and cheddar cheese casserole, placing it on a plate along with some fruit, and handing it to her.

Josie demurred, "Mace hasn't proposed."

"He needs to," I said, dishing up more pieces for the kids who lined up. "You're living in his house, taking care of these heathens. You have him by the balls. If you left, this place would descend into chaos in a matter of hours."

"On the vein of not falling into chaos, Otis and Theo are participating in a summer art camp they found," Mace informed me.

"It's for our business," Otis said excitedly as he and Theo dug into their food. "We're selling T-shirts online."

"Because that's not sketchy," I said. "Is that even legal?"

"I helped them set up a corporation," Hunter said, scooping fruit onto each of the kids' plates who he felt weren't eating enough plant matter. "If you don't want to be useful, you can go back to Manhattan and stop wasting space."

"Fine. I will be soccer mom this afternoon."

"We'll get you a minivan," Mike said with a smirk.

"The billionaire playboy gets domesticated," Josie said with a grin.

Greg scowled. "He's not that domesticated if he's orchestrating prank calls like a child."

CHAPTER 3

Hazel

threw down the phone as soon as I ended the call. Then I screamed, "Oh my God!"

When I decided to call that morning, I was assuming Sexy Sunglasses, or rather, Archer, I guess his name was, wouldn't be awake. He didn't seem like the early-riser type. I was certain I would just leave a voicemail. I had even written out what I was going to say. But when his brother answered the phone, my script completely flew out the window.

I had been so humiliated. Then I was furious. How dare Archer play a joke on me? Stupidly attractive, huh. Actually he was just another stupid idea, just like my art education, just like the Art Café, and just like this Hail Mary grant I was hoping to win from the Art Zurich Biennial Expo.

I took a deep breath and tried to channel my inner boss babe as I grabbed a broom and went out into the early morning to sweep the sidewalk in front of my café.

"'I am an entrepreneur doing big things. These are four-inch stilettos, so don't even waste your time trying to bring me down,'" I quoted. But I wasn't wearing any stilettos, just my red slip-on Toms.

I looked down at my scuffed-up shoes. It was another reminder of the disconnect between who I wanted to be and who I actually was.

"I want pancakes. Raspberry dark chocolate soufflé pancakes," I yelled out to the empty street. One of the problems with having a failing café was that I ended up eating all the leftover food. And there was a lot.

"Don't make pancakes. Don't stress eat." I looked down at my white overalls. Slouchy artist had become my signature look since opening the café. Not because of any real conscious decision, but because I couldn't really fit into my other nicer clothes.

For a few weeks when I first opened, I had tried to serve breakfast, but I never attracted enough customers. I looked over at the brick building next to mine. A sign on the front said, *Grey Dove Bistro, Coming Soon!*

That was the other reason why I knew I was in the death throes of a failing business. Chloe Barnard, popular contestant on *The Great Christmas Bake-Off* and dessert-maker extraordinaire, was putting a franchise in Harrogate. And of course it was going right next to my business. Talk about a real boss babe. She was building an empire of cool restaurants. Her Instagram game was on point. She had a gorgeous billionaire boyfriend, Jack Frost, and an impeccably decorated penthouse.

When the Grey Dove Bistro opened, no one would ever come to my little café. I slumped down on the stoop.

The train from Svensson PharmaTech rumbled down the street. It was another quirk of Harrogate that I loved, the freight train that rumbled down Main Street several times a week. I waved to the train conductor, and he blew the horn. I sighed as he passed. I would miss that if I lost my café.

What I wouldn't miss were the several idiots who had taken to racing their motorcycles down the street in the middle of the night. I had to wake up early to make the sandwiches that Ida sold at her general store. On top of the humiliation from Archer's practical joke, I had a headache from lack of sleep.

"Did you call him?" Jemma called, walking down the street toward me.

"Keep your voice down," I hissed and pulled her inside the café. "I did call," I said.

"You did?" she squealed then added, "But it's early. He might have still been asleep."

"That was the plan," I replied, going to the large fridge to take out the deli meats, cheeses, and locally sourced vegetables to make the sandwiches for Ida. Jemma washed her hands and put on an apron. "But it was a joke," I continued, angrily slapping the loaves of bread onto the counter.

"What?" Jemma exclaimed as she started slicing tomatoes.

"He gave me the number to his mean older brother, and let me tell you, he was not amused I called him Donut Danish."

Jemma started laughing and almost dropped her knife. "You didn't!"

"Now I'm going to have to listen to my sister give me a lecture about not trusting Svenssons."

"At least he bought a painting!"

"He came in here like he owned the place," I grumbled. "He's just like those horrible art collectors in Manhattan."

"Money is money."

"I'd rather not take his money," I said. "Especially if Archer's just going to use it as an excuse to be a douche."

"We should have known," Jemma said. "Who wears sunglasses at night, right?"

"At least I have Ida as one nice customer."

"Ida said she wants as many sandwiches as you can make," Jemma told me as I smeared various fancy aiolis on the slices of bread. "Apparently a lot of people from Svensson Investment are coming into her shop to buy them. They like the cute names and the Instagram-worthy labels."

"Ida is so sweet."

"Olivia says Ida's driving her crazy. She said she's heard way too much about her grandmother's sexcapades."

I laughed, some of the tension easing out of my back.

Jemma and I spent the next few hours finishing the sandwiches.

When they were done, I wrapped each in brown butcher paper and tied them with baker's twine. The cardstock tags that were tied onto each tasty package were letterpressed with a watercolor design of that particular sandwich and a quirky but inspirational quote.

Then Jemma and I loaded the boxes of sandwiches into my bike trailer and hauled them to Ida's General Store. I huffed as I pushed my bike, dragging the heavy cart behind it. I wiped the sweat out of my eyes. It wasn't even nine in the morning, and it was already boiling.

"Hey, look!" Jemma said as we turned on a side street. "That building's done. They have all the paper out of the windows." We stopped to peek inside.

As I looked through the windows, my heart sank. "It's a gallery."

"It's not as nice as yours," Jemma said as we peered inside. Except I knew she was lying. It was a beautifully decorated gallery with gorgeous art.

"What am I going to do?" I moaned. "This is turning into one of the worst days of my life." A woman came out of the back room.

"I think she sees us," Jemma said and started to pull me away.

I knew she did. The tall, waifish woman with the perfectly straight blond hair sneered when she recognized me. There was a real boss babe, in her designer clothes and mile-high stilettoes. She even walked like she ate men for lunch.

"McKenna?" I asked when she opened the door. "What are you doing in Harrogate?"

My nemesis from art school stood framed in the doorway, hand on her hip, towering over me. She had made art school miserable by sabotaging my work, making hurtful comments about anything I produced, and spreading rumors about me. When I moved home, tail between my legs, ego stinging from the failure of not making it in the New York City art scene, my only consolation was that I would never have to see McKenna again.

Yet here she was. Scratch what I said before—this was *the worst* day of my life.

"If it isn't Hazel." McKenna flipped her glossy hair.

"Why aren't you in Manhattan? Why do you have to be here?"

She inspected her perfectly manicured nails and smirked. "Harrogate is a happening place. There are lots of people with money from Svensson PharmaTech here."

"Oh, of course, we should have known—you're here for a Svensson billionaire," Jemma shot at McKenna. My friend had been there through the years when McKenna's nasty comments had caused me to call Jemma, crying, from the bathroom.

"Unfortunately the Svenssons here are a little out of your league," my friend continued. "They like women with souls, not plastic harpies."

McKenna looked down her perfect nose at Jemma.

"Billionaires like the Svenssons want women they can show off at parties, not ones who serve the food at the parties." She looked pointedly at the cart of sandwiches. "Are you a caterer now, Hazel?"

"She owns a café," Jemma said. "And it's very successful!"

That was an oversell, but hey, thanks for sticking up for me, Jemma.

"Do you?" McKenna sneered and looked me up and down from the top of my frizzy ponytail to the rolled-up hems of my white overalls that were admittedly a little snug on the boob and hip areas. "You do know you're supposed to sell the food, not eat all of it?" With that she swept back inside the gallery.

Feeling dejected, I pushed the cart after Jemma.

"Don't worry. The Art Café is so much better than her little gallery," Jemma assured me.

"Except it's not," I said sadly. I had done what I could with the café, but my real vision was exactly what McKenna had done to her gallery. I wanted those pristine white walls, the impeccably restored stamped-tin ceiling, the terrazzo floor, the minimalist paintings like bright spots of lipstick on an attractive man's shirt collar.

Stop. You are not thinking about Archer.

"I know what you're thinking," Jemma said.

"I'm not thinking about Archer!" I shrieked.

"Whoa, that was not where I was going," Jemma said, "but good to see your libido hasn't completely shriveled up and crawled into a ditch to die. I was just saying you have to put McKenna out of your head. Haters are the reminder that you're doing something right."

I tried to relax and only channel positive energy into the universe when Jemma and I rolled the cart into Ida's General Store. Ida hustled over and hugged us.

"My favorite artist and my favorite shop girl!"

"We have sandwiches."

"They're so cute!" Ida said. "Look at how pretty you wrap them."

"It's the same as always," I said.

"But they look amazing. You're so talented and creative!" Ida said. The older woman was like a cool grandmother, and she always pumped up my spirits. "Stand in front of the display," Ida said, pulling out her phone. "I want a picture. I've got an Instagram account, you know. Josie helped me set it up. I have to post every day. It helps give the general store that personal touch. I have two hundred followers!"

I posed awkwardly in front of the sandwich display and made a peace sign.

"Smile and stick those tatas out! Be proud of what you got!" Ida exclaimed as she snapped the picture.

"All these creative little labels are really putting me in the mood for the art retreat this afternoon," Ida said excitedly as she took close-up shots of the sandwiches. "All the girls are. I told Dottie you were going to have live nude painting."

"That's not the kind of art retreat we're having," I said, blushing as my thoughts took a hard right to Archer. *No, brain. Bad brain.*

I stuffed down thoughts of Archer posing nude. I didn't even like him. He was a terrible person, and having him nude in my café would be a terrible idea.

"Something to consider," Ida said. "Stay for a drink? Art's been making mead."

"Jemma and I have the art committee meeting," I said. I didn't understand how Ida could want alcohol this early in the morning.

"Make me proud!" Ida called after us as we walked as quickly as we could in the heat to city hall.

"I hope this isn't going to take too long," I said to Olivia when Jemma and I met her in front of the ornate city hall building. Inside was a gorgeous mural of Harrogate in the early eighteen hundreds, when it was first founded. That was really the type of art I liked though it would have me tossed out of the art world. Real artists weren't supposed to like, let alone create, paintings that looked like photos. But that was my style.

"So I saw something weird today," Olivia said as we went upstairs to one of the conference rooms.

"Was it McKenna?" Jemma asked.

"Yes! Isn't that the stuck-up snooty girl who was mean to you in college, Hazel?" Olivia asked. "Why is she here? I thought her family was rich. Harrogate seems a little on the small side for her. What's she up to? I don't trust her."

"Maybe she's here to stalk me," I joked.

"I think she's here to stalk Archer," Jemma said, holding out her phone. There was a picture of McKenna in a dress that looked like it cost more than I'd made in my entire career as a painter. Standing next to her was Archer, handsome in his tux. I felt a little nauseous.

"She would be exactly the type of girl guys like Archer go for," I said irritably.

"Let them have each other," Olivia said. "They're two horrible people who deserve to make each other miserable."

"Archer has terrible taste."

"He bought one of your paintings."

"It was probably a joke like the phone call." Promising myself I would never have to see him again, I said, "Let's get this over with. I have to be at the café at eleven a.m. to start setting up for the lunch trickle."

"You always sell out of sandwiches at the general store at least," Jemma said helpfully.

"Maybe Ida's Instagram post will make more people come. But probably not," I said as I pushed through the tall wooden door into the ornate conference room that looked out over the town square.

I stopped in the doorway, and Jemma slammed into me.

"Move," Jemma said.

But I couldn't. There, sitting at the table, was Archer.

CHAPTER 4

had had very little sleep the night before, and I was dragging. I was hoping to nap out in the sunshine on the terrace while the kids played. But I knew Greg was right, as much as I hated to admit it. If I could score the Art Zurich Biennial Expo, that would put my conference center on the map. It would be wildly successful.

I was still daydreaming about how awesome my conference center was going to be when I sat in one of the large leather chairs in the conference room that looked out over the town square. Josie had to go to Manhattan, and I wondered just how organized this art committee was going to be. I bet it was a pack of senior citizens who thought a couple of high-school-level murals were enough to make Harrogate attractive to the Art Zurich crowd.

I yawned and then almost choked when the door opened and a familiar poofy-haired brunette walked in. She saw me, and I resisted the urge to clap a hand over my balls. The look Hazel gave me said she would gladly remove them for me.

"What a pleasant surprise," I said, turning on the charm.

"You mean unpleasant," Hazel replied. "How dare you show up in my committee meeting?"

"Your committee meeting? Josie said I was going to be running this."

"No, she didn't," Hazel sputtered.

I laughed. "Relax. I'm not trying to steal your committee. I'm here to offer my much-needed expertise."

"Expertise in what, being a jerk?"

"It was just a joke," I told her. "Anyways, you were the one who offered your nighttime services."

"That was a *joke*," Hazel shrieked.

"See?" I said. "We both do sexual things we regret."

"I didn't do anything sexual with you."

"You said I made you wet."

"You made me sweaty."

"Got her all sweaty," I said to her friends, who each had a hand over their mouths, I supposed to keep from laughing or screaming.

"It's not like your phone sex doesn't leave a lot to be desired," I told Hazel.

"You heard that?" she asked, horrified.

"You called a random stranger and gave him phone sex?" Jemma asked her friend in confusion.

"Not just a stranger, my half brother," I said.

"I didn't do that. He's lying! I just introduced myself and asked for you by the dumb nickname you gave because you can't say your name like a normal person." Hazel's cheeks were flushed, and tendrils of her curly hair had escaped from the ponytail to frame her face.

"Greg's face when you called him Donut Danish." I started snickering, which made her even madder. "I can't." I wiped away a tear in an exaggerated gesture. "It was priceless. Really worth not getting any sleep."

"Get out," Hazel said flatly.

"No," I said, leaning back in my chair. I thought I saw her eyes flick to the tattoo on my chest right under my collarbone. "I need us to win this Art Zurich Expo. And we need to do a better showing than the giant vegetable exhibition or the butter-carving contest."

"If you're trying to insult my Etsy painting—"

I held up a hand and choked down a laugh. "I wouldn't dare. That painting of the naked baby in the squash bucket was a masterpiece. The way you captured the look in his eyes, like he just had a premonition of the apocalypse, was masterful."

"Stop mocking me."

"I'm not mocking," I said, standing up. "I am a gentleman and an art scholar, which is why I really need to be on this committee. See, you don't understand—that man you called and harassed this morning?"

"That was you!" she shrieked.

"Hazel, honestly. Greg won't pay for the Mast Brothers' chocolate factory site unless we win this expo."

"You don't know the first thing about art," Hazel huffed. Her friends looked back and forth between us.

"I know *everything* about art. My hotels are filled with art. That's one of the things Greyson Hotel Group gets high reviews for. You know Fang Fei?"

Hazel nodded uncertainly.

"I made her. I saw her work, bought up every piece of it, and spun a narrative about how she was the next big thing. Boom, all her paintings are worth millions now."

Hazel's eyes widened slightly.

"Everything I touch turns to gold, and I'm about to do it with Harrogate."

"We don't need your help," Hazel said defiantly.

"Oh, I think you do." I fussed with my collar, exposing more of the tattoos she seemed so entranced by, and watched with satisfaction as her eyes followed the gesture, went down, then flicked back up to my face.

"I can offer money and expertise, and as soon as I have the Mast Brothers' chocolate factory under option, we can have a huge fancy gala there. You have to have a fancy gala with art people. You know that. We'll even buy all of you, since you're on the committee, very nice dresses."

"Fancy ones?" Jemma asked.

"Very fancy," I assured her. "Couture."

"Jemma, have some integrity," Hazel hissed.

"Speak for yourself," her friend snorted. "Dude wants to buy me a fancy designer dress, I'm taking it. You can show up to the gala in overalls and no bra, but I won't."

"You're not wearing a bra?" I blurted before I could kill the words.

Hazel looked at me in shock.

Well, shit, there goes my conference center.

Then her eyes narrowed, and she unhooked the buckle of her overalls and pulled her shirt down to show me the lace bra she was wearing. If I didn't know any better, I thought I saw the barest pink crescent of nipple before she released the collar of the springy shirt.

Now I was the one to be awkward and tongue-tied.

"I can't believe you just flashed a strange man," Hazel's other friend shouted.

"People in the subway do it all the time, Olivia," Hazel remarked.

"No one should be flashing you in the subway," I growled.

"I don't need you to look after me," Hazel reprimanded, "and we don't need your help in Harrogate. Harrogate is already great." Hazel glared at me. "We can win the Art Zurich Expo without you."

I looked at her. I was starting to see what the deal was.

"Possibly," I said slowly. "But can *you* win without me?"

Hazel looked slightly guilty.

"I know exactly why you want Harrogate to win the biennial expo," I continued. "There's an individual grant that only five people receive, and one of them goes to an artist in the winning conference location. You want to be one of them. You don't actually care about the town winning the grant."

Hazel opened her mouth.

"Don't protest," I said, cutting her off before she could speak. "We're all here for our own self-interests. No judgement from me."

"In Hazel's defense, Olivia's pursuing it too," Jemma said.

Hazel kicked her friend and pursed her lips. "Fine, yes, I do want to win it."

I grinned and took a step toward her. "It'll be fun, Hazel. You and me, the dream team, making art together."

"I thought we were the dream team," a sultry voice said.

Oh shit.

Mckenna, my ex. I don't know if I should call her an ex-girlfriend, because girlfriends don't do what she did to me. She was more of an ex-parasite.

"Worst day of my freaking life," Hazel said under her breath.

"No kidding," I muttered. Hazel scowled at me.

McKenna sauntered into the room. She looked the same, walked the same, and smelled the same. She sidled up to me and reached up to kiss me on the cheek. "It's been such a long time, Archer."

"So, you're a stalker now."

McKenna laughed. "You're always such a jokester. No, I have a gallery in town. I heard you're going for the Art Zurich Biennial Expo. As an art gallery owner in this town, it behooves me to make sure Harrogate puts their best foot forward."

"We have it under control, McKenna," Hazel said. "I'm sure you have other more important things to do like scare small children."

McKenna looked down her nose at Hazel. I tried not to smirk. So Hazel had some spine.

"We need to start the meeting," Hazel said. "I have to open my café for lunch soon."

"Lunch?" I said. "I hope it's as good as the popcorn you made me last night." I was teasing her partly because it was funny to see her blush and partly because I knew it would make McKenna insanely jealous. "It was a magical evening, wasn't it, Hazel?" I prompted, hoping she would join in. Clearly she didn't like McKenna any more than I did.

But it seemed Hazel was still mad about the phone call prank. "We weren't doing anything," she scolded. "That was a business transaction."

"I can't believe you thought of it that way!" I exclaimed. "I poured out my heart and soul to you."

Hazel rolled her eyes. "If we could commence with the meeting. Some of us have real jobs," she grumbled.

We sat around the table. McKenna bullied her way into a seat next to mine. I scooted the chair as far away as I could.

"I'll go over some background information since this is your first meeting," Hazel said. Her hair was escaping its ponytail, and I itched to tuck it back in place. "We're in a competition with several other locations to host the Art Zurich Biennial Expo in two years. The search committee is trying to find unique places to host it instead of the usual big cities. We have the Harrogate Trust, which has some funds for improvements. But we don't have an unlimited budget. So I was thinking more along the lines of strategic interventions, like murals, gallery visits, and Olivia offered to lead a tour of historic Harrogate architecture."

I waited a beat. "That's it?"

"We have a limited scope to work with," Hazel protested.

"Small, dinky, and uninspiring," McKenna sniffed. "I'm glad I came today."

"Why don't you go back to Manhattan?" Hazel hissed at McKenna.

"I like it here," she said and flipped her hair.

"Look," I said. "I need to win this expo at all costs. I have funds. We need big ideas, emphasis on big. Money is no object."

"Are you sure?" Hazel asked me.

"Why don't we meet separately and report back?" McKenna breathed and trailed her hand on my wrist, "since we're obviously the most qualified people here."

I jumped up.

"Actually that's a fantastic idea," I said as I hustled to the door, "except instead of small groups, we'll just all brainstorm alone and report back."

CHAPTER 5

Hazel

After Archer made his abrupt exit, I went back to my café for the lunch trickle. I wished I could have a true lunch rush, but no matter how many power poses I did in the morning, the café wasn't that busy. As I prepped for lunch, I thought about what we could do to make Harrogate appealing for the Art Zurich search committee. If Archer was paying the tab, I had some big ideas I was itching to implement.

A few people trickled in mainly to grab to-go orders. They were all professionally dressed, healthy-looking people. I knew the majority of them worked at Svensson PharmaTech, making the big bucks while sitting in air-conditioned comfort.

I slumped down at a table after the last person left. I didn't have to count my earnings to know I was in desperate need of more customers.

"It could have been me," I said sadly, thunking my head on the café table. "I could have gone to accounting school and found gainful employment at a corporation."

Instead I had to prepare for the art retreat that afternoon. When I first opened the Art Café, I thought having people there painting would add a cool atmosphere. It would be like having live music, but you could actually talk to the person next to you. I had a grand vision of an active three-story café. But the only live painting was the veggie-patch baby. The art retreat was an attempt to recoup some money.

Olivia: *My grandma said to remind you about finding a nude model. She thinks you should invite Archer to do it.*

Hazel: *Tell Ida this is a wholesome art retreat.*

Olivia: *Really?? Because you flashed him. She thinks it's only fair.*

Hazel: *I can't believe you're telling people about that! Please put me on an ice float and send me out into the Atlantic.*

Olivia: *It's the middle of summer. Besides I thought it was a total power move. You know, show dominance. It's like those hyenas that pee on things. Also it's already on the Harrogate Facebook group.*

Hazel: *Stop! You're making it worse. People are going to think I'm crazy. You need to cut me off when you see me starting to derail. This is why I'm lonely and single.*

Olivia: *I didn't realize Archer was on the table. Now that I know, I'll be a better wing girl. I'll only let you bat your eyes and make* appreciative noises when he makes inane comments comparing the size of his portfolio to his dick.

Hazel: *I refuse to acknowledge how attractive he is. Also he's a massive douche and I am not that desperate.*

Olivia: *Except we are pretty desperate. We need his money if we want a chance to be the host city for the expo. Plus you need that grant.*

Hazel: *You have a better chance of winning than I do.*

Olivia: *Neither of us has a good chance. The snobby Art Zurich snobs probably want to give it to people like McKenna.*

Hazel: *If she wins it I will die.*

Olivia: *Put good vibes into the universe. And think of things to spend Archer's money on.*

Hazel: **sigh* right be positive. Maybe the stupidly attractive guy will treat you like a joke and your terrible menace from college will appear in your safe space.*

Olivia: *Turn that desperation into determination!*

I hated to admit it, but Archer was right. We did need him to win the Art Zurich Expo. Grand ideas were what would put Harrogate on the map, and Archer's money and influence would help make the ideas a reality. More importantly, I needed Harrogate to win so I would score one of the coveted individual grants. It would be enough money to pay off my building and jump-start several of the art programs I wanted to host.

The art retreat was a big piece of my grant application. I had billed it as a way to connect people to an authentic place and their heritage through art. In reality, there weren't a lot of cool thirtysomethings who wanted to paint and talk about art. Instead it would mainly consist of day-drinking octogenarians.

"At least they're paying," I reminded myself as I went upstairs to set up for the art retreat. My three-story brick building had the café on the bottom, gallery space in the middle, and my studio apartment on the third floor. The whole place reeked of acrylic and desperation. I opened the large floor-to-ceiling glass windows and listened to the noise from the street below while I set up easels and chairs.

Even though the retreat goers were less than ideal, I was still looking forward to the retreat.

"Hello?" someone called up the stairs.

"I'm coming," I shouted and ran downstairs. "Please look at the menu—oh, hi, Meg."

"I came in to buy a sandwich," my sister said.

"You don't have to buy pity sandwiches from me. Besides, once the Grey Dove Bistro gets here, I'm dead in the water anyway."

"I heard you sold a painting," Meg said, sitting at one of the metal café tables. "Congrats."

"Word sure travels fast."

"It's all over Facebook," Meg said. "Ida was very excited."

"You could buy a sandwich at her general store," I said.

"I'd rather buy it fresh from you."

I stared at my sister for a moment. "You just want to hear about the guy."

"Ida was under the impression that you practically ripped off your shirt and had sex with him on the floor."

"Ida wasn't even here," I complained as I took out the ingredients for Meg's sandwich. "Prosciutto and buffalo mozzarella arugula sandwich with pesto aioli?"

"You know it! You make the best sandwiches," my sister said. Then she prompted, "Ida said the guy was a Svensson and he left a card?"

"Yes and yes, but don't worry. He's clearly a piece of shit, and I will never get involved with him."

"Good," Meg said, looking relieved. "Svenssons are bad news."

"I know. I was there." It went silent for an uncomfortable moment. Meg didn't like to talk about what had happened between her and Hunter Svensson.

"Minnie and Rose miss you," Meg said, breaking the silence. "You should come by for dinner. They're almost in high school. Soon they'll be off to college." She took out her credit card to pay me.

"You don't have to. It's not going to keep," I said.

"I'm paying you anyway," Meg said firmly. "You're running a business."

I always felt crappy when my older sister treated me like a child. It felt condescending. However, the cold hard truth was that I really didn't have much to show for myself.

"This was a mistake," I said, wrapping up the sandwich. "What?"

"All of it. Just go ahead and say, 'I told you so.'"

Meg looked sad. "It would have been fine if Uncle Barry had done what he promised our parents and used the inheritance to pay for your college education like he was supposed to."

"Where is all the money?" I asked, handing Meg her sandwich.

"I don't know." Meg pursed her lips. Along with Hunter, Uncle Barry was a sore point. Our father hadn't legally left my sisters and me anything when he'd died. Uncle Barry was left in charge of all the funds and property from my father. Barry was nice enough, but he was starting to grow a little senile. I had long ago given up hope that he would see me and my sisters as anything other than cute but useless little girls.

"You should be mayor," I grumbled. "Uncle Barry is barely cognizant. There should at least be a term limit or something. You do all the work. And he treats you like a secretary."

"That's just how it is," Meg said brusquely, standing up to leave. "Don't forget about dinner."

I sulked after Meg left. It seemed like she and I could never have a normal sisterly conversation without it derailing.

Ever since our parents died, Meghan had been irritable and stressed out. The only time I really saw her relaxed and happy was her brief stint with Hunter. Of course it had all gone horribly south. Was that what happened with the Loring girls? Were our lives destined to be train wrecks?

Another Svensson wandered into my thoughts as I finished setting up the second-floor studio. I forced myself not to think about him. It was just his tattoos; I was attracted to the pictures.

Right, Hazel, of course. I couldn't think about Archer. I had bigger problems.

"Yoo-hoo!" Ida called. "I'm ready to do some nude painting."

Olivia's grandmother huffed up the stairs. She was wearing a stereotypical painter's outfit complete with a beret and striped tights.

"Sorry it's a little warm up here," I said.

"Why don't you make us some cocktails?" Ida suggested with a wink.

"Isn't it a little early?"

"I bought the alcoholic beverages package," the old woman said.

"There wasn't really one…"

"Yeah, but that was the extra I paid," Ida said, showing me the email receipt.

I inspected it. Apparently she had paid extra.

"Besides," Ida continued, "I told everyone there would be booze. That and the nude painting is why all the girls signed up."

I felt a little faint. "I don't have a nude model."

"Yet," Ida said. "What about your boyfriend?"

"I don't have a boyfriend."

"Archer Svensson. Josie is dating his twin, you know."

"I didn't know Mace Svensson was a twin. He and Archer seem like complete opposites. Mace is an upstanding citizen, and Archer is a jerk. Jemma told you about the mean trick he played on me, right?"

"It's because he likes you," Ida insisted. "Men are basically twelve-year-old boys inside. But not on the outside. If you know what I mean."

I did know.

"I'm going to go make some drinks," I chirped, hoping to cut off the conversation before it could wander into the dangerous territory of how much of a man Archer was on the outside.

I went downstairs to make pitchers of vodka lavender thyme lemonade. More of Ida's elderly friends arrived. They all were very excited about drinking. Painting, too, but mostly drinking.

I placed the drinks in the dumbwaiter to move upstairs. The dumbwaiter was another of my favorite elements in my building. Did McKenna have a dumbwaiter in her building? I thought not. But she did have Archer. Screw him. They could have each other and make perfect artistic babies.

The door opened. A breeze cooled the back of my neck.

"Go on upstairs. Drinks are coming, but there's no nude model today," I called out as I fiddled with the dumbwaiter.

"I can volunteer my services," said a familiar male voice. "I've been told I look pretty good without any clothes on."

CHAPTER 6

When I still resided in Manhattan, I spent a large amount of my free time at the Grey Dove Bistro, sampling Chloe's cooking. Duck-fat roasted potatoes, cheesy pasta, all-you-can-eat desserts—she was cooking my kind of food. The portions were huge, which I also appreciated.

Svensson PharmaTech did not serve anything remotely close to the Grey Dove Bistro fare.

I had headed over there after the art committee meeting. Seeing McKenna had rattled me. I browsed one of the break-rooms. Mace provided snacks for his employees, but instead of donuts, he had fruit, fishy-smelling seaweed crackers, and yogurt. I took a VitaMeal smoothie from the fridge and pretended it was that popcorn Hazel had made.

Hazel. Now there was something to distract me from McKenna. She was feisty and clearly could give as good as she got. She was one of the first single women I'd met who didn't immediately seem to want me for my money or status. Hell, it seemed like Hazel actually wanted me to go away. It was too bad I screwed up with the prank. Hazel might have actually been kind of fun. And I did want to see what she looked like under the overalls, with her hair down.

After finishing my health drink, I went on to my other favorite distraction—messing with Mace. We all had our scars from our terrible childhood. Mace was a control freak and a classic middle child. I enjoyed nudging him out of his comfort zone; I felt like it was my duty. I wished Josie, who was an admitted candy addict, would have broken his desire for healthy food, but baby steps.

I had commandeered Josie's old office ever since her replacement was arrested and put into prison. Long story. Because her office was originally meant for the CEO's assistant, I had to walk through Mace's office to reach it.

My identical twin gave a long sigh when I walked in. "You own two hotels in this town," Mace said, looking up from his computer screen. "Why don't you go use the offices there?"

"Because my employees are using them," I said as I started to rearrange the contents on his desk. "The Harrogate hotels are on the smaller side, and the offices don't have any windows. Also you're not there." I hugged my twin and ruffled his hair, messing up the carefully arranged style. "Someone has to make sure you don't spiral into a pit of obsessive-compulsive behaviors and scare Josie away."

"You're one to talk. I'm the one who has a girlfriend," Mace said smugly. "Or as you referred to her, the future Mrs. Svensson. She'll be the first. Maybe you can find a girlfriend. You could be a kept man."

I thought briefly about Hazel then shut that down. No more crazy art girls.

"You're already planning to propose? That's not the cautious, gun-shy Mace we all know and love!" Mike announced as he, Hunter, and Greg walked into Mace's office.

"I'll be so glad when you have your own offices in Harrogate," Mace grumbled as we went next door. "That conference center can't happen soon enough."

"You wound me, Mace," I called out. "You should be glad to have me around."

"Don't forget you're supposed to take Otis and Theo to the art camp," he warned me before shutting the door.

I flashed him a thumbs-up through the glass wall and flopped down on the beanbag chair I'd had delivered to the office.

"We need to discuss the strategy for winning the Mast Brothers' chocolate factory property," Greg said, opening up his notebook.

"Is Meg going to be at the presentation?" I asked aloud.

"It's a city property. She probably will," Mike said.

"Then should we really bring him?" I motioned to Hunter.

"Mayor Barry says I'm his favorite Svensson. He's the one who will ultimately be making the decision," Hunter said, back ramrod straight in his chair. "Besides, Archer is the one who needs to not go. Especially after that stunt he pulled with the phone prank."

"It wasn't that bad."

"It was terrible. Garrett isn't pleased."

"Fuck, I don't need Garrett on my case."

"You better be careful," Mike said. "He's still in a bad mood about the cell phone ban—said it ruined everything. He's out for blood."

"Hazel wasn't that upset. She flashed me instead of crying when I saw her this morning."

"She flashed you?" Mace yelled from next door.

"Stop eavesdropping," I yelled back.

Hunter scowled. "I thought you did a better job of keeping things in line in Manhattan," he said snidely to Greg. "And yet here's Archer, acting like a fool."

Greg seethed.

"Archer doesn't actually have to be there," Mike offered. "I own Greyson Hotel Group too."

"It was my idea," I exclaimed. "And you might think it's crazy, but when we make a lot of money, I'm going to say I told you so and rub it in your faces."

"Hunter will go, but if Meg is there," Greg warned, "don't even look at her."

"Don't tell me how to do my job," Hunter growled.

"I'll stop when you stop fucking up my business deals," Greg snapped.

"So," Mike said, trying to defuse the tension. "This is what I have for the presentation." He swiped at his tablet, and on the large TV on the wall was a picture of the nine-teenth-century industrial complex of the Mast Brothers' chocolate factory. It was going to be my *pièce de résistance*. I couldn't help but grin.

Hunter was skeptical. "And we want this place why?"

"It's cool, in a word," I said. "It's authentic, and it's going to be a groundbreaking conference center."

"Carl just brought in a whole new set of investors," Greg said. "They are very interested in having their money capitalized. They like how innovative Frost Tower is. They're showing interest in a conference center, if we can make the numbers work."

"We have schematic floor plans and some renderings," Mike said, flicking through the presentation.

I whistled. "Slick. Very impressive."

"We need to have a better idea of where we're going to put the hotels," Mike reiterated.

I opened my mouth to complain.

"If we bring this factory land under option from the city," Mike said, cutting me off, "we need to spend some time investigating. The Art Zurich Expo regularly attracts over sixty thousand people. We will need at least eighty percent of that number in keys."

"Did you look for the owner of the strip mall site adjacent to the factory?" Hunter asked.

"I did some cursory searching; I think the city owns it, but I'm not sure. There was a random shell LLC listed as the property owner, but they haven't paid taxes. Usually in that situation, the property reverts to the city at some point. It's complicated," Mike said. "I'm having our interns look into it."

"What interns?"

"Eli and Tristan," Mace said, sticking his head in the room. "You need to be more of a team player and help out with the younger brothers."

"I'm better than those losers in Seattle," I protested.

"Marginally," Mace said, looking at his watch. "You better leave now. You're going to be late for art camp."

I raced back to the estate to pick up Otis and Theo. They were waiting impatiently on the front stoop.

"You're so cute with your little easels and paint boxes."

"We're trying to make a marketable product," Otis said. "It's not a joke."

"Right, right," I said. I looked at my sports car.

"There are three of us, and you have two seats," Otis said unhelpfully.

"I can do math."

"Can you?" Theo sniffed.

"I liked you better when you were small and didn't talk back," I growled at them, looking around.

Eli and Tristan were pulling out of the back drive from the large garage that had the extra cars in it. They were in one of the stocky sedans Mace liked to buy.

I stepped in front of the car. Eli rolled down the window.

"I need that," I told Eli.

"This is the last car!" he said, gripping the steering wheel. "Mike said we needed to go do research for him!"

"I don't care. I'm older and bigger, and I need it. It's mine. Move."

"I'm telling Hunter," Eli complained as he and Tristan climbed out of the car. Tristan was staring too intently at my sports car for my liking.

"Don't touch my stuff," I warned as I helped Otis and Theo load their art equipment in the trunk.

"Where is the retreat?" I asked, opening up my map app on my phone.

"You can't use the phone while driving," Otis said.

"Right. The rule from Meg."

"Mace said she implemented it to mess with Hunter." He was quiet for a moment then added, "Garrett's not happy about it."

"Garrett's not happy about a lot of stuff."

"I can't believe Mace let you have a phone," I said to Otis as he directed me through town. "I didn't have a phone when I was your age. Mace is really slipping."

"They all have GPS trackers. Blade made him an app to show where everyone is," Theo said.

"Because that's not creepy. It's not enough that you live on a haunted estate. Now peeping Mace is tracking our every move."

"He's tracking the cars too," Otis said helpfully.

"Of course he is."

"Turn right," Otis said. "We're here." He unbuckled his seat belt as I pulled into a parking space across the street from a very familiar brick building.

"I, ah—are you sure this is right?"

The kids had already run across the street to the Art Café, calling, "We're late!" as they rushed inside.

I followed, squinting when I walked in out of the bright sun. There was Hazel, wearing those overalls. One of the straps had fallen off her shoulder. She was wearing a cropped shirt. I wanted to run my hand across the strip of bare midriff. Instead I offered to be a nude model.

"I can't believe you'd make that comment in front of those children," Hazel scolded. She peered at Otis and Theo. "They aren't your kids, are they?"

"You wound me, Hazel. I'm not that old. They're like—" I waved my hands around and pulled a number out of thin air. "Ten?"

"We're twelve!" Theo said.

"Right, right."

"You don't even know their ages?" Hazel admonished, huffing as she pulled the rope on the dumbwaiter. "Are you here for lunch? Because I actually have an art retreat, though I guess I could start Ida and her friends with their drinks and make you guys a quick bite." She yanked on the rope.

She was so short that the dumbwaiter wasn't really going up that far.

I stepped beside her and took over the pulley. "Your arms are so short we'd be here all day."

Hazel snorted, hands on her hips. Her thumbs were right at that strip of bare skin at her waist. I wanted to press my mouth to the spot. I forced my gaze back to the dumbwaiter and hefted it up.

"Just wrap the rope around the—"

"I know. I own a number of hotels in historic buildings that had similar features. Though eventually I converted them all to be automatic because I'm not a masochist," I said as I locked the break.

"Do you need a sandwich that bad?" she muttered.

"We're not here for lunch. We're here for the art retreat," Otis exclaimed.

"You are?" Hazel asked. She looked a bit put out.

"We want to learn how to make designs for our T-shirt business," Theo said excitedly.

"My brothers are budding entrepreneurs, just like me!" I grinned at her. She scowled.

"The art retreat is upstairs. I have alcoholic drinks for the adults, but I guess I'll make you two some juice."

"You're not going to offer me a beverage?" I asked.

CHAPTER 7

Hazel

"No, I'm not going to offer you a beverage," I hissed at him as we followed his little brothers upstairs.

"We're committee coworkers, Hazel," Archer said. His breath was slightly cool against my neck. He was way too close to me. "We should clear up some of this *tension* between us."

I cleared my throat and hurried to the front of the room.

"Thank you so much for participating in the first artists' retreat at Harrogate. This is a gathering of creative minds. Everyone here has something to contribute. I'll be showing you various techniques over the next few weeks. Let me know if there's anything I can do to make this a fun, creative experience."

Archer watched me with an amused expression from the corner of the room. He leaned against the wall, posed alluringly like Michelangelo's David except he was wearing too many clothes.

"Use this as an opportunity to be inspired," I finished lamely, still staring at Archer. "Any questions?"

Ida stood up. "I feel like I speak for everyone when I say nude models."

The older women cheered. Theo and Otis looked a little concerned.

"We won't have any nude models," I said hastily.

"Booo!"

"Or if we do, it will have to be a separate session for people who don't feel uncomfortable with that type of art," I added. The grin on Archer's face was Cheshire sized.

He mouthed, *Private session*, to me.

The blush crept up on my cheeks.

"You need a drink, hotcakes?" Ida called over her shoulder to Archer.

"It's three in the afternoon," he said. "Of course!" Archer sauntered up to the front of the room, where I had the glasses and pitcher of vodka lavender thyme lemonade.

I could swear he was posing as he poured a cup and took a sip.

"Exactly what I was craving," he said, looking straight at me, his eyes flicking back and forth between my nose and my chest and my mouth. I could feel the nervous sweating start. Archer was so unfairly attractive, and he clearly enjoyed teasing me. I, however, was terrible at flirting. I slapped the thought down. That wasn't what this was.

"If I could please sit on you," I said.

"Anytime," Archer called out.

"That's not what I meant!" Why did he have to be so stupidly attractive? "If you could please take your seats, and

I could have your attention," I said carefully, "I will start the lesson."

A slow smile spread across Archer's face. I wanted to punch it.

No, you want to sit on it.

Archer grinned, almost as if he knew what I was thinking.

"I'll sit on your face if she won't," Ida stated.

"See, Hazel?" Archer said. "Someone here appreciates a fine work of art."

When he was seated on the couch in the back of the studio, I explained, "Today we are doing a still life. This exercise is about capturing light and shadows. Using only one color, paint this pitcher of water on the table."

I demonstrated on the canvas I had set up.

"This is a very quick exercise. Don't overthink it. Just act and capture the essence of what you see." Everyone seemed like they were into it once they started. Of course the seniors had all been drinking enough that they seemed pretty loose, which with this type of exercise, was a benefit.

Otis and Theo were having a little trouble understanding the exercise.

"You have to paint around the light," I told them, taking the paintbrush and showing them.

I could see Archer out of the corner of my eye sitting on the couch. I froze as he lazily surveyed me. For a moment I thought maybe he saw something he liked. Then I remembered he used to date McKenna. He probably still hooked up with her occasionally. She seemed like the type who would be up for that, not that I was judging, except that I kinda was.

"Are you going to sit there the whole time?" I snapped.

"I'm not a retreat member. I'm just trying to make sure you don't corrupt these innocent minds. Nude models, alcohol in the afternoon, flashing strange men. It's shameful, Hazel." He took a sip of his drink.

"I didn't flash you! You barely saw anything," I hissed, taking two steps toward him.

Archer leaned forward and whispered, "I grew up in a sexually repressed religious doomsday cult. I saw enough to be sent to hell for all eternity." He smirked.

"It was like I was wearing a bathing suit," I retorted.

"It was more titillating than that," Archer said in a low tone. "Did you get it? Isn't that a great play on words from someone who is stupid attractive?"

"Yeah, real sharp. You should get a cookie for your effort," I said dryly.

"You have cookies?" He perked up.

"No."

"You can't tease a guy like that, Hazel," he complained. "Also I can't believe you turned down my offer to be a nude model."

"The art retreat is just fine without you."

Archer grinned and leaned back on the couch. "You know," he said, "I think I will be a retreat participant. Art is very inspirational. Did you know there's a vault in the Vatican of explicit sexual art? There are paintings of people having sex with nymphs and goats and whatnot."

"Goat sex?" Ida yelled out.

"I thought you said your hearing aid wasn't working," I shot back to Ida.

"Naw, that's just what I tell my sister, Edna, when I don't want to listen to her badgering me," Ida said.

A smile played around Archer's mouth.

"It will be nice to have a man participate in the retreat," Ida continued. "You know, offer another perspective on things."

"Yeah, Hazel, how about it? Do you have any *wide-open* spots in your retreat?" Archer looked smug. I cursed my attractive-male-afflicted awkwardness. Also, why was it hot in here? I mentally put central air on my wish list of things to buy if I ever won that Art Zurich grant.

Begrudgingly, I checked the roster. "It looks like we have some spots still open."

Archer handed me his credit card. "It's heavy, isn't it?" he asked.

"You're inappropriate."

Archer clasped a hand to his chest. "That isn't what I meant at all, Hazel. Honestly, there are children and elderly present. I merely was making polite conversation. "

I clamped my mouth shut tight as I ran his card through the card reader on my phone. Or tried to. "It won't fit."

Archer smirked.

"Stupid knockoff card reader. Last time I buy something from China," I muttered. I entered the number manually.

"You're going to be very impressed with my art," Archer said as he signed the digital receipt. "You should see all the ink I have on my body."

He followed me into the storage closet, where I pulled out an extra easel and a canvas for him. He picked them up easily.

"You should come sit near me, sugar buns!" Ida called as Archer set up his station.

"Why don't you have another drink, Ida?" I offered, hoping to distract her.

"Don't mind if I do."

I floated between each of the retreat goers, providing tips and guidance. The entire time, I stole glances at Archer out of the corner of my eye. He had rolled up his sleeves, and I could make out the tendons on his forearms. While he was a pretty picture, he did not seem like he knew what he was doing.

"I thought you said you were good at painting?" I whispered over his shoulder while I inspected the dumpster fire on his canvas. I was satisfied to see him shiver slightly as my breath caressed his neck.

"I'm good at finger painting," he replied, scooping up paint on his brush.

My hand itched, and I reached out and grabbed the paintbrush before he could glop all the paint on the canvas. My fingertips grazed the back of his hand.

"I knew you secretly like me," he whispered. "I bet you do naughty things with this paintbrush when you're all alone."

I flicked his earlobe.

"Ow! That's not what I meant at all, Hazel." Archer turned around, horrified, and I started to feel a little bad for hurting him. Those bad feelings turned to exasperation when he continued, "I meant that you probably draw pictures of me nude of course, with a comically large, throbbing—" I clapped a hand to his mouth before he said the word.

"Cock!" Ida shouted out gleefully. I looked at Archer's brothers in horror. Fortunately they were wearing headphones and listening to music.

"How did you even hear that, Ida?"

"Cranked that hearing aid up, baby. You can call me the CIA because I will come in Archer."

Archer looked up at the ceiling. "Granted, I grew up in a cult in the middle of the desert, so I didn't get the best human anatomy lesson, but I don't think that's how any of this works."

"That's it, Ida," I told her. "You've had enough to drink." I went over to take the glass out of her hand, but she downed it in one go.

"I'm begrudgingly impressed," Archer said after a beat.

"I have no gag reflex," Ida bragged. "I can give you pointers, Hazel."

"I don't need them—"

"Also if you drew naughty pictures of him, you have to show me, okay?"

"I'm not drawing naughty pictures of Archer."

"That's too bad! You should. I hear people make a lot of money drawing porn online."

"I'm a serious artist! I'm not drawing porn, especially not of Archer."

But I stole glances at Archer through the rest of the afternoon.

The way the light streaming through the large windows illuminated him like a Dutch master's painting, I sort of did want to draw him. Not in a pornographic way—I wanted to see how far that tattoo went on his chest. Not because I wanted to see the outlines of the muscles and the V that went down to... well, you know. The craftsmanship of the tattoos was what I was interested in.

Then I thought of McKenna. She had been awful to me in college. I had purposefully lost track of her—I didn't want to know how successful she was. The article about McKenna and Archer said they'd had only a few dates. And Archer was probably flirting with me, though it could have just been his personality or another joke. I looked down at my paint-smeared overalls. I certainly wasn't dressed to impress. Who was I kidding? There was no way Archer was into me.

CHAPTER 8

Archer

Hazel had been so flustered during the retreat. It was endearing and a little intriguing. I chuckled to myself as I drove the kids back. They chattered excitedly in the back seat of my car.

I pulled up in front of the large estate house, and Otis and Theo hopped out. Adrian and Tristan were standing around my sports car, taking pictures of Eli posing behind the wheel.

"Don't even think about driving my car," I growled at them, hurrying over.

"I told them you would be mad," Adrian said.

"But look how cool Eli looks," Tristan said, showing me the pictures he had taken of Eli in too-large sunglasses making nonsense hand signs.

I resisted the urge to roll my eyes. Was I that insufferable when I was that young? How was I acting so old now? Next thing I knew I was going to be going to bed before midnight and yelling at the kids to get off my lawn.

The whining started as soon as I walked into the house.

"I'm hungry!" Henry complained.

"Is Josie cooking?" I asked hopefully.

"She's not here," Garrett informed me. He was sitting at the dining room table, poring over spreadsheets. "She and Mace went on a date."

"Mace took her on a date night? I'm a little hurt."

"I'm surprised you aren't out on a date. McKenna is in town," Garrett said nastily. He held a grudge in the best of times, and none of my brothers had forgiven McKenna for what had happened.

"How did you even know she was here?"

"I make it my business to know," Garrett said. I liked to stir up trouble, but I stayed far away from Garrett. He had a habit of screwing you over if you crossed him.

A notification popped up on my Instagram feed. I scrolled through the photos. Chloe had a slideshow of photos of her restaurant. I salivated when I saw the picture of the duck confit and asparagus she had made. The next post was a picture from Josie of her and my twin on their dinner date.

"I'm hungry," Henry whined. It was giving me serious flashbacks of being in the compound and not having any food.

"I'll cook something," I assured him.

"You don't know how to cook," Garrett said derisively.

"I could cook if I wanted to. Or you could cook," I told Garrett.

He stared at me, his eyes a flat gray.

"Some of us have to make sure that this family doesn't go down the toilet. Hunter is off, probably giving Meg more ammunition to ruin my life, like she did with the cell phone law," he said in a clipped tone. "In addition, you and your conference center have messed up my schedule. Someone has to find money for that abomination."

"See if you can find money for a zoo while you're at it," I told him. "Maybe we could have penguins."

"Or goats," my older brother Remy said, coming into the room. "If we had goats, we could just go make cheese."

A picture popped up on my phone.

Josie hearts this.

It was a picture of Hazel standing in front of an impressive array of sandwiches.

"Are you going to cook?" Nate asked me, tugging on my pant leg.

"No, I'm not going to cook," I told him. He looked sad. I chucked him under his chin, and my little brother frowned. "I'm a billionaire. I'm going to use my money to make this problem go away."

I clicked on the picture. The post contained a link to Hazel's Instagram. I sent her a message.

Archer: *Need food for 40.*

I looked at the kids. They all looked hungry.

Archer: *Scratch that. 50. Anything you have.*
Name your price.

My phone rang a few seconds later.

"You should call ahead for catering," Hazel said. She sounded irritated but a little breathless.

"We're starving. It's an emergency," I begged, batting away Henry's hand. He was trying to dig in my pocket for nonexistent food.

Hazel sighed. "My café is supposed to be open for happy hour right now."

"I'll pay you for lost wages."

"You can't just snap your fingers and expect people to jump. I have customers," she said.

"Put out a sign that says, 'Closed for Private Event.' And for the record, I'm not snapping my fingers; I'm throwing a wad of money at the problem. You'll be very well compensated—unless you're one of those artists who live on sunshine and exposure. I myself always prefer money. Besides, this is a good deed. There are starving children here. We even have a military veteran." Remy flashed me a thumbs-up.

"I don't know if I have enough to make a cohesive meal," Hazel said. I could tell she was wavering.

"They will literally eat anything, and I will pay you literally for anything if I don't have to cook it. Shoot, you could just make a ton of that popcorn, and we'd be fine."

"I'm not feeding your little brothers popcorn," she scoffed. "I'll see what I have and be over in forty-five minutes."

"I'll pay you double if you come over here in twenty. You make house calls, don't you? Surely you don't just service people in your café."

"You are so gross."

"You said I was attractive last night."

She hung up.

"Problem solved!" I crowed.

Garrett stared at me. "You need to check your attitude. I will not have you turning this into another Hunter situation."

CHAPTER 9

Hazel

I couldn't believe Archer. The nerve of that man. But then I looked around my building. I could at least charge him several hundred dollars to cover the next month's utilities. I didn't feel right charging more than that. It would more than cover the cost of the food and labor and closing the Art Café—not that I made all that much money off of the restaurant. Though I did occasionally have a couple people come for happy hour drinks.

If Archer did open the conference center, maybe he could hire me as a caterer since, by that point, my building would be taken back by the bank.

"No." I cut off the negative thoughts and struck a power pose. "You are creative. You are strong. You are going to win that grant, and everything is going to be okay! Archer is throwing you a very small life preserver. Don't blow it."

I didn't want to feed his brothers popcorn, but I didn't have much in the fridge. I couldn't make sandwiches, because

I needed all of those ingredients for the food I sold at Ida's General Store.

But what else did I have?

I smiled. Pancakes—specifically savory crepes. I had a ton of ham, cheese, and eggs, plus all the vegetables from the farm co-op that were delivered this morning. It was another of those things I signed up for back when I was a starry-eyed newbie café owner.

Croque-madame and croque-monsieur crepes along with a nice salad with fresh lettuce would make a yummy dinner. I loaded the ingredients and the large griddles I would need to cook everything into my bike trailer.

Yes, I rode around on a bike. It was either buy the building or a car. I had found the bike while dumpster diving and fixed it up. That was one useful thing about art school— they taught us how to do metalwork and welding—so I was able to make the bike and the trailer functional. I started the long hot ride to the Svenssons' estate.

I swept my sweaty hair out of my face when I pulled up at the ornate gate. I was about to push the button, then I froze. What if this was another of Archer's elaborate pranks? I squared my shoulders. If he thought he was going to prank me again, he had another thing coming. I would absolutely go complain to his older brothers. The gate swung open before I could even push the intercom button. I guess I was expected after all.

The front door opened when I pedaled down the drive to the huge manor house. I hadn't been to their estate before. My friend Olivia was the architect. She had shown me pictures, but they didn't do justice to how huge the building was.

As I pulled to a squeaky stop in the roundabout, I gaped up at the house. The facade was a dark-gray stone. My gaze swept over the large metal windows that gleamed in the evening sunlight. Archer stood in the front doorway impatiently. A small child clung to his legs.

"Thank God you're here. I thought they were going to kill and eat me," he said then yelled over his shoulder, "Go help her with her stuff if you want to eat!"

Smaller versions of Archer swarmed my bike, picked up everything, and ran inside. I followed Archer's little brothers into the house.

"Welcome to the estate. That's the gremlin who lives in the attic. His name is Garrett," Archer said as we walked through the dining room. Garrett grunted but didn't look up from his computer. "We'll throw some scraps at him later. This is Remy, the best Svensson after yours truly." Remy gave me a hug. He had a huge bushy beard and was like a giant teddy bear.

"Welcome, Hazel," he said.

"Sorry, I'm sweaty," I said, slightly smashed against the big man's shirt.

"Kitchen is here," Archer said, shoving Remy off me.

"Wow, this kitchen is amazing!" I gushed. "It's bigger than my café!" The gleaming kitchen had a huge island that looked like it could seat most of Archer's brothers. There were four ovens, an eight-burner range, and gleaming white terrazzo on the floors. Against the opposite wall was a bank of refrigerators and freezers.

"I could live in this kitchen." I looked around the room. I was practically salivating to use the appliances and sprawl my ingredients on the pristine white counters. Along with my dream of being a famous artist, I also dreamed of an awesome apartment. I would hang up expensive art, display sculptures, and host cool parties. My dream kitchen looked a lot like this one.

"Do you need help?" Otis asked me.

I looked around. "I guess so. You might eat faster."

I was expecting to have to supervise more, but the kids seemed like they had some experience in a kitchen. They washed lettuce and grated cheese while I made the béchamel for the croque-monsieur and croque-madame crepes and preheated the griddles. I was preparing to mix the savory batter by hand, when three of Mace's brothers came out of a large pantry with stand mixers in various colors.

I tried not to drool. Stand mixers were not in my café's budget. I relied on arm strength and a whisk.

"I'm going to Venmo you money," Archer said, slumped artfully at the kitchen island. "There's cash in the safe, but Garrett won't give me access."

"I can't imagine why," I said tartly.

"I feel like you're trying to insult me, but I might be too stupid attractive to figure it out," he said with a small grin, his head resting on his hand. Archer followed my movements as I dumped flour, oil, water, and eggs into the metal bowl and set the mixers going.

I poured the first layer of batter onto the hot griddle and used a crepe squeegee to make it a thin layer. Normally making crepes was a tedious process. But I had found a set of long griddles on which I could make a huge sheet of crepes and cut them into sections. I could make ten crepes at once. The tricky part was flipping them.

"That smells delicious," Archer told me. "Whenever you get tired of day-drinking art retreaters, you should just come here and cook full-time."

"So instead of listening to inappropriate comments from Ida and Dottie, I'd have to listen to your obnoxious comments? No thanks."

"Me?" Archer asked in mock indignation. "You were the one flirting with a student."

"I wasn't flirting with you."

Archer raised an eyebrow. "You were so flirting, and it was so hot."

I smelled smoke. "Crap! The crepes are burning. Go set the table," I ordered him. "You're distracting me."

Archer smirked. "You find me distracting." He pulled at his shirt collar.

"You're doing that on purpose."

"I'm just trying to get a little air. It's getting a little hot in here," he said over his shoulder as he went into the dining room.

I fanned myself. It was a little warm. The crepes were salvageable, so I placed thin slices of ham and nutty Gruyère cheese on them, folded them over, then set them on the large metal sheet pan and moved to the next batch.

The stacks of hot crepes piled up. I had a nice assembly line going. When I had sixty crepes made, I slathered them in the creamy béchamel sauce and slid them under the broiler. The fact that the Svenssons had four ovens made the process painless.

I topped half of the crepes with fried eggs and tossed the salad with a vinaigrette.

"Dinner!" I announced as a few of Archer's little brothers helped me carry the trays into the dining room.

The kids all crowded around the platters.

"Salad," I ordered. "You can't just eat crepes. You need something green."

Archer scooped a hot crepe from the platter. "This is so good," he said around the hot food. "I think I could just marry you right now."

Garrett walked up to the line. "Croque-monsieur crepes, croque-madame crepes, or both?" I offered. "Madame has a fried egg."

Garrett looked from the platters to me.

"*Problem?*" Archer growled from his spot at the long buffet serving the crepes.

"I'm just shocked that you were able to make all this. I'm impressed," Garrett said to me with a nod. "The crepes are all uniform, and everything looks equally high quality. It is very efficient."

"You just received the highest compliment," Archer said, elbowing me gently in the side.

We sat down at the table. Archer surveyed the younger children and groaned.

"Y'all, I am trying to be the fun older brother, but if you keep eating your salad with your hands—Henry, yes, I am looking at you—I will be forced to be the mean older brother who no one likes." He stuffed a fork into Henry's hand.

A commotion in the hall resounded through the dining room door.

"I feel bad. Maybe we should have brought them something," we heard Josie say as she and Archer's identical twin, Mace, walked into the dining room and stopped short.

"You made this?" Mace asked in disbelief.

"Of course Archer didn't make it," Garrett said snidely as he stood up to take another crepe. "Hazel made it."

"Archer paid me," I clarified. I didn't want Josie to think I was moving into her territory or anything.

"Hazel Loring?" a man stated. I looked up. From another entrance to the dining room, Hunter Svensson watched me warily.

My eyes narrowed when I saw him. Though I teased Meg about sleeping with him, I didn't think he should actually get back together with her. I still remembered how upset she had been after what he had done.

Hunter's face was a blank mask. "How is Meg?"

"She's still mad at you," I blurted out.

"Does she know you're here?" he asked, his expression unreadable. "I highly doubt she wants you to get in some sort of tryst with a Svensson, especially not that one." He motioned to Archer.

"We're not in a tryst," Archer corrected. "I'm paying her."

The way he said it made it sound cold and impersonal. I didn't know why I was thinking things were any different. Maybe because of the flirting earlier that day? Then he sent me the Instagram message, and part of me thought Archer and I were maybe becoming a little friendlier. But I guess not.

"I have to go," I said abruptly, pushing back my chair, ignoring Archer as he called after me.

The Svenssons' voices tapered off as I fled the large estate house. That was the lesson Meg was always trying to teach about the Svensson brothers—don't trust them.

CHAPTER 10

Archer

"I hope you're not involved with her," Hunter said in a clipped tone as soon as Hazel left. "She's the deputy mayor's sister."

"Yeah, I got that," I told my older brother. "She's on the art committee with me."

"Hunter, *you* are the only person Meg has a problem with," Garrett said, returning to the table with more food.

"You know, for someone who wasn't being all that helpful earlier, you sure are eating a lot," I told Garrett. He ignored me.

"Aren't you trying to convince the city to sign off on your conference center?" Hunter demanded.

"Yeah, so?"

"Meg will go scorched earth on you if she thinks you're after her sister," my older brother stated.

"Of course I'm not after her. Not that she would even have me after that prank I played."

"Wait, Hazel was the one you tricked into calling Greg? Archer," Mace said reproachfully, cutting a bite off my crepe. I resisted the urge to stab him in the hand.

"You might as well just pack up and go back to Manhattan," Garrett said. "There's no way you're winning that conference center."

"I didn't know Hazel was Meghan's sister at the time!" I protested.

"Just help Harrogate win the Art Zurich Expo, and I'm sure all will be forgiven," Josie assured me. "Also this food is amazing."

"Did Mace not feed you? I thought you had a date night," I said.

"Yes, but I always have room for a cheesy crepe," Josie replied. "You need to talk Hazel into making Nutella crepes next!"

I stayed up late going over the presentation with Mike and Greg, and the next morning, we headed over to city hall.

"These renderings look so good," I said, admiring them as I placed the computer illustrations of what the conference center would look like on the easels we brought.

"They better. We spent a fortune on all this stuff," Mike replied.

At the front of the large room in city hall was a long table. Five minutes before we were scheduled to present, the door opened, and Mayor Barry walked in, followed by another older man who I recognized as Amos, a descendant of the factory's original owner, and Meghan.

"Deputy Mayor!" I said enthusiastically. "When can we expect your Supreme Court appointment?"

Meghan half rolled her eyes. "I hardly think I'm qualified."

"Please, you'd be the best judge to ever judge." I almost saw a smile, but then she and Hunter locked eyes, and a blanket of tension settled over the room.

"Hunter, my boy," Mayor Barry exclaimed jovially, seemingly oblivious to what was going on between Hunter and Meghan. The mayor was a large man and wasn't in the best of health, so Hunter crossed the room to shake his hand. "So glad to see you," Mayor Barry said. "We're very excited to see what you have to propose. We like Harrogate to be as business friendly as possible."

"While still making sure it is friendly for all residents," Meghan added.

"We worked hard to make sure that our design was something all residents of Harrogate could be proud of and benefit from," Hunter all but spat. "Of course you can make up some imaginary reason to reject this project."

"Shut up," Greg hissed at Hunter.

The tension didn't ease as we ran through our presentation, emphasizing the creative vision for the project. Mayor Barry nodded along and made appreciative noises when we showed the floor plans and explained how we would have room for the food hall in addition to some office space and, of course, all the exhibition space. Neither Meg nor Amos smiled once.

"We're even planning on having a Grey Dove Bistro franchise in the food hall," I added, knowing the mayor was a big fan.

"Delightful!" the large man said, clasping his hands together.

Meghan frowned. "All right, I've seen enough. Your team can wait for us to call you back in. We have lunch provided next door."

We waited around in a large meeting room overlooking the town square while the Harrington investment team gave their presentations. Along with bottles of water on a table in the room, there were sandwiches wrapped in brown butcher paper tied with string. They had little colorful hand-painted cards.

"Prosciutto and buffalo mozzarella sandwich with pesto aioli. Your favorite," I said to Hunter, waving it in his face.

I took a turkey bacon sandwich. "This is amazing." I looked at the card that was tied onto the sandwich wrapping. The style was familiar. It was one of Hazel's sandwiches. I felt oddly happy knowing that.

"I think we have this in the bag," I said cheerfully.

"The Harringtons are going to put up a good fight," Mike said, swallowing his bite of sandwich.

"Meghan's not going to select them," Hunter said. "She doesn't like the Harringtons. They treated her poorly when she worked at the law firm."

"Yeah," I said, "but she hates you." Hunter turned on me, face furious.

"Stop it, Hunter," Greg snarled at him.

"We're ready for you unless you want to have a brawl in the middle of city hall," Meghan stated from the doorway.

We walked into the large presentation room. The Harrington Investment team was in there too.

Amos addressed both teams. "My great-grandfather founded this factory. He was a traditional man. I feel like the factory complex is part of my family. And just like I wouldn't have given my blessing for my daughter to marry some skeezeball salesman, I'm not going to carelessly hand the land over to your development companies." He looked at Meghan and Barry. "Now I know the city technically owns this land," Amos continued.

"It was a generous gift to the city," Meghan said smoothly.

"And a tax burden they can't afford," Mike muttered to me.

"I was under the impression that you would be selling it to a developer with my blessing," Amos complained.

Meg nodded. "Absolutely."

"I don't want to give my land that's been in my family for generations over to some slick-haired wheeler-dealer. I need to see heart and soul in this project."

"Here's the deal," Meghan said to us. "Both of your firms are qualified to do this project from a financial and a logistic standpoint."

Hunter leveled his gaze at her. "We are far superior to the Harringtons. Between Svensson Investment and Greyson Hotel Group, we have ten times as many successful projects in our portfolio." I nudged my brother, hoping he would get the hint to shut up.

"I understand," Mayor Barry said. "Unfortunately, the city isn't sold on the vision yet."

"Barry is being polite, but I'm too old to be nice," Amos said loudly. "I hate those rendering whatchamacallits you all showed." He stabbed a finger at one of the boards. "This looks like some crazy futuristic land. I want to see vision. I want to see the human touch. These things look like something out of Asia. It's like a video game. I hate it."

"Obviously, the final product wouldn't look like that," Evan Harrington said.

"Why don't you all come back with a better vision of what it will look like? Those video-game things are hard to read," Barry said, smiling. "You're bright young people. Especially you, Hunter."

Meghan sniffed. "You have two weeks to come up with something of vision and substance to present."

CHAPTER 11

Hazel

A fter running away from the Svenssons' house, I slunk back to the Art Café.

Slumping at one of the café tables, I checked Venmo. Archer had actually paid me at least, and it was way more than I was going to charge.

"Wait, he paid me three thousand dollars?" I felt bad. I didn't really do that much work, and his younger brothers had helped. "And of course I said something dumb around him. He must think I'm an idiot."

I collected the stack of mail from the floor and threw it in a drawer, not looking at it. I knew they were late notices for my loans and utilities.

Setting up my easel in the café, I decided to take my mind off things by finishing a painting. It was an inspirational painting of my café illustrating how I wanted it to look when I finally had money to fix it up. I touched up the flowers in the window boxes and went to work on the tree I was going to put in the foreground to draw people's eyes into the painting. But all I could think about was Archer. The particular shade of gray of his eyes, the cut of his jaw, the sinew on his neck against the expensive suit fabric.

Sometimes I would get this rush to paint, like I had to, like my skin was going to come off if I didn't. The image of him was burned in my mind, needing to come out. I had the sudden urge to paint Archer, to capture the striking black of his expensive suit against the old brick. It would look like a Dutch master's portrait, the black of his clothes almost fading into the background, the light sculpting the planes and angles of his face and the intensity of his eyes.

"I just need to paint him, then I'll forget about him," I said, though in reality, I wanted Archer to climb out of the painting like Pygmalion's statue and sweep me off my feet. After hours of working, I put the finishing touch on Archer's hair. I had placed him in the sunlight that washed over the front of the building and mixed a series of dark yellows to capture the gold in his hair. Then I placed the painting upstairs in my private studio. There was no way it could ever see the light of day. I would die of embarrassment.

I half hoped to see Archer and half didn't want to see him at the retreat the next day. I was frazzled the next morning as I made Ida's sandwiches then suffered through the lunch trickle.

Archer stalked in that afternoon, sunglasses planted firmly on his face. He seemed like he was in a bad mood.

"Today we're doing impressionist-style painting. I have some flowers here, donated by Ida's General Store." The seniors clapped lightly.

I passed out glasses of sangria. The older women sipped as they used large brushstrokes to paint the flowers.

"Need a drink?" I asked Archer. He was sitting on the couch, arms crossed, watching his little brothers paint.

"No, thanks," he said. I wondered if he was mad that he gave me so much money for the food. Maybe I didn't do a good enough job cooking.

"Look," I told him. "I think you might have given me too much for dinner yesterday."

"No," he said. "Keep it. You helped me out of a tight spot. We just had a bad meeting today. Don't worry about it."

"Anything I can do to help?"

"I'll take that drink. Also I think I might buy you an air-conditioning unit. It's sweltering in here."

Archer took a sip of the sangria. I noticed he had unbuttoned his shirt even more. Archer smirked as he caught me staring.

"You want me to take it all the way off?"

Ida wolf whistled.

"I don't think she could handle it," I said, blushing. I told myself it was the heat.

"Really?" Archer asked. "Because I bet I could be really inspirational."

"It's already too hot in here," I muttered.

"I think I will paint actually," Archer said, smile widening. "Maybe I'll be inspired." He walked up to the blank canvas I had set out for him and proceeded to take off his shirt. The senior citizens all screamed and whistled.

"This shirt was pricy. I don't want to ruin it with paint," Archer said with a wink.

I slapped a hand to my eyes. I would be lying if I said I wasn't peeking. The fine line-work tattoos made a geometric pattern over his chest. They were well composed and done by an artist knowledgeable about their craft. They disappeared into the waist of his dress pants. I wondered how far down the tattoos went.

"I have an apron," I told Archer firmly.

"Boo," Ida said. "I was promised nude models."

I hurried to the storage closet and pulled out a smock. "Here," I said, thrusting it at Archer. "If you're worried about paint, you can wear this."

"You want to cover all this up?" Archer asked, pretending to be offended.

"Yes." *No.*

Somehow the smock made it worse. For one, it was too small on him. His muscles bulged under the fabric, which rode up whenever he moved his arm so that I could still see his abs.

Archer was in my brain for the rest of the afternoon. Ida would periodically lead a chant of, "Take it off! Take it off!" Archer would obligingly start to lift the smock, and I would yell at him to put it back on.

At the end of the retreat, I was ready to make myself a drink.

The chime at the front door sounded.

"Drinks?" Olivia called as she settled back in a chair.

"Definitely," I said as I pulled out the liquors and started the deep fryer for snacks.

"Someone has men on the brain," Olivia said when she walked over to one of the small tables with the drinks and a plate of Vincent van Goat cheese fritters smothered in local honey.

"I'm not the type of girl Archer wants."

"Uh, I wasn't talking about you. I was talking about my horny grandmother. Ida went on and on about how her Facebook friends are so jealous that she has access to drinks, snacks, and a hot piece of ass, as she put it."

I winced. "You need to control your grandmother."

"And you need to value yourself. You're a bartender and a cook. What man doesn't want that?"

"You mean what man doesn't want a girl who can't even keep her business afloat?"

"Archer has money," Olivia said. "The car he drives could probably pay for this building, pay for the upkeep, and let you have all the paint you desire."

"I don't want a handout or a man to just buy things for me. I want to do this on my own and be successful," I said, biting into the gooey goat cheese fritter.

"I have some good news that will cheer you up!" Olivia said. "A client of one of my friends from architecture school has an art gallery in New York City. She said you could come by tomorrow to show her your paintings."

I squealed and thanked the universe. "You're the best, Olivia. Maybe this was my big break!"

"We need to figure out what paintings you should take," Olivia said as we walked up to the third floor, where my studio was. "Oh my God, what is this? Is that Archer Svensson?" my friend exclaimed, grabbing my arm when she saw the painting of my café I'd been working on yesterday. I tried to hide it.

"This is borderline creepy," Olivia said, laughing. "Does he know you've been painting him?"

I shuddered and pulled the canvas away from her. "I would die if he found out."

Olivia flipped through my stack of canvases. "You should bring these idyllic town scene paintings," she said. "Instead of the weird abstract ones."

"No one wants those. They're just paintings I made for me."

"You could sell them to a hotel."

"A motel maybe."

"Actually the one you did with Archer is probably the best of the bunch. I really think you should try and sell it. People like images of other people they know."

"I cannot bring that painting," I said, shoving the painting behind the couch.

Olivia helped me select ten paintings and carefully stacked them in my large portfolio.

"All done," she said, zipping it up. "Too bad Archer isn't here. He could kiss it for good luck!"

CHAPTER 12

Despite teasing Hazel, I couldn't help but mope after that horrible development meeting with the city.

"I can't believe they didn't like the renderings. Seriously, who refuses to sell based on a rendering?" I complained to Mace that evening in the clubroom. It had a built-in bar and was completely clad in wood. There were priceless antiques that made Mace's eye twitch whenever I touched them.

"What does that even mean, the renderings look too 'futuristic'? What am I going to do?"

"You think you have problems? What am I going to do about the kids? Josie is going to revolt," my twin replied, settling into one of the large leather chairs, drink in hand. We kept the liquor in the clubroom so the teenagers couldn't get to it. As such, it was where all my adult-aged brothers tended to congregate after a long day.

"I thought Josie liked cooking for large crowds," I said, quoting her.

Mace grimaced. "The novelty is wearing off. Plus all the college kids eat so much food. I forgot how much they eat. I thought Josie was going to kill Eli when he sat there and ate an entire loaf of banana bread she had just made."

"We can go eat at restaurants," I said. I had been in Harrogate for weeks, yet I still didn't have my conference center. All my effort, down the drain—and the kids were driving me crazy. I missed the nightlife in Manhattan. There was no nightlife in Harrogate. Instead I was stuck at home with the kids. I was used to breezing in, stirring the pot, then leaving since I didn't actually live at the estate house. Now, though, I stirred the pot and had to clean it up when it spilled over.

"Just because that's what you do, doesn't mean the kids should be eating out for breakfast, lunch, and dinner," Mace said with a frown.

"If Hunter hadn't screwed things up with Meg," I said casually, "she and Josie would make a great team."

"I don't want to hear another word about it," Hunter snapped from the corner of the room, not looking up from the documents he was marking up. "I'm sick of you thinking you can slide in here and hang around like you're on vacation. It's incredibly inconvenient."

"Really? Is it an inconvenience? Like the cell phone law?" Garrett sneered. "I got another ticket, by the way."

"I'm really questioning the decision to have Hunter at the meeting today," I said.

"The only reason Meghan didn't completely throw you all out was because Mayor Barry likes me," Hunter snapped, setting down his papers.

"This small town is an incestuous cesspool," I complained, leaning back in the leather chair.

"Speaking of people who are related, we need to come to a consensus about the food situation," Mace announced.

"There are an awful lot of adults sucking up food and oxygen here," Hunter added.

Garrett mumbled something about Hunter, and our older brother stood up. Garrett stared him down from his chair. I seriously needed a break from my family.

"If you're going to be here full-time, Archer," Mace continued, "I think we should take some of the load off Josie. Maybe we could come up with a schedule—"

I groaned dramatically.

"Why don't you go back to Manhattan if you don't like it here?" Hunter asked tersely.

The reality was, I was sort of tired of the shallow Manhattan life. McKenna also had a hand in souring the city for me. I was not going to admit it, but I was also a little jealous of what my twin had with Josie.

"You never do anything," Hunter continued. "You refuse to take interns. You don't cook. After all I have done, after everything I have sacrificed, I consider it a slap in the face."

Garrett snorted. "Give it a rest, Hunter."

"Is Archer part of this family or not?"

"I am, but I'm going to need a break," I said, standing up.

"Freedom!" I sang as my sports car roared down the road. But it didn't feel as great as it usually did. I had sent a few feelers out to people I used to party with. They sent me offerings of new clubs, gallery openings, and exclusive parties. I scrolled through them on my way to the elevator after I parked the car in the parking deck below my condo building.

None of the events seemed all that interesting. I half wondered what the kids were doing. Did they have anything to eat? Did Mace make them his signature dry, flavorless chicken and vegetable pan dinner?

"Nice to see you again, Mr. Svensson," the doorman greeted me when I walked into the expansive lobby.

It was the first project Greg's investment company had funded. As such, the lobby style was a little dated; it was very 2009. A handful of my brothers had their Manhattan base in this tower. The biggest selling point, though, was that Greg didn't live here. He could be overbearing and controlling at the best of times. The man had no sense of humor and tended to take things literally.

"I'm going to enjoy my peace and quiet," I told myself when I punched the key code to unlock my condo. The large metal door slid open. It was one of my favorite features of my condo. I settled on the couch. Though my condo was posh and high-end, it felt cold and empty. The only sound was the AC unit kicking in.

I checked the fridge. No food. I wanted some of the popcorn Hazel had made, or one of those sandwiches. My mouth watered. What had she put on that sandwich? I had saved the little card. I took it out of my pocket and stared at the illustration. Hazel really did have a good eye for color and composition. Maybe I could have her design the menus or signage for my hotels. People went crazy for Instagram-worthy touches like that.

That still didn't solve my food problem. But I had an ace up my sleeve.

Archer: *Will look attractive for food.*
Chloe: *You can come if I can take a nice photo
     of you to put on Instagram.*
Archer: *Done.*

"These pigeons are conspiring against us," a homeless man told me very seriously as I walked down the wide busy New York City street on my way to Frost Tower.

"It's good to be back in Manhattan!" I yelled. The passersby ignored me, and I laughed.

Chloe's restaurant was hopping. She gave me a warm hug when she saw me then shoved a box in my hands.

"Sample cookies for your new hotel," she said. I took out one of the cookies.

"They're almost too pretty to eat." They were decorated like my newest hotel that had opened a few blocks away.

"How's the new franchise in Harrogate coming?" I asked Chloe as I took a bite of the cookie.

"Slow. I have too much on my plate. I want to open up a bar next door, then I have two other franchises opening in New York City."

"You need to hire some more people," Chloe's friend and coworker Maria stated.

I pulled at my shirt collar and tried to look innocent and attractive. "I kind of already promised that you would put a booth in the food hall in my conference center," I said in a rush.

Chloe shook her head slowly. "I don't have the woman power."

"That's why you need to hire more people!" Maria called out again from behind the bakery case.

"I'm trying! I have both Maria's and Nina's whole families basically employed now."

"There's a labor shortage," I told Chloe, eating another cookie. "I'm having trouble at my hotels too."

Chloe plucked the cookie out of my hand and put it back in the box. "I thought you wanted dinner," she admonished, waving me into the kitchen to pick up a large tray of pasta, blackened fish, and a grain and grilled vegetable salad.

"Jack already grabbed a table," Chloe said. "He's out there somewhere."

I walked through the large restaurant at the base of Frost Tower. Jack, Chloe's boyfriend, was sitting opposite Liam, my half brother, at a table near the window.

"I heard Hunter kicked you out," Liam said by way of greeting.

"Vicious rumors," I said. Chloe came over with a bottle of wine and sat down next to Jack. She cut off a piece of the fish along with some of the pasta, put it on a small plate, and slid it over to me.

"Try this," Chloe said. "I found a new fishmonger, and I'm trying out some new recipes."

"How come you're giving him food?" Liam complained.

"I give you free food all the time, and you just wolf it all down before giving me a good commentary."

"I tell you it's delicious," Liam countered.

"She needs a more refined palate," I told him and took a bite of the pasta.

"Handmade tortellini, slightly chilled, with a fresh pesto," I said, spearing another bite. "It's like you put summer in a salad and put it on my plate. And look at the crust on this fish. Did you just catch it this morning? Look at how flakey that is. Look at it, Liam!"

Liam snapped it off my fork.

"Heathen."

"See?" Chloe said. "That's just what I needed to hear."

"You better be careful," Jack warned me, "or you might be the next judge on *The Great Christmas Bake-Off*."

"They're doing that again this year?"

"Of course. Gunnar said he made mad money on that show. Dana is concocting some scheme to make it bigger and better."

"They need to find someplace else to have it other than Jack's tower," Chloe said. "I already rent that kitchen space to make Greyson Hotel Group's cookies."

"As you should. Those hand-decorated cookies we give each guest every day are a huge reason why people stay there."

"The best part is," Jack said with a grin, "my tower is a hundred percent leased."

"Nice," I said, fist-bumping him. "Though I think you mean that the best part is that Greg is off your case. I wish I could finally close on this conference center. Greg and Hunter are driving me nuts."

"Maybe when you get that conference center, Dana and Gunnar can have *The Great Christmas Bake-Off* there," Liam joked.

"Ah, I don't think it will be ready by then." Truth was, I had heard from Liam how insane *The Great Christmas Bake-Off* was last year. I did not need that in my life.

After staggering out of Chloe's restaurant, having been stuffed with food and loaded down with a bag of desserts, I forced myself to walk the thirty minutes to my closest hotel.

It gleamed from down the block. I loved seeing my hotels. I always chose beautiful old historic buildings, or if one wasn't available in the location I wanted, I had a luxury building built. In the first floor or two, I would put galleries, restaurants, high-end bodegas, or nice retail stores to make the hotels feel more a part of the neighborhood. They were nice amenities for the community and made hotel guests feel like they were having an authentic experience.

When I walked into my hotel, I greeted the staff and answered questions. We had a celebrity with a big baby shower coming in the next few days, two weddings that weekend, and a prom. I had expert staff, and I was pleased with the plans they showed me. I set my bags of food in my office—I had an office in every hotel I owned. Then I wandered the hallways under the guise of quality control and looked at all the expensive artwork. It was collectively worth a fortune. I wondered if Hazel would like it. I wished she were here so I could see her reaction.

Going back to my office on the third floor of the hotel, I settled down on the couch and pulled out my phone. I swiped at my phone, ignoring all the messages from people begging me to come party and instead pulled up Hazel's Instagram.

It wasn't even midnight when I fell asleep, scrolling through the pictures of her.

"I hope you didn't sleep here like a homeless person," Mike said the next morning as he shook me roughly awake.

I blinked and yawned. "Why are you here so early?"

"We need to get the conference center under control," Mike said, opening the curtains, letting the light stream in through the window.

"I have a plan," I assured him, pulling a cookie out of the bag of baked goods Chloe had given me and taking a bite.

"That's not the point. You can't just neglect the other hotels," he said.

"I'm not neglecting them. They're running great!"

"Yes, for now. But part of what makes Greyson Hotel Group special is our attention to detail. You can't do that when you're in Harrogate all the time."

"I'm going to go through the New York City hotels today," I promised.

"No, you're not. We have the interns," Mike said, snatching the cookie out of my hand.

"What interns?" I asked, trying to decide if I had enough energy to fight him for it.

Mike frowned. "Our brothers who are interning at our company. Do you pay attention to anything?"

"Ugh, I thought that was a joke."

"No. And Hunter wants them to be supervised. There have been complaints of them riding their bikes up and down Main Street at all hours. We need to start training them. They can't turn into useless playboys."

"All right, maybe next week." I yawned.

"They're here now, Archer," Mike said. Several of my brothers poked their heads around the doorframe.

"Cookie?" I offered. Mike made a disgusted noise.

My brother tapped his pen on the desk impatiently while I made myself as presentable as I could. Then we went on a tour to several other boutique hotels that our company owned nearby. On the way, I made us stop by several of my favorite food trucks.

"You can't get empanadas like these in Harrogate," I said, blowing on the crispy pastry. I munched on the food as our group followed Mike to our newest hotel.

"Can anyone tell me why we chose this location?" Mike asked. Eli raised his hand to answer, and I tuned them out. I looked through the window of the retail space. There was a restaurant on one side of the entrance and an art gallery on the other. And who should I see through the window but Hazel.

CHAPTER 13

took an early train that morning—you never knew with the train system—and I arrived in New York City with an hour and a half to spare.

I decided to stop by to see a couple friends of mine from art school. I had some ideas for how to make Harrogate appealing to the Art Zurich Biennial Expo search committee, but I needed some help.

"How's the restaurant business?" Katie asked. She worked in a shared sculpture studio in the Bronx.

"Oh, you know," I said. I didn't want to go into how badly I was failing. "So I have a job for you."

"Wait, you mean someone actually wants to pay us for our art?" Katie asked, walking me back through the large warehouse space. There were several sculptures out.

"I know, right? What a novel concept," I said, taking a few pictures.

"I don't know. I like to deep-fry exposure and eat it on a taco."

"You'll get exposure with this project, but you'll also get money," I told Katie as she rounded up several other artists we went to school with.

As we stood around a large ornamental outdoor firepit, I told them about my ideas for bringing art to Harrogate.

"I'm pitching it at our committee meeting tomorrow," I told the group. "Once Archer Svensson signs off, we'll have you come out, see the site, and let me know which spot you want. We want to make a statement, so bigger is better. Our timeline is pretty short, too, so there will obviously be a fee to expedite the work."

Several of the artists pumped their fists. Like me, I knew they were pleased with the idea of some extra money.

Katie walked me out after the meeting. "So, Archer Svensson, huh?"

"You know him?"

"I know of him. He made Fang Fei famous. I thought he was dating McKenna. I'm glad you're moving into her territory."

"I'm not moving into her territory," I scoffed. "I don't want anything to do with Archer. He's obnoxious."

"But he's so good-looking." Katie sighed. "And he appreciates art."

After hugging Katie goodbye, I hefted the heavy portfolio. I didn't have money to take a car, so I was forced to jostle onto the subway. I had to walk several blocks from the closest subway station to the gallery and was out of breath and sweaty when I arrived.

The gallery was at the bottom of a fancy hotel.

"Hello?" I called when I walked into the air-conditioning.

"You must be Hazel." A tall, thin older woman approached me, hand outstretched.

"Hi, Lucy?" I asked in a rush, shifting my portfolio to my other arm and shaking her hand. "Sorry," I said after accidentally banging her with the portfolio. "Thank you so much for meeting with me."

"We sell quite a bit of art to investors," Lucy bragged. "Fang Fei used to show with us before she was discovered." I remembered what Archer had said, how he had made her famous. Maybe a billionaire would walk into the gallery and make me famous.

The gallery owner gestured to my portfolio. "Let's have a look."

I started to lay out the paintings. The abstract collage canvases looked like they belonged in Lucy's gallery, I thought as I arranged them on the table. I took out one that was charcoal with spatters of yellow and laid it on the table.

"Oh," the gallery owner said. She was looking at the next painting in the stack. My stomach churned. It was the realistic one of my café with Archer front and center.

"That wasn't supposed to be in there," I said, hurrying to hide the painting.

"That man looks familiar," Lucy said, trying to get a closer look while I floundered.

"It's my boyfriend, Archer Svensson," a woman said from across the room.

I whirled around. "McKenna?"

"Lucy is my aunt," McKenna said as she slowly circled the table to inspect my paintings. McKenna and her aunt tsk-tsked as they reviewed my work.

"Unfortunately, I'm not that impressed," Lucy said after several minutes. She took off her glasses and looked at me. "You know, I don't ever see you at art functions in Manhattan."

"I live in Harrogate," I explained. "It's difficult to come into the city."

"I see. Well, there are trends, and I'm afraid your work is not in vogue right now."

"Thank you for your time." I looked down at my shoes, ordering myself not to cry. "I never should have come here," I muttered as I carefully placed the canvases back in the portfolio.

Lucy and McKenna whispered behind the reception desk. Couldn't they have at least waited until I left to make fun of me?

I jumped when someone banged on the glass.

"Archer?" I mouthed. He grinned. I felt something jump in my chest.

The tall man opened the door and sauntered into the gallery.

"Why do you always have to appear in my life at the worst possible times?" I whispered furiously.

"I own this building," he said smugly.

"Mr. Svensson!" Lucy said, hurrying over. McKenna sashayed behind her. Archer struggled to maintain composure.

"Archer," McKenna purred, pressing herself lightly against him, and kissed his cheek. Really, it was practically his mouth. "So good to see you."

"It's so wonderful of you to stop by," Lucy said. "Are you looking for a new artist?"

That shit-eating grin spread across his face. "As a matter of fact, I am," he said. He turned to me. "What do you have?"

I was mortified.

"Please, we have several new artists in," Lucy practically begged, motioning me to get the hell out of her gallery. I was happy to oblige.

Archer blocked my path. "I'd like to see what she brought in," he repeated.

"Surely not!" Lucy said, horrified.

He ignored her and opened my portfolio. McKenna looked on in annoyance as Archer carefully went through the paintings.

I prayed he wouldn't see the one where I had painted him without his permission. Unfortunately I wasn't going to be so lucky.

"Now this is art!" he said when he saw the painting of him in front of my café. I wanted to sink into the floor and die.

"We have some great paintings by a young Brazilian artist," Lucy said faintly.

"I'll take this one," Archer said.

"Wouldn't you rather—" Lucy said.

"How much?"

"I…" Lucy looked at me, then she looked at Archer.

"Fifty dollars," McKenna said nastily.

"Two thousand," her aunt cut in.

"Sold," Archer said. "Here's my credit card."

In shock, I watched as Lucy carefully packaged the painting and ran Archer's card. "As usual, thank you for your business," she said, smile plastered on her face. "Where shall we have it sent?"

"Have it delivered to Svensson Investment," Archer said. He took a piece of paper and wrote a note. "Frame it first, would you? And please include this note. You have my billing information."

"I can't believe he just embarrassed you like that," McKenna said softly, inspecting her nails as Archer talked to her aunt. "But you know those billionaires."

"Maybe I should put more of your art up," Lucy said uncertainly after Archer left. I couldn't even look at him.

"Don't bother," McKenna said. "He was just trying to humiliate her."

CHAPTER 14

I f I had known McKenna was going to be there, I wouldn't have even gone in the gallery. But Hazel had seemed upset as Lucy looked through her paintings. I knew how snooty art-world people could be. I couldn't resist pulling one over on them.

I hoped Hazel wasn't too upset with me. It was just a joke. Plus her painting did look nice.

When I walked into my condo, I was greeted by complete quiet. My entire childhood and my early adulthood I'd had to share a room with a person or ten. Now it seemed the ultimate luxury to have all of this space to myself and in one of the most expensive cities in the world.

It was still empty though. I missed my family, as much as I hated to admit it. I had planned to spend several days in Manhattan at least, but now I found myself repacking my bags and heading down into the parking garage at the base of the building.

"I'm just doing this because clearly Mace is preoccupied and someone has to take care of my little brothers," I assured myself.

"You were always so considerate. That's why you were my favorite child."

"Mom?" I said, whirling around.

"My darling baby," my mother said.

Unlike Payslee, one of my father's other sister wives who was now thankfully in jail, my mother, Merla Vee, was fairly stylish and healthy. She approached me, her high heels clacking on the concrete parking deck floor.

"Hi, Mom," I said, hugging her. I felt a little guilty. All of my full-blooded brothers had basically cut our mom off. When we were kids, she just left one day, said she couldn't take being with my father anymore. She abandoned us at the compound. Being in a doomsday polygamist cult must have been hard for her. I couldn't blame her for leaving. My other brothers blamed her, though. Shortly after Merla Vee left, our father kicked me and my brothers out to fend for ourselves in the desert.

Still, she was my mother, and I couldn't abandon her.

Merla Vee reached up to pet my hair. "Look at my big, strong, handsome son," she said, smiling. "You were always my favorite."

My mother had been unhappy being a sister wife in a polygamist cult for obvious reasons. When I was a child, I would always try to cheer her up. Normally she would take her frustration out on her kids. I was the only one who could make her laugh.

"You know you shouldn't be here; my brothers could see you," I reminder her.

"You should tell them to call their mother," she said with a pout. "I'm so proud of everything you have accomplished."

I basked in the praise even though I knew it was false. She was flattering me so I would give her money. And it was working. The only time she contacted me was when she needed cash.

"We could grab dinner," I offered. "I could tell you about what's going on in my life." Even as I made the offer, I knew she wouldn't accept it.

"Oh," Marla Vee said with a laugh. "I know you're busy. I don't want to bother you. I only wanted to mention this company I wanted to invest in." She always claimed to have investment opportunities though I had never seen any real information on them. I knew my mother was spending the money on clothes and jewelry.

"Sure," I said, trying not to show my disappointment. "How about I give you a few thousand now, and we can talk more in detail later?"

"You're so generous," Merla Vee said, hugging me and kissing my cheek. "That's why you're my favorite son."

She tried to hide her impatience while I sent her three thousand dollars over Venmo.

"Thank you, sweetie! We'll be in touch," she said as she walked out of the parking deck with mincing steps.

I sat in my car after she left. A part of me wanted to call my twin and come clean, but Mace was busy with Josie, and he was finally happy. I knew this would send him into a tailspin after what had happened last month with Payslee.

I turned on the radio, hoping the music would lift my mood. I tried very hard to always be upbeat and fun. It was part of my persona. In the break between songs, the announcer said that all the trains heading west out of the city were down.

"So glad I have my car," I said, patting my dashboard. Harrogate was on the west commuter line. "Sucks for those people."

And one person in particular. A dejected-looking Hazel stood at a bus stop several blocks away with her huge portfolio. I pulled up beside her.

"The trains are down," I called through the window.

"I know," she said and looked away from me.

"Do you want a ride?" I prompted.

"No, thank you," she said.

"Look, I'm sorry about earlier in the gallery. I wasn't trying to be mean. I just thought it would be funny."

"It wasn't," Hazel snapped.

Someone behind me honked. I blared my horn back.

"Could you just get in the car, please?" I snarled.

"I don't get in the car with assholes," she yelled at me.

"You won't be able to go home," I told her.

She didn't budge.

"If you don't want a ride, at least let me put you up in one of my hotels." I looked up at the sky. "I think it's going to rain. You don't want all your paintings to get wet."

Hazel stared at the dark clouds gathering over the city. Then she huffed as I popped the trunk and ran around to take her portfolio from her and stow it in the car.

She sat in the passenger seat, arms crossed. "Thank you for the ride."

"You're not going to call me an attractive idiot?" I asked as I pulled out into traffic. "I'm a little disappointed."

"I don't want to boost your ego anymore," Hazel said. "You already know you're attractive."

"She thinks I'm attractive!"

"I also think you're an idiot."

"I'm sorry. Truly I am. I didn't mean to hurt you."

"You didn't hurt me," Hazel scoffed. "I'm not that thin-skinned. I did spend four years of my life in art school being berated for the fact that my paintings looked too realistic and derivative. Because if you can count all the toes on a painting of a foot, apparently that's terrible and you're dragging the art world down."

I laughed. "Art school professors are the worst. I gave a lecture once at an art school in California with Fang Fei, and the professors kept asking me all these gotcha questions to trip me up and make themselves look smart. It's like, seriously, guys, get a life."

Hazel smiled. "It's because the stakes are so low. Aside from the handful of people who make it big, anyone else in art can't really hope for much besides a part-time teaching position if they're lucky."

"You're making it as an artist," I reminded her. "You have the Art Café."

Hazel snorted. "Yeah, making it."

"I like you and your paintbrush," I said lightly.

"I thought it was *your* paintbrush we were supposed to be concerned about," she quipped.

"Concerned? Hardly," I said lightly, hoping the joke meant she wasn't mad at me. "Though if you are concerned about it, I *am* pretty good at finger painting, no brush needed."

I thought I saw her try not to smile. "I'm not going to encourage you. Speaking of art, when did you start collecting it?" Hazel asked. "It doesn't seem like something a Svensson would do."

"How many Svenssons do you know?"

She crossed her arms. "I just can't see Hunter collecting art."

"I'm not sure how much of the sordid Svensson brothers' history you know."

"Some."

"Right, small town. Well, we grew up in a polygamist cult in a compound in the middle of the desert and lived in a cramped, crumbling house. Then when Hunter helped us all escape to the outside world, there was TV and snacks and nice clothes and art. I just wanted something beautiful in my life. I might have gone a little overboard," I admitted. "I like collecting art and displaying it. Full disclosure, that's the reason I developed my first hotel. I wanted to show off all the art I was able to buy."

Hazel lightly touched my arm. "Of all the ways to go crazy after your ordeal, art is probably more wholesome than alcohol, fast cars, and women."

I smirked at her. "I went crazy on all of those things too."

Now that we cleared Manhattan, it was smooth driving. Hazel clutched the door as I sped up, the road stretching out in front of us. "You're going to get a ticket," she warned.

"I thought you were friends with the police. If we're pulled over, you can put in a good word."

"Doubtful," she said. "Maybe if I were driving."

"You have a driver's license?"

"Of course I have a driver's license."

"But you pulled up on a bike."

"If you don't want me to drive your car, just say so," she said.

"This is my baby." I stroked the dashboard.

"You insulted me."

I pulled over. "Fine. Drive."

"Seriously?"

I nodded, a little apprehensive at the gleeful expression on Hazel's face as I stepped out.

"Oh boy." Hazel rubbed her hands together as she sat in the driver's seat.

"Gimme your sunglasses," she said, plucking them off my face. She put the car into gear and floored the gas. The sports car jerked forward. Now I was the one gripping the door.

"I thought you didn't like to go fast," I said over the roar of the engine. Hazel whooped as we raced down the road to Harrogate. We beat the storm to her café.

She pulled to a stop in front of the Art Café right as the first few raindrops hit the windshield.

"You're going back to work?" I asked. "It's late."

She shrugged.

"I can drop you back to your house," I offered.

"This is fine," Hazel insisted as she popped the trunk and opened the car door.

I jumped out and followed behind her with the portfolio.

"I'll take it up for you," I said, heading to the narrow stairs, taking them two at a time.

"Stop. You don't have to," she insisted, scurrying up after me.

The third floor was a mess—paintings everywhere, piles of canvases. Through an open door, I saw a bed stuffed into what looked like a storage closet.

Hazel huffed up beside me. I peered at her. "You don't live here, do you?"

"Go away."

"Seriously, let me book you a hotel room," I offered.

"I don't need your charity," she yelled, pushing me toward the stairs. "Just go away."

I headed back to the car, dodging the fat, slightly cool raindrops.

I should have stayed in Manhattan. And I can't even go to Hazel's bar because she's mad at me for some reason.

I was so lost in my thoughts that I almost ran into McKenna, who was standing in front of my car.

"Archer," she cooed.

"I thought you had finally given up on Harrogate," I said coldly.

She laughed brightly, then before I could stop her, she wrapped her arms around me and kissed me. "Hardly," she said against my mouth. "I wanted to rekindle what we had."

CHAPTER 15

Hazel

Maybe I had been too harsh on Archer. He did give me a ride and let me drive his car. I looked out the window to see if it was too late to run after him. That's when I saw him and McKenna kissing. It was a hot, movie-worthy, steamy, summer-rain kiss. I was instantly jealous.

> **Hazel:** *Archer's making out with McKenna in front of my café.*
> **Jemma:** *??? Why is he in front of your café?*
> **Olivia:** *McKenna's trying to send a message.*
> **Hazel:** *Archer drove me home from Manhattan.*
> **Jemma:** *So why is he kissing McKenna? He clearly wants you.*
> **Hazel:** *He was just being polite.*
> **Jemma:** *Did he ask to come inside?*

Hazel: *Came inside then I threw him out. He saw my closet bedroom and figured out I live in my café. I don't even have a house. He offered to give me a hotel room.*

Jemma: *You're killing me. I'm literally dying on your behalf. If a good-looking guy offers to put you up in a hotel he owns you should at least consider it. You definitely don't kick him out!*

Olivia: *If you hadn't he would be kissing you instead of McKenna. This was the universe giving you an opening and you blew it.*

Hazel: *Or what if all the flirting was just for show? Maybe he doesn't want someone like me.*

But did I want someone like him? I mean, who was I kidding? Of course I did. He was attractive, fun, cared about his family, and appreciated art.

The next morning we had an art committee meeting scheduled. I was there early and watched Archer stumble in late. He was followed by McKenna. Had they been together? Why did I even care? I seriously wished I hadn't kicked him out.

"Let's call this committee meeting to order," I said, trying to keep the annoyance off my face as McKenna smiled softly at Archer.

Did they or didn't they? I gripped the pen.

"The Svenssons have contributed a large amount of funds for improvements to help Harrogate win the Art

Zurich Expo," I said. "Let's all present our ideas for how to best allocate these funds for maximum impact."

"First," Archer said, "we should have some marketing collateral about how easy it is to navigate around the city and how easy it is to reach Harrogate from the international airport."

"Maybe Josie can help us with presentations and brochures," I said, writing a note.

"We should do a bike share," Jemma added.

"Just have free bikes," Archer said, "like those scooter companies. It's easier to manage than an actual bike share. Paint them cool colors or weld interesting metalwork on them, and boom, it's an Instagram moment. Then it won't look so corporate. We can also have individuals or businesses sponsor a bike."

I hated to admit it, but it did sound like a better plan.

"The next idea is murals," I said.

"You need to be careful with the murals," Archer warned. "They need to be nice murals not sucky ones. Either go basic with text and color blocking, or go for abstract murals."

"We should keep the color palette similar as well," I added.

Archer grinned at me. "You and I are on the same wavelength."

McKenna jumped in. "Someone with *talent* needs to paint them."

"I have several friends from art school who are muralists," I said. "They would be willing."

"I went to school with you too," McKenna snapped. "There's no one in our class who is worthy of painting the murals."

"Then you find someone," Jemma cut in.

"We also need to have a big moment, like an art trail or something," I said, hoping to avoid a fight. "New York City has the High Line. Atlanta has the BeltLine. Harrogate needs something similar that is a big public moment to showcase art."

Archer was nodding along.

"Maybe we could tie it in as part of Archer's conference center?" I said sweetly. Jemma pulled up the map we had made of the potential route on her tablet. "We could have the art trail run from the conference center through the train park and connect to the green space by Svensson PharmaTech."

Archer looked thoughtful. I held my breath, wondering if he would go for it.

"We need it built by the time the Art Zurich team arrives," McKenna scoffed. "It will never work."

"No, we don't," I said. "The search committee is trying to find up-and-coming places. We only need a part of the trail built with plans for the rest. Surely we can build a little bit, maybe on Svensson PharmaTech's property?"

"Done," Archer said.

"Are you sure?" I asked. "Don't you want to ask Mace?"

"It's a great idea."

"Don't you need a permit?" McKenna countered.

"Hazel's great-uncle is the mayor. We can push something through quickly. It's a sidewalk and some gravel," Archer said. "How hard can it be? The big thing is, we need some art on the art trail."

"I've already reached out to sculptors I know from art school," I told him.

McKenna made a face. She stroked Archer's hand, and I resisted the urge to throw my pen at her. "Archer, you have your own sculpture collection. Why don't we use those?"

"They're investment pieces," Archer said, frowning.

After the rest of the meeting, in which McKenna would slyly touch Archer whenever possible, Olivia and Jemma followed me to the Art Café.

Bouncing on the balls of her feet, Olivia asked, "How did it go yesterday at the gallery?"

I sighed and ushered them inside. "I made a sale."

"Which painting did the gallery buy?" Olivia asked nonchalantly.

"The one that you put in there."

She grinned. "The nice one! You should make more of them!"

"Archer bought it. He did it as a joke," I said flatly. I looked down at the floor. His actions had stung more than I cared to admit.

My friends gasped when I told them the story.

"McKenna's a witch, and Archer's a sociopath," Jemma assured me.

"Maybe he's being mean to you because he likes you," Olivia said.

"That's how little boys behave. Men shouldn't play games like that," Jemma retorted.

"I'm trying to look on the bright side," I said. "I sold a painting, and I'll hopefully sell a ton more at the art fair this weekend."

"I wish I hadn't sent you over there now," Olivia said, expression guilty. "I didn't realize the gallery owner was related to McKenna."

"She just seems like she keeps popping up where we don't want her."

"If you're not super mad," Olivia said, rocking back on her heels, "can you come over to the Svensson estate? I need your help on selecting colors. It's for Josie's cottage."

I pretended to be annoyed, but secretly I loved helping Olivia on her architecture projects. Also she had a car with air-conditioning, so I didn't have to bike over there—not that I didn't need the exercise.

We drove up to the house and parked in the roundabout. Olivia headed to the front door.

"I can't go inside!" I protested. I did not want to see Archer.

"We aren't just going to creep around. We have to go through the house. They need to know we're here."

I slumped.

"Come on, Hazel! Please? We're just going to pop in. You're going to tell me the perfect primer and topcoat to use, and then we're out of there. Easy peasy."

The front door opened to several little blond heads peeking out.

"Hi!"

"Are you here to cook?"

"Olivia's not here to cook. She's... oh hey, Hazel." There in front of me was Archer. He was shirtless. I gulped. Archer smirked as he noticed my gaze travel down the path of his tattoos on his chest to the V that disappeared into his low-slung trunks.

"It's really warm. We're all outside," he said, a lazy grin on his face. "We've bought a Slip 'N Slide."

I stared up at the ornate ceiling. I wasn't giving him the satisfaction of seeing me drool over him.

"I was telling Mace about the art walk. It will get built one way or another," he said confidently as we followed him to the backyard. I nodded, keeping my mouth firmly shut.

The Svenssons were all sitting outside. The kids were cute as they splashed in the Slip 'N Slide. The adult males were all shirtless and smoking fucking hot.

Someone save me. I'm dying.

Archer gestured to his brothers.

"This is Mace. You know Garrett. That's Mike. We'll pretend Hunter doesn't exist, and that's Greg. You guys met on the phone."

The awkward comments were beating down the door from my brain to my mouth. As soon as I saw Greg, I immediately said, "Donut Danishes are soft and squishy, which you are definitely not. I don't know why Archer thought it would be funny."

There was silence. I clapped a hand over my mouth. Archer collapsed next to me, roaring in laughter.

"I am so sorry," I said, mortified. "I act weird around attractive men."

Why did you have to say that?

Now all of Archer's brothers were laughing.

"You're probably the only person who finds Greg attractive," Archer said.

Greg was annoyed. "I look like all of you."

"Not Archer," I said.

Stop talking, Hazel!

"Yes, I'm special," Archer said, waggling his eyebrows at me over the top of his sunglasses.

"You're just slightly less better-looking," I said.

Lies. The tattoos on his chest were calling my name.

Greg smirked as Archer pretended to be offended.

While the Svensson brothers bickered, I escaped with Olivia to the cottage.

"This is not a cottage," I said when we stood in front of the house that was larger than my childhood home. "Cottages are supposed to be one room with a thatched roof. This is a mansion."

"The Harrogates built this estate and all the outbuildings in the late eighteen hundreds," Olivia explained. "The Harrogate patriarch had these houses built for in-laws, cousins, and other various family members who he didn't want in the main house."

"This is gorgeous," I said, following Olivia into the cottage.

"It feels a lot smaller after the nightmare of restoring the main house," she said. "Anyway, come help me pick paints for the main rooms."

I looked around the room then at the paint samples.

"Use these for the primer," I said, holding up some warm peach tones. I leafed through the paint colors.

"Let me see this navy and this green." I held the swatches up to the wall.

"They're not too dark?"

"No. They will look nice against this white trim. I need to see the colors painted on the wall before I can give you a definitive answer," I warned.

"Stay for dinner!" Archer called out as I followed Olivia across the expansive backyard to the estate house.

"He wants you to stay and cook," Mace added dryly. "Josie's thrown in the towel. She's working, believe it or not."

"I believe it! She's in high demand, I hear," Olivia said. I was so envious of Olivia being able to talk to the Svenssons so freely.

"We have sandwich stuff…" Archer interjected.

"Make McKenna do it," I said nastily and hurried off to stunned looks.

CHAPTER 16

Archer

"You're back together with McKenna?" Greg asked coldly when Hazel was out of earshot. Otis and Theo insisted on walking her out. I hoped they didn't pester her with too many questions.

"I'm not back with her," I said, glaring at my brother. "She accosted me in the street. It was an ambush!"

"Wait, she's here in Harrogate?" Mace asked with a frown.

"She's been here for almost a week," Garrett said. He was under an umbrella, fully clothed, with his laptop.

"Why didn't you say anything? After what happened with Payslee..." Mace clamped his mouth shut.

"McKenna's not like Payslee," I hissed, hoping the kids didn't hear. I didn't want to spook them.

"You have the worst taste in women," Hunter said, settling back in his chair with his newspaper.

"And Mace has the best taste," Mike said as Josie walked out onto the terrace with a large package under her arm.

"A courier brought this," she said. "It's for Greg. The courier said Marnie told him it was extremely urgent. Otis is finding some scissors."

Greg frowned. I tried to keep my face neutral. It was *the painting*. I couldn't wait to see his face when he opened it. The note I'd written had made it sound like the painting was some urgent thing. I knew Marnie, Greg's assistant, would make sure he opened it. And she, as a stellar assistant, had it sent over to the estate.

"Did you figure out your rendering situation?" Josie asked as she came and lay down next to Mace on the lounge chair.

"We'll need to see if the architects can redo the renderings," Mike said.

"We can't just let them loose," I argued. "We should decide on a style. We need to figure out what Amos will like."

"He said he wanted the human touch," Mike added.

"Do you draw?" Greg asked Josie.

"No," she said. "I'm not that talented."

"You need to stop volunteering her for your work projects," Mace complained. "I never see her as it is."

Otis came out with a knife, and Greg opened the package. As soon as he pulled the painting out of the box, I started snickering.

"What the hell?" Mike asked.

Greg frowned as he studied the painting. My face beamed out from the canvas.

"This is exactly what we need," Greg announced, holding up the painting.

"A picture of Archer's face?" Mace asked, confused. "This is a new level of narcissism, even for you, Archer."

"It's not for me!" I said, hopping up and crossing the terrace to the table where Greg had the painting propped up. "I'm giving it to Greg. It's a present so you'll always remember me."

I stared at the painting. It was weird to see myself painted. I didn't think I'd ever experienced that. It was somehow more intimate than a picture, like the painter, well, Hazel, had truly seen me.

"It's perfect," Greg said.

"It is?" Mike said.

"Just cover up Archer, and look at the rest of it," Greg said, tearing off a piece of the brown wrapping paper and covering the portion of the painting with my face.

"Hey now!"

"Is that Harrogate?" Josie asked, coming over and peering at the painting.

"Right," Greg said with excitement. "This painting is basically a rendering of Harrogate. Look at the light, the trees, and the nice-looking shops. It's Main Street but comes across as very high-end yet still has some authenticity and character. This is the feel we're going for in the convention center. We need renderings like this for the project."

"It does seem like Amos would appreciate this style," Mike said. "What artist did you hire, Archer? Would he have any availability?"

Otis and Theo giggled to themselves.

"What's so funny?" Greg asked them.

"The artist is a girl," Otis said, pointing to Hazel's signature in the corner.

"Yeah and Archer's girlfriend," Theo said.

"She is not my girlfriend," I countered though a part of me wondered if that would be such a bad thing.

"I certainly hope not," Greg said. He looked down his nose at me and shook his head slowly. "How disappointing. You take after Hunter."

"Hey! You take that back."

Greg glared at me. "You are exactly like him. You can't treat women with respect. You insulted and played a mean practical joke on Hazel, and now she's going to screw over a major business deal. You're *exactly* like Hunter."

"You can't just blame everything on me, Greg," Hunter growled.

"Yes, I can."

I flopped back down on the lawn chair. "I'm not going to end up like Hunter, though. I'm charming and attractive, and I am going to beg and grovel until Hazel does the painting because I have absolutely no shame."

CHAPTER 17

Hazel

tried to stay calm when Olivia dropped me off at the Art Café. As I unlocked the door, I noticed that more demolition work had been done next door on the future Grey Dove Bistro. I tried not to seem morose as a few people trickled in for a drink.

> **Hazel:** *I still can't believe Archer was making out with McKenna of all people.*
>
> **Jemma:** *She's awful. She was in the general store today complaining that we didn't have a specific flavor of La Croix. Like go back to Manhattan.*
>
> **Olivia:** *She's obnoxious. Just concentrate on the art fair this weekend.*

I tried to send positive energy out to the universe. It must have worked because I received a notification from the bank that the money from the gallery was deposited into my account.

I sat back in my chair, thinking. Archer had bought yet another one of my paintings. Along with paying me to cook dinner for his brothers, he had been coming through for me. Of course he was probably also coming in McKenna, but it wasn't like I wanted Archer anyways.

Okay, yes, actually I did want him, but not as a *boyfriend*. I knew he was too out of my league for that. But maybe as an artfully arranged tasting menu?

Thinking about putting my mouth on his bare skin made me a little too hot. I set up a canvas to paint. The idea for the art walk had inspired me. Several ideas floated around in my head. The art walk would be really beautiful, like a fairy path. My imagination bloomed as I started to paint. The path would weave around the sculptures and huge trees. I painted glowing chandeliers hanging from the branches.

I painted for hours, and it grew dark out. I stopped to let the paint set before I did any more work. Though the canvas was looking good, it didn't make me any less annoyed with McKenna.

"Haters mean you're doing something right," I chanted as I lit some candles. I like candles, mainly because they gave me an excuse to burn things.

"Let the negative energy flow out of you," I said, closing my eyes and doing some yoga poses on the cool floor. "I am inspiring the universe, and the universe is inspiring me."

"I'm not the universe, but I am feeling very inspired, though maybe that's not the right word for it."

I shrieked and fell over. Archer grabbed me before I hit the floor and swung me easily to my feet.

"You startled me," I gasped.

"Sorry," he said, face serious. I fussed self-consciously with the buckle on my overalls. I wished I had worn something nicer. Archer's eyes followed my hands as I refastened the strap around the curve of my breast.

"Don't look at me like that," I scolded him. He held up his hands.

"Look," he said, "I'm extremely sorry about the phone call, just like I'm sorry about embarrassing you at the gallery. But I really need your help with a project."

I glared up at him. He was so unfairly tall. His hair hung in his face. I itched to reach up and smooth it back.

"Don't stand there and ask me to help you after you flirt with me then hook up with McKenna," I said hotly.

"Whoa, no! No." He shook his head. "None of that is true, okay? Well, the flirting is true, but I did not hook up with McKenna."

"I saw you with her."

Archer frowned. "McKenna is under the impression that we are getting back together, but that will never, ever happen."

"Oh," I said, needing to sit down for a moment. My legs shook, and Archer put a hand on my waist and guided me to a chair.

"Are you all right?"

"It's just hot in here," I said. Archer went to the bar and poured me a drink. Bringing it over, he held it to my lips, cupping my chin. "I'm fine," I said, feeling dumb. "Sorry for overreacting and for painting you like a stalker."

"I don't think I've ever had a woman pay that much attention to me before," he said. "I kind of like it."

Archer pulled a chair out and turned it, straddling it. I forced myself not to stare at his crotch.

"Trying to sneak a peek at my paintbrush?" he teased. "Do I need to sit the other way? I can go get a fig leaf to cover up."

"You would need a pretty big fig leaf," I said before I could stop myself.

His grin was predatory.

"Because fig leaves are actually on the smaller size," I amended hastily, trying and failing to not be creepy. "They might cover a smaller man just fine, but I think you need an above-average fig leaf." I made a face.

"No complaints here, Hazel. You can talk about the size of my paintbrush any day," Archer said, resting his chin on his hand. My eyes dipped down, traversing the length of his body.

"I need you to concentrate, Hazel," he said, his voice low. "The fate of my company rests in your hands."

Archer pulled out his phone and showed me the presentation for the design for the Mast Brothers' chocolate factory.

"You're putting in a food hall?" I asked excitedly. "That's really cool. I like the design for the signage and the way you integrated the landscaping into the existing industrial elements."

"The city doesn't seem to like it. We were told that the design had no human touch. So can you do something like this, but nice, like the painting you made of me?"

I did want to paint the factory. An excuse to do a painting in the style I loved and get paid for it? Yes, please. Except...

"Why should I help you after you were mean to me?" I countered.

"You help me, I help you," Archer said. "You want that art trail? My brothers aren't going to pay for squat if I don't win this factory. So, what do you say, Hazel, one boss to another? You want to do business?"

I did want to win that Art Zurich grant, and Archer was offering to pay. Beggars couldn't be choosers. I wasn't sleeping with him or anything. Meg would understand. It was just business.

"How much are you going to pay me?" I asked, hoping I sounded like a self-assured boss babe.

Archer shrugged. "We'll pay whatever you ask. Within reason, of course. Greg's already mad at me."

"Ten thousand?" I said.

Archer didn't even blink. "Done."

"And materials," I added.

"Double done."

He reached out his hand to shake. It was firm and strong and large. I wondered what it would be like to have that hand other places, sliding down my back, in my panties.

I stomped on the thought. Archer was now technically my client. Professional women shouldn't sleep with their clients even if they really wanted to.

"Celebratory drink?" I asked, standing up in what I hoped was a sultry motion. Except I almost fell to the floor when my leg got tangled up in the wrought-iron chair leg.

"Still afflicted with attractive-man syndrome, I see," Archer said, hand on my waist, guiding me to the bar.

"Don't flatter yourself. It's residual from being around your brothers."

"Cold, Hazel, very cold."

"What can I get for you?" I asked, going around to the other side of the bar and collecting an armful of cocktail supplies. Archer tugged the bottles and glasses out of my arms, causing the buckle on my overalls to come undone.

Archer set the bottles on the bar top then reached over and clipped the buckle back together.

"Might be a safety hazard," he said as the warmth of his fingers barely grazed my breast.

He's a client, Hazel, a client.

"Another Norman Rockwell Old Fashioned?" I asked, trying to ignore the buzzing feeling between my legs.

"What's your favorite drink?" Archer asked.

"I like Her Paintbrush."

"Shouldn't it be 'His Paintbrush'?" Archer asked.

"That would be too sexually suggestive. This is supposed to be a wholesome bar." Archer bit his lip. I wanted to lean over and press my mouth to his.

"A truly sexually suggestive name would be 'On His Paintbrush.'"

"Now that really would be a step too far," I said lightly. "You might start to give people ideas."

"Ideas like what?" he asked, his voice still that same low rumble. I let it wash over me as I mixed the blackberry liquor and bitter orange for a Her Paintbrush cocktail.

I poured the drink into a tall glass and finished it with a little mint and a bamboo stirrer then slid it over to Archer. He stirred it, swirling the colors.

"See?" I said. "It looks like paint."

Archer took a sip while he looked straight at me. "Tasty. You know what I really crave?" he asked, his voice low. It rolled around the room. I was breathless. I could see my chest rise and fall as he leaned forward.

"It's something I haven't been able to stop thinking about. I dreamed about it last night."

"What do you want?" I asked in a whisper.

"Some of that popcorn and a sandwich." He sat back, a self-satisfied look on his face.

"Oh my God."

"But I can give you a demonstration of my paintbrush skills later, if you're up for it."

"The question is, are you up for it?" I asked, crossing my arms.

Archer clutched his chest. "It was a drink idea, Hazel! You have a dirty mind, though if you're really that hot for me, I guess we could go a round."

I made the Jackson Pollock popcorn, dousing the kernels in truffle butter and finely shaved parmesan. Archer snacked on it while I made him his sandwich.

"This is amazing," he said, taking a bite. "It's literally the best thing I've ever eaten."

I felt a rush of pleasure seeing him eat the food I made. I liked feeding people. That was the one thing food and art had in common. I loved seeing people experience joy from something I made with my own hands.

I stole a handful of popcorn and asked, "So no one in that giant house of yours ever cooks?"

"Not since Josie moved in, but I think she's about to stage a mutiny."

"None of the rest of you do anything?"

Archer made a face. I had always been curious about the Svenssons. They seemed so mysterious behind the gates of their estate. I saw the younger ones when I took Minnie and Rose to school, but being around Archer had been the most I interacted with the family of billionaires.

"Mace sort of does. It's just hard. I don't think any of us are really disciplined enough to essentially cater three meals a day every day."

"You manage to have successful businesses," I countered.

"Yes, but that's business. It's almost in some ways easier than family. You put in the work, and money and power and respect come out. With the kids, you put in work, and it seems like you are always falling behind."

"I'm sure they like having you around," I said. "Also, you wouldn't have to cook every day. There are lots of Svensson brothers. You guys could rotate."

Archer grimaced. "Very few of us actually stay at the estate for any extended amount of time."

"You just leave your little brothers alone?" I asked. Archer scowled.

"Hey, I'm not judging. My little sisters are alone with Meg and Uncle Barry. I should probably do more," I said with a guilty shrug.

Archer nodded. "Our childhood was rough. We lived in an old trailer home. There was never any room; we had nothing. Then you leave the compound, and it's like, there's this whole wide world out there with flowers and cupcakes and cars and money and nice clothes and swimming pools, and the last thing you want to do is stay cooped up in a house with two dozen rowdy kids who remind you too much of your terrible childhood."

"Your older brother Hunter does it."

Archer grimaced. "Hunter sacrificed everything. He's been stuck here for years. He's never done anything for himself. I bet he thought that he was just going to take care of my generation and then he would be done. But the kids kept showing up once my father figured out that he could pawn them off on Hunter." He shook his head and took a long drink. "Mace helps. I should do more, I know. I try not to think about it. It's a lot of bad memories."

"Sorry," I said. "My sisters and I also were left high and dry when my parents died."

"But your great-uncle's the mayor," Archer said.

I didn't know if I wanted to go into how difficult it was with Uncle Barry. "It's complicated."

"Yeah, complicated," Archer said and snorted. "Manhattan is easy—make money. Annoy Greg. Be the billionaire. Here you'd think a small town would be simple, but really it's just free of distractions and forces you to confront who you really are. I'm not sure if I like him all that much." Archer looked down at his drink.

"I like you," I said, resting my hand softly on his.

"You do?" He grinned. There was that jump in my chest. "I guess you would have to if you're painting that lovingly detailed picture of me."

I blushed.

"I like you too, Hazel," he said, leveling his gaze at me. He took another sip of the drink.

"I didn't think you liked me, because you were being mean to me," I admitted.

"No," he said. "I'm just an idiot." Archer leaned toward me slightly. My eyes traveled down the flash of exposed skin. The way he was leaning over the bar, I could see the outline of one of his pecs through his shirt.

"My eyes are up here, Hazel," Archer said wryly.

My eyes met his, and my chest clenched. I thought maybe he would lean over to kiss me. I wanted him to. Instead I broke the tension. "But I wanted to look at your paintbrush!"

CHAPTER 18

had been more honest with Hazel than I had with anyone else. I was a little worried it would be weird between us. McKenna certainly hadn't liked it when I acted like anything other than the aloof billionaire. But Hazel smiled up at me and squeezed my arm when she saw me at the art retreat the next afternoon, like I was the highlight of her week.

"I saved you a sandwich," she said and pressed a brown paper package into my hand. It was such a thoughtful, sweet gesture. I ate it while Otis and Theo excitedly set up their paints and canvases.

"I need to go to the site soon," Hazel said to me.

I nodded, my mouth full of sandwich. "We can go over whenever you want," I said after I swallowed.

"I have to get ready for the art fair first." She chewed on her lip. I wanted to press my mouth to hers.

Don't. You've technically hired her. You could put her in a bad spot. Don't prove Greg right.

"Are you making more apocalyptic babies to sell?" I teased her.

She stuck her tongue out at me. "No, just kittens and puppies. Corgis especially are popular, along with my inspirational paintings. Not that I expect any of that to interest the big bad hotel boss and art collector."

"You don't know. Maybe I'll have a cat-themed hotel one of these days," I said and devoured the last bite.

"You ate that quick," Hazel said, nodding to the sandwich wrapper.

"I eat a lot of things quickly."

"That's too bad. I was hoping you would eat slower."

I coughed. Normally I was the one to start the sexual-tension laced teasing. I really should dial it back. Hunter made it sound like hellfire was going to rain down if Meg even *thought* I was after her sister.

I looked at the card on the sandwich. "What kind was this one?"

"I made it extra special for you. It doesn't have a name yet. I was thinking of calling it the cat's meow because I really want to see your face when you have a mouth full of—"

"Hi, you two love birds."

"Ida, hey!" Hazel said like she hadn't just implied she wanted me to eat her out. Had she been implying it?

"Drinks?" Hazel asked.

"Yes, please. It's sweltering out," the older woman said.

Several other seniors filed in, and they busied themselves with pulling out their painting supplies. There was something different about them, though.

Hazel and I noticed at the exact same time. "What are you wearing?"

Ida posed. "Isn't it marvelous?"

Each elderly woman was wearing a shirt with a crop of the painting Hazel had done of my face superimposed on a stylized night sky. The script on their shirts said, *Svensson Gazing*.

"We made them," Otis said proudly. "They're really popular shirts."

"What the—"

Otis interpreted my shock as pleasant surprise not, oh my God, that's a creepy shirt.

"There's a factory nearby that does print-on-demand shirts," Theo said. "We collected orders through Facebook!"

"You can't just take a painting that someone else did and sell it," I said, trying to find some way of keeping that shirt out of circulation.

"We made the star background," Otis said defiantly.

"But Hazel painted that picture of me," I scolded. "You don't have rights to it."

"Actually you do," Hazel said. I looked at her.

"When you bought it, you also bought all the rights to distribute and replicate it."

"Well you two didn't ask me for the rights," I told my little brothers. "I should start charging you."

"We're trying to run a business!" Otis complained.

"I'm just kidding," I told them, ruffling their hair.

"We're very happy customers," Ida said. "We started a fan club. Also, Otis, you and your brother should branch into body pillows."

"Ida!" Hazel said, horrified. Ida poured herself another drink.

Hazel clapped her hands. "Today we're going to do some landscapes. A nice thing that I like to do before I start being creative is to do a little motivation. It can be a phrase, an idea, a painting you like..."

Ida's hand shot up. Hazel smiled blandly at her.

Ide stood up. "My inspiration is men." She sat back down. All her fellow retreat goers nodded appreciatively. Ida stood back up. "Preferably naked," Ida said. I tried not to laugh as Hazel struggled to keep a pleasant expression on her face.

"Right, okay, well, on that note, watercolor!"

"Will we ever be painting a nude model?" Ida interrupted.

"Painting live figures is very difficult," Hazel explained. "Today, you're going to be doing a painting of a scenic landscape."

She talked through how to paint grass, trees, and mountains and how to use a minimal color palette. Every so often she would sweep her finger around her shirt collar to pull up her bra strap or fidget with the high-waisted pants she wore that barely met the hemline of her cropped shirt. Every time she raised her arm, I saw a slip of creamy midriff. I didn't even bother paying attention to her instructions. There was no way I was going to have the mental control to concentrate on painting today.

"You're not going to paint?" she asked, coming up beside me.

"It's hard to concentrate," I said.

"I know." She shuddered. "I could barely give the lesson what with a dozen sets of your eyes staring at me from those shirts."

CHAPTER 19

Hazel

I didn't know what had come over me to flirt that blatantly with Archer. He seemed surprised and intrigued though, like I was interesting and fun and cool.

Ida hung back after the retreat. She stood next to me at the window as we watched Archer escort his little brothers to his car.

"I have to admit, he is inspirational," I said with a sigh.

"Yes, he is," Ida said. "It's good you're feeding him. A way to a man's heart is food and sex—lots of sex. Ask me how I know."

"I'd rather not—"

"Me and Bert, let me tell you!" Ida said, barreling on. The Svensson PharmaTech train rolled down Main Street, the clanking of the wheels drowning out the most gratuitous details of the perils of sex in one's seventies. "Yoga," Ida finished as the train passed. "That's the secret."

While the train spared me the details, it didn't spare me from the young blonde woman waiting across the street for it to pass.

"Ugh, McKenna."

"She's after your man," Ida commented, glaring out the window.

"Archer's not my man."

"You need to jump on that, then," Ida admonished. "If you insist on wearing those overalls, at least wear some cute panties under them so it's a nice little surprise when he sticks his hands down there."

I was trying to decide whether it would be worse to continue listening to Ida, go downstairs and confront McKenna, or just throw myself out the window.

McKenna made the choice for me. She stomped up the stairs, her stilettos clapping on the hardwood treads.

"You can't steal Archer from me," she said, stalking across the room. "You're a bad influence. He's heartbroken. He misses me, and you're trying to take advantage of him. Archer and I are going to be married. He's in love with me."

"Really?" I asked. "Because from what he said, he doesn't care for you at all."

"You can't just steal other people's boyfriends," McKenna huffed.

"He's not your boyfriend," I countered.

"That's right, missy!" Ida chimed in. "Archer wants someone who butters his artisanal bread."

I slapped a hand to my face. I did not need Ida escalating the situation.

"Look, McKenna," I said, trying to defuse the situation. "Archer is over here for a legitimate reason. I'm doing some work for him."

"Yeah! Working that paintbrush! *Woo!*" Ida exclaimed, pumping her fist.

"Is that what you're doing? How am I not surprised?" McKenna sneered.

"That's not—Ida, please—"

"He's just using you, you know," McKenna said, tapping her expensive designer shoe on the floor. "Even if you two are having some sort of affair, Archer is a billionaire and a Svensson. It is highly unlikely that he truly wants anything to do with you. He can't take you to parties or a nice restaurant or show you off to investors. He wants someone like me." She preened.

"Then why does he spend all his free time with Hazel?" Ida shot back. That was the wrong thing to say. McKenna's eye started twitching.

"We have a history," McKenna said. Her tone had a slightly hysterical edge. I was worried she would go all final destination and throw Ida through a window or something.

"You *are* history," Ida said. "Archer's clearly moved on to bigger and better things."

McKenna looked me up and down. "Bigger, yes. Better, I'm not so sure." Then she turned on her heel and left.

"Don't let her drag you down," Ida said, patting me on the back as I tried to shake off McKenna's comments. "Men like a little junk in the trunk. Trust me."

I finally shooed Ida out after giving her the rest of the alcoholic drinks to go.

I was wiped after the art retreat, and I was, for once, thankful not to have a big happy hour rush. In between serving the trickle of customers, I ran up and down the stairs to choose paintings I would take to sell at the art fair that weekend.

When the last customer left, I tried to do another puppy painting to sell, but I wasn't feeling it. Was McKenna right? Was Archer just using me? The time I had spent with him last night had seemed genuine, though. However, the conversation with him had reignited the guilt about my little sisters.

I hung up the Closed sign on the door. Then I took my bike and some leftover food to my childhood home. A pair of motorcycles blew past me.

"Stop speeding!" I yelled at them, but they were already several blocks away. I was still grumbling when my little sister Minnie opened the front door.

"Hazel!" my younger sister shrieked. Rose came running. They were in junior high. Most of the time, they were surly teenagers, but there were still moments when they acted like sweet little girls.

"Did you come to save us?"

"Can we come live with you?" they begged.

"I don't have any room," I told them, coming inside. "I brought you food though!"

"I have healthy food made," Meg said.

"I almost got run over by some motorcycles. I deserve something fatty, salty, and savory," I retorted.

Meg shook her head. "Susie says it's some of the Svensson boys back from college break for the summer. She's already complained to Hunter—not that it did anything."

"Maybe it's payback for the cell phone ban?"

Meg sniffed. "The cell phone ban makes everyone safer."

"Where's Uncle Barry?" I asked.

"He's at a city meeting," Meg replied. "We didn't know you were coming."

"I thought I'd surprise you all," I said, unpacking the food from my bag.

"You're hardly ever over here," Meg said.

"'Cause she's with her boyfriend!" Minnie said, giggling as she opened up the deviled eggs I'd brought. "Yum!"

"And I have sandwiches. I brought your favorite," I said, waving Meg's sandwich in front of her nose.

"Ugh, fine."

"She's hangry," Rose told me, pulling out plates and napkins. "And she's mad she had to see Hunter the other day."

"Maybe you could give him another chance," I said carefully, scooping out some pasta salad on my plate. "It doesn't sound like he's moved on, and neither have you."

"I could move on if I wanted to," Meg said. "There are a lot of eligible guys in Harrogate now."

"You never go on any dates," Rose scoffed.

"I'm busy," Meg said, forking some salad onto Rose's plate.

"Can you come swimming with us tomorrow?" Minnie asked me.

"I have an early start to a long day tomorrow," I said. "I'm doing the rendering for Archer's convention center. Apparently whoever is approving it said it didn't have the human touch."

My older sister pursed her lips. "Amos didn't like their renderings. I'm on the decision committee." She frowned. "You know, Hazel, Archer probably hired you because of me. I bet he thinks I'll give them the job because of that."

I felt a tear prick my eyes.

"Sorry," Meg said, seeing the hurt on my face. "I didn't mean it like that. I know you're a good artist. But you can't trust those Svenssons."

CHAPTER 20

"Hazel's doing the paintings!" I crowed, walking into the large home office. "Did you hear?" I asked Hunter. He grunted and didn't look up from his screen.

The man was crazy organized. In the office was a whiteboard with his neat handwriting. A large calendar that was color coded and tabbed hung on one wall. There was a bookcase with identical gray binders that each had one of my brothers' names on it. I went to the shelf and pulled mine.

"Don't touch that," Hunter ordered. Garrett was at his desk, studiously ignoring me.

"It's my binder. It has my name on it." I flipped through. "You don't have a section in here about how awesome I am."

"I'm not going to give you a pat on the back for doing your job," Hunter said. "Speaking of, I hope you made it clear that you weren't hiring Hazel because of her sister."

"Uh... I didn't even think of that. Surely she knows I hired her because of how good a painter she is."

"I'm not sure we should trust his judgement on anything," Garrett said, standing up. His military-short hair made him look dangerous in the evening light. I thought Garrett and I were on somewhat good terms, but I realized as he advanced on me that maybe we weren't as good as I thought. "Did you think I wasn't going to find out?" Garrett asked, his tone clipped.

"Find out about what?" I asked, slowly backing away.

"Mom." He stuck his tablet in my face. There was video footage from the parking deck of me and Merla Vee hugging.

Hunter stood up. "After everything that happened in the last few months, you do this?"

"I'm sorry I can't just cut out people I love, unlike some people," I said angrily. "I believe in second chances."

"This is more than a second chance," Garrett said. "You've been giving her tens of thousands of dollars."

"It wasn't that much!" I protested.

Garrett turned the tablet around, swiped, then stuck it back in my face. "As I said..."

"I can't believe you've been in my bank accounts," I said, incredulous, staring at the column of numbers. I guess a few thousand here and there really did add up.

"Of course I'm in your bank accounts," Garrett said, plucking the tablet out of my hands. "Someone has to make sure your company is solvent. Mike, bless him, he tries, but he's far from qualified to manage the financials of a major real estate group."

Hunter pinched the bridge of his nose.

"You need to cut off Mom," he said. "Stop giving her money. Stop talking to her. Stop enabling her."

"If I want to try to have a relationship with our mother, I should be able to do that. I'm not just going to cut her off like some people."

Hunter glowered at me. "Shut up."

I didn't. "You could give Meg another chance," I said hotly.

"You think I haven't tried?" Hunter raged. "We live in the same damn town. I've tried multiple times to apologize. I've begged. I've pleaded—" He clamped his mouth shut. "It doesn't matter."

Garrett narrowed his eyes at Hunter. "You need to deal with that situation, or I'll do it for you." He turned his steel gaze on me. "I finally have Mace at a point where he's not jeopardizing Svensson PharmaTech with his obsessive-compulsive tendencies. He's almost, dare I say it, *normal* with Josie around. It's already difficult enough being the CFO and dealing with all of your terrible financial decisions. I don't need him going into a tailspin. Do not keep giving Mom money. I'm watching you," Garrett warned.

I stalked out of the office. The worst thing was I knew they were right. I'd known for a while I should have cut off our mother. I also knew they were right that Mace could never ever know.

My twin was sitting in the dining room. I leaned against the doorframe. Mace looked so relaxed and happy. Otis and Theo were regaling Mace and Josie with their business plan for T-shirt world domination.

"We have shirts with memes and micro-target people with designs," Otis was explaining.

"I want to have a business," Nate said.

"Me too!" Peyton cried, bumping against Otis.

"You can't be a part of our business."

"Start your own business," I told them from my spot in the doorway.

"Doing what?"

"You could have a lemonade stand," Josie suggested.

"Or even better," I said, "you should sell popsicles. It's hot enough."

"We can put candy inside of them!" Josie said gleefully. "Call it popsicle surprise."

"That sounds dirty," I said.

"Only to dirty minds," Mace retorted.

"You need a sign. Otis and Theo can make you shirts. You can have a little cart and walk around and sell them," I told my little brothers. "Man, I'm on a roll. Maybe I'll start selling popsicles."

"It's our business!" Nate said, trying to tackle me.

The rest of the evening, I helped Nate and Peyton test out various popsicle recipes we found online. We even roped in some of the older kids to help. It was nice to hang out with them. Doing fun projects was something my mother had never done with me and my brothers though I had longed for it as a child.

The next morning, I waited in front of Hazel's Art Café to take her to the Mast Brothers' chocolate factory site. I was stupidly excited to see her when she walked out of the café. Her hair was in a messy French roll. She was wearing breezy ankle pants and a soft cropped shirt. Flashes of her midriff showed as she locked up the café.

I stowed her easel and painting supplies in the trunk then sat in the car.

"What's that?" I asked as she sat in the passenger seat with a wicker basket.

"I made you a picnic," she said, smiling at me over her sunglasses. "I might be a while. I don't want you to starve to death."

I leaned back in the driver's seat and pulled onto Main Street. "Did you turn this into a date, Hazel?"

"No, this is a professional courtesy."

"So the painting I commissioned from you comes with food," I said as we approached the Mast Brothers' chocolate factory on the north end of town. "Good to know."

"I love these old buildings." Hazel sighed as I drove up to the ornate factory gate. It was already unlocked so that the workers could set up for the art fair that weekend.

"Look at the detail on this wrought iron," she said, hanging out the window of the car. I forced myself to look at the gate detail and not her ass. "See? They put in chocolate candies and the tools for the trade. People really had an eye for detail back then."

I parked in front of an expansive brick building with two-story-tall windows.

"This is where I want to put the food hall," I told her, leading her through the building. We passed a large statue of a meerkat.

"Oooh, it's Mast the meerkat!" Hazel squealed. "I used to come here when I was a kid. They had this little train that ran underground to a museum. It had these creepy animatronic puppets. I would always be so freaked out, but then I would get free candy at the end of it."

"The puppets are still down there," I said. "And they are still just as terrifying. All of this space," I said as we walked into another large building that used to house the chocolate meerkat manufacturing, "is going to be exhibition halls."

"It's beautiful!" Hazel said. She spun around in a circle through the spots of light from the high clerestory windows. I couldn't help it. I swept her up in my arms and danced us around and around the room.

Hazel was slightly breathless when we stopped. My hands were resting on her hips. Her skin was soft and warm. All I wanted to do in that moment was kiss her. Hazel licked her lips and stepped back, pulling at her shirt.

"So," she said. "What do you want me to paint?" She turned to walk to the heavy wooden barn-style doors at the end of the building.

"The train used to roll straight inside the warehouse for loading and unloading," I explained. "We could do a painting from here. But maybe you want something with a little more perspective."

Hazel looked around. "Can we access that roof?" She pointed through a window to the adjacent building.

"There are stairs on the other side," I said, picking up her equipment and leading her across the courtyard. She followed me, stopping every so often to look out one of the windows.

"Admiring the view?" I asked.

"Among other things."

The building was eight stories tall and gave an impressive view of the complex.

"Amazing," Hazel said as we stood at the edge of the roof. I had an arm firmly around her waist.

"I'm not going to fall," Hazel scoffed as we walked around the perimeter of the building. She immediately tripped, and I hauled her back against me.

"Maybe you should do a view from the ground."

"No, this is perfect, see? I can include those huge doors, and we'll put some landscaping there on the side. Then we have a row of restaurants along those tall windows," she said.

I set down her art supplies.

"You don't have to stay if you don't want to," Hazel said, looking up at me. "I'm sure you have a lot of important things to do."

"This is the most important thing right now," I said as she set up her easel.

"Yeah, but I can do it myself."

I snorted. "I'm not leaving you at an abandoned factory site alone. Besides, you made me lunch." I spread out a blanket on the wooden walkway on the roof. "Also I think I need to hire you to make lunch once a week at least, maybe more. Mace has it in his head that we need to rotate to give Josie a break on cooking."

"And of course you're going to outsource it."

I opened up the picnic hamper. "Hazel, I am a god among men and good at a great many things, but cooking anything more than a burnt omelet is beyond my capacity. I already sent you money for ingredients. No take-backsies! Make me proud."

"I can't cook for your family! I'm busy. There's this painting and the art retreat and the Art Zurich Expo."

"Just make us extra sandwiches," I said, taking a bite of the Cat's Meow she had packed. It had tomatoes, cream cheese, and smoked salmon on an everything bagel.

After I ate, I dozed in the sunshine, listening to the birds chirp and Hazel's paintbrush scrape against the canvas. I woke up with Hazel gently stroking my face.

"All done?" I murmured.

"I have a rough sketch of the light and shadows, and I took some pictures. I'll have to come back a few more times, of course."

I felt relaxed and happy as I drove away from the factory site.

"Nude painting tomorrow?" I asked as I stopped the car in front of her café.

She looked at me wide-eyed.

"You know, for the art retreat," I prompted, trying to keep a straight face. "Though I suppose I could do a private session if you so preferred. I feel like I need to pay you back for eating your pussy, sorry your sandwich, the Cat's Meow."

A flush bloomed over Hazel's cheeks and her breasts, the mounds peeking up over the low scoop of the soft shirt. I walked her to the door, wondering if I pushed too hard. Hazel turned to me after she unlocked the door.

"I'm not sure the retreat goers are advanced enough for nude painting," she said. "You'd need someone with a little more experience."

"Are you experienced in nude painting?"

"Very," she said. "Maybe sometime I'll give you a demonstration of my skills."

She slipped inside and shut the door, leaving me frustrated and slightly confused. I never spent this much time going after a woman. Normally they were happy to throw themselves at me. But Hazel was something else.

As much as I complained about Harrogate, one advantage it had was that I could just take off and drive through the countryside. It made having a sports car worth it. I pulled away from the curb with a roar of the engine, intending to stay out for hours.

CHAPTER 21

Hazel

I couldn't believe I had just been blatantly flirting with Archer. Was he into me? He had said McKenna wasn't in the picture at all.

Then there were a few times where I thought he was almost about to kiss me. Why didn't he? When he was sleeping there on the roof, all I wanted to do was straddle him and run my hand down his chest. I wished I hadn't chickened out when he dropped me off at the Art Café and had pulled him upstairs instead of shutting the door in his face.

I went up to organize the paintings I would be taking to the exhibition the next day. It was in the Mast Brothers' chocolate factory, in one of the abandoned factory buildings, like it was every year. And like every year, I went and sold an array of bland paintings of kittens, puppies, and soft landscapes. Though I wished I could sell my avant-garde paintings for millions of dollars, I had to make do with selling boring paintings for a couple hundred, if I was lucky.

"At least you're able to sell your art," I told myself. I did a power pose in front of the splotchy antique mirror I'd rescued from a dumpster. I knew I should try to do one last painting, but I was still too frazzled from my afternoon with Archer. I couldn't get out of my mind the feel of his sun-warmed skin, the planes of his jaw.

Hazel: *I touched Archer's face today.*

Jemma: *...okay well I think you're supposed to do something else with him but that's a step in the right direction.*

Olivia: *Maybe in another five months you'll finally get around to seeing him naked.*

Hazel: *Ha ha. You guys are supposed to be supportive. It was to wake him up from a nap. I didn't want to surprise him awake.*

Jemma: *Show up at his house without any underwear and tell him you have a surprise for him.*

Hazel: *I can't do that! He lives with his little brothers. That would be weird.*

Jemma: *As opposed to creepily watching him while he sleeps.*

Olivia: *This is why you've had such a dry spell.*

Jemma: *Maybe she's acting crazy because of the dry spell.*

Hazel: *I'm going dumpster diving.*

Olivia: *And... maybe this is why you haven't gotten any...*

I grabbed my bike and hooked up the trailer. We were going to be making stained glass at the retreat tomorrow, and I needed materials. On principle, I refused to buy glass just to break it. I also needed to find some metal I could melt down for the solder in between the glass pieces.

My first stop was Svensson PharmaTech. Sometimes they put out scraps. There was some office furniture but not anything I could use for an art project.

I pedaled down Main Street. There were workshops at the edge of town; sometimes they had scraps. The large wholesale store was that direction too. In the evenings, they threw out crates of food. I had a hankering for avocados. Maybe I would be lucky tonight.

Motorcycles revved in the distance as I pedaled along. Honestly, at the next town hall meeting, I was going to complain about those. Whoever was riding their fancy bikes down the street needed to stop.

There were a few cars on the road, but most people were at home by now. I signaled that I was turning onto one of the streets that led to the outskirts of town. Away from the bustle of Main Street, it seemed dead. It was also a little creepy. I had the distinct feeling like someone was watching me.

You're being dumb.

Harrogate was so much safer and more affluent than it was when I was a girl. I looked over my shoulder. In the distance behind me were headlights.

"They're probably just going home," I told myself.

All the buildings I passed were dark. If something were to happen, I would be all alone. Cursing all my student loan debt and my decision to buy the café building instead of a car, I turned onto the short road that led to the wholesale store. Then I waited a beat and looked over my shoulder to see the same headlights swing into the driveway. There was no way that person was going to the store. It had been closed thirty minutes already.

"They're picking up someone," I told myself firmly as I parked my bike near the dumpster. "If you want to be anxious about something, be anxious about the fact that you're about to lose your home and your business."

Looking to make sure no employees were out, I stood on top of an empty milk crate and eased the top off the dumpster and used my phone to take pictures of the inside. Score! Not only was there a whole pallet of raspberries, I also saw a box of broken glass plates. It took me a few tries to jump up to actually get inside the dumpster. I was struggling, reaching for the box of plates.

"Almost got it…"

Muscular arms wrapped around my waist and jerked me backward. I screamed and attacked the man holding me.

"Stop!" Archer said, batting away my fists.

"What are you doing?" I shrieked. "You can't just grab someone like that!"

"You looked like you were about to fall headfirst in there," Archer said, frowning. "What are you even doing? What could you possibly need in that dumpster?"

"Broken plates," I said defiantly. "And raspberries."

"I will buy you raspberries and break some plates for you if you stop digging around in the dumpster like a raccoon. Honestly," he said, tugging me back to his car.

"I don't need you to buy me anything," I said.

"How did you even get over here? I thought you didn't have a car."

"I took my bike."

Archer swore and looked up at the night sky. "It's pitch dark, and we're miles outside of town. You could have been hurt."

"It's Harrogate, not Manhattan," I scoffed. "I'm perfectly fine." He released me, and I hightailed it back to the dumpster. "I need those plates for the art retreat."

Archer swore again. "Someone spare me from crazy art girls," he said into the dark. Then he marched over to me. "I will get it out for you." He was tall enough that he could easily stand on the milk crate and reach inside, plucking out the boxes of broken glass plates.

"Nice!" I said, inspecting them. There were two boxes, a set of mottled-blue glass plates and a box of purple and silver. "These will be perfect." I looked up at Archer. "Can you get my raspberries?"

"You are not eating raspberries out of a dumpster," he said, taking the plates in one hand and me in the other. "I'm taking you home."

"I have my bike," I protested. "And I need to find some scrap metal."

Archer ignored me as he took my bike, unclipped the trailer, and loaded them into the trunk of his car. Even though the sports car had trunk room, the bike still stuck out awkwardly.

"See, I should just ride my bike."

"It's fine to stick out like that. It's not a long drive."

"But I need—"

"If we stop at whatever metal scrap yard, will you please let me drive you home and then stay there?" he begged.

"I think you're overreacting," I told him as I sat in the passenger seat.

"This is a perfectly reasonable reaction," he said as he pulled onto the road.

Archer stood around as I picked through the scrap metal at one of the metalworking shops down the road. I knew the owner, and he was nice enough to let me take some scraps when I needed.

"That it?" Archer asked as I put the metal in his trunk.

"It's a little dirty," I said. "Sorry about your car."

He shrugged. "It needs to be detailed. My little brothers already scuffed it up."

"Siblings, huh? Always ruining your stuff," I said.

He laughed.

"Are you coming to the art fair tomorrow?" I asked as I sat back in the car.

"Maybe in the afternoon," he replied.

"All the good stuff is in the morning," I said. "If you want to pick up a Hazel Loring original of two very adorable corgi puppies, you better arrive early."

"I'm not much of a morning person. I'm a creature of the night," he said.

He looked it in that moment, one hand on the steering wheel, hair fluttering slightly in the breeze from the open car window.

I looked down at my overalls. "I need to start dressing better around you," I said. "I mean, wearing paint-spattered overalls and a cropped shirt is probably not the standard you're used to." Archer flicked a quick glance at me and then looked back at the road. "I feel like I made a terrible impression. I'm not usually this much of a disaster," I said, rambling.

"I never knew I needed girls in crop tops in my life before I met you. It's a welcome addition."

"So if I wear this shirt again," I said, sliding my fingers up his bare forearm to the rolled-up sleeve, "you'll come dumpster diving with me?"

"How about if you wear that shirt with nothing else, I will buy you your very own dumpster, and you can fill it with whatever you want?"

"I want to fill it with raspberries and marshmallows and stuffed animals!"

Archer laughed. His voice was so deep, and I shivered slightly.

"I wish you had rescued the raspberries." I sighed, looking out the window. We were almost back to my café. "I would have made you raspberry white chocolate soufflé pancakes."

Archer pulled up in front of my café and parked the car.

"I also wanted to make a raspberry muddle. It's really tasty," I told him as he unloaded my stuff from the trunk. "It has sparkling water, a little lime, some mint, and a lot of vodka."

"Sound delicious," Archer said, turning around from setting my bike down on the sidewalk and walking me to the door.

I unlocked it then turned around, leaning back against it. "Normally I don't have a lot of desserts on the menu," I said to him. "But I'd make an exception for you."

He rested a forearm on the door above my head and leaned over me, his body barely touching mine.

"Do you want to come inside?" I whispered and licked my lips. "For dessert?"

Archer stared at me, his gray eyes silver in the street light. "Keep it on ice for me," he said and kissed me softly on the cheek, then lightly nuzzled my neck. I gasped, wanting him to kiss me for real, but he had already stepped back.

I was in a state of mild shock as he drove off, leaving me to wonder, *Why did he leave?*

CHAPTER 22

It took every ounce of willpower I had to walk away from Hazel after her offer of dessert. The past week I had been going round and round in circles, thinking that I was misreading the situation. Maybe Hazel thought I was annoying yet attractive but didn't really want anything to do with me. Maybe it was too complicated of a situation. I had hired her to do a painting, and there was the bad blood between our families.

Now that it was very clear she did, in fact, want me, I wasn't sure what to do. I wasn't any stranger to hookups. I would meet an attractive girl at a swanky party. We would get shit-faced drunk, hook up at my place or hers, and then go our separate ways. A few of them had stuck around, like McKenna, but that wasn't the norm. None of them were like Hazel. They were models or socialites—tall, lanky, and smooth haired. Eventually they all started to blur together. Hazel was a shock of difference, the softness of her body, her flyaway hair, and the nicest pair of tits I had ever seen. They were full and round, and I wanted to suck on her nipples through the soft crop top she always wore.

I was afraid if I hadn't left, I would have taken Hazel upstairs to the couch, buried my face in her tits, and buried my cock inside of her. But she was a cute small-town café owner. That might have been too much for her. Besides, I wanted to savor the experience. I wanted to study Hazel like a fine piece of art and discover all the hidden secrets and meaning.

All the spinning about Hazel left me hot and dizzy. I cranked up the AC and took a cold shower but couldn't calm down. I finally snuck upstairs to the clubroom. Several fingers of whisky later, and online shopping for a crate of the most expensive raspberries I could find, I had calmed down enough to finally fall asleep.

The next morning I was woken up roughly. I blearily opened my eyes. Tristan was hovering over me.

"What?" I growled at him.

"Mike says we all have to go to the art fair. It's part of our Greyson Hotel Group internship. He wants to see how the space performs when there are a lot of people in it."

"Whatever," I said and rolled over to go back to sleep.

"Archer, *get up*." This time it was Hunter.

"I need my beauty sleep. I'm not getting any younger." I put a pillow over my head to block the light as Hunter wrenched open the curtains.

"You're also not getting a convention center if you keep acting like this," he said and pulled all the blankets off of me.

I showered, dressed, then went down to the kitchen and dug around in the fridge for the sandwich half I had hid in the back from the picnic Hazel had made me.

"Uh," Josie said. She looked at me sheepishly. "Sorry," she said, holding out the half-eaten sandwich.

"I told her she could eat it," Mace said, sipping his bulletproof coffee.

"That's my sandwich."

"It's a really good sandwich," Josie said, looking only slightly guilty. "Is this one of the ones Ida sells?"

"Yes, but she buys them from Hazel's Art Café."

"Oh really?" Josie asked, taking another bite.

"The space does flow very nicely," Mike said as we walked into one of the large factory buildings that were being used as exhibition halls. Tristan and Eli took pictures while Mike and I walked around the booths. Otis and Theo wanted to tag along too. They were looking for inspiration for their T-shirts, and they darted down the aisles of art displays.

"We were thinking of using this building for large lecture rooms," Mike said as we walked, "but maybe we should flip it with Building C. This works really nicely for tables."

"Would you like to buy a painting of two kittens and a ball of yarn?" I heard a familiar voice call.

Hazel—she was sitting behind a table surrounded by paintings of baby animals. Ida was there, too, along with Jemma and Olivia. Ida was taking a long swig out of a thermos that more than likely did not contain coffee.

"Someone's suddenly perked up," Mike commented when I turned and headed over to Hazel's table.

Her hair was in a messy topknot. She was wearing tight black yoga pants that accentuated the curve of her hips and another one of those scoop-necked cropped shirts that drove me crazy. The peak of her lace bra showed slightly when she moved or readjusted the shirt.

"I'm just very inspired by art," I said. Mike snorted.

"If I'd known you were going to be here," Ida cooed at me, "I would have brought all the old girls with me and worn my fan T-shirt."

"T-shirt?" Mike asked.

"Ida is the president of my fan club," I bragged.

"You have a fan club?" Mike said incredulously.

"I'm very popular in Harrogate," I replied.

"He's the cat's meow," Ida said. "There's a petition going around to have Hazel quit her job drawing puppies and start drawing porn."

"You're posing nude?" Mike asked, incredulous. "Does Greg know about this?"

Ida turned to Hazel. "I bet you'd make a lot of money off of him."

"Excuse her, please," Olivia said to us. "She's been morning drinking."

"Pregaming for the art fair," Ida said with an exaggerated wink.

"The art fair already started, Ms. Ida," I said.

"So it has." She peered around. "Would you like some, Mr. Svensson?" she asked, shaking the thermos at Mike.

"No, ma'am, thank you," Mike replied. Ida shrugged and took a swig from the thermos.

"Thank you for helping us on the rendering," Mike said to Hazel. Tristan and Eli chose that moment to saunter up. They seemed a little too excited to see Hazel and her pretty friends.

"What painting?" Ida slurred. "You doing nudes without me?"

"She is really deep in the sauce," I commented. "And it's only"—I lifted my wrist to look at my watch— "nine thirty a.m."

"You shouldn't be doing nudes without me," Ida said, wavering slightly on her stool.

"What is in that cocktail?" Mike asked.

Olivia took the thermos and tasted it. "I don't think it's a mixed drink. I think it's just a bottle of liquor she dumped into a thermos."

"Are you part of the art retreat?" Tristan asked, looking too long at Hazel for my taste. I grabbed him by the collar and shook him. "Behave."

"You know if you need a model," Eli said, waggling his eyebrows, "I'm available."

Olivia couldn't contain herself anymore and started laughing.

"Eli, Tristan," I barked. "Stop it. That's rude, and ineffective." I flicked Eli's ear.

"Ow!"

Tristan laughed.

"Don't bring your dumb college behavior here," I warned them. "You know better than that."

"I'll paint you," Ida said, leaning forward in her seat. Hazel snickered. Eli and Tristan looked a little apprehensive at Olivia's grandmother's offer.

"Um, no, Grandma, no. He's like fifteen," Olivia said with a snort.

"I'm not!" Eli retorted and puffed out his chest. "I'm an adult."

"He's barely old enough to drink," I said. "Barely."

"We're finishing college early though," Eli bragged.

"So, what he's saying is that they're smart but have zero social skills," Mike remarked.

"You sure have your hands full," Jemma said.

"They're our interns. We're trying to teach them to be productive members of society."

"Aww!" Hazel cooed. "You have interns! That's so adorable!"

"Are you interning too?" Jemma asked Otis as he and Theo walked up with bags of paintings. Hazel held out her arms, and Otis and Theo gave her hugs.

"I like your puppy paintings," Otis said.

"See? Everyone likes puppies," Hazel told me.

"Can I buy the one with the corgi?" Otis asked.

"You can have it," Hazel told him, "because you and Theo are my favorite students."

"What am I?" Ida squawked and almost fell off her stool.

"A drunk," Olivia said.

"No," I told Hazel. "Don't give your work away for free. Ring it up. Pick the one you want, Otis."

"What? I want a painting," Eli said.

"Fine, you know what? Paintings for everyone. Mike, do you want a painting?"

"Sure, why not?" my brother said with a shrug. "Do you have anything gothic or like a skull or something?"

"I have puppies, kittens, babies, and flowers," Hazel replied.

"You have the chunky raccoon," Olivia reminded her.

"I want it!" Theo and Otis scuffled.

"If there's a chonker raccoon, I want it," Mike said, breaking up the fight.

"You should offer to let him compensate you with something else," Ida said too loudly as I pulled out my wallet.

"Hush," Olivia hissed to Ida.

The old woman whispered loudly, "Put a ring on it!"

Hazel was studying me. Then she reached out and ran her fingers through my hair. "I wanted it out of your eyes."

I smirked. "I would say something really filthy," I stage-whispered to her, "but there are children and elderly present."

"I'm not elderly!" said Ida.

"Hah!" Olivia exclaimed.

"Don't hah me, young lady," Ida scolded and took another swig from the thermos.

Hazel rang up the paintings and turned the tablet toward me.

"Ohhh," Olivia's grandmother said loudly when I handed Hazel the credit card. "Is that an American Express Black?"

"Grandma," Olivia warned. I struggled to keep a straight face. I knew exactly where the old woman was going. It was a classic joke.

"Is it going to—"

"Don't you dare!" Olivia said.

"Actually," Hazel said, taking the card, "it isn't going to fit. We've tried this before."

"You have?" Mike asked, looking at me.

"Yes, we have," I said firmly. "And while it was a little touch and go, we figured out a way that was comfortable for both of us."

Hazel rolled her eyes and typed in the credit card number while Olivia packed up the paintings. "You are so juvenile," she said to me.

"Yeah, Archer," Tristan said, taking the paintings. "Have some respect. There are ladies present."

Eli took Olivia's hand and kissed it. She struggled not to laugh.

I looked at my younger brother in disgust. "You're going to be single and alone the rest of your life."

"Speak for yourself," he retorted.

Call me, he mouthed to Olivia.

"Enjoy your paintings, boys," Hazel said, waving as we left.

Mike and I walked through the other exhibition halls. Four of the large buildings were packed with booths.

"The site doesn't seem like it has any issues accommodating all these people," Mike said. "And they don't even have a parking deck or anything."

"I'm sure a lot of people must come in by train," I told him. "I know my two hotels in Harrogate were booked up for this art exhibition months in advance."

"I'm going to talk to the event coordinator," Mike said, handing me the paintings and walking over to talk to a man with a clipboard and a walkie-talkie.

I sent Eli and Tristan off to take pictures of the on-site parking while I stayed with Otis and Theo. They were looking at metal bug yard art. I told Theo he could have some if he bought three and periodically hid them in Mace's room. I chuckled. Mace would have a fit.

While I was waiting for him and Otis to pick out their sculptures, McKenna came hurrying over to me. It was too late to hide behind a booth. She was elegant in all black, her hair a curtain framing her face. She was a contrast to Hazel with her soft messiness.

When I'd first met McKenna, Greyson Hotel Group hadn't yet become profitable off its portfolio of unique boutique hotels. I was trying to lose the roughness of growing up in a doomsday cult. McKenna and her elegant sophistication had seemed intriguing. Now after having to stroke the egos of those types of people day in and day out, I just wanted someone honest. McKenna certainly wasn't.

"Archer," McKenna said, looping her arm around mine. She looked down at the paintings wrapped in the familiar paper and string, with a handmade card containing Hazel's loopy signature. "Don't tell me you bought one of those paint-by-numbers canvases."

"McKenna, we're done," I hissed at her. "You need to let it go."

"Archer, darling, don't say that!" McKenna batted her eyes. She could play the part of being genuine, but I was at the point where I saw through the charade. "I am so sorry about what happened." Her eyes were large, her face a fake mask of innocence.

"You lied and tried to alienate me from my family," I said flatly. "What you did was unforgivable."

"Archer, I love you." Her eyes shone with tears. "I want us to be together."

"Absolutely not. You need to stay away from my family," I said, shaking her off. "You tried to ruin my relationship with my family once. I will never let you have that kind of power ever again."

"You can't mean that!" McKenna said. "I did what I did because I loved you."

"That's not how you treat someone you love."

"I'm going to make you take me back," she said, her expression flipping from sad and loving to bitter and vengeful in an instant. I watched her warily. "You think Hazel cares about you?" she spat. "She's just using you. You'll see. You're going to come crawling back to me."

CHAPTER 23

Hazel

sold out of paintings by that afternoon. I packed up the extra wrapping paper. Though I made some money, I was still feeling stressed. I needed to have made more if I wanted to save my café.

"Since I'm here, I want to get some more work done on the painting for Archer's convention hall," I told my friends. Jemma and Olivia hoisted Ida upright.

"I'm taking her home to sleep this off," Olivia said, sounding mildly disgusted.

Taking my easel, I managed to sneak up a fire escape on the other side of the building and set up at the spot where I was doing the rendering. I immediately relaxed once I started painting. The late-afternoon light was amazing. It bathed the site in a warm glow with crisp shadows. It was like a Dutch master's painting laid out before me.

I had always romanticized painting at an easel, sitting outside. Though all the pictures of puppies and baby animals were from photographs, I didn't like painting from photos if I could help it.

I worked quickly, capturing the play of light on the buildings. I wasn't working on the whole painting but spot painting, which I would fill in later. I just wanted to capture the various moments.

I sighed as the sun set behind the ten-story brick building, the largest on the site. I packed up the painting, careful not to smudge anything. I felt invigorated from all the creative energy—and from seeing Archer.

The way he walked through the space like he owned it, which if I did my job right, he soon would, was magnetic. He was also adorable with his brothers. As much as Meg and I sometimes fought, I would do anything for my sisters. I appreciated that Archer felt the same way about his brothers.

I biked back slowly to my café. I was sweaty and grungy. All I wanted was a hot shower and some chocolate raspberry cheesecake. I wished Archer had let me take those raspberries. They were perfectly fine.

The pipes clanked as they slowly pumped the hot water to my shower. I had my tiny bedroom in a closet on the third floor. Yes, I was back in a closet, but at least it was my own closet. It even had a skylight. Next to it, in its own closet, was a crumbling acrylic shower. The toilet was in yet another closet and had one of those pull chains from the nineteen twenties. The cracked pedestal sink sat outside in my studio space.

All in all, my third-floor studio apartment was not the glamourous space I always wanted to live in. The whole place was tiny and gross, but as soon as I had enough money, I was going to gut it, fix all the plumbing issues, and design a beautiful light-filled studio and living space.

At least the water was hot. I stepped into the shower, letting it wash the grime off of me. As I stood under the spray, the relaxing hot water suddenly turned freezing cold. Screaming, I struggled to jump out of the shower, swinging the door out and stumbling into the open studio space.

Gasping from the shock of the cold, I pulled a towel around me. The towel rack pulled out of the wall and clanged to the floor. I screamed again out of rage.

"Why doesn't anything go right?" I wailed.

I heard a bang and froze. Someone was in my building. Did I lock the door? I couldn't remember. If I had, how had they gotten in? I looked around in a panic for a weapon as I heard footsteps pounding up the stairs.

I scrounged the metal towel bar that had fallen off the wall. Clutching my towel against me, I hoisted the metal bar and hid behind the shower door. The bar was heavier than it looked, and my arm was trembling.

The footsteps came closer, and I peeked around the door to see a black-clad figure turn around the wall at the stair landing. I swung. The man ducked, and the towel rack embedded into the wall.

"What the hell?" Archer yelled.

"What are you doing here?" I shrieked at him.

His eyes widened when he saw I was in a towel. He clapped a hand over his face.

"I thought you were being attacked!" he said. "I heard you scream. I thought—I'm sorry."

"Hand me my clothes," I said, scurrying into my bedroom closet. My voice was trembling. "I wasn't attacked," I said when he handed me the yoga pants and crop top I had worn earlier and thrown on the floor because I didn't think a man was coming into my apartment.

"My water heater went out," I said to him. "It was freezing."

Archer swore.

"How did you get in here? I locked the door. You better not have broken my door," I warned.

"I hope you aren't relying on that lock to keep you safe. All I needed was my credit card and a good shove to open it," he said. "Also," he continued when I walked back into my room, tying up my hair, "why is your shower in a closet?"

"We can't all live in fancy houses," I told him. "It's fine. It's historic. Stuff breaks, yes, but it's part of the charm."

"Let me take a look at it."

"What can you do?" I scoffed. "You're some fancy-pants billionaire. You don't fix stuff."

Archer was incensed. "I own a billion-dollar hotel company. The majority of our hotels are in historic buildings. I better know how to fix stuff," he said as he took off his jacket.

Suddenly I was very aware there was a man in my apartment.

"See something you like?" he asked, slowly unbuttoning his dress shirt. He removed it, his undershirt, and his watch, laying them on the couch. Then he walked over to me, bare chested. His muscles rippled, and suddenly I was very glad I'd had a cold shower. I was thinking I might need another one. "As much as I want to act out a seventies porno flick with you, in the starring role of the plumber, I'd like for you to have hot water," Archer said lightly.

I followed him downstairs. He took a toolbox out of the back of his sports car.

"Take me to your boiler," he said.

"This is really something," he remarked after I led him to the ancient nineteen-thirties tankless water heater in the basement. "When was the last time this thing was serviced?" he asked.

I shrugged. "Decades?" The water heater was crusted over, but I could still see a hint of the intricate design stamped in it. "A factory in town used to make them."

A giant cricket jumped out from under the heater. I screamed.

"It's not going to hurt you," Archer said. "They don't bite." He flicked the bug off his pants leg. "You need to spray."

"I hate coming down here," I complained.

"Go upstairs, then. I'll take care of it," he said and turned back to the heater.

I didn't want to go off and leave him alone, so I waited in the hallway of the café that led to the basement stairs. I texted my friends while listening to the banging and clanking.

Hazel: *Archer showed up at my apartment.*
Olivia: *No! He just showed up?*
Hazel: *Water heater issues. He's fixing it.*
Jemma: *OMG he's fixing your water heater.*
Hazel: *He took his shirt off to do it.*
Jemma: *Holy testosterone.*

I had to admit I was glad Archer was there fixing it. I didn't know how to do it, and I certainly didn't have money to pay someone to do it.

After about fifteen minutes, Archer came back upstairs. His hair was messy, and he had streaks of dirt on his face and chest.

"I guess it's a good thing you took off your nice shirt," I said.

"You just wanted to see me with my shirt off," he said with a crooked smile.

"Did you fix it?"

"The heater is covered in mineral deposits. I need to flush it. Do you have vinegar?"

I lugged out a jug of white vinegar and handed it to him. He poured it in the tank along with some boiling water and let it sit.

"We don't want to leave it in there too long. The tank will corrode," Archer said, setting a timer on my phone and sitting down at one of the tables.

I was suddenly very aware of him shirtless in my café.

"I hope no one comes in here expecting a drink," I joked. "This might be a public health hazard."

He raised an eyebrow. "I think actually having sex in here would be a public health hazard."

I gulped. Was it flirting? An offer?

"You're going to make some girl very happy someday. You're like a perfect-ten boyfriend," I said, trying to sound flirty and not desperate. "Fixing my heater, running to protect me from the cold water, and you aren't afraid of crickets."

He smiled grimly. "Yeah, I've had a little too much experience with crickets." He looked back at the basement door.

"Like on *Fear Factor*?" I joked. "You have a ton of money. You should just pay someone to deal with crickets."

He looked back at me.

"Not *Fear Factor*." He looked down and rubbed at the dirt on his hands. "I guess I shouldn't tell you this…"

"Tell me."

"Never mind."

"I'm not going to judge you," I said, sitting down next to him. "You've seen the state of my life. I don't even have a real bathroom."

Archer glanced quickly at me then out the window. "At the compound, my father would fly into these rages if we put a foot wrong. There was this hole in the ground. He would lock me in sometimes if he thought I was being too obnoxious. It was infested with crickets because it was damp," Archer said, trying to sound as matter-of-fact as possible.

I felt tears prick my eyes. "That's awful," I said, leaning over to hug him. He held me tightly, and I buried my face in the crook of his neck.

"I should be over it. I am over it," he said lightly. "What doesn't kill you makes you stronger, right?"

"Yeah," I said, "but sometimes it doesn't make you stronger. It just makes you sad."

"I upset you," Archer said, rubbing away a tear. "Wait, here's a joke. What is warm, wet, and pink?"

I started to feel a little wet.

He grinned. "A pig in a hot tub."

I laughed. "Since you gave me hot water, I thought you were going to ask me for something else as a thank-you present," I said. "I want to make you feel better."

"Look," Archer told me seriously, "if you can pull off these paintings and win me the chocolate factory site, I will get on my knees and literally eat you out until my jaw locks and then cook pizza rolls for you."

CHAPTER 24

Archer

She stammered unintelligibly after I made my offer. Was it a joke too far? Except I wasn't really joking.

Hazel was looking up at me, panting slightly. Her nipples were hard through her shirt, little pebbles against my chest. All I wanted to do was kiss her then take her like I would take her mouth. The phone alarm shrieked.

"Better flush out your water heater before the acid eats it away," I growled.

Hazel nodded as I stood up. Her eyes were a little dilated.

The hot water heater looked about as good as could be expected for something almost a hundred years old.

"You're probably going to need a new one soon," I told Hazel as I tested the sink at the bar to make sure the water came out hot.

"I guess I'll take a shower now," she said. "I'm still a little wet."

I blinked. I wanted nothing more than to let my fingers trail up her leg and see just how wet she was.

"I mean wet like sweaty because I was outside all day and I started to take a shower but it was cold." She gulped. I wanted to push her against the bar, pull down her panties, and fuck her tight, hot pussy until she screamed.

"I should go shower too," I said, turning abruptly to walk upstairs.

"You're showering here?" she squeaked.

"Hardly. I'm going home to shower. I don't think I'd fit in yours."

"You'd fit."

I quirked an eyebrow.

"Oh, you meant the shower." Her face was flushed as she handed me my clothes.

I looked down at her. If she asked me to stay, I was going to push her into that dinky little bed and fuck her all night.

"I guess I'll see you tomorrow," she said.

I felt jumpy, like I could twist out of my own skin, as I walked to my car. I didn't like that Hazel felt sorry for me. I wanted her to desire me. I had half a mind to go back to her apartment, push her against the couch, and kiss my way down to the wet pink flesh and—

McKenna jumped up from behind my car when I beeped it open with the key fob. I swore as she came around the car to me.

"I already told you," I warned.

"Archer, I miss you," she begged.

"No, you don't. You don't even like me," I countered. I looked back up, hoping Hazel wasn't seeing this.

McKenna grabbed my jaw, sinking her nails into my skin. "Don't think about her. Think of me. Archer, we were good together."

"Stop," I told her, pushing her off, getting in my car, and racing home.

I couldn't sleep that night between wanting Hazel and then being angry about McKenna.

After tossing and turning, I got up early and went out for a run. There were lights along the trails that crisscrossed our estate. Since it was summer, the sun rose early. I stood on the terrace and watched then went inside to scrounge for breakfast.

"I thought you went back to Manhattan," Hunter said when he saw me sitting at the table. He placed a box of food on the table.

"What's that?"

"Hazel sent food. Apparently you ordered it?"

"She was here?" I looked wildly around. Why hadn't she come to talk to me?

"No. A courier left it," Hunter replied, throwing me a bagel. "But now I see why you're still here. It's that girl, Hazel."

"No, not Hazel. I have to be here for my conference center," I lied.

"The presentation is not for another week and a half," Hunter said. "You're neglecting your real business. Mike has lodged several complaints with me."

Traitor.

"I have the art committee and the art retreat," I said around a mouthful of lox bagel.

"Someone else could do that," Hunter replied. "You can't bank everything on winning this convention center. Meg might give it to Harrington out of spite."

I snorted. "Hazel is painting away. She's fast and good. Go ahead and buy the champagne for that factory site because we're going to win it."

"As long as she delivers a superior product to whatever Harrington is going to show. But know this; once this is all wrapped up," Hunter warned, "you need to go back to Manhattan."

Back to Manhattan? I would need to find some way of convincing Hazel to come along. I wanted her around. But she might not want to leave her friends and her sisters.

"Are you paying attention?" Hunter asked.

I looked at him blankly.

"I don't know what's gotten into you."

"It's McKenna. She's been following him around," Garrett said.

"Stop talking about me like I'm not here."

"Then act like an adult."

"Fine. McKenna is not a problem. She'll get bored and slither back into her hole in Manhattan."

I spent the morning holed up in Mace's office. I would periodically poke my head around the door and shoot a little paper ball at him through a straw. My aim wasn't all that great. I was rusty. Sometimes the paper pieces would just bounce on the floor.

"Stop it," Mace warned.

"Just trying to keep you on your toes," I said.

Garrett knocked on the glass wall of Mace's office. He had a crate in his hand. He looked annoyed. "I'm not your mail boy," he said icily.

"What is that?" Mace asked.

"You're not the only one who plots and plans," I said, taking the crate from Garrett gleefully. "Hey, Mace, do you want a sandwich? I feel like a sandwich."

"Anything to get you out of my office."

CHAPTER 25

Hazel

had Archer on the brain. I also wondered why he hadn't kissed me. It felt like he wanted to.

Hazel: *Do I smell bad?*

Olivia: *No? You smell like bread and deli meats.*

Jemma: *But in a good way. Guys like that.*

Hazel: *Archer fixed my heater then he left. I'm a mess.*

Jemma: *Call him back over and tell him it needs fixing again then open the door in sexy lingerie.*

Hazel: *I don't think I have any properly sexy lingerie.*

Olivia: *Cut some holes in your panties.*

Hazel: *I can't…*

Jemma: *Take control. Be the change you want to see in your life!*

I could not sleep that night at all. I had fitful dreams that Archer was there. I would wake up, see that he wasn't, need a very cold shower, go back to bed, and repeat the process. I was relieved when the sun shone through the skylight in my bedroom closet.

I made sandwiches, all while thinking of Archer's comments about sex in the café. "I seriously need to get laid," I said out loud.

"Amen!" Jemma said as she walked in and headed to wash her hands. "At least he fixed your hot water."

"I needed him to fix something else," I grumbled, and I quickly finished the sandwiches. I also made a box for the Svenssons since Archer had paid me for food. After another sweltering walk to Ida's General Store, I returned to my café and started prepping for the lunch rush, or rather the lunch trickle.

There was a blank spot on the wall where the large collage trash painting had hung. My painting of the art walk was dry, so I decided to hang it in the blank spot. I was tired of pretending to be the type of artist I wasn't. I stood on a ladder to adjust the picture wire hanging from the picture rail. The ceilings were tall, and my ladder was more of a step stool that I had pulled out of a dumpster.

Crack.

I shrieked as I fell, squeezing my eyes shut. Strong arms grabbed me. I opened my eyes.

"I swear," Archer said as he set me down safely on the floor. "I can't tell if it's you who's accident-prone or this café."

"It's my stuff," I said helplessly. "You get what you pay for, and I found this stool for free in a dumpster."

Archer looked at the ladder then up at the picture wire. "I wanted to hang this."

Archer looked at the painting. "Is this the art walk?"

I nodded.

Archer reached up easily, fixed the picture wire, then hung the painting. He stood back and really looked at it. I watched Archer study my painting. His eyes wandered over every brushstroke, taking it in.

"That's mesmerizing," he said finally. He turned to me, his eyes wandering over me as closely as they had the painting.

Take control. The first brushstroke is the hardest. Don't overthink it.

I closed the distance between us. I reached up on my toes—*he was so tall!*—and kissed him softly on the corner of his mouth. His fingertips rested lightly on my waist.

"I wanted you to do this yesterday," I whispered to him.

Archer slid a hand on my waist, tilted his head, and kissed me. His lips were slightly cool from the air, but when he deepened the kiss, his mouth was hot. He kissed me like he wasn't in any hurry, like he couldn't care less that we were in full view of the window to the street. I wrapped my arms around him, not wanting it to end.

"I *wanted* to do this yesterday," Archer said, his voice husky. "But I felt like I should do it properly, you know, take you out on a date first."

"Mm-hmm," I said, "but you really should test-drive the paintbrush before you buy it."

He looked slightly confused. "I think that's the wrong metaphor," Archer said, his thumb running lightly on my neck.

"No," I said, "it's like when you go to an art store, you should try out the paintbrush before you buy it."

"I'm not selling my paintbrush. I'm giving it away for free."

"That's too bad," I said, resting my chin on his chest, "because I make really nice packaging."

He laughed.

I looked over at the bar. There was a wooden crate on it. "What's that?"

"I told you I would bring you raspberries," he replied. I ran over to the box and opened the lid. Inside were handfuls of perfect, plump raspberries. I grabbed several and popped them in my mouth. The juice exploded on my tongue.

"Yum." I moaned. "So freaking good."

Archer walked over and kissed me. The juice of the raspberries mingled with the taste of him.

"They are pretty good," he said, his voice rumbling through my chest. His head dipped down again to kiss me, his muscular arms crushing my body to his.

"Pancakes," I gasped when he released me. "I'm making pancakes."

"You don't have to cook. We could go out," Archer said with a frown. "I have restaurants at the bottom of my two hotels in town."

I looked at him askance. "You can't bring me amazing berries and then be like, 'Hey, let's just ignore these and let them wilt in the heat.' They must be worshiped."

A smile quirked at the edges of his mouth.

"Sit," I ordered him. "I'm never able to do a lot of baking. Mainly all I make is alcohol and sandwiches. People don't come here for dessert. I'm going to enjoy every minute of this."

I went to my storage room and pulled out all my baking equipment. It wasn't high-end—I didn't even have a stand mixer. But I had my soufflé rings and a nice whisk I had inherited from Melvin.

"Well," Archer said. "Since you have all your stuff out, can I have some popcorn?" He wrapped his arms around me, kissing up my neck to my jaw. "Please? Pretty please?"

I turned around and kissed his mouth, still a little shocked that this was actually happening. But his mouth was very real, pressed against mine. His tongue stroked the inside of my mouth, like he could stand there all day, pressing me against the bar. My hands traveled up the ripple of muscles on his back. They went lower to his belt—but Archer released me before I could throw caution out and suggest sex in the café.

I shooed him to the bar stool, poured in the oil and popcorn kernels, and set a large popcorn pot on the gas stove. I had to fiddle with it a little to make it work. Maybe one day I would have a nice kitchen.

The café was arranged so that the kitchen was open to the dining space. Archer watched me with interest. "Wait, that's how you make popcorn?" Archer asked, looking over. "That's really cool."

"How do you make popcorn?" I asked as I turned the wooden handle.

He shrugged. "A bag?"

"This is so much better," I said. "Want to try?"

Archer joined me behind the counter. "Just turn it slowly," I instructed. He started cranking the wheel like he was trying to start a motorcycle.

"Slowly," I said, resting my hand on his. "You want to let the kernels sit in the heat just long enough to get a little jumpy then rotate them so they don't burn. Nothing worse than burnt popcorn."

I set the truffle butter to melt in a little pot on the stove then chopped some parsley. All the while, I snuck glances at Archer, admiring the lines of his body. He had his weight shifted on one leg, the sleeves on his white dress shirt rolled up. The tendons and veins on his forearm flexed slightly as he rotated the handle.

"There is something wrong with me if I'm getting turned on by this," I muttered.

Archer grinned. "What was that?"

"Nothing. We should have some alcohol with this, shouldn't we? Alcohol makes any situation better," I said, hastily grabbing mixers and liquor and setting them on the counter.

I grabbed handfuls of the raspberries and put them in a glass pitcher, muddling them with a wooden spoon. I didn't want to make jam, just to release the juice and the flavor. I added in club soda, vodka, a hint of lime, and some local honey. I tasted the concoction. It had a bright, summery flavor.

I poured the drink into a glass and held it up to Archer's mouth. He took a sip.

"These are the best raspberries I've ever had. You don't need sugar or anything," I said.

"It's very refreshing," he said, leaning down to kiss me. The popcorn rattled around in the pot.

"Keep stirring," I told him.

He kissed me again then took another sip of the drink.

"It's not too sweet, is it?" I asked. "Are you one of those guys who doesn't like sweets?"

"Hardly," Archer scoffed. "Give me your cookies, cakes, and pies. I will eat them all. My friend Chloe has a bakery, and she always gives me free stuff. I have the Grey Dove Bistro make hand-decorated sugar cookies that look like each of my hotels. We give them out instead of chocolates. The free Instagram publicity we get from them is nuts. I'm thinking about having her do a special Christmas version of the cookies, you know, with the hotels all decorated and snowy with lights."

The vodka churned in my stomach when I thought of Chloe. Her bistro would absolutely put me out of business. I forced myself to calm down.

Positive energy! I have a sexy guy in my kitchen. I'm going to bake. Don't freak out. Don't be weird. Don't blow this.

"I'm glad you like sugar," I said lightly.

"I like eating all sorts of sweet things," he said, his deep voice promising more pleasure than chocolate cake.

"These raspberries sure are sweet," I said, shoving a handful in my mouth. The juice ran down my chin.

Archer leaned over and licked it off lightly. The popcorn in the pot went crazy.

"I think it's ready," I said, shoving a bowl in between me and Archer. "Where did you even find the berries?" I asked as I poured the truffle butter over the popcorn, tossing it once.

"You can buy anything online," Archer bragged as he held the bowl while I grated the parmesan. "Weirdly enough," he continued thoughtfully, "I found them on this one website that was dedicated to all things raspberry. They had raspberry candy, edible raspberry lingerie, and edible raspberry-flavored body paint."

"That sounds…" *Erotic? Sexy? Something I wanted and needed?* "Interesting," I said lamely.

Archer smirked like he knew what I had been thinking. "It was all organic."

"I don't understand how edible lingerie works," I said as I sprinkled the finely shaved parsley and some French sea salt on the popcorn. "Like, do you eat the whole thing? Is it like a Fruit by the Foot? Also what about the edible body paint? Isn't it just like a raspberry reduction? I feel like I could make that."

"Anytime you want to cover me in raspberry sauce and lick it off, I am totally game," Archer said, his hand trailing down my waist to rest on my hip. "Hell, maybe you could start a side hustle doing that."

"I don't know if I can make sex toys."

"Sex food," Archer corrected, feeding me a bite of popcorn. "Didn't Ida say you were drawing porn?"

"I'm not drawing porn!" I said, almost choking on the popcorn. I had to take a swig of the raspberry vodka muddle.

"If you were, you could draw little demonstration pictures to go along with your products."

"I'm running a wholesome establishment here."

"You're serving alcohol to the elderly at two in the afternoon," Archer said with a snort. "You're already well on your way down the road of debauchery. Might as well embrace it wholeheartedly!"

"You mean like sleeping with one of my art retreaters?" I asked too casually as I organized my ingredients for the raspberry cheesecake pancakes.

He shrugged and threw a handful of popcorn in his mouth. "You suggested it, not me. I was thinking of something less blatant and more artistic. Perhaps nude models with, like, tastefully displayed little cakes and chocolates and things. You know, like they do with sushi in some clubs?"

"What clubs are you going to?"

"Don't act like you've never eaten a piece of food off a good-looking man, Hazel."

I pursed my lips as I separated the eggs for the pancakes. I was making Japanese-style pancakes, which were more like soufflés.

"I'm not some playboy billionaire running around, buying crates of raspberries and impulse shopping paintings," I said.

"You should try it," Archer said as he unbuttoned his shirt.

I swallowed. "I'm cooking," I croaked.

He smirked. "So you are. And it sure is heating up in here. I guess I'll be the one eating off of you." I was beating the egg whites and sugar into a meringue. I couldn't stop because it wouldn't set right, and I wanted the pancakes to be fluffy. Ideally they should be two inches high and jiggly. I shivered as Archer set a raspberry on the soft spot where my neck and collarbone met. He leaned down and licked it off, his mouth pressing to my skin.

"Tasty," he murmured in my ear as he nibbled the lobe. Now that there was a very real possibility that Archer and I would... you know... I was starting to freak out.

"Well, these look nice and stiff. You want the erect peaks," I said, folding the meringue.

Archer snickered.

"I mean," I said, starting to get tongue-tied. He was right next to me. If I wasn't mistaken, I could feel something stiffer and more erect than the meringue in the bowl against the back of my thigh. "I want really thick pancakes."

"Like a good nine-inch stack?" Archer asked, stepping back to give me some breathing room.

"Something like that," I rasped as I turned on the griddle to get hot and mixed the egg yolks with flour and milk. I stirred the raspberries in then folded the meringue and the pink-streaked batter together. Finally I carefully poured it into the round molds on the griddle.

"These have to cook for a while," I told Archer as I measured out heavy cream for the ganache to pour over the pancakes instead of syrup.

"So that they're really thick and stiff. Got it," he replied.

I slurped some of the drink. The alcohol cooled my throat and loosened me up. I tried to concentrate as I chopped up chocolate.

"So you are making edible body paint," Archer said as I mixed the chocolate and cream together in the double boiler.

"It seems like ganache would be a little too sticky," I said as I stirred it carefully in the double boiler while the pancakes slowly cooked and puffed in their molds.

"What would you suggest, then?" Archer asked as I pulled out the chilled whisk and metal bowl from the freezer. I poured whipped cream and powdered sugar in and started beating. "I think this actually would be better. Goes on smooth. You can lick it off in one swipe."

"Only one swipe?" Archer asked as I crushed raspberries and folded them into the whipped cream. "It would be better to sit there and work it with your tongue, don't you think?" he asked, scooping up some of the whipped cream and licking it slowly off his finger.

"Pancakes are done," I said, almost dropping the whipped cream bowl. I stacked the pancakes on a plate, layering the whipped cream between the tall, fluffy golden pancakes and drizzling the ganache on them.

Archer took a bite. "Perfect," he said and set his fork aside. Walking around the counter, he pressed me to him. "Thank you for the pancakes," he said, tilting his head to kiss my neck then up to my mouth. I moaned against his mouth and pulled him down to me. "I don't know about you, but I like to have a main course before dessert."

His hands ran slowly up and down my back, sliding over my hips, caressing my thighs. A part of me didn't care if people could see into the café. I just wanted to strip off my clothes so I could feel him. His hand crept up my leg. Suddenly it was all too much.

"Sorry. Can't. Actually have a busy rest of the evening planned. Need to do some painting," I croaked, slipping out of his arms. I grabbed a brown paper takeout box and used a spatula to scoop the pancakes inside.

"But—" Archer said as I all but shoved him out the door and handed him the box.

"Thanks for stopping by. Come back and see us again!" I said and slammed the door, then I ran and hid behind the counter. "What is wrong with me?"

CHAPTER 26

"I thought you were bringing me a sandwich," Mace said irritably when I walked into the living room.

"Find your own sandwich," I growled at my twin.

I was still sort of fried from Hazel. I half assumed that after all of that, I would eat her pancakes then take her upstairs, or ideally take her to my hotel, but I wasn't going to be too picky, and eat something else. But as soon as things became hot and heavy, she slapped my leftover pancakes in a box, shoved them in my hands, and then shoved me out the door.

"What's that?" Mace asked, nodding to the box in my hands.

"Is that food?" Henry asked as he and Arlo ran up to me.

"You guys are like scavengers."

"No kidding!" Josie said. Her feet were in Mace's lap, and he was kneading them slightly. "I think I cooked enough food to feed a battalion, and it's all gone. So if you're hungry, we have nothing here to eat."

"I already ate. Had pancakes."

She gestured to the box. "Leftovers! You know I want a bite." Josie opened up the box and gasped. "These are so pretty! This is a cake not pancakes."

"Did Chloe make that?" Mace asked.

"Chloe's not even here," I said. "Hazel made it."

"The art sandwich girl?"

"She likes to bake."

Josie cut off a huge chunk and stuffed it in her mouth. "So freaking good."

As if they had a sixth sense that there was more food in the house, the rest of the horde of my younger brothers came padding into the room and crowded around Josie.

"You guys are so creepy!" I said, shooing them away. Josie started cutting off pieces of the pancake.

"That's mine," I complained.

"Honestly, Archer," Hunter said, coming into the living room, disapproval clear on his face. "You never exercise, and you eat junk food all day. I think you can share."

"I work out! I just do it at night."

Josie was carefully partitioning off my leftovers and giving each kid a bite. The last bit she reached out and fed to Mace.

"It is good, and you know I don't like sweets that much. But I would eat more of that," he said.

"Hazel made that especially for me!"

Hunter glared. "You need to stop distracting her. She's supposed to be making a painting for the convention center, not feeding you."

Peyton ran into the room with a popsicle and almost crashed into Hunter. "We're selling these tomorrow!" he announced excitedly.

"You are?" I asked as Hunter grabbed him.

"I don't want you dripping that on the carpet. It's all over your face. How are you coming along with the Art Zurich Expo campaign, Archer?" Hunter asked, wiping at Peyton's face with a napkin.

I took out my phone and swiped to the picture I'd taken of Hazel's art walk painting.

Hunter grunted.

"Is that an impressed grunt? Or an annoyed grunt?" I asked him.

"Let me see," Josie said, making a grabbing motion with her fingers. "Ooh!" she exclaimed, studying the photo. "I love the chandeliers! Weston and Blade want their company, ThinkX, to sponsor a conference. A great marketing angle would be to bill it as inspiration in an inspirational place. If Harrogate is known as a cool art town and has a unique conference center, it would really help drum up interest. When are you going to start designing? We need to make sure there are Instagrammable moments on the art walk."

"I made some calls to landscape designers I've used on my hotels and sent them the picture," I explained. "They're coming out to Harrogate in the next few days to look at the site."

"How much is this going to cost, exactly?" Hunter asked.

I shrugged. "You and Garrett can figure that out. You're the finance people."

"This is your project, Archer," Hunter said. "What were you doing all day at Hazel's if you weren't even working on this project?"

Oh, I don't know, making out with a hot girl...

As if he could read my thoughts, Hunter's eyes narrowed. "So that's what you were doing. I warned you about becoming involved with Meg's sister. You really do have the worst taste in women."

"The popsicle is melting on your suit," I told him. His jaw clenched, and he carried Peyton to the kitchen.

I escaped to the clubroom. I needed a drink and a distraction from my obsession over what had happened with Hazel. Was Hunter right? Was that why Hazel had pushed me out? Was she concerned about what Meg would think?

That couldn't be it—Hazel was her own person. She was a business owner, and she unashamedly dumpster dived. She didn't strike me as someone overly concerned with what people thought.

Maybe it was me? Maybe I moved too fast. I did my usual shtick. Maybe it was too much. I thought she was having fun.

Focus, I told myself. *There are other women if Hazel is tired of you.*

But I didn't want another woman. I knew I could have any of the ones who threw themselves at me in Manhattan. Hazel was different. And that kiss, well all of those kisses, were amazing. She was so soft and curvy. Hazel wasn't the type I usually went for, no. But seeing how badly it went with McKenna, something different was just what I craved.

Seeing Hazel the next morning at the committee meeting was torture. I tried to keep it together as I gave an update about the art walk and showed off Hazel's painting. McKenna was clearly annoyed.

"I have designers I could call on, Archer, to refine this idea."

"It's fine, McKenna. I already have it under control."

"But we should think about the design. This chandelier tree is hideous and derivative."

"Josie seems to like it, and she's the head of the Harrogate Trust," I said, leveling my gaze at her.

McKenna sniffed. "If you all want to lose the bid for the expo, then fine." She grabbed her bag and walked out. "You're all going to be sorry you didn't listen to me."

I grabbed Hazel by the arm after the meeting was over. "Did I do something wrong?" I asked her softly.

"No," she said, looking up at me through her lashes. "I just really want you. It was a little overwhelming."

The breathless way she said it, the honestly in her face, was too much. I leaned over and kissed her, pressed her back against the door. I felt myself growing hard, listening to her whimper. Her hand tangled in my hair as I nuzzled her tits, feeling her rock-hard nipples through her shirt. I let my hand drift down under her skirt to press between her legs. Her panties were wet, and it was all I could do not to turn her around and bend her over the table.

She pushed me off and visibly swallowed. "Someone might come in," she said. Her eyes were dilated, and I could smell the hint of lust wafting off of her.

"I don't care," I whispered, running my hands under her shirt to cup her tits. "I want you, Hazel," I whispered in her ear. She moaned and strained against me. Before we could go any further, we heard yelling, and Hazel pushed me off and ran to the window.

CHAPTER 27

Hazel

A crowd was gathered in the square outside city hall. "What's going on?" I asked, peering out the window, trying to see.

"I don't know. Isn't there anything more important?" Archer asked. I was satisfied to see that the normally self-composed man seemed like he was losing a bit of control.

"Aren't you curious?" I teased as he followed me out of the room.

"Not that curious," he said, his hand on the small of my back. But he snapped his attention to the crowd as soon as we walked outside into the sunshine.

"Are those your brothers?" I asked. Archer's younger brothers were milling around. A dark-green bus was parked on the street. I waved to Remy. Archer and I followed the yelling. My sister Meg and his brother Hunter were going at it.

"They aren't allowed to sell food items without a permit," Meg was saying.

"It's a popsicle stand run by children, Meghan. Be reasonable," Hunter replied. "Oh, wait, I forgot. You're totally incapable of that when it comes to my family. You just can't help but be petty."

My sister, like me, tended to be on the shorter, wider side. And Hunter, with his height and broad shoulders, loomed over her. I was nervous for a second.

"He's not going to hurt her, is he?" I asked Archer uncertainly. Archer's face went dark, and he strode over to Hunter. I trotted after him.

"Stop it, Hunter," Archer snarled at his brother, grabbing his shoulder.

"She can't just run this town like her own personal kingdom," Hunter said, shaking off Archer.

"I'm not doing it to be arbitrary," Meg said. "It's the law."

Ida walked up, her phone out, filming us.

Hunter turned to the camera. "As you can see, the town of Harrogate is letting idiocy reign over common sense. No one should have a problem if innocent children are trying to sell wholesome homemade popsicles on such a hot day."

"You're trying to shut down the boys' popsicle stand?" Ida asked Meg in shock.

My sister scowled. "You don't know how clean their kitchen is. They could make people sick. I'm not banning them—they need a permit."

Susie, one of the police officers, showed up, followed shortly by Mace.

"This is getting out of hand," I muttered to Archer.

"Mr. Svensson," Susie said, her voice carrying over the din. "What is going on?"

"They need a permit to operate a food truck," Meg said.

"It's not a food truck," Hunter retorted. "You're just doing this to mess with me."

"They do need a permit," Susie said firmly. "Go talk to the health department."

Hunter opened his mouth to argue.

Mace grabbed Hunter. "Stop it." Hunter clamped his mouth shut and glared at my sister.

"Sorry," Mace told Susie. "They didn't know."

"We have a new food stand legislation where you don't need to go through as stringent of a process as if you were opening a restaurant," she offered. "The health department just comes and takes a look around your house to make sure you're not cooking in your bathroom."

"It's not a problem," Mace assured her.

Hunter shrugged him off. "This is outrageous. We're suing."

"Now who's being unreasonable?" Meghan shot back.

I helped Archer shoo his little brothers back into the old green school bus.

"As much as I like the fact that it drives Mace insane," Archer said as Remy drove off, "I really wish they'd do something with that bus. It's an eyesore."

Hunter and Meghan were still arguing about some obscure legal terms.

"I was going to have a meeting with him," Archer said, "but from the looks of things, he's going to be occupied the rest of the afternoon."

"I half wish they would just sleep together and end the sexual tension," I said as Hunter strode across the street to the courthouse, threatening to file a lawsuit. Meghan ran after him.

"Lawyers," Archer said, shaking his head.

CHAPTER 28

Speaking of sexual tension," I said softly in Hazel's ear, "are we going to finish what we started?"

She shivered. "I have to go to the café and get ready for lunch," she said.

"Well if you're craving big thick—"

"Big thick what?" Ida asked. Crap, I forgot she was still here.

"Pancakes," Hazel said firmly.

"You make pancakes?" Ida replied.

"She makes soft fluffy pancakes that I want to bury my face in."

Hazel shoved me.

"Oh, I see." Ida tapped the side of her head knowingly.

"I'll see you later," Hazel said. Before she could leave, I swept her into my arms and kissed her long and slow.

Ida whooped and hollered.

"I'm off to my conference center," I told her.

I was already thinking of it as mine. I knew the city had to approve the sale, and then Mike and Greg needed to be convinced that it would actually make money. But I was confident the conference center would happen. Mike was slowly getting on board. I needed to find a spot to build more hotels.

On the other side of the future conference center was an old strip mall site. I figured the city owned it, but no one could confirm. Hopefully Hunter hadn't aggravated Meg too much. Maybe I would have to organize a romantic dinner for them to grease the wheels. Hunter could be charming if he was motivated enough.

I parked my car and explored the strip mall site. It was flat, and I climbed up on a roof to look around. I could see the factory building rising up above the tree line behind the abandoned buildings. Another point in the strip mall site's favor was that it was far enough away that the tall hotel buildings wouldn't clash with the historic factory site or overwhelm the town of Harrogate.

"Maybe I can build out the art path as a connection to ferry people between the strip mall site and the factory," I mused, checking the map on my phone with what I saw before me.

"Factory, check. Hotel site, check. Sexy curvy girl on my arm, check!" I said, whistling as I walked around the abandoned retail building to my car.

You know what wasn't on my list? My mother. The nice Mercedes that I had bought her was parked next to my sports car.

"Mom."

Merla Vee simpered, "Archer, honey, how's my favorite kid?"

"What are you doing here?" I hissed. I looked up. I didn't see any cameras on the light poles with the blown-out bulbs. But I knew Garrett was probably going to find out about the meeting somehow. Did he have drones in the sky? "You cannot be here," I told my mom.

"You haven't been returning my calls," Merla Vee said. I tried not to scowl. The voicemail messages she left were all thinly veiled attempts to ask for money.

"What do you want?" I asked harshly. "Money? I don't have any more."

"It's that girl, isn't it?" my mom hissed. The pleasant expression on her face fell and let me see the angry, rage-filled expression she wore most of the time we lived in the shack in the desert.

I flinched, half expecting her to throw something at me, like she used to when I was a kid.

My mother saw my distrust and relaxed her features. "Archer, baby, my favorite," she sang. "You know your mamma loves you."

I shook my head.

"There's this great business opportunity," Merla Vee began.

"No," I said.

"But, Archer—"

"No," I said more forcefully. "I'm done. I'm cutting you off."

"You can't cut me off," she snarled.

"Yes, I can," I said flatly. "I've given you a lot of money over the years. You've never once asked me how I am or showed any real interest in me. You just want me to support your lifestyle."

"I took care of you," she shouted. "I sacrificed every-thing for you boys."

"You were a terrible mother. Hunter did more than you. After Dad kicked me and my brothers out, Greg and Hunter lied to us and said we were on a fun camping trip. We were out in the highlands, basically hunting and fishing. I thought it was a great adventure—until winter hit."

"Greg is Athlyn's son," Merla Vee protested. "He's not my son. He's not my problem. I raised you boys right. I told your father not to take up with Athlyn. You think I wanted that life?"

"You sure kept around like you did," I said.

"Your daddy kept promising things were going to get better. I was a victim," she said, beating her chest.

"So were your children!" I shouted. "The kicker is that Hunter and Remy were only sixteen, and Greg was a few months younger. I couldn't imagine how they managed. They were kids. You escaped. You could have taken us all with you. You could have done *something*."

"My boyfriend didn't want that," my mom said, her mouth a thin flat line.

"Right, uh-huh. Well, maybe you can go back to him and beg him for money."

When Merla Vee realized I was serious, the anger consumed her face. My mom glared at me, and she wrenched her car door open.

"You're going to regret this," she said, wagging her finger. "I raised you better than this."

"Stay out of Harrogate," I told her.

I had been planning on surprising Hazel that afternoon, but now I was too worked up. Instead I drove over to the Mast Brothers' chocolate factory. I was building a better future for my younger brothers. The convention center was part of it. I wanted Hazel to be a part of it. I walked around the grounds, making notes for how I wanted the design to work. I smiled when I spotted a figure on the roof.

CHAPTER 29

Hazel

After lunch I went to the Mast Brothers' chocolate factory center to paint. I would never admit it to Archer, but it was a little creepy being there by myself.

I painted the rest of that afternoon. The rendering was really coming together. I had the base of the buildings done. Now I was adding in the landscaping, trees, and making sure the glass looked nice. I wanted the whole rendering to have a sharp but ethereal feel, like a Vermeer painting, where the light was so perfect.

I didn't notice Archer until he was right behind me.

"Crap!" I yelled, jostling the canvas. Archer grabbed it and me. I laughed.

"I was actually trying not to startle you, believe it or not," Archer said.

I had worn a skirt that day to try and catch some of the breeze, and I smoothed it down.

"So this is the painting," Archer said, studying the canvas. "It seriously looks good."

I felt a rush of pride. "So pizza rolls and you eating me out until your jaw locks are in my future?"

"I did promise," he said, his voice dangerously low. His hand released its grip on my waist and pressed between my legs. I whimpered. He wrapped an arm around me. His other hand slid under my skirt. He tipped my head back and kissed me deeply.

"We shouldn't do this here," I gasped.

"No rooftop finger painting sessions?" Archer asked.

I bit my lip.

"Keep biting your lip like that," he whispered, "and I'm going to fuck you right here on this rooftop."

I shivered. I really was horny if I was starting to think rooftop sex was a perfectly fine and dandy idea.

No rooftop sex, Hazel. Bad, bad idea.

I packed up the easel and my supplies. "I wish more people wanted this style of painting," I said.

"There's a buyer for everything," Archer said as he picked up the case and wrapped a hand around my waist, guiding me to the stairwell.

"I'm not so sure."

"You should talk to Josie about marketing," he said. "Or Chloe."

Right, Chloe.

"I don't need an escort," I said crossly as Archer grabbed my bike and rolled it to his car.

"Of course you do. Because when the escaped felon comes and kidnaps you, everyone's going to be like, 'Who was she last seen with?' And then other people are going to be like, 'Archer,' and then I'll never be able to sleep in my own pantry again."

"Your own pantry?" I asked.

Archer kissed my cheek. It was barely a brush, but I wanted to strip all my clothes off and throw myself at him. My panties were wet and hot as I fidgeted in the passenger seat of his car. I half wanted him to pull over, park the car, and show me his finger painting skills firsthand.

Soon we were pulling up in front of my building. I watched like a creep as Archer set my bike on the curb and carried my easel inside.

"Upstairs?" he asked, half turning toward me, one foot on the staircase.

"Yes, please," I said, my voice catching in my throat.

Then he was standing in front of me in my studio. It was one thing to paint someone, but to have him there, standing in front of me, knowing he wanted me, was another.

"Drink?" I asked. "Though I guess I should have asked when we were downstairs."

Stop rambling, Hazel!

"How about something better?" he offered, encircling my waist with his large hands and pushing me back gently onto the couch. "I wanted to do this in the conference room," he said, kissing me, his hand pressing between my legs. "And when you made that stack of very sexually suggestive pancakes and then that night when you jumped out naked at me."

"I was wearing a towel," I said and whimpered, arching against his hand.

"It was the skimpiest towel I've ever seen," he whispered in my ear, stroking me through my panties.

Where previously Archer had been playful, now he was all serious desire. He kissed me, his tongue stroking the inside of my mouth. I leaned back against the couch as Archer pulled at my top. The flowing fabric yielded easily. He pulled my breast out, sucking on it, his tongue and lips rolling the hard nipple. I moaned, my head leaning back.

"Archer," I whimpered. I spread my legs to give him easy access to me. His hand pushed under my panties.

"You're so wet," he groaned. His fingers curled, stroking me. His mouth moved back to my breast. My hips bucked against him as he stroked and teased me, his mouth sucking and biting at my nipple.

"I told you I was a good finger painter," he said, kissing back up along my jaw to my mouth. "But I also have other mediums I excel at."

He knelt down slowly. I was breathing hard as he kissed his way up my inner thigh, and I felt the heat of his breath through my soaking-wet panties. He eased them off of me, then he pressed his face between my legs.

"That feels amazing," I moaned. His hands were on my legs, spreading them. I leaned back into the couch pillows.

He reached up, his hand finding my breast, pinching the nipple, rubbing it as he licked and sucked. His tongue found my clit, and I cried out.

"You're making me so hard," he mumbled.

I tangled my fingers in his hair. His large hands held my hips steady as he licked and teased me, trailing his tongue to my opening and then back up the slit to suck on my clit. He slipped two fingers in my opening, curling his fingers, making me gasp.

My belly tightened, and my legs trembled. "I want your cock," I begged.

He ignored me, continuing to lick me. His tongue did this twisting thing around my clit. I clutched at his hair. I came with a cry, Archer drawing out the pleasure.

"You should have said you wanted to be on my paintbrush," he told me, kissing a nipple then kissing up to my collarbone.

"You're a really good painter," I slurred, running my fingers down his skin, tracing the tattoos through his open shirt collar and down the column of buttons. His zipper was half undone, and he was hard.

"I feel like you didn't savor it enough," he said, voice gravelly with desire. "The craftsmanship of good art needs to be appreciated."

I squeaked as he grabbed my waist and spun me around so I was face-first in the couch. He pushed up my skirt and pressed his face against the sensitive flesh. My back arched, and I gasped.

"I want you to fuck me," I moaned. His large hands gripped my hips, and he stroked me with his tongue slowly and deliberately. My fingers gripped the arm of the couch.

One of Archer's fingers teased my clit while his tongue dipped in and out of my opening. His fingers moved up to pinch my nipple, rolling the pebble-hard pink nub.

"Please, fuck me!" I begged Archer. He seemed content to explore every inch of the flesh. His fingers moved back to my opening, his other hand still playing with my nipple. He inserted two fingers in my opening, stroking me.

"You mean like that?" he asked. His voice was so deep. I moaned, grinding back against his hand.

"I want your cock," I said hoarsely, my head tipped back.

"I want to make you come again first. I love those little noises you make," he said, his fingers moving in and out of me. I whimpered.

His fingers went away, replaced by his mouth. He went after my clit, nipping and sucking until I was a sweaty, writhing mess. I bucked against him, but his large hands held my hips in place as I came with a curse.

"Crap, that was good."

"I told you I was a good painter."

"Yeah, but you didn't tell me you were that good," I said, standing up. "I still want your cock," I told him, turning to set my hands on his broad shoulders.

But between the heat and the pleasure, I felt a little dizzy. Archer caught me around the waist and laid me back on the couch.

I told him, "Just give me, like, five minutes…"

CHAPTER 30

I was totally obsessed with Hazel. I was also a bit miffed she just fell asleep. Should I be proud? Sure, I would take it. I watched her sleep, sprawled on the couch. I dragged a blanket over her. I didn't want to leave her by herself. Would it be weird if I stayed and watched her sleep? Probably.

My phone buzzed.

Carl: *Did you all see? We're all over the news. Greg is not pleased.*

Garrett: *Greg is too "busy" to text for himself? Shocking.*

Mike: *The publicity is all on our side at least.*

Blade: *Josie says that contentious publicity like the popsicle lawsuit is not good publicity.*

Weston: *Yeah some of us are trying to run businesses and make money here.*

Mace: *I still am not ok with the fact that you all see more of Josie than me.*

I closed the app and put the phone in my pocket. With so many brothers, the best way to communicate was massive group chats. Normally I enjoyed them, but right now I did not need the drama.

Speaking of drama, there was McKenna, waiting for me outside.

Is she stalking me?

Her lip trembled when she saw me. "Archer?"

"I don't have time for this."

"You were with her, weren't you? Tell me!"

"It's not any of your business," I said brusquely. "Don't you have a gallery to run? You have money, a nice family. You have everything. Why are you acting so irrational?"

"But I don't have everything!" she cried. "I don't have you."

"McKenna, we're done."

"Your mom thinks we'd be good together."

I stopped cold. "Why are you talking to my mother?"

"We had coffee," McKenna said. "She thinks Hazel is a bad influence." She reached up to stroke my arm, but I pushed her off and got in my car. "I can't deal with this right now."

My phone was buzzing in my pocket with messages on the various group chats I was on with my brothers. The vibrating was not helping the fact that I did not get to have Hazel on my paintbrush, so to speak. I gripped the steering wheel as I thought about her straddling me, riding me.

I need a good, cold shower and a stiff drink.

I would be receiving neither of those. I walked into the house, and it was chaos. Greg and Hunter were practically at each other's throats. Garrett was standing at the top of the stairs, looking like a vampire about to wreak havoc over the village. Mace's fists were clenched. The kids were running around like wild goats.

"What the hell?" I asked Mace over the din.

He shook his head. "At least Josie isn't here to see this. She'd run screaming back to Manhattan."

"I cannot believe you! It's all over Facebook," Greg yelled at Hunter.

"The popsicle stand?" I asked.

"Ida posted it online. The news media picked it up. Josie is in Manhattan doing damage control. Fortunately between her and Gunnar, they have some media contacts. They're trying to kill the story." Mace ran a hand through his hair and looked at his phone.

"Josie thinks we should do a press conference," I said, reading over his shoulder. "People all seem like they're on our side."

"We have to work with the city of Harrogate," Mace said. "This could jeopardize my company."

"They should be working with *us*," my younger brother Weston called out as he came into the house followed by his cofounder, Blade.

"Don't come here if you're just going to stir up shit with the city," Garrett warned. "You don't even live here."

"If Archer develops that conference center, I'm going to be here more often," Weston countered. "Now that you all have high-speed internet installed in Harrogate, you have faster internet here than in Manhattan."

"And," Blade said, "it's actually faster to travel to an international airport from Harrogate compared to Manhattan because it's a straight shot to Newark."

"Our consultants travel the majority of the time," Weston continued. "Manhattan is expensive. The public schools are bad. Blade has been making a very compelling case for moving ThinkX to Harrogate."

"You can't move here," Hunter said flatly.

"Why?"

"Because you aggravate me."

"See, this is why—"

"Shut up, Greg."

There was about to be a nuclear war, so I shooed my little brothers into the conservatory while Hunter and Greg argued.

"You should have started a T-shirt business," Otis was lecturing Peyton as I settled all the younger boys in the conservatory and pulled out some art supplies from the cabinet Josie had stocked. It should keep them occupied.

"You can still have a popsicle business," I told Peyton and Nate. "What you need to do is sway public opinion to your side."

"Greg's not going to like that idea," Nate said uncertainly.

"Which is exactly why it's a good one," I said gleefully. "Trust me. On many occasions, I wanted to put a hotel in an area where people didn't want any development. But with a little magic, promise some fancy amenities, and boom, they're eating out of your hands."

Remy came in, bushy beard framing his face. "You, me, popsicle protest, tomorrow afternoon."

"Are you seriously stirring up shit?" Garrett demanded when he stalked into the conservatory.

"No swearing," I said, mimicking Hunter. "That will be a hundred dollars." The kids laughed. "Relax, they're just doing some art therapy," I lied.

"Oh, that's too bad," Garrett said. He looked at me expectantly. "This might play nicely into a plan I have running."

I grinned. "Lucky for you, I am the recent recipient of three whole art classes. We're going to make some awesome signs."

"They cannot protest," Mike said, setting his coat down as the kids scrambled to make signs. "We still need Meghan to sign off on my convention center. We also need them to sign off on the strip mall site if the real estate gods are gracious."

Garrett's expression remained flat. "They'll sign off. Meg's sister is tied up in this. She's not going to jeopardize it. And Hunter needs to be taken down a peg. He's been aggravating lately and won't listen to reason."

"You mean he won't listen to you!" Remy laughed.

"After all of this, there is no way Meghan gives us that factory," Mike said, pulling me aside. "She's already mad. She's not returning my calls about the strip mall site."

"We have Hazel. She's the secret weapon."

Mike cocked his head. "And apparently we have Archer Svensson."

"What's that supposed to mean?" I asked.

"You turned the charm up to eleven and convinced Meg's sister to do the painting," Mike elaborated. "That was devious and underhanded, even for you."

"That's not why I'm with her," I snarled.

He raised his hands. "Calm down," he said. "It's just, you're a use-them-and-toss-them kind of guy."

"No, I'm not!"

"Yes, you are."

"I've changed."

"I hope so," Garrett interjected. "Because if Meghan decides you are after her sister for all the wrong reasons, the Svenssons will never be able to do business in the city of Harrogate again."

woke up the next morning lying half naked on a couch. My face was plastered onto the pillow with drool. I sat up and wiped my face off, blinking in the morning sun.

"She's alive!"

I shrieked as I turned and saw Ida, Jemma, and Olivia standing there, looking at me.

"Rough night?" Jemma asked.

"We were worried," Olivia said. "Jemma came by to make the sandwiches, but you didn't answer the door. It didn't look like you were even here."

"I told them you were probably away, having a soaking-wet evening with Archer," Ida said. "And you did!"

I wrapped the blanket around myself and shuffled to my shower closet.

"So," Ida crowed, "how was it?"

"Grandma, don't you have to take care of the general store?" Olivia asked. "Hazel's obviously fine."

"She's more than fine, I'll say," her grandmother replied.

"Come on. I'll drive you back," Olivia said, rolling her eyes.

"Dare I ask?" Jemma said when I was showered and downstairs making sandwiches. "How was it?"

"Pretty good."

Jemma cackled. "I feel like Archer's going to be upset if you describe him as pretty good," she said, clapping her hands together.

"Was he a good finger painter?"

I nodded. "And tongue painter."

"Wow, he gave you the all-star treatment."

While I basked in the afterglow of the admittedly pleasurable evening, I did wonder how Archer would react when he saw me that afternoon for the art retreat. I had fallen asleep on him after all.

"Stud muffin!" Ida called out when Archer walked upstairs, younger brothers in tow. "I see you've been sampling all Harrogate has to offer."

"Ida," I exclaimed, horrified, "you can't just spread everyone's business like that."

"I'm sure she was just talking about sandwiches," Archer said, smirking at me. "You know how much I love to eat sandwiches." His phone rang, and he stepped out to take the call.

"Making him work for it—good for you," Ida said, taking a swig of her drink.

"I'm going to replace that with water," I warned. She clutched the glass to her chest.

"Today," I told the group, "we're exploring stained glass. This is a very popular medium, and it looks beautiful in your house."

I helped them score and break the pieces of colored glass and showed them how to solder the pieces together.

"Not something you should do tipsy," Ida said as she took another swig of her third or fourth drink.

"No, it's not," I said, feeling slightly alarmed as the old woman waved the soldering iron around drunkenly. "You could burn or cut yourself."

"I'm making a penis," Ida announced.

"Please don't."

"But—"

"You know what?" I said, throwing up my hands. "It doesn't even matter at this point." I poured a drink of my own.

"At this point, Ida's art is the closest any of us are going to get," Dottie said.

"Hazel's getting enough action for everyone."

"Did it look as great as this one?" Ida asked, holding up her stained-glass art.

The penis was constructed of purple and blue stained-glass chips. The metal holding the pieces together wasn't all that straight.

"I didn't actually see it," I admitted.

All the elderly women gasped. "You need to make sure it's adequate," Ida said. "You know, scope it out. See how it measures up."

Archer walked back in, phone in hand.

"You'll tell me if mine looks all blue and purple like that," he whispered to me.

I was wrung out by the time we were done with the art retreat. Trying to make sure they didn't set the place on fire was exhausting. I was disappointed Archer didn't hang around. He waved to me when he left, little brothers trotting behind him. He was on the phone again. But he was a business man, so I supposed his time was in high demand.

It was just as well. I needed to finish the painting of his conference center. I put the Closed sign out on the Art Café. I had to finish the painting tonight. The Svenssons's presentation was tomorrow.

I went back upstairs and looked at the painting, making notes of what all needed to be touched up. Because of the heat, the oil paints were curing nicely. I only had a few more hours of work.

There was furious knocking at the door. My heart leaped as I hurried downstairs. Was it Archer? Nope. McKenna glared at me through the window.

"Let me in!" she shrieked.

"No," I said through the glass.

"You think because you're sleeping with him that it means something?" McKenna hissed at me. "You're all going to be sorry for humiliating me."

"You're doing that all on your own," I retorted. "You can't keep stalking people. I know you showed up in Harrogate because you heard Archer was here."

McKenna sneered at me. "He's just using you," she said. "Trust me. Archer Svensson loves *me*. As soon as you help him win that bid for the chocolate factory, mark my words, he's going to dump you on the side of the road with all your garbage art, and he'll be jetting off to Manhattan with me."

I refused to let her see how much the words stung.

"You're going to turn into Ida," McKenna continued. "Hobbling around Harrogate, making lewd comments, and telling everyone about the time you banged a billionaire."

"Archer's not like that," I said defiantly.

"Of course he is. Men like that don't become powerful billionaires by being nice," she said, her nails tapping against the glass like some sort of evil fairy.

I turned abruptly and went back upstairs. Through the window, I watched McKenna stalk off down the street. As soon as she disappeared from view, I threw open the windows to try to catch a cross breeze. My apartment was boiling hot. The air outside was still, and I fanned myself.

Still hot, I tore off my clothes and my bra. The underwire had ripped out and was poking me. Of course I couldn't afford a new one. I had to mute all the banking apps because I would continuously receive notifications that I was overdue on payment. The money Archer had paid me was already swallowed up.

I threw on a silky spaghetti-strap undershirt and walked around in it and panties, painting touch-ups over the next few hours and listening to music. I was so wrapped up in the work, I didn't even hear the footsteps on the stairs.

CHAPTER 32

Archer

All the talk of dicks during the art retreat made me want one thing. But I already had plans that afternoon.

"Are you two ready for the protest?" I asked Otis and Theo. They nodded happily.

"I have my sign!"

I was used to stirring the pot then vamoosing. But now I was going to have the opportunity to experience the fruits of my labor.

City hall was several blocks away. When I parked the car, Otis and Theo grabbed their signs to join the dozens of blond-haired kids marching in the square. Remy was in the center of the mass with a bullhorn. Several news crews had cameras, and reporters were out. Hunter stood to the side, arms crossed, sunglasses on. I snickered to myself as I sat back on one of the stone planters under the tree and watched, sipping on the drink I had snagged from Hazel's restaurant.

A car roared up and screeched to a halt on the street. Greg stormed out, coming over to me.

"Have you lost your mind?"

"Why are you blaming me?"

"Anytime there's trouble afoot, it's usually your doing."

"I just helped them make the signs," I told him, trying to keep the smile off my face. Perpetually stressed from managing a multibillion-dollar investment firm and chasing after his wayward younger brothers like yours truly, Greg was always on a hair trigger. As much as I felt it was my duty to help him release his anger, I still needed him to sign off on the financing for my convention center.

"Do you take anything seriously?" Greg asked, voice cold.

I gestured dramatically with my drink. "Dude, Garrett wanted this."

"Oh." Greg was momentarily speechless. "Did he say why?"

"All part of his master plan with Hunter."

If he were Mace, I would have messed up Greg's carefully parted hair. But Greg was grouchy during the best of times.

My older brother shook his head. "I can't believe you're so shortsighted and immature."

I snorted. "Please. I always have an ulterior motive. I'm thinking bigger than the convention center. We need the city to sell us that strip mall site."

"This is not going to make them think favorably of you," Greg warned.

"Actually, this is going to ensure they give me the land," I said. Greg was skeptical.

I continued. "The popsicle fiasco makes the City of Harrogate look petty. Once the hate mail flows in, they will want to make nice. In exchange for staging a photo op with New York State's cutest children, I will suggest they sell me the strip mall site for a fair price."

"That is such a terrible idea. How you even managed to successfully grow and maintain a multibillion-dollar hotel group is beyond me."

He stood up, and I jumped up after him. "Just hear me out—"

"Don't," Greg said, cutting me off. "I need to go do damage control." He inclined his head slightly, and I followed his gaze.

Meghan marched out of the city hall building and stalked over to Hunter.

"This is very mature," she said as we walked up. "Using your little brothers as props."

My older brother uncrossed his arms. "I'm teaching my little brothers about the public process and peaceful protest. My brother Remy did several tours in Afghanistan fighting for their rights. Maybe you could show a little respect."

I wish I knew what exactly had happened to cause so much bad blood between them.

"It's a health safety issue," Meghan said, trying to keep her face neutral. Hunter's jaw was set, his expression stubborn.

"We understand," Greg interjected. "I'll handle this."

Meg nodded. "I look forward to watching you lose the lawsuit, Hunter." Then she went to talk to one of the news crews.

"Hunter," Greg's voice was dangerously low, "you need to stop this now. I can't believe I had to come in from Manhattan to deal with this. You look like an idiot."

"Yeah, Hunter, the law is very clear," I said. "But look on the bright side. At least the kids got some fresh air."

Greg turned his icy gaze on me. "Get the kids back on the bus, and then get out of my sight."

I gave him a mock salute and walked over to Remy. "We have to shut 'er down."

"Great protest, everyone," Remy announced through the bullhorn. "Greg's mad?"

"Isn't he always?" I replied.

"He needs to get laid," Remy said sagely as the kids filed onto the bus.

"Don't we all?"

Hazel didn't answer when I knocked on the locked café door. Music blared from the open windows. She was clearly in, so I jimmied the lock and went upstairs.

She was engrossed in her painting. Seeing her barefoot and wearing this silky tank top that barely covered her panties, all I wanted to do was pull down the slip of fabric and press my mouth against her. It was hot in the apartment, and I loosened my shirt collar.

I didn't realize Hazel had no idea I was there until I pressed myself against her and murmured into her neck, "Is it distracting when I do this?"

Hazel screamed, the paintbrush jerking up and hitting me in the face. I grabbed her hand to keep her from taking my eye out.

She turned around in my arms. The outlines of her nipples were visible through the sheer fabric. I assumed it was something vintage. They sure did have good taste back then.

"I really want to suck on your tits," I told her, trying to regain some semblance of control, "but I think I probably owe you an apology first."

Hazel clapped a hand to her chest. She was breathing hard; her tits rose and fell.

"You're the one who is going to be sorry if your rendering is ruined the night before your big conference center presentation," she said.

I tipped my head down and kissed her. My hands slowly caressed her ass, sliding up her back to crush her to me.

"But apology accepted I guess," she said when I released her.

"How's the painting coming?" I asked, inspecting the canvas.

"I'm almost done," she said, turning back to the painting and dabbing little bits of color here and there. "You can't be here if you're going to distract me," she said as I kissed her neck to her shoulder blades, letting my hands slide up between her legs.

She turned to bop me on the nose with the paintbrush. "Go sit on the couch."

"I can't believe you're more interested in that store-bought paintbrush than a homegrown one."

"You need to leave if you're going to be disruptive."

"I'm not here to distract you. I'm here to inspire you," I told her.

"Oh yeah?" She set the paintbrush down and picked up a different brush to add little bits of yellow to the canvas.

"You said you would paint me nude."

"Did you want me to make a nude painting of you or literally paint you nude?" she asked, still studying the canvas with an expert eye.

"Your choice."

Hazel turned her head slightly and smiled at me. She might have thought we were flirting, but I was very serious.

I watched her fuss with the painting a little more. Then she stepped back. "I think that's it."

"Great!" I said. "Let's go on a date to celebrate. We could go dumpster diving, or I could watch you bend over a dumpster."

She smacked me lightly.

"The presentation is tomorrow," Hazel said. "I need to watch the painting and make sure everything is drying okay."

I raised an eyebrow. "So you'd literally rather watch paint dry than come out with me?"

She looked at me askance. "You *hired* me to do a job. There's a lot riding on this for you. What if while we're out, a pipe breaks or a giant bird flies into the room? No. I can't leave."

She went to the sink to wash off her brushes. I used the opportunity to strip down. We weren't going out? Fine. I could be very entertaining inside too.

I debated. Should I leave the boxer briefs on? No, I shouldn't.

She turned around, carrying a jar with brushes in it. She almost dropped it when she saw me posed in front of her.

"I wasn't kidding about the nude painting."

CHAPTER 33

Hazel

A rcher had kept hinting at the nude painting bit, but I didn't quite expect it. Not that it was unwelcome seeing him standing there in front of me.

"You're wearing too many clothes," he told me, setting the glass mason jar I was holding aside.

I could only stare at him. "I really do want to paint you."

Archer's eyes narrowed slightly. I was sort of used to the playful Archer. This one was all desire. His cock was erect. The heat from his hands almost burned through the sheer slip I was wearing.

My panties were soaking wet. Archer's eyes flicked down to the outline of my nipples against the thin fabric. He pulled me to him. His hard cock pressed against my bare thigh.

"I didn't get to fuck you last time," he whispered to me, his hands sliding down the sheer fabric, catching on the lace.

The muscles on his back rippled under my palms as I ran my hands over the smooth skin.

"Don't rip off my slip," I told him. "It's vintage."

"Then take it off," he murmured.

I pulled it over my head and let it fall in a pool on the floor.

Archer kissed me. It was deep and powerful. His hands roamed over my skin, and I reached down between us to feel him.

"You make me so hard," he growled in my ear.

"I can tell," I said as his head dipped down to nip and kiss a nipple.

"I knew you only invited me up here for my big thick cock," he said, his voice deep in my ear. He picked me up easily and tossed me on the bed in the next room. "Your tits are amazing," he said, kissing and licking my nipples, then going down, down. I pushed his head, needing his tongue on me. He mouthed at my panties.

"Just take them off!" I gasped.

He made a throaty noise against me. "I love how wet you are," he said. "Maybe I should just fuck you with them on."

"I want you," I whimpered.

"Next time perhaps," he said then slowly and deliberately slipped the soaking-wet fabric off. I spread my legs, hooking one knee around his shoulders as he dipped his tongue in the hot pink flesh between my legs, teasing me. He slipped two fingers inside me, his tongue still drawing little circles on my pussy, going daringly close to my clit but not quite there. I was sweaty and moaning, my fingers tangled into his hair. My hips made little thrusts against him.

"I need to come," I panted. "I want you to fuck me."

I heard him chuckle deep in his chest. The vibrations went right through me.

"I love listening to you beg for my cock. Maybe we'll make a whole evening of that."

"Stop teasing," I said and moaned.

Archer stroked me with his hand as he licked and sucked my clit. I was making high-pitched little cries as he turned me into a sweaty, whimpering mess. His tongue made two swirls around my clit, and I came with a cry.

I lay there panting and reaching for him. "I want you."

"You want me to fuck you?" he asked with a hiss as I ran my hand down the length of his cock. It was hard and thick. Even though I had just come so hard I saw Van Gogh's Starry Night painting, I needed to feel him in me.

He pressed his cock into the slickness between my legs, playing with it in my pussy. I moaned, arching my back. One of his hands caressed me down the length of my torso.

"I really want to fuck you," he said, his voice low and rough with lust.

"Do it."

"You want me to fuck you with my big, thick hard cock?" he asked, kissing me hard. Archer drew back from me, and I watched, my eyes heavy lidded, as he put on a condom. Archer looked at me, a self-satisfied smile on his mouth while he rolled the rubber onto his cock.

"Are you still wet for me?" he asked, teasing me with his fingers.

"Fuck me, please!" I gasped. He hooked one of my legs over his shoulder then slipped inside me in one smooth motion. I cried out as I took the length of him.

"You're so tight," he groaned, kissing my neck as he slowly pulled out then slid back in. "Your pussy is so hot and tight."

He found a rhythm, and as he fucked me with his cock, his fingers stroked my clit. I was still relaxed from his hands and tongue, and my hips could only make little circles, pushing against his hand and cock.

"Can I fuck you harder?" he whispered, talking dirty in my ear. "I want to fuck that tight hot pussy."

"Fuck me," I said, whispering against his mouth. I barely had the wherewithal to kiss him properly. Archer's hand moved from between my legs. He placed it next to my head, his other hand grasping the thigh of the leg that was hooked over his shoulder.

My breath came out in mewling gasps as he fucked me, jackhammering into me. I clutched at him. The old metal bed frame creaked as he thrust into me. I could feel his cock slide against my already sensitive clit with every thrust, bringing me to the edge. When I came, it was a torrent of *ohmygods* and curse words. He kissed me as I came, and then he lazily fucked me a little longer, drawing out my pleasure until I finally felt him shudder and come.

We were sweaty from the exertion and the summer heat. Archer flipped me on my side and held me against him, kissing my collarbone.

"That was worth the wait," Archer said into my hair.

My heartbeat returned to normal, and my brain rebooted. I looked around. Archer's face was pressed into my neck. His strong arms held me tenderly. Instead of feeling like an amazing sex goddess, I remembered my sister's words. Archer was bad news. I didn't know anything about him except that he wanted to put in a convention center and didn't seem bothered by whatever cost it took.

Maybe this was part of some grand scheme of his. Was he sleeping with me so that Meg would approve his factory?

CHAPTER 34

Archer

It was dark when I woke up, with a thin stream of light coming in from the roof. For a second I thought I was back in the hole in the ground, and I sprang up and threw myself against the wall. There was a splintering sound, and a woman screamed.

Hazel flipped on the light. I winced as I looked at the hole in her wall.

"Sorry, forgot where I was for a second," I mumbled.

When my brothers and I first escaped from the compound, I would get nightmares about being locked in the hole in the ground when I misbehaved. I thought I was over it by now, though. I was a billionaire. I ran a successful company. Women threw themselves at my feet. The fight with my mother must have triggered it, I decided.

I snagged Hazel around the waist and threw her back onto the bed. The metal frame groaned under the force.

"You know," I told her, "I've done a lot of questionable things for sex. But this is the last time I fuck you in this closet."

"It's not that bad," she said as I kissed down her neck to her soft, full, round breasts.

I owned two hotels in Harrogate. Why we did this here was beyond me. "Next time," I told her, "it's you, me, and the presidential suite. Huge bed, killer view."

I kissed her deeply, and she pushed me off before it went too far.

"You have the presentation," she gasped, pulling out her phone from the pile of clothes smushed between the bed frame and the wall. "You're going to be late."

"No, you're going to be late," I said, kissing her one last time.

"Me?" she asked, her voice cracking. She cleared her throat. "I don't know anything about the project."

"You made the painting. They've already seen our presentation about the design. Besides, you're related to two of the people on the decision board. You have to be there," I told her.

"I don't have anything to wear," she fretted. "I need to shower."

"Me too. Just grab your stuff. We'll change at the estate. Besides, I don't even think I can fit into that cave of a shower. I don't know how you do it. You need to do some renovating."

"Er, yeah," Hazel said and went to look at the rendering she'd done of the convention center. In the daylight, it was even more spectacular.

"This is so cool," I said.

"I hope your brother likes it," Hazel replied, placing the canvas carefully in a wooden box.

"All that matters is that Amos likes it. And I think Amos is going to love it."

My phone was awash in messages from my brothers on the group chat.

> **Greg:** *Archer where are you? The presentation is in a few hours.*
> **Mike:** *Seriously Archer.*
> **Mace:** *Archer don't forget you have to cook tonight.*
> **Garrett:** *It was on the schedule. Don't say you didn't know.*
> **Mace:** *We are not asking Josie to do anything more.*
> **Liam:** *You better not! I have a big marketing campaign coming up. You useless idiots need to man up and cook your own food.*

Fuck.

I looked at Hazel. "I have one more job for you…"

We drove back to the estate with the painting, Hazel's clothes, and boxes full of sandwich ingredients in tow. Greg and Mike were already up, sipping coffee and going over the strategy for later that morning.

"There you are." Greg's irritation was visible on his face. "I thought you weren't going to show up."

I yawned. "Had to pick up the painting. And the artist."

"All night?" Mike asked skeptically.

My grin got wider. Hazel blushed. She held up her garment bag. "My shower is not the greatest, and Archer said I could shower here." The words came out in a rush. "He said you wanted me to come to the presentation?"

Greg looked at her critically. I was going to jump him if he said anything mean to her.

"Probably a good idea," he said thoughtfully. "The Harringtons won't have a real-life resident of Harrogate on their team."

"Let's see the rendering before you two disappear again," Mike said. Hazel blushed.

When I unveiled the painting, I saw an actual genuine smile break out on Greg's face.

"Wow," he said. "The rendering looks amazing. You could just walk right into it."

"You did all this in three weeks?" Mike asked in disbelief.

"I'm wondering," Greg said, "if maybe we should just have Hazel present. It's not like we hit it out of the park the last time."

"No way," Hazel said. "I don't know enough about the project."

"You can talk about the vision," I told her. "You just have to sell it."

"Not by myself."

"We'll be there too," Greg said. "But you will need to walk them through the painting. That's really all that we're presenting—the vision for the place."

"I guess."

"Don't be nervous," I told her. "You stood up in front of all those old drunk women and taught them how to make stained-glass penises."

"Wait, what?" Josie asked, coming into the dining room with a large mug of coffee topped by a tower of whipped cream.

"I'm running the worst art retreat of the century. They're making dildos and nude paintings. What's worse is they want Archer to be a model," Hazel said.

Josie laughed gleefully.

"Don't sound so excited," Mace said, following her into the room and turning to look at Hazel's painting.

"If we win this project," Greg said, "Archer can pose for whatever you need."

Mace snickered.

"They want him to pose nude," Hazel clarified.

"Oh, well, never mind, then."

"Oh no, you already promised. We win, you'll get the full frontal Svensson treatment," I promised Hazel.

"Please don't," Greg said.

"This was your idea," I reminded him.

"We're not going to do anything if you make us late," Mike said.

"All right, all right!"

"And don't take three hours in the bathroom," Mike added. "I don't know why it takes you so long."

"Come on, Hazel," I said, ushering her away from my family. "These people don't understand the creative process. It takes time to look this good."

"This is an amazing house," Hazel gushed as I led her through. She took in the wide hallways, the priceless antiques, and the paintings on the walls of long-dead Harrogates.

"Just a few ghosts of billionaires past," I said as we walked past one particularly creepy painting of a thin woman flanked by her two twin daughters.

I showed Hazel to one of the guest bathrooms.

"I am dying of envy right now," she said, slowly walking into the large marble-clad room. For a moment I wondered if she would invite me in. I wanted to push her up against the cabinet and fuck her and listen to her moan in my ear. But I wasn't sure exactly how she felt about last night.

You need to win this convention center, I chanted to myself.

"I'm down the hall," I said, walking out of the guest bathroom. "But I'll meet you downstairs."

As I showered, I tried not to think about how it had felt to be inside of Hazel.

You need to focus on winning the factory site, I told myself. Normally I wasn't this affected by a woman. I was very good at compartmentalizing my night pursuits versus my business. But Hazel was bleeding into everything.

"It's just because she's doing work for you," I told myself. Normally I had strict rules about fraternizing with anyone who could be construed as an employee. I didn't want a lawsuit. But Hazel was different; she broke down all my defenses.

I stood in front of my closet, trying to decide what to wear. *What would Hazel want to see me in?* I mused. I settled on charcoal-gray pants, a white shirt with some sheen, and single-button suit jacket with a green silk pocket square I was sure Hazel would like.

Someone knocked on the bedroom door, and Hazel poked her head into the bathroom.

"You're not even dressed," she said.

"I have on underwear," I countered, circling my arms around her. She was wearing a pencil skirt and a sleeveless shirt with a pussy bow that emphasized the swell of her breasts. Her hair was pulled back into a low bun, and I longed to take it out and bury my hands in it.

"We're going to be late," Hazel said.

I turned back to the mirror. She watched me as I fixed my hair.

"How do you get it to do that?" she asked.

"The trick is to blow dry it when damp," I said, combing it back with my fingers. "Then I use this magic hair product I had my annoying chemical engineer brother develop for me."

"Mace?"

"No, I actually have a number of weirdo engineers in my family. Parker made it. I had to resort to extortion, but it was worth it." I bent over so that gravity would pull my hair forward and swiped in the paste, back to front. I stood back up and adjusted my hair. I was gratified to see Hazel's eyes quickly flick up to the ceiling. Someone was admiring the view. "That's pretty much it, really. It helps to have hair that grows in long and thick. It also helps to have naturally great highlights." I blew myself a kiss in the mirror.

"That is incredibly narcissistic," Hazel said.

When we walked into the auditorium in the town hall, Harrington's team was setting up.

I was pleased to see Hazel's rendering was a thousand times better than what the Harringtons had. Theirs was some sort of watercolor and ink-pen illustration. It was fine, but Hazel's painting had light, depth, and evoked emotion.

Greg was wearing his professional face. Hunter stood beside him and studiously ignored Meghan. I greeted Meg, Amos, and the mayor.

"You have ten minutes," Mayor Barry said. "I have golf in an hour and a half."

Harrington presented first. Their vision sounded corporate. It was the same thing I saw at warehouse redevelopments around the country. I bet it was a rehash of what they had presented the last time, because Amos didn't look all that pleased.

"And now for Svensson Investment," Meg said.

Hazel stepped up. "This warehouse complex is unique. All through history, people have had a connection to place. The Svenssons' vision for this site is to foster that reconnection to place, preserving as much of the historic structure as possible, not as a monument but as a place to live and go about life." She sounded authoritative and assured.

Amos came over to inspect the painting. "This is exactly what I wanted!" he said. Pleased, he shook Hazel's hand. "I'm glad the Svenssons chose you for the team."

"She's been fantastic," I said smoothly.

"Wow, I could just look at this all day. If I may speak for the committee," he said, turning back to Mayor Barry, who nodded. "The project is yours on one condition—have these framed and hung up at city hall."

"Absolutely."

Meg looked down her nose at us.

"You can't say we don't deserve this development," Hunter said to Meg.

She pursed her lips then said, "We're going to give the project to Greyson Hotel Group and Svensson Investment."

I pumped my fist as the Harrington team filed out in annoyance.

"Thank you very much. We look forward to working with the city."

But when I glanced over at Hazel, she didn't seem all that happy.

CHAPTER 35

Hazel

"**B**reak out the champagne. We are in the convention center business!" Archer hollered as we walked into the Svenssons' estate house.

"You are so obnoxious," Greg said, walking in behind us.

"So that's that. You have your factory," I said.

"Worried you won't see me as much?" Archer asked, laughing as we walked into the kitchen.

"She's probably tired of you," Hunter said. "I'm about to have you shipped back to Manhattan with Greg."

"We still have a lot more together time, Hunter," Archer said, slipping off his sunglasses. "Currently we have the factory site is under option. It's a period where we have first right of refusal. Normally you use that time period to convince banks to loan you money. Lucky for me, I'm dealing with the Bank of Svensson."

He slapped Greg on the back. Greg growled at him, and Archer snatched his hand back.

"Stop being so cocky. We need to make sure this is actually going to work," Mike warned. "We need to nail down a site for the hotel rooms to serve the conference center."

Mike turned to me. "If you know of a secret interdimensional portal where I can put a bazillion rooms, let me know."

"So it's happening!" Josie said, coming into the kitchen from the conservatory.

"All thanks to Hazel," Eli said, carrying in the posters and plans from the presentation.

Josie hugged me. "Now we can have the big fancy gala there!"

"Hell yeah. I love a party," Archer said, rubbing his hands together.

"No swearing," Hunter chastised.

"Yeah, Archer, no bad language!" Henry and Peyton shouted, running over and throwing themselves at Archer as he handed Hunter a credit card.

"What's that for?" I asked.

"Swear words are a hundred dollars each," Hunter said, swiping Archer's credit card. He had a name-brand cell phone card reader, I noticed. I resolved to keep my language clean. I could not afford a surprise hundred-dollar fine.

"There's the resident artist," Remy said. He had on sturdy boots and canvas pants. He was a contrast to his brothers' impeccable suits and shined wingtip shoes. "And our resident cook."

"I'm hungry," Henry whined.

"It's Archer's turn to cook today," Hunter said.

"And I am prepared." Archer gestured with his arms, framing me like I was a game show prize.

"I can't believe you're making Hazel cook," Hunter admonished. "She's a guest."

"I'm paying Hazel to cook," Archer said. "She has the magic touch."

"Actually that's you," I said.

"I feel like all our interactions revolve around food," Archer said as he mangled a tomato I had told him to cut.

"And sex," I deadpanned.

He coughed. "Hey, I have no complaints. We should up the ante," he purred, "and combine food and sex."

"Like what, you want me to eat a piece of cheese off you?"

"I wonder if you can make edible cheese underwear," Archer said thoughtfully.

"Um, gross."

"But you would be fine with me licking, say, honey or whipped cream off of you?" he asked.

I shivered. "I wouldn't say no. Have you had edible underwear?" I asked Archer.

"You mean, like, did I own it?"

"I mean, like, have you eaten it?"

"Just by itself with a glass of wine?"

"No, like off of someone."

"Can't say that I have," he mused. "If I'm raring and ready to go, I'm not sure I would sit there and take the time to consume an entire set of women's underwear. Like, would she find it arousing to watch me sit there and waste time eating her underwear when I could eat her out? Does she get off on watching me chew? Plus what do they even put in it? It has to be shelf-stable, right?"

"Maybe you're just supposed to nibble a few strategic holes," I said, cutting more bread. "But if it's made out of Fruit Roll-Ups, then it could get gunky down there. You'd have to sit there and really lick it off."

"I can't say that I'm not getting a little hot and bothered watching you make those sandwiches," he said.

"So you'd go for edible panties made of a sandwich?" I asked.

Archer snorted. "Why go to the trouble of fashioning it into lingerie? Just lay there naked, and put the sandwich in a strategic location."

"Need any help?" Josie asked, walking into the kitchen, wearing a swimsuit and matching cover-up.

"Yes," Archer said. "What is your opinion on edible underwear made from a sandwich?"

I slapped a hand over his mouth. "You are so inappropriate."

"I haven't had any edible underwear that has tasted good," Josie said.

"The kids are starving, Archer," Mace said, poking his head around the door. "Also edible underwear?"

Archer wrapped his arms around his twin, leaving streaks of tomato juice on Mace's face. "My poor naïve, inexperienced twin."

"I can buy some edible underwear for you, if you want," Josie said to Mace. "But it tastes like sweet plastic."

After finishing the sandwiches along with a salad and roasted vegetables, we set everything on a long table buffet style on the outdoor terrace. The kids had little picnic blankets set up on the lawn and terrace. The adults sat at tables and in lounge chairs on the stone terrace overlooking the expansive backyard.

"There's a prosciutto and buffalo mozzarella arugula sandwich with pesto aioli," Archer said to Hunter. "Your favorite."

"Really?" I asked. "That's Meg's favorite."

Hunter grimaced.

"So you've gotten the full Svensson treatment now, Hazel," Mace said, wiping his hands.

"I sure did."

Archer almost choked on a piece of roasted asparagus. Mace thwacked him on the back. "You need to chew your food."

Josie laughed. Mace looked confused.

"You're so slow on the uptake," Josie said affectionately.

"What? Oh. *Oh*... I didn't mean it like that. I meant..." He gestured to two small blond-headed Svenssons squabbling on the steps.

"I love how close you guys are," I said to Archer.

Archer wavered his hand. "Some of us are closer than others. There're close to a hundred of us scattered around the Eastern seaboard. Then there are the black sheep."

"Still, it's good that you prioritize family."

We spent the afternoon out on the terrace. The Svenssons already had the perfect outdoor retreat. My building had a side yard that, in my dreams, had cute outdoor seating with lights and café tables and planters. Of course that was looking less and less like a reality.

"It's nice to have another girl around," Josie said from the lounge chair next to mine. She had lent me a bathing suit.

It was a little snug, but the way Archer looked at me in it was all that I needed. For once I wasn't tongue-tied. Probably because I was very drunk.

I had made pitchers of mixed drinks, and periodically Archer or Mace would come by and fill up our glasses.

"This is the perfect spot for a big barbecue," I told Josie.

"When we win the Art Zurich Expo," she said, "we're going to throw a massive party."

"If we win, you mean."

"I think we will. You and Archer are a dream team."

Archer was definitely dreamy. I didn't want to leave him that evening. He pushed me against the wall in the expansive entryway, kissing me in the dark.

"I told you," Archer said in my ear. "I'm not fucking you in that closet anymore. So I can fuck you here or in my hotel."

"I can't go to your hotel," I whispered to him. "It's late at night. People would know we're there for one thing."

"Here it is, then," he whispered back.

I followed him up to his bedroom. Archer pressed me against the fancy wallpaper. I moaned, wrapping my legs around him. He unzipped his pants, and the hard length of him throbbed against my wet panties. I ground my hips against him as he carried me over to the bed, his large hands caressing my ass as he easily laid me down. He pulled off his shirt and pants. He was hard through the boxer briefs.

"I want you to fuck me with that thick cock," I whispered against his mouth as he crushed it against mine and pushed up my skirt, his fingers stroking me, teasing my pussy.

"I love how wet you get," Archer said in my ear, still stroking me. "I can't wait to stick my cock in you." He pulled at my blouse, unbuttoning two buttons and then yanking so the rest of the buttons popped off. He pushed down my bra, exposing my breast.

Archer sucked on a nipple, rolling it with his tongue as his fingers teased my pussy, dipping in my opening then stroking my clit. Archer moved up to kiss along my jaw to my ear. "One day," he said, his voice deliciously deep, "I want to watch you tease yourself, stroke your clit, with your legs spread while you moan and tell me all the dirty things you want me to do to you."

"I'll tell you right now," I said, grinding against him.

His hand left me, and he opened a condom packet, rolling it on.

"I want you to turn me around, push my panties to the side, and fuck me with that huge cock of yours until I scream."

He kissed me, grabbed my wrists, and pinned them above my head lightly with one hand, then pulled my panties down with the other. "Good to know," he said. "I'll file that away for future use."

I spread my legs, arching against his hand. Archer pushed inside of me, silencing my moan with a kiss. I strained against him as he thrust into me, his cock sliding against my clit, my sensitive nipples brushing his muscular chest with every thrust.

One hand fondled my breasts while the other grasped my hip.

"Faster," I begged, needing to feel him.

I wrapped my arms around his neck, nipping his lips and biting his chin as he fucked me. One of his hands gripped the headboard for leverage. I made high-pitched little whimpers every time he thrust into me. His hand moved to my clit, his thumb rubbing it as he kept fucking me. I moaned, biting his ear. I came, arched against him, the cry silenced with his kiss.

I lay there, panting. He gently kissed my breasts. "You have the most amazing tits." It felt magical being with him.

"I'm glad you're staying in town for a little while longer," I whispered to him in the dark.

"A little while at least," he murmured into my hair.

I felt weird, though. Why did he say only a little while so matter-of-factly? Was McKenna right? Was Archer just using me?

CHAPTER 36

I t was pitch dark when I woke up. My nose was freezing. There was something soft and warm next to me. I buried my cold nose in the softness. It shrieked and slapped at me.

"Why is your nose cold? It's the middle of the summer," Hazel complained as my eyes adjusted to the early-morning light that seeped in under the curtains.

"It's called air-conditioning," I said. "So you're not hot and sweaty while you sleep."

She waited a beat. "I thought you liked me hot and sweaty."

"I'll make you hot and sweaty," I growled, pushing her back against the pillows.

"I love your bed," she said.

"You'll love it more after I fuck you in it again," I said, kissing her. She shivered from the cold or from my touch. She was warm and still slick from our lovemaking the night before. I stroked her, slowly and deliberately, watching the pleasure bloom on her face. "As much as I enjoy making you come undone," I whispered to her, "I really think I want to fuck you again."

Hazel nodded slowly as I rolled on a condom.

"You're so hot and tight," I groaned as I pushed inside of her. She moaned as I thrust into her, her silky wet pussy making my abs clench. "Do you like this?" I whispered to her, loving that I was the one who could make her come undone.

Her hips pushed against me. The moans and whimpers she made as I thrust into her were intoxicating. She cried my name when she came, and I used my fingers to draw it out, feeling her shudder. I kissed her deeply as I came then wrapped her in my arms.

We lay there, breathing heavily. Hazel cuddled against my chest. She smiled at me and kissed along my jaw to my ear and down my neck.

"Maybe we should have gone to a hotel," Hazel said. "I don't have a change of clothes, and I don't want to do the walk of shame in front of your family."

"Only Greg will judge," I said lightly.

"Ugh," Hazel said, crawling out of bed. "I don't have any clean underwear."

"We should bring some of your clothes over here," I said from my vantage point on the bed, admiring the sight of her curvy figure walking around my bedroom, every so often bending over to pick up an article of clothing.

"I can't just move into your brothers' house," she said, horrified.

"Hey, this is partially my house," I sniffed. "It's owned by a trust, and I sit on the board."

Hazel looked at the ripped shirt in her hands. "What am I going to wear? I can't go home like this!"

"You're leaving now?" I asked, sitting up. "What about breakfast?"

"We just had it."

"What about second breakfast?" I asked, swinging my legs over the bed and walking over to her to wrap my arms around her, running my hands over her naked body. "I can make you some of those phallic pancakes."

"I'd like to see you try!" She laughed. "You'd splash batter over everything."

"Hazel, I'm offended. All my batter remains firmly in the condom."

She rolled her eyes. "You're the worst."

I handed her one of my shirts, and she pulled on the pants she had worn when she came over yesterday morning. I smirked to myself as she dressed.

She turned, eyebrow raised. "Do I even want to know what you're thinking?"

"We've had sex twice in two days now," I said with a grin. "We should make it every day for the rest of our lives."

A broad smile bloomed on her face. I couldn't help but scoop her up in my arms to kiss her, swinging us around slowly.

"Come on. I'll make you breakfast," I said. I took Hazel downstairs through the back staircase that led into the kitchen. Josie was there, staring into the fridge.

"This is awkward," Hazel said after a moment.

"I am the queen of awkward," Josie replied.

"I'm making breakfast," I said proudly.

Josie looked a little worried.

"How about," Hazel said, "I cook, and you help? Do people here like eggs benedict?"

Hazel had the militant precision of a woman who had spent years working in food service. Even Josie was impressed.

"You and Chloe should hang out. She's putting a store in Harrogate."

"Uh-huh," Hazel said as she snapped the ends off the asparagus and coated them in olive oil, salt, and pepper. "Her store is going in right next to mine."

"You're going to be neighbors!" Josie said in excitement.

"Yeah, neighbors." Hazel filled a pan with English muffins and toasted them in the oven. She checked on them periodically as she made poached eggs in several large pots of boiling water. A literal vat of hollandaise sauce was on the counter, and I stood at a griddle, babysitting the Canadian bacon because, in the words of Hazel, it was literally impossible to screw up.

"I'm a little put out," Josie said.

"Sorry," Hazel said. "I don't mean to take over your space."

"I didn't mean it like that," Josie said. "I just—" She looked around the kitchen. "It's like a military operation."

"I'm used to cooking for a large number of people," Hazel explained. The asparagus went into the oven at high heat.

"So am I, but I'm *never* this organized," Josie said, making pitchers of mimosas.

"It's like a painting," Hazel said. "You can't just slap paint on the canvas. You have to plan, think about where it could go wrong, and do it in stages."

I stole bites off the tray as I helped transport everything to the dining room, where my starving brothers waited. Hazel assembled the eggs benedict as each Svensson brother came up.

After everyone was served, I made mine and slathered everything in the creamy, slightly tangy hollandaise sauce.

"Is that really necessary?" Hunter asked as I slurped up a bite.

"Don't be jealous because my girlfriend can cook and yours hates your freaking guts."

"See, Hunter?" Garrett said, neatly cutting his food. Hunter looked up at the ceiling and silently counted to ten. "You could have been a nicer person, and we'd have good food and be able to talk on the phone and drive."

"Driving while using a cell phone is dangerous," a woman said.

Hunter jumped up, and several of the kids screamed as Meg walked into the dining room.

"Deputy Mayor Loring is here," Remy said, walking in behind her and making a beeline for the food. Meg's eyes narrowed when she saw Hazel spooning hollandaise sauce on Remy's plate.

"Breakfast?" I offered.

"No, thank you." Meg pushed an errant curl of her hair out of her face, and Hunter watched her like a parched man in the desert.

"You should really have something to eat, Deputy Mayor," I said. "Let your favorite Svensson brother fix you a plate."

"You are not my favorite Svensson if you're sleeping with my sister," she snapped. Meg turned to Hunter. "You better not let this get out of hand. Otherwise the popsicle lawsuit will be the least of your worries."

"He wants her to lick him like a popsicle," I sang softly under my breath.

Meg froze. Hunter growled and lunged at me. I screamed dramatically. "Meghan, save me!"

"You're all going to sober up once I tell you why I'm here," she said.

We looked at her.

"I have some bad news." She pulled out some paperwork from her bag. "You asked me to look into the strip mall site. I instructed Mrs. Levingston to do some research. We thought the city owned the site, as it has been abandoned since the last recession. However, it hasn't quite been long enough for the city to take it back through eminent domain. There were a series of shell LLCs that owned the property over several years' time. They were more than likely used to tax dodge. We finally managed to track down the owner."

"Great. So we'll buy it from them," I said.

"The owner is McKenna Madden." The room was dead quiet. I felt like throwing up.

"I hear you two have a history," Meg said.

"Can't you just, I don't know, not tell her?" I pleaded.

"I am legally bound to inform her," Meghan said, "but I'm telling you first as a courtesy."

"Guess you're not getting that conference center after all," Hunter said.

CHAPTER 37

Hazel

I left with Meghan after she broke the news to the Svenssons. Archer seemed shaken, and the rest of his brothers were angry.

"I don't understand," I said as I got into my sister's car. "McKenna is a soul-sucking dementor, but she's also greedy. The Svenssons can pay her for the property. Problem solved. Why are they so upset?"

"Who knows?" Meg asked. "It's not your problem."

"I care about Archer, and I don't want him upset."

Meg sighed. "You need to be careful with the Svenssons. The little ones are cute, but the older ones are devious and underhanded."

"Remy seems nice," I countered. "And so does Mace. I know you always said the Svenssons are terrible people, but honestly, they weren't that bad to hang out with."

"I don't want you to be hurt."

The unspoken words, *Like I was,* hung in the air between us.

Meg dropped me off at my café. I wasn't expecting any customers. The Coming Soon sign for the Grey Dove Bistro was a looming reminder that I couldn't worry about the Svenssons. I had my own problems to deal with. I picked up the pile of envelopes on the floor that were shoved through the mail slot earlier that day. I sorted through them—notices from the student loan company about missed payments, notices from the bank about the mortgage, late notices about the power bills.

I shoved everything into my drawer of shame. I could barely close it. My phone dinged with a notification. There was money in my Venmo account from Archer.

The description said, **Paying you back for the sandwiches. Also a little extra for edible panties.**

I groaned. All my Venmo friends were going to see that.

Jemma: *Edible panties???*
Hazel: *It's not what you think! Besides I've heard edible panties don't actually taste that good.*
Olivia: *I don't think you're supposed to sit there and eat them...*
Jemma: *If anyone can make edible underwear actually edible, it's Hazel!*

Could I? I needed to try and figure out how I was going to save my business. But deep down I knew there was no saving it. The only hope was to win the grant.

The box of raspberries Archer had given me still sat on the counter. What would I do with the fruit? It wouldn't last forever. I wanted to cheer him. Could I use them to make edible underwear? In art school, we had to do a class on basic fashion design.

It wasn't hard to make costumes out of nonfabric material like paper or plastic sheets. Maybe a fruit leather would work. It would be stiff enough to hold its shape. I boiled down the raspberries and pressed the juice out, then poured the mix on a jelly roll pan. I didn't have a dehydrator, so I stuck it in the oven on low heat.

There was a fair amount of the raspberry juice left. Thinking I would use it as a simple syrup for mixed drinks, I strained it and added a bit of sugar.

"It looks like paint!" I said, testing the rich-red liquid with a spoon. I giggled and spread a little on my bare arm. Then I licked it. It tasted pretty good.

I wonder what it would be like licking it off of Archer.

I shivered, remembering the last two nights I had spent with him. It was scary how much of an about-face I had done with him. I had turned off the oven and let the fruit leather slowly cool down and was pouring the raspberry syrup into a little vial when the door to the café opened.

"Just a second," I called, not looking up.

"What are you making?"

I jerked and almost dropped the vial. Archer reached out to steady my hand.

"I was making simple syrup, but now it's edible body paint. It's vegan."

"Yes," Archer said. "But how does it taste?"

He picked me up in his arms, kissing me.

"You know, I swore I wasn't going to do this in your closet," he said against my mouth as he carried me upstairs. He laid me down on the bed. "We're going to my hotel next time," he said in between kissing me and taking off my clothes.

"Since we're in my painting studio now," I said, showing him the red raspberry syrup, "might as well take advantage."

Archer leaned against the pillows, looking like a Michelangelo painting.

I straddled him. "You're the best-looking canvas I've ever seen," I told him. I dipped my finger in the syrup then began to paint. Archer's muscles jumped as I slowly traced my finger down his chest.

"What are you painting?" he murmured.

I leaned over and kissed him. "It's a surprise."

He bit down a curse as my fingers moved over his skin to paint a flower. The petals curled over his pecs. He craned his head down. "Are you painting roses?"

"It's a pink liquid, so flowers obviously. You have a choice of flowers, puppies, or an inspirational quote."

My finger trailed down his abs.

"I think that's enough painting," Archer said, one large hand grasping my thigh.

"Wait," I said, pushing him back down on the bed. "I need to lick it off because I don't want to ruin my sheets." I slowly ran my tongue through the sweet sauce.

Archer swore as I licked up every bit of pink flower. "You're a tease," he said.

I licked down, down.

"Okay, that's enough," he rasped, turning us over. He kissed me, starting at my neck then along my collarbone. I was wet and hot in anticipation.

"Hurry up," I panted.

Archer lingered, his mouth moving to suck my breast, rolling the nipple with his tongue. His hand came up to stroke me, and I pressed against him.

"You're mean."

"Fair is fair."

"I want your cock," I moaned. "I'm so wet for you." Archer flipped me over. He dipped his fingers in me, and I arched my back. "Please, fuck me."

He ignored me in favor of light kisses and hints of tongue trailing across my back. I moaned as he kissed my hips, coming closer to where I wanted him to be. I spread my legs further, inviting him. I cried out when he pressed his mouth between my legs. His strong hands grasped my hips, and I moaned, letting him hold me up as he licked and kissed the pink flesh.

He moved back and forth from my clit to my opening. All I could do was moan and plead.

"I need you to fuck me!" I begged as his tongue trailed in my pussy. I wanted the release. He tore a wrapper and put on a condom. "I'm so hot and wet for you. I need your thick—" I let out a long moan as he pushed inside me. Having him fuck me at this angle felt wanton, as the Victorians used to say.

My hips ground against him. I had to rest on my forearms; I could barely hold myself up. Archer had one hand on my waist, one hand working my clit. I bucked against him.

"Harder," I moaned. "I want to feel all of you."

I came hard, and his fingers drew out the pleasure. In a few quick thrusts, Archer came too. I felt him shiver, then he kissed my shoulder blade up to my neck.

"That was fantastic," he murmured in my ear.

It was fantastic, but I was wondering if the sex should just be that—fantastic sex. Was a relationship even in the cards? Archer had hired me to paint and to come over to his house and cook. I met some of his family, and he had met mine though maybe that shouldn't count since this was a small town.

"Stop thinking," he mumbled into my hair.

I tried. I really did. But the doubts kept coming.

CHAPTER 38

Archer

I pushed Hazel back onto the bed and was about to start round two when I heard the unmistakable roar of motorcycles.

"Ugh, that is so annoying!" she said, pushing me off and grabbing her clothes. I shrugged on my pants and shirt as Hazel stomped over to the stairs.

Does Hazel have some sort of crazy motorcycle gang ex-boyfriend? I wondered as the engines roared through the open window of the third-floor studio.

"Who is that?" I growled at her, fully prepared to take out the nutcase.

"Your brothers!" she yelled at me.

I blinked. "Oh, hell no." I pulled on my boots and ran outside just in time to see two motorcycles race down the street toward the café.

"Stop," I said, stepping out into the street in front of them.

Hazel screamed. The motorcycles screeched to a halt inches from me. I shook my head.

Eli took off his helmet. "Bro," he said.

"Don't bro me!" I yelled at my younger brothers. "Do you have any idea what time it is?"

"Dude, you're like really harsh right now," Eli said.

"You sound like Mace," Tristan said, pushing up the visor on his helmet.

"This happens all the time," Hazel yelled, waving her arms. "All hours of the night." I could tell she was furious, and honestly, so was I.

"You're going to be hit by the train," I warned them. "It drives right down this street."

Eli scoffed, "This is a Bugatti. It can outrun a train."

"No," I ordered. "No one is going to outrace the train. Stop riding around. Walk those bikes back to the garage and go to sleep. You work for me now. I am the CEO of Greyson Hotel Group, and you need to be well rested tomorrow."

"Now you really sound like Mace," Eli complained.

"Yeah, and honestly I'm starting to have a little more sympathy for him, which is not something I ever wanted to say, and now you made me say it, so you are doubly on my shit list!"

Eli looked between me and Hazel. He waggled his eyebrows and opened his mouth to make an inappropriate comment.

"Don't," I told him. "Don't you dare."

I watched my brothers walk their bikes down the street. When I was sure they weren't going to jump back on, I turned back to Hazel. "If they bother you anymore, let me know."

Hazel was standing in the café doorway, barefoot, her hair in messy waves around her face, her arms crossed over her white shirt to hide the fact she was braless underneath. Suddenly I wanted nothing more than to feel her tits, feel the hot wet heat between her legs. Her eyes were dark as I walked over to her. She stepped back until she bumped into a table.

"Turn around," I whispered.

"Someone could see!" she protested, but I could see she was excited.

"It's dark inside. Besides, this will be fast and dirty," I whispered into her ear. She bit her lip. I could tell she was wavering. The lust was clear in her eyes. I trailed a hand up her thigh to the heat between her legs.

"You're wet just thinking about me bending you over and fucking you."

Her breath hitched slightly. I grabbed her around the waist and kissed her, then moved down to suck her tits through the thin fabric. She moaned softly, her fingers carding through my hair. I kissed down. Her legs trembled as I pushed up the fabric to lick her slit.

"That feels so good," she moaned, her head tipped back.

I unzipped my pants and rolled on a condom. Hazel's chest rose and fell rapidly.

"Still on the fence?" I asked.

"I want you to fuck me," she moaned. It made me so hard. I turned her around, pulling down her panties, then pushed inside of her.

"You feel so good," I groaned. As I thrust into her, she whimpered, bracing herself on the little café table. "Your pussy is so hot and wet," I said in her ear as I kept up the fast pace. Her back arched, and Hazel moaned as my hand gripped her hip as I fucked her. I played with her tits, kissing her neck, my cock sliding in and out of her tight pussy.

Her breath came out in little high-pitched pants as I thrust into her. My hand went down to stroke her clit, and she gasped. Her legs trembled, and she leaned completely over the table, spreading her legs wider.

I held her hips and fucked her. The way her legs were trembling let me know she was close. Teasing her clit, I leaned down, pulling her head to the side slightly to kiss her mouth. She whimpered as she came, her ass pressed against me. I came soon after, the feel of her pussy clenching around me sending me over the edge.

I gathered Hazel in my arms as she breathed hard. I took her upstairs and laid her down, wrapping around her.

"You know," I said, not sure if she was asleep.

"Hmm?"

"I forgot to get your panties."

The undergarment was found the next morning by Hazel's friend Jemma.

I sat shirtless and yawning in the café at the very table I fucked Hazel at last night. Jemma looked between me and Hazel and the scrap of fabric in her hand.

"Give me that!" Hazel said, running up to her friend and snatching the panties.

Jemma laughed. "Based on our text conversation, I was thinking these would be panties of the edible variety."

Hazel turned beet red, and I grinned slowly.

Jemma fanned herself. "You should build a little porch or something outside," Jemma said to Hazel, "and just park him outside shirtless. I bet you'd draw in a ton of customers!"

"They'd probably all be Ida and her friends." Hazel snorted.

"You should try and sell them some of your edible body paint," I told her. "Seniors like to get down too."

"You're going to be hearing a lot about it at the town meeting, I'm sure," Hazel said.

"Are you going?"

"I have to present about the efforts to win the Art Zurich Expo and try and drum up support. You're on the committee, so you should be there too."

After Hazel and Jemma finished making the enormous stack of sandwiches, I drove them over to Ida's.

"My favorite Svensson!" Ida crowed. "Wait, take a picture with this sandwich," she said, handing me one of the neatly wrapped sandwiches.

"If I model with it, can I eat it?" I asked.

"You can eat anything in here you want," Ida declared.

I looked at Hazel. "There's only one thing in here I want to eat…"

Hazel started to turn red.

"And it's this sandwich!" I finished.

Hazel groaned. I took off the wrapping while Ida snapped a picture.

The old woman whooped, "Yeah, baby, spread those buns!"

CHAPTER 39

Hazel

W e had to go to the art committee meeting right after Archer finished making love to the sandwich.

"I can't believe you ate another sandwich, Archer. You already ate breakfast," I said as Jemma wedged next to me in the passenger seat.

"I worked up a big appetite from last night," he said, looking over his sunglasses.

"You need a bigger car," I told Archer. "I don't see how you function with a two-seater sports car with all your brothers."

"We should probably walk," Jemma said, smooshed beside me. "But I am so happy to have AC even for a little bit."

Olivia was already in the room when we walked in. I tensed up, wondering if McKenna was going to be there, but she didn't show up.

"We're still a few weeks out from the Art Zurich visit. How are the milestones coming?"

Archer set out his tablet and flipped through pictures and plans of what his landscape architect had drawn up.

"My brother is down with us putting the first mile of the art walk on his property. This is where the landscape architect recommends it going. We'll have this all up at the town meeting tonight, along with Hazel's painting."

"Will they be able to complete it in time?" I asked.

"The path, yes, but we need some artwork to make it awesome." Archer looked at me. "I know I'm good with my hands, but we might need some actual sculpture artists."

Jemma mouthed to Olivia, *Edible body paint.*

I kicked my friend under the table and said, "I have some friends who are starting work on several large sculptures for the trail."

"They should be lit nicely," Olivia said. "And I love the idea of the chandelier tree. In addition to fairy lights in the trees, the chandeliers should mark the beginning of the art walk."

"And my brother is paying for the power. He wants to put up a big sign about how it's green energy from the hydroelectric plant," Archer said. "But we'll hash all that out. We may want a few other meetings with the Svensson PharmaTech leadership and the Harrogate Trust board."

I was feeling relaxed and pumped about all the art that was going to be displayed around town. That was until we stepped out into the grand lobby space and were confronted by McKenna.

"Archer," she said, sidling up to him and running her hands down his chest.

"Don't touch him," I snapped, yanking him back.

McKenna smirked. "I have something Archer wants, so I think actually I will touch him—that is if you still want that strip mall site that *I own*."

"Why don't you call my company, and we'll set up a meeting to see if we can't come to some sort of agreement?" Archer said in a slightly bored but professional tone.

"I am not going to call your secretary like I'm some hussy you picked up in the park," McKenna screeched. "You want to do business? Then I need real offers from the CEO, not one of your interns."

She reached up and grabbed Archer by the shirt collar. His hands twitched like he wanted to shove her off. He was too polite to do that, though.

"I finally have all the power," McKenna said. "I already know what I want—you."

That evening before the town meeting, I was still rattled from the confrontation with McKenna. Her words implied that she didn't just want money, she wanted Archer. Now she was sitting in the front row of the large meeting hall, smirking.

"McKenna always does this!" I fumed. "She always finds some way to ruin my life!"

"As long as she doesn't ruin the Art Zurich Expo bid," Olivia said.

"I need to find some way to force her to sell," I muttered.

"Let the Svenssons handle it," Jemma said. "They seem to have things under control. Archer has a lot of resources—I bet they just buy her out. It will be fine! Now go drum up support for the Art Zurich Expo!"

I stood up, wiping my hands on my skirt, and went to stand next to my sister.

"Thank you for coming to tonight's meeting," Meg said. "While we're going to address the grievances like the motorcycles and the fact that Art still needs his distillery—yes, we know, Art—we're going to start off with the Harrogate Trust's latest project to bring the prestigious Art Zurich Biennial Expo to Harrogate. Here to talk about that is Hazel."

Jemma flashed me a thumbs-up. McKenna glared daggers in my direction.

Be the boss babe.

"Thank you for coming," I said, trying to project confidence. "As you've seen on the posters, we're making arts and culture improvements to Harrogate. Some of you have been participating in my art retreat."

"Woo! Dildos!" Ida yelled.

Her sister, Edna, shot her a scathing look. "We're trying to make Harrogate a place of high culture, not some sort of back-alley porn shop, Ida."

"Maybe that will be my new business," I said with a laugh. Crickets. "It was a joke." I gulped. I risked a glance at Archer. He was shaking with silent laughter. Hunter elbowed him.

"These posters show the headliner project. It's an art trail sponsored by Svensson PharmaTech."

The crowd applauded.

"It's going to be built soon," I said to the several raised hands. "It has to be. The judges are coming in a few weeks, so we need all hands on deck. Svensson PharmaTech is doing a day of service this coming weekend. I see some of the PharmaTech employees here, so thank you."

"Hey, this is going to raise my property values, so sure I'll put on a sun hat and some garden gloves," one man said, eliciting laughs from the audience.

"That's the spirit! We have online signup sheets on the tablets near the entrance. Please sign up. We need help prepping sites for murals. The historic buildings need to be cleaned, plus there are flowers to plant. To welcome the judges, we will also be hosting a black-tie gala at the Mast Brothers' chocolate factory. Tickets are on sale. All proceeds go toward the Harrogate Trust."

"You were great!" Archer said when we were back in front of my café. He'd driven me home after I fielded questions for an hour after the town hall meeting.

"I just hope we have a lot of volunteers," I said as I unlocked the door.

"Am I invited inside?" he asked, leaning over me, his forearm resting on the brick wall. His expression was warm and somewhat dangerous.

"You're always invited," I said, pushing the door open.

"I'm not fucking you in that crappy rickety bed anymore," he growled as he nipped my ear and wrapped his arms around me. His hands slipped under my shirt to cup my breasts. I moaned against his mouth. "Have I told you how much I like your tits?" he asked, kissing my ear and pushing me up against the counter.

Right as I was about to suggest another round of sex in the café, someone yelled outside.

"What was that?" I gasped.

Archer tensed up. "Just—I'll be back later. Don't wait up." He kissed me and left.

What the hell?

CHAPTER 40

heard my mother outside. After unceremoniously shooing Hazel upstairs and cursing the fact that I had yet again not fucked her in a hotel, I went outside, locking the door and softly closing it behind me.

My mother was standing out on the sidewalk. She hurried over when she saw me. "Archer! Baby."

"Stop," I ordered, pushing her away. "I can't believe you."

"I just want what's best for you." She started to cry.

I was unmoved. "You want money."

"I want you to be happy! This girl, Hazel, isn't going to make you happy. You need to be with McKenna. She would be good to you. I saw videos of you two all over the gossip websites. You're great together."

I blew out a breath in annoyance. "Never going to happen."

My mother started to protest.

"Stay away from McKenna if you care about me at all," I told her.

I watched her wander away in her high heels. I wondered if I should tell Garrett our mother was still here. I didn't want to deal with them all jumping down my throat like they had when Meghan told us about the fact that McKenna was the landowner of the strip mall.

Hazel was sprawled on the couch asleep when I went upstairs.

"We seriously need a different place to hook up," I muttered as I picked her up and put her to bed.

When I woke up the next morning, Hazel was already up and gone. Yawning, I wandered downstairs. Hazel had a pile of sandwiches sitting on the counter in front of her.

"Geez, do you always wake up so early?"

Hazel blinked at me. "I've already made five hundred sandwiches, emailed with several muralists, and been on the Facebook group of the art walk sculpture artists."

I reached out to grab a sandwich.

"These are for selling," she said lightly, batting my hand away.

"Ida won't mind," I said, snatching a sandwich. "She likes me."

I snapped a picture of myself shirtless and texted it to Hazel's phone. "Show that to Ida if she complains."

Since Hazel was on a roll for the Art Zurich Expo, we went over to the Mast Brothers' chocolate factory to brainstorm for the gala.

"Ah!" I said, inhaling when we stepped out of my sports car. "Soon you will be mine!"

"I thought you said it was under option," Hazel said, hopping out of the car with an enormous bag filled with lord only knew.

"I'm buying it," I said. "I don't care what Greg and Mike say. They're Debbie Downers."

"Where should we have the gala?" Hazel asked, pulling a notepad out of her bag and flipping to a blank page.

"I think in Building A. It has these really cool windows," I said, "and a mezzanine that looks out over the space."

We walked around the large building. Hazel took pictures and notes. Then she stood in the space, sketching. The sun streamed in through the windows, lighting up the halo of hair in her messy French roll.

"I want another vantage point," Hazel said, heading to the mezzanine stairs. "This is safe to use, right?"

"Olivia came out and did an assessment," I said as we walked upstairs. Lining the mezzanine were the old supervisors' offices. They'd been cleared of most of the furniture; however, the antique oak desks were still in the offices.

Hazel looked out over the courtyard space with the old railroad tracks. "This is such a great complex."

I was too busy admiring her curvy figure to look outside.

Hazel turned slightly and caught me staring. "You know," she said. "This convention center still needs to be christened."

"Why, Hazel," I said, trying to keep my voice steady as she slowly unbuttoned her blouse. "I do believe I might be a bad influence on you."

Hazel leaned against the desk. She took a breast out of her lacy bra and pinched her nipple. I was immediately hard.

"Isn't this what you wanted to see?" Hazel asked. "You wanted to watch me touch myself."

I swallowed. My pants were uncomfortably tight. I eased the zipper down. Hazel slowly teased up her skirt to expose the lace panties she was wearing.

"You wanted to watch me do a little finger painting. Thinking about you bending me over and sticking that big cock inside me makes me so wet," Hazel purred. She pulled her panties to the side and stroked herself.

Something exploded in my brain.

She bit her lip and moaned softly. "This feels so good." Her head tipped forward. "Thinking about you fucking me, your hand on my clit—"

I couldn't take it anymore. I growled and took two steps, then I was on her, kissing her mouth, my tongue tracing her mouth as my fingers pushed under her panties, stroking her. She moaned as I rolled on a condom. I didn't bother pulling down her panties, just thrust inside of her.

"You feel so tight," I groaned as I fucked her. Hazel's legs were wide, giving me easy access. I tipped my head down, sucking on her breast, rolling the nipple around with my tongue.

I moved back to her mouth. She strained against me as I gripped her hips, sliding in and out of her tight pussy. My cock rubbed against her clit with each thrust. Already half gone from the tease show she'd given a few moments ago, her body trembled, and I could tell she was close. Hazel made these little gasping noises that drove me wild.

Her nails dug into my scalp as she came. The little whimper she made and her pussy getting so tight made me come as well. She breathed hard, her nipples still hard against my chest.

"This is a very nice factory," she whispered in my ear.

"We should go to my hotel," I told her, kissing her neck. "Then you'll really be impressed."

"I still have things to organize for the Harrogate work day," she told me.

"Right. That."

"It's important. And your business will benefit," she said lightly.

CHAPTER 41

Hazel

Archer drove me back to my café. During the entire drive, his phone beeped and rang.

"Something wrong?" I asked.

"No," he said, kissing me. "Just business that I've been neglecting."

"We shouldn't have stayed so long at the factory. You didn't have to come. I could have gone myself," I said, feeling guilty.

Archer took my hands in his own larger ones. "Spending time with you is never a waste," he said, uncharacteristically serious. In the next moment, the loopy grin was back. "My hotel group is basically on autopilot. I have a ton of employees, even if my interns are less than stellar."

"Still, you have a lot on your plate," I said as Archer walked me to the door. "What with McKenna and the strip mall site."

Archer leaned down to kiss me. "I'll handle it. Don't worry," he said.

After Archer drove off, I sat at my computer, answering emails and questions about the art walk. A knock on the front door interrupted me.

"Did you forget something?" I called, thinking it was Archer. But when I opened the door, there was a blond woman outside.

"Did you come for lunch?" I asked, confused.

The woman smiled, but it didn't reach her eyes. I held the door open, and the woman brushed past me into the café.

"So this is Hazel," she said, looking me up and down. It was obvious she wasn't impressed.

"Who are you?" I asked, trying to remain civil.

"Merla Vee. I'm Archer's mother," she preened. She was tall and thin and wearing designer clothes. In her heels, she towered over me.

"Nice to meet you." I stuck out my hand.

She ignored it. "I'm going to get straight to the point. I don't think you're good enough for my son."

"I'm sorry you feel that way," I said.

"He is a billionaire, an art collector, and a real estate developer," Merla Vee continued. "His hotels are impeccable. Have you stayed in one?"

"I can't say that I have," I replied, starting to wonder if I could legally throw her out of my business. Maybe if I said it was for insurance purposes?

"Archer needs a woman he can show off, who he can take to a fancy party and make all the men envious. You"— she looked me up and down again—"don't fit that bill."

"Why are you telling me this?" I demanded. "Why do you even care?"

"I'm not doing this to be mean," Merla Vee said, widening her eyes. "I simply want to make sure you aren't hurt. It's clear to me what Archer's doing."

I tried to keep the shock off my face. Merla Vee looked at me in wide-eyed sympathy. "I'm his mother. I know him better than anyone. You're allowing yourself to be used. He clearly has no intention of anything serious with you. How could you possibly think you were worthy of my son, with your terrible art and your failed café?" She laughed.

"I have some work I need to finish," I said weakly. Archer's mother breezed out of the café, and I had to sit down.

I know Archer isn't close to his father, but maybe he is close to his mother.

If so, where did that leave me? I had heard horror stories about crazy mothers-in-law.

You're jumping the gun, I admonished myself. *It's not like Archer's proposed.*

I opened my laptop, hoping to find something to distract me. All I saw was a stack of angry messages from creditors. At least my utilities hadn't been shut off. With the last bit of money Archer had sent me for cooking, I had paid off my utility bills for the next month. After that though? Who knew? The money I had from Archer hadn't gone far. By the time I spread it around to my various creditors, it was like the money never existed.

"Who am I kidding?" I groaned. "I'm not a boss babe. I'm a dumb girl who can't get her life together." I stood up and went to the fridge. "Time to eat your feelings."

The raspberry fruit leather was sitting on the glass shelf, taunting me. It looked dumb. Archer wouldn't be excited by that. I grabbed the milk, butter, and eggs then slammed the door.

Pushing aside the thoughts that this may be one of the last times I made a meal in my building, I set out making raspberry bomb muffins.

First I made a glossy chocolate fudge sauce, mixing good dark chocolate, butter, evaporated milk, and a little sugar over the double boiler. I set it aside to cool.

Then I sifted the flour, baking powder, and sugar then mixed in cream cheese, a little cream, and eggs. Working carefully, I folded the last few handfuls of raspberries into the yellow batter. The fudge wasn't quite as runny, and I used a small ice cream scoop to place a bit of fudge in the middle of the half-filled muffin tin then covered it with more batter.

The muffins rose beautifully. That was the nice thing about muffins. They cooked quickly. I took pictures for Instagram while they cooled. Then I took a bite of the raspberry cream cheese muffin. The chocolate fudge in the middle exploded in my mouth. The sugar hit my system, and I started to feel better.

"Be optimistic," I ordered myself. "No hurdle is too high for my heels! Even if I'm not actually wearing any."

Shaking off the lingering webs of self-doubt, I took the large platter of muffins upstairs to continue planning for the Art Zurich Expo. Harrogate needed to be as artistic as possible. Hopefully it would be enough for our city to win and, more importantly, enough for me to win the grant to save my business.

CHAPTER 42

Archer

A s much as I wanted to spend the rest of the day with Hazel, I needed to solve the McKenna problem. I needed the conference center, and I needed the strip mall site for the hotels for the conference center.

Mike's text message had said to come meet him at Svensson PharmaTech. He was sitting in Garrett's office. Garrett was behind his desk, tapping it with his pen.

"You're late," he said in a flat tone.

"I was busy." I grinned at my younger brother. When we were kids, I like to tease him until he freaked out. One day I pushed him too far, and he put a snake in my bed. Ever since, I tried to steer clear of the bright-yellow line Garrett had painted in the sand. Though my younger brother was strange, he was remarkably effective. Which was why I was hoping I could convince him to solve my problem.

"We need to discuss the McKenna situation," Garrett said finally.

"Garrett's helping," Mike said to me.

"Did you have to sell your soul?" I whispered to Mike.

"Stop being dramatic," Garrett said. "Of course I'm helping. The McKenna situation should have been dead and buried long ago"—I wondered if Garrett meant literally—"and yet here we are."

"I'd like all ideas on the table. McKenna cannot be underestimated."

I opened my mouth.

"Don't even waste your breath on whatever inane comment you were going to make, Archer. This was a purely rhetorical statement. McKenna is not allowed to run roughshod over our family. Greg and Hunter don't seem like they're taking this seriously, which is unsurprising," Garrett said in a clipped tone. "And Mace is too lovesick to be of much use, not that he is generally a useful person."

"Can't we just pay her off?"

"No, Archer, we cannot just pay her off. She is like our father—obsessive, fixated, in a word, crazy. I have a character profile on her."

Mike snuck a glance at me. He had the deer-in-the-headlights look most people had when dealing with Garrett.

"Now, I've looked into the paperwork. McKenna does have legal ownership of the property. She has enough money from selling paintings on commission that she can more than afford to pay the fines and fees the site has racked up if she so chooses."

He tapped his pen on the desk. "Then she would proceed to string us along for years, potentially."

Mike gulped.

"What's the plan, oh great one?"

"I have several options. The easy one is to trick her."

"Trick her?" Mike asked.

Garrett nodded sagely. "All Archer needs to do is convince her that he's planning on rekindling their romance."

"That seems like it could backfire," Mike said slowly.

"I can't imagine Archer would mess up a fake relationship."

Yeah, that isn't going to work for me. There's no way I can do that to Hazel.

"McKenna's going to want some consummation before she agrees to anything," I said.

"And?" Garrett retorted. "Is there some medical issue that will prevent you from doing that?"

Geez, I forgot just how much talking to Garrett felt like making a deal with a demon. "That's not going to work for me," I said. "What's my other option?"

"Blackmail," Garrett replied.

"Blackmail?"

"Yes."

"Now you've really lost it."

"Do you even have any dirt on her?" Mike asked.

"She plagiarized a paper in high school and slept with one of her college professors for an A."

"That hardly seems enough to force her hand," Mike said. "Also this seems highly underhanded and illegal."

"There's a little gray area between making a deal and extortion. That's where I operate. I've told you my terms. Neither of you has the wherewithal to do what needs to be done."

I started to protest.

"Get out of my office," Garrett said and turned back to his computer.

"Garrett is nuts," Mike said as we walked across the hall to Mace's office. "We need to look at alternative sites."

"We're so close!"

"There's always Option One."

"I can't," I said sharply. "I can't hurt Hazel."

"Holy smokes!" Mace said, coming around from his desk. "You like her!"

"Of course I like her," I replied. "Hazel is a very likable person."

"I mean *like* her," Mace insisted. I sighed. Mace slung an arm around my shoulder. "My baby's all grown up and settling down."

"That's my line! Get off," I complained to my twin. He stepped back, grinning.

"Besides, what's not to like? She's a great cook. She's good with our little brothers. She's not a skeeze, out for my money, and she has her own business. She's perfect. Unlike you, I know a good thing when I see it. I'm not going to screw it up."

The rest of the day, I couldn't stop grinning whenever I thought about Hazel. I knew I should be worried about McKenna and my conference center, but I was still awash in the good feelings. Even a mandatory family meeting didn't kill it.

We all assembled in the large ballroom on the third floor of the estate. Ever since I read the story about what happened to Wes Holbrook in his family ballroom, I was a little antsy in the space.

Remy had a projector and screen set up. I scooted around it and sat next to Mace. "I can't believe I have to come to this meeting. I was just at the family meeting in Manhattan." Greg would force us to have family meetings in Manhattan, but usually it was a little more free-form and included alcohol.

"And now you're here," Hunter said at the front of the room. The screen flashed to an agenda.

"First order of business—the motorcycle racing."

"Archer, you ratted us out?" Eli exclaimed.

"You can't drive your motorcycle in the middle of the night," Hunter told them. "I've told you to stop. I better not hear one more complaint. Eli, you and Tristan are on notice. Next." Eli glared at me. I bared my teeth at him, and he quickly turned around and looked straight ahead.

"I love watching your inner dad come out," Mace whispered to me. I kicked my twin.

"Dentist appointments are coming up," Hunter was saying. "I have a whole day booked. Everyone is waking up early."

"Are we going to talk about the elephant in the room?" Garrett asked, interrupting Hunter.

"Which one of your many complaints is it, Garrett?" Hunter asked, clearly annoyed.

"McKenna—"

"That is a business matter," Hunter said.

Remy's hand shot up.

"What is it, Remington?"

"I have us down for the volunteer day."

"Remy, that's on the agenda. All of you can see the agenda. It's right here on the screen. We are going in order. Now, moving on."

Remy's hand shot up again. I stifled a laugh at the expression on Hunter's face.

"I need goats."

"What the—" Hunter clamped his mouth shut. "Why?"

"To eat the weeds on cleanup day. A pack of goats is just what we need to clear the way for the art trail."

"Is it?" Mace asked.

"Remy." Hunter pinched the bridge of his nose. "There is no scenario where I agree to purchase a pack of goats."

"A herd," Garrett said.

"Excuse me?" Hunter hissed.

Garrett looked at him blankly. "It's not a pack of goats. It's a herd."

CHAPTER 43

Hazel

was eating the last muffin—yes, I ate the whole plate—when Archer came up the stairs.

"You should stop breaking and entering," I told him.

"You should install a new lock," he teased back. He looked at the plate covered in crumbs and muffin wrappers. "I thought I smelled something good."

"They're all gone," I said guiltily.

"I can't believe you didn't save any for me," he said, reaching out to caress me. His hands slid under my T-shirt dress. "I guess I'll have to eat something else," he murmured in my ear. I moaned as Archer kissed my neck then tipped my head back to kiss my mouth.

His fingers pushed under my panties.

"I want you," I said. I turned around and leaned over the small table I used to hold my paintbrushes. "I have one more muffin left for you to eat."

Archer knelt behind me and pulled down my soaking-wet panties. His tongue traced a stripe down the wet pink slit between my legs. I whimpered as he licked and nipped me. His tongue went up to tease my clit then back to dip in my opening. I tried to buck against him, but his large hands held me steady. He dipped two fingers in me as his tongue made this twisting movement around my clit. He crooked his fingers, and I came with a cry.

"Fuck you're so good at this," I panted as Archer rolled on a condom. He stroked me with his fingers. My legs trembled, and my chest clenched. Archer teased me with his cock.

"You're not the only one who's good with a paintbrush," Archer whispered in my ear. Then he was in me. I cried out and gripped the table. It was pretty rickety, and I didn't think it would hold my weight. One of Archer's large hands gripped my hip. The other reached up to my nipple to pinch it.

I whimpered as he thrust into me. His hand moved down to stroke my clit. I ground against his hand, loving how huge his cock felt inside of me. I was a sweaty, moaning mess and begging him to make me come when I felt my body tighten and release. Archer's fingers dug into my ass as he thrust in me a few more times then came.

"No bed?" I asked after he untangled himself from me.

"I told you, no more of your crappy bed. You should come to my hotel."

"Right now? I have to work," I said. "I can't take a vacation. We have the art retreat tomorrow."

"Skip it," he said, pulling me in for a kiss.

"They're paying customers." *And the only reason I haven't been evicted from my building, but Archer doesn't need to know that.*

I didn't want to ruin this time with Archer with negative thoughts. *You will win the grant, and everything will be okay.*

"Besides," I continued, trying to sound light and breezy. "The art retreat is a big part of my individual grant application. The judges are going to come look at my studio, my work, and my students' work."

"You better hide the stained-glass penis, then," Archer joked.

"I'm feeling pumped and creative!" Ida said at the art retreat the next afternoon.

"And drunk," Archer whispered to me.

He hadn't spent the night. Apparently his twin was working on some big project, and he had to babysit. Now he was sprawled out on the couch, fielding frankly lecherous looks from the old women in the studio.

"Another drink there, hotcakes?" Ida asked.

"Don't mind if I do," Archer replied as Ida, slightly wobbly, poured him a generous glass of the mixed drink.

"I hope you're not too drunk to make ceramics," I said, gesturing to the pottery wheels.

"How hard can it be?" Ida exclaimed. "Spin the wheel—make magic."

"It's a little more complicated than that—"

"Did I ever tell you about my first husband?" Ida asked Archer. "He used to call me spinner because he could set me on his lap and spin me around, and magic would happen. Can't do that now, of course. Too old—my knees. Though I've started doing more advanced yoga poses. Bert is pretty impressed. I could show you some yoga poses sometime. Maybe we should have a sexual yoga retreat, Hazel."

Archer was struggling to hold back a laugh. "I wouldn't want you to overextend yourself."

I cleared my throat, trying to put the image of Ida spinning around slowly on Bert's lap out of my mind. "Let's turn our attention back to a different kind of spinning," I said hastily, motioning everyone back to their seats.

"This is an ancient art. The pottery wheel was invented several thousand years ago," I said, giving my pottery wheel a spin. "People back then used pottery for carrying food and water, storage, cooking, or as decorative art. Today we're going to try and make a simple vase. First, take your clay and set it firmly on the wheel. Wet your hands a little bit."

"I'm all wet," Ida said.

Archer grinned and took another sip of his drink.

"You're not making pottery," Ida said.

"I don't want my hands covered in clay. I'll watch. I love a woman who's good with her hands." He cast a smoldering look in my direction and took a slow sip of his drink. The elderly women all cheered, and I winced.

"So put your hands around the clay," I said, demonstrating.

"It's so thick," Dottie said, oblivious to the double meaning. Archer silently choked on laughter. I prayed his little brothers were too focused on making sure their pottery wasn't wonky to pay too much attention to the comments.

"Now push forward," I instructed.

Yeah, baby, Archer mouthed. He really needed to participate. It wasn't right that he was sitting there, distracting me for his own amusement.

"Now press your thumbs around the tip of the clay," I said, regretting my word choice as soon as it came out.

"But not too forcefully, right?" Archer said in a fake innocent tone.

"Interlock your hands like this," I said, trying to ignore him. "The wheel should be spinning, and you should see the clay grow long."

"Long and thick or long and skinny?" Archer asked, clearly enjoying every minute of this demonstration.

The seniors were having a little trouble. It took a bit to get the hang of it.

"Mine's flaccid!" Dottie complained. I looked over, and sure enough, her clay was long and flopped over the wheel.

"Just smoosh it back down," I said, coming over to help her.

"I don't want to make a vase," Ida declared. "I want to make a dildo."

Frazzled as I ran around, trying to keep clay from flying all over the walls, I said, "You know what? You go right ahead."

"I'm going to put big veins and huge balls on it and everything!" Ida said, beaming.

"Just remind me to hide that away before the Art Zurich people see it," I said to Archer as I passed by him on the way to help Otis with his vase.

"Who knows?" Archer said after thinking for a moment. "They may think it's a well-thought-out piece of commentary on the sexual urges of senior women. You might even win a prize," he said to Ida.

"You hear that?" Ida crowed to Dottie. "I could be a world-renowned artist!"

CHAPTER 44

"It's cleanup day!" Remy bellowed in the hallway as he opened my bedroom door and flung open the window curtains. I pulled the covers over my head.

"It's too early."

"It's six a.m.!" my older brother said cheerfully.

"Okay, it is way too early."

"We're all volunteering for you, Archer," Remy said, picking me up and half dragging me off the bed like he used to do when we were kids. I pulled all the covers off with me and curled up on the floor. The carpet was really soft. I had it put in especially for my room in the estate. I had slept in worse places.

Remy snatched the covers off of me. I groaned.

"Don't wear your fancy clothes. Here, I brought you a pair of my canvas pants and work boots."

"Spare me," I said, peering at the scuffed-up clothes in his hands. "I cannot wear that. I have standards to uphold."

"We even have team T-shirts," Remy said. "Otis and Theo made them." He held up the shirt. It read, **This Svensson is the GOAT**. There was a picture of a goat wearing a hard hat.

"Isn't it cute?" Remy asked, grinning through his bushy beard. His wild hair was pulled back into a ponytail. "Do you get it? Because GOAT stands for Greatest Of All Time, and our mascot is a goat." Remy beamed at me.

"Is it? Did you run that by Hunter? You know how he feels about goats."

I put on the shirt. I was begrudgingly impressed with the quality of my little brothers' artwork, though the colors could stand a redo. It was all neon pink, green, and blue. It definitely wasn't my style. It clashed with my hair, my eyes, and well, everything really.

After I finished dressing, I walked into the dining room. I grabbed one of Remy's famous breakfast burritos from the stack on the buffet. My other brothers were already up and wearing their shirts. Even Hunter was wearing a shirt.

"You look stylish," I said to Hunter, trying not to smirk.

"Shut up," he said.

Remy pulled the bus into the roundabout in front of the large estate house, and we all filed in.

I slipped on my sunglasses, slumped in my seat, and slowly ate my breakfast burrito. "Does the cleanup seriously start at seven?" I complained.

"Don't want to waste the daylight!" Remy called out over the roar of the engine.

I had to admit, once we arrived at the staging area and joined the crowd of people, I was feeling pretty pumped.

"This is such a great turnout," Hazel gushed when we arrived. She turned to Mace. "Thank you so much for putting this out to your employees."

"My pleasure. Svensson PharmaTech is glad to be a member of the Harrogate community."

"Spare me the corporate mumbo jumbo," I said, shoving him. "Let's start asking the important questions. How are we feeding all these people? It's an all-day thing, right?"

Hazel nodded. "We have sandwiches. Jemma and I were up all night making them. Ida donated snacks. Also, you're on the art committee, so you get a lanyard!" I had to bend down so that she could drape it over my neck.

"What do you need me to do?"

She flipped through the pages on her clipboard. "You can hang with me. We're going to be delivering people the tools and supplies they need."

I followed her to a golf cart.

"The PharmaTech volunteers are clearing the path near their offices for where the trail is going. I can't believe we already secured a permit. This afternoon they're going to take the bulldozer to it to clear it and lay the gravel down and trench for the electrical wire for the trees," she said as she checked items off on her list. "There's also the bike painting for the bike share going on. Lots of families with young kids are doing that today."

Her phone beeped with incoming texts. "Edna is overseeing flowers in the town square," Hazel explained. "She needs some more fertilizer. Apparently not enough was set out."

I loaded the bags in. Then we hopped in the golf cart, and I hung on for dear life as Hazel raced through the staging area and over to the town square.

"I'm starting to think it was a good idea for you to not have a car," I said, gingerly stepping out of the golf cart. "You're a crazy driver."

"I'm a great driver!"

"You're aggressive," I said, hauling the bags of fertilizer out of the back of the golf cart.

"Nothing like a big strong man!" Ida said when I walked up with the bags.

"Ida," her sister, Edna, snapped. Edna was a judge in Harrogate, and no one wanted to end up in her courtroom. She was known for making grown men sob like little babies.

"This is looking good!" Hazel said. There was an array of flowers in a gradation of oranges, pinks, and yellows.

"Yes, we needed to spruce the place up a bit," Edna said. "It would be great if more people would help instead of lollygagging about."

"I'm working," Ida grumbled. "Hey, when's lunch?"

After several more harrowing golf cart rides to drop off more paint, tell the people prepping the mural areas to confirm the sizing, and give Olivia a ride to several of the historic buildings to make sure people were pressure washing them correctly, we took glass cleaner and newspaper inside the historic city hall building. My brothers were all scurrying around inside, on ladders, cleaning the huge windows.

"I see streaks," Hunter said, his low voice slipping throughout the large room.

"Why do we have to clean?" Otis was whining.

"Part of the Art Zurich tour is to take the people through these historic buildings," Hazel said. "It's what makes our town unique."

"It's so much glass." Peyton sighed, squirting more Windex on his newspaper.

"Well, hop to it," I told them, "because there's three times as much glass in the exhibition hall, where we're holding the gala."

Otis looked at me in shock.

"I'm just kidding," I said, laughing. "I'll hire a cleaning firm for that!"

"The windows look great!" Hazel said to my brothers. They beamed. The hall did look nice. The sun streamed through the sparkling windows and lit up the mural on the opposite wall.

Hazel checked her clipboard as we left the building. "It's almost time for lunch. Because we didn't want people leaving the work site," Hazel said, "we're bringing the lunch to the different workers."

When we arrived at her café, she loaded me down with boxes of sandwiches, and we zoomed around, delivering drinks, chips, and sandwiches.

"I didn't put nice labels on them," she fretted as I took several boxes to the families painting the colorful bikes.

"I think people are going to be so happy to have some-thing to eat, they won't care," I assured her while trying to sneak a sandwich.

"Those are for the volunteers!" she said.

"Then maybe I'll eat something else," I whispered, leaning over to kiss her.

Most of the teams wrapped up a few hours after lunch. Many people went up to Svensson PharmaTech to see the progress on the main attraction.

In addition to the volunteers, Mace also had a construction crew on-site.

"So the land is pretty well cleared of debris," the foreman was saying to Mace as Hazel and I walked up. "We're going to start digging the pathway."

"Is the concrete going to be set by next week?" Mace asked.

The foreman nodded. "We're going to dig today and start laying gravel while we have daylight. Tomorrow I have concrete trucks scheduled. We'll pour, and while it's curing, the electrician will start pulling the wire."

"This is going to be so cool!" Hazel said, her eyes lighting up when we saw the cleared path for the art walk.

"It's actually a really nice amenity for my workers," Mace said. "There have been several requests to make all the green space and woods around the company more usable. People are really excited about the path."

We gathered on the roof with Mace's other employees and my brothers. "You survived cleaning the windows," I said to Otis.

"At least they aren't jumping around," Hunter said. "Though they did have enough energy to insist we come watch the earthmoving equipment."

"They aren't tearing down any trees," Hazel asked me, "right?"

"No, the landscape architect has the path going around them," I assured her.

My little brothers cheered as the bulldozer cut through the dirt. The path started to take shape. Svensson PharmaTech was on a hill, and from the roof, we could see across town to my future convention center.

"This is going to be perfect," I said. "I don't even care that McKenna owns the strip mall site. Garrett's going to fix it."

"He will?" Hazel sounded doubtful. "A lot hinges on her acting like a rational person. I have my doubts."

"I told you not to worry about McKenna." I pulled her close to me and nuzzled her hair. It felt nice just hanging out with her and my family.

CHAPTER 45

Hazel

"I think beautification day went well," I said at the committee meeting that Monday. I had decided to just give up on the café. Aside from making sandwiches for Ida, I didn't have time to sit in an empty café and wonder if a customer was going to wander in. My last Hail Mary shot was winning this art grant. I had to be firing on all cylinders—hence the multi-hour meeting scheduled for today.

Pulling up my spreadsheet, I said, "The art walk has the remainder of the concrete getting poured today," I said. "I have the sculpture artists meeting this afternoon. They're bringing in their sculptures. The boxes of lights to string up arrived in the mail yesterday."

"The buildings are mostly all cleaned," Olivia said. "Edna has sentenced several teenagers who were caught underage drinking to community service. They will be finishing up any remaining cleaning in lieu of fines or jail time."

"The flowers are all planted and looking awesome. The muralists are out right now, working," Jemma said.

"The bikes are done and decorated and out," Olivia added. "There are already people using them, which is great. I have the historic-building tour ready to go. I even made little booklets about the buildings of Harrogate."

"These are nice," I said, flipping through a little square book with glossy pictures.

"I have the gallery walk itinerary," McKenna said. I hated that she was in the meeting. Archer obviously didn't want her there either. "Obviously mine will be last, to leave a good impression. I hope you have that rickety café cleaned up, Hazel. I have half a mind to scratch it from the tour."

"It's going to have my art retreat paintings up," I said to her. I was going to try and ignore how terrible she was for the good of the Art Zurich bid.

"How's the gala planning coming?" I asked Archer. "You're supposed to be in charge of hotels, meals, hospitality, and the gala."

"I have a block of the nicest suites in the Corentin Hotel reserved—that's the art deco hotel on Main Street and Tenth. I even had some of the more prestigious artwork moved there from one of my other hotels in Manhattan for the occasion. The judges won't pay a dime. I have all the meals, and alcohol, of course, covered. The work crew is in the Mast Brothers' chocolate factory cleaning and starting to set up. We have hundreds of tickets sold. It should be a great event. I have Zoey from Weddings in the City planning the event."

Now there was a boss babe I wanted to emulate. She had her own wedding-planning business and did weddings for the wealthy and elite in Manhattan. Her Instagram was amazing.

"She just dropped everything and planned a party?" I asked.

Archer shrugged. "She said she was happy to not have to deal with bridezillas for once. But that's not all!" Archer continued. "I have a really cool surprise. Get this—I convinced Chloe to come do catering! Isn't that awesome? I have to pay her out the wazoo, but rumor has it that one of the judges' wives who is coming along is a huge fan of *The Great Christmas Bake-Off* and of Chloe. So this will be perfect. She's doing all the breakfast catering and a couple of the lunches. The other lunch and the dinners will be local farm-to-table restaurants, which are already booked. Zoey's going to be doing some decorating there too."

Archer was rambling on about the upcoming festivities, but all I could think was that *Chloe was coming*. She and the Grey Dove Bistro were going to put me out of business.

"Well isn't that great?" I said faintly. Jemma looked at me in concern.

"She's coming this afternoon," Archer said. "She needs a place to cook. I told her she could use your café."

"You did?"

"Yeah and she might need some help. I told her you were a great cook," he said. "Isn't this awesome? We're so going to win!"

After the committee meeting, I went over to my café. I looked around. I had already started hanging the best of the art-retreat paintings and pottery, with little signs about the students.

Hazel: *I can't believe Chloe is coming. This is terrible!*

Jemma: *Archer didn't mean anything by it I'm sure.*

Hazel: *I know. It's not like I told him about how my business is failing. At least I paid the gas bill for this month so Chloe will actually be able to cook.*

Olivia: *Just focus on winning the grant. That's all you need. Then you can pay off the mortgage on your building and renovate it. Even if you can't have a café, there are a lot of tech startups here because of Svenssons PharmaTech. You could at least rent out the space as an office.*

Hazel: *But where would I live? I can't move back in with my sister.*

Jemma: *Duh move in with the hot guy you've been banging.*

Hazel: *I don't want to be his charity case.*

Olivia: *If you help him win the art grant you just handed him a billion dollar conference center on a silver platter. He wouldn't be able to win it without you.*

Hazel: *And all of you.*

Olivia: **heart**

After taking out cleaning supplies, I scoured the stove and tried to calm down.

"For every time there is a season," I told myself. "Sometimes your business fails. A true girl boss picks herself back up. This is a minor setback. Maybe this will be a good thing. I'll win the grant. Maybe I won't have a café, but I can do something else with this space. Everything will be fine. I have to believe that."

After spending several hours cleaning, my café sparkled. I wished it was better decorated. I had seen the to-die-for pictures on Chloe's Instagram from her impeccably decorated restaurant in her boyfriend's tower.

> **Archer:** *Chloe's here. We're on our way. Also had to bring some of my brothers. Don't worry they are the small ones. You'll barely notice them.*
>
> **Hazel:** *Okay I'm here.*

I made popcorn and Magritte Martinis. Then I fretted as I walked around the café, swiveling the tables if they seemed a little wobbly. A black SUV pulled up in front of my café. Josie climbed out, followed by a short blond woman in sunglasses.

"Hi, you must be Hazel!" she called when I opened the front door. "I'm Chloe. We're going to be neighbors!"

Archer sauntered in. "This, Chloe, is my home away from home. Hazel is the woman who makes the pancakes and sandwiches."

"They're amazing pancakes. I saw them on your Instagram. They're gorgeous!" Chloe cooed. "Oh, look how cute it is in here! I love the exposed-brick walls. That's what I wanted in my restaurant in Manhattan, but of course the building was all concrete. I love these historic buildings."

"I have drinks and some popcorn ready if you guys want a snack," I said, trying to sound upbeat. "As you can see, the setup is pretty straightforward. Hopefully this will work for you."

Otis and Theo went upstairs to work on their paintings, taking cups of the popcorn with them. Henry clung to Archer.

"You want some popcorn?" he asked. Henry nodded. Archer fed him popcorn while Chloe, Josie, and I discussed the menu.

"So there is the lunch when the representatives arrive then breakfast the next three days," Chloe said. "I love making breakfast food. I hear you make a mean crepe, Hazel. I think we should have crepes one day. We should do pancakes another day; the Japanese ones you make are great. Let's serve them with eggs benedict so it's like a fun little sweet treat to go with the savory meal. What do you need for the dish? Berries? Josie was saying you guys have a great farm co-op out here."

"Wait, you actually want me to help you?" I asked.

"Of course!" Chloe said, taking a handful of popcorn. "I can't spare anyone from my restaurant. I'm a little worried about the franchise out here. My friend Nina was supposed to run it, but now we're opening one in Brooklyn and another one downtown that she is going to run. So I don't know what I'm going to do here. I'm a little short-staffed. Besides, your food looks awesome! The judges will love it."

"What about lunch?" Josie asked.

"You should just have sandwiches," Archer said.

"I had one of your sandwiches. We stopped by Ida's," Chloe said.

I had a horrified thought. "I hope Ida was on good behavior."

"Nope," Chloe said. "She's a riot! I love her. She told me to eat the *bánh mì*—it was amazing."

"I wish you'd had a fresh one and not one that was sitting in a case," I grumbled.

"You make really fancy sandwiches, and it's hot out. I think they would be perfect to serve for lunch with some salads," Josie suggested.

"I make a really good pasta salad," Chloe said. "And there are so many fresh vegetables with the farm co-op. And of course I'll make desserts."

Archer set a box on the table, and Chloe opened it, displaying perfectly decorated cookies that looked like places around Harrogate.

"These are beautiful," I said in awe.

"I'm having Chloe make a box of these for each person, to be waiting in their hotel rooms," Archer said, reaching over and snagging a cookie.

"What about the signature cocktails?" Josie asked. "Archer was telling me about your artist-themed cocktails. We should serve those!"

"We need to serve something better than just wine and beer," Archer added.

"Hazel shouldn't be tending bar during the party," Josie said.

"I have caterers for the gala," Archer told her.

"I can just give them the recipes," I said. "And make some signs for the drinks."

"Great, it's all settled," Chloe said, closing her notebook. "I'm back and forth to Manhattan the next few days. This is going to be amazing!"

She was so bubbly and fun to be around. I couldn't hate her for moving in next door to me. Chloe was such a nice person, even if she was going to cost me my café.

If she helps you win the grant, that's all that matters.

CHAPTER 46

Archer

"I swear, the only reason I'm giving a presentation," Mace said to Josie, "is because I need Archer to not set up shop here."

I was holding court in Mace's office. After the welcome lunch, we had several presentations scheduled to introduce Harrogate to the Art Zurich judges. Eli and Tristan were there too. Since they were Greyson Hotel Group interns, I decided I might as well put them to work.

"This is good practice for you guys," I told my younger brothers. "Though our big business is hotels, we make a huge percentage of our profits due to events like conferences, corporate retreats, and weddings."

"First, taking Otis and Theo to the art retreat, then taking interns under your wing. Look at you being helpful raising the next generation," Mace said.

"What? I participate."

"Sometimes, but it's like pulling teeth."

"It's just business. If I die from choking on a fish McBite, someone has to carry on my legacy."

"Hazel's been a good influence on him," Josie said.

"Stop acting like proud parents."

"But we are proud," my twin said, trying to smooth down my hair.

"Get off. It took me thirty minutes to make it do this."

"Hazel's been influencing his waistline a bit too," Eli said.

"Don't even," I warned then looked down at my waist and gingerly poked my abs. Did they feel a little less washboardy?

"The weight looks good on you," Josie said, trying not to smile. "You look nice and round, like a dad."

I freaked out and jumped up to examine my reflection in the floor-to-ceiling glass windows. Josie and Mace leaned against each other, laughing.

"Ha ha, very funny. I look outstanding."

After the meeting at Mace's, I dropped Eli and Tristan off at the Corentin Hotel to start prepping for the Art Zurich judges' arrival.

Is Hazel changing me? I wondered. I certainly was spending the longest chunk of time in Harrogate I ever had. I had been here longer than Christmas. The slower pace of life, being with Hazel, being with my family—I felt more grounded.

When I walked into my office at the Corentin Hotel, McKenna was there waiting for me, perched on my desk.

"Archer."

Crap.

"Did you think about my offer? Maybe we could go somewhere and talk about it," McKenna suggested.

"I'm not interested."

"If you want this convention center to happen, you need to be."

"Fine," I said. "What do you want?" The displeasure was clear on my face.

"I know you want to settle down," she said. "I think it should be with me, not Hazel."

"No."

"Just give us another chance, Archer," she pleaded. "We were good together."

"I would so much rather be with Hazel than you, McKenna. She would never use me for money or influence. She has her own successful business. Hazel and I make perfect sense together."

"I have my own gallery," McKenna insisted. "I would be better than some cook who does terrible paintings."

"Hazel makes great paintings. She also makes paintings she can sell. There's nothing wrong with trying to do what's best for your business. I'm not going to begrudge someone success," I said.

McKenna sniffed. "If you're such an alpha billionaire business man, then you can see that you need me to make this deal happen. One date, Archer, that's it. We don't even have to have sex though I know what you like."

"Go away."

"Just think about it. You, me, a long weekend. Give me a chance to make everything up to you. *Shh*," she said, pressing a perfectly manicured finger to my mouth to silence my protest. "Just think about it."

As she left, she looked over her shoulder at me and winked.

I just stood there. What was I going to do?

For a brief moment, I considered going on a date with McKenna. Maybe it wouldn't be that bad. Then I thought about Hazel. There was no way I was going to hurt her like that. It wasn't even an option. I needed to find another way.

CHAPTER 47

Hazel

"After finishing meeting with the various muralists around town, I stopped at my café to sign for a food delivery before the next meeting about the art walk. I couldn't wait to see it.

I quickly loaded the boxes of vegetables, eggs, meats, and other supplies into the large walk-in fridge. When I came back out into the café, there was Archer's mother, stuffing something in her purse.

"Sorry," I said forcefully, "we're closed." *Probably forever.*

Archer's mother looked at me haughtily. "Since you're someone who is trying to scam my son out of his money, I suppose I shouldn't expect you to be pleasant and friendly."

I sputtered, "I'm not trying to scam him!"

"Of course you are. I know girls like you. You're after his money."

"No, I'm not. You're going to have to leave," I told her. "I have another meeting."

I tried to calm down as I biked over to the art walk on the Svensson PharmaTech campus. Archer was there when I slowly climbed up the hill to the trailhead. Construction workers were stringing up the chandeliers and fairy lights.

Archer smiled when he saw me and pulled me in for a kiss. "I need to buy you a car," he said.

"I don't need a car. My bike is fine," I said in a rush, his mother's accusations of my being after Archer's money still fresh in my mind.

I turned to look at the art walk. Caution tape was up so people wouldn't step on the concrete. Wooden benches sat waiting to be installed.

"Concrete takes a good thirty days to fully cure," the foreman said, "but within the next few days, since it's so warm and humid, it should be hard enough to install the benches and the sculptures in."

"Do you think the lights are too janky?" I asked Archer as we watched the workers hang the chandeliers on two large trees that framed the entrance to the art walk.

"Honestly, no," he said. "I think it's actually going to be cool. It's a nice Instagram moment, as Josie likes to say."

I took out my phone and snapped a picture. "I can't believe they built this much so quickly," I said.

We walked on the cleared dirt alongside the concrete path. It went a good mile, then it stopped at a large sign that had the map of the full extent of the trail as well as some renderings. As we walked back, I showed Archer the pictures of the sculptures and the spots where they would be installed.

"You're not going to put up Ida's dildo?" he joked.

I shuddered. "She made me take it to be fired in a kiln. She painted it glitter green with the veins a blue. She calls it the hulk. She said she has jewels she's going to bedazzle it with."

"Sounds fascinating."

Otis, Theo, and Garrett were waiting by a Tesla SUV when we walked to the parking lot from the art walk.

"We're going to be late for the art retreat," Otis said, glaring at Archer.

"Garrett could have taken you."

"I'm busy trying to fix your mistakes," Garrett said.

"Yeah, how is that coming?" Archer asked, tone flat. Archer stared at Garrett. Garrett stared back. The two brothers did that silent alpha-male communication thing that I had no patience for.

"The McKenna issue? I'm sure you have it under control. Now don't worry, Otis. I'm running the art retreat, and if you arrive when I do, then you're right on time!"

Archer picked up my bike and loaded it in the SUV. Then he pressed a button on his key fob, and the falcon-wing doors swung up. Though I didn't consider myself a car person, I was begrudgingly impressed.

"If I have to drive an SUV, I have to get the most overkill one possible," Archer said as we climbed in.

"I can't believe you gave up your sports car," I said, buckling up. "You're such a hockey mom," I teased.

"SUVs are nice. You're higher up," Otis said. "And it's battery powered, so it's better for the environment."

"Yeah, yeah," Archer said as we drove down the winding street into town.

Ida was standing behind the bar when we walked into the café.

"That alcohol is for the Art Zurich retreat," I said, trying to wrestle the bottle out of her arms. She was surprisingly strong for an old woman.

"You have to sample it to make sure it's good," Ida said, taking another sip. "If anything, I'm doing you a favor."

"If you're back there, I'll take a drink," Archer said.

"At this rate, we're going to have to give the judges water and juice boxes," I complained.

"Just expense it," Archer said. "I basically gave Harrogate a blank check for this Art Zurich Expo bid. I'm putting it under marketing."

"Don't drink too much," I chastised them. "We're doing pop art today."

"Is that the one that looks like a comic book?" Otis asked.

"Someone's been doing their homework!"

"Sweet!" The boys ran upstairs, and Archer offered Ida an arm to steady her.

"You found yourself a keeper here, Hazel," Ida said.

"Sure did! He's good with kids, eats my food, and is nice to sweet old ladies."

"He's not helping me because I'm old," Ida complained. "He's helping me because I'm drunk as a skunk."

"How long were you here drinking?"

"Not long enough. I had to listen to Dottie tell me all about her hemorrhoids."

"I'd need a drink after that too," Archer muttered.

I could tell the drinking was going to be a problem when the seniors started painting. We were doing paintings in the style of Roy Liebeskind. He used dots and thick black lines for paintings to make them look like frames of comic books. Only Otis's and Theo's paintings looked decent.

"Your circles are so nice and even," I praised them. "You don't want to paint, Archer?"

"I know how to quit before I'm kicked," he said, taking a sip of his drink and motioning to Ida. Her dots were not even. In fact, some of them just looked like amoebas. Dottie's lines were wandering over the page, and Bettina had fallen asleep at the canvas.

I sighed. "I was hoping to have something nice to show for when the Art Zurich representatives come to Harrogate," I said.

"You have my dildo," Ida said and burped.

"You made these a little strong, Ida," Archer said.

"Otis's and Theo's paintings look nice at least," I said. "They're my star students."

CHAPTER 48

Archer

A s we raced toward the arrival of the Art Zurich representatives, the artistic vision of Harrogate really came together. The only problem? McKenna. I couldn't tell if she was stalking me or if it was just bad luck that she seemed to appear wherever I was.

I was on-site at the Mast Brothers' chocolate factory meeting with Zoey to finalize the event space layout, décor, and program.

I parked the SUV, and there was McKenna, like an infection that wouldn't go away.

"My offer stands," she said when I got out of the car. "You want that hotel site. I want you. You can even keep Hazel as your little side piece in your Podunk town."

"If you don't like it here, then leave," I told her.

She made an annoyed sound.

"Or are you trying to sabotage this expo bid?" My eyes narrowed.

"I also applied for the individual grant," McKenna said, tossing her curtain of glossy hair. "So, no, I don't act against my own interests. Or yours. I'm here for you, Archer. I'm trying to support you."

"That's a complete turn of events from how you were a year ago," I retorted.

"I want us to be successful. We're a power couple."

"We're not a power couple," I told her. "You tried to destroy my family. You turned me against them and accused my brother of something horrible."

"I did it for you, for us! You'll see. Harrogate will win the Art Zurich Expo. I'll win the individual grant, and then the only thing standing between you and a billion-dollar conference center is me. And I want you between something else." She leaned against me, running her nails lightly down my neck.

"Never in a million years."

After the meeting with Zoey, I went to see Hazel. She was in her café sitting at a table with her laptop, typing furiously.

"They're coming in two days," she said, chewing on her bottom lip. "What if this doesn't work?"

"Of course it will work," I said, rubbing her back. "The art walk looks great."

"There are still a couple sculptures that need to go up. I swear, working with artists is the worst sometimes. I had one person on the phone with me for an hour complaining that the concrete their sculpture is supposed to be bolted on is too aggressive of a gray. Like, it's concrete, people. We're paying you for your art. Get it up and shut up."

I laughed, hugging her and planting a kiss on her head. "You know," I said. "Not to stress you out, but there's one very important thing you forgot."

"I forgot something?" she asked, tensing up and pulling away from me. Hazel picked up her clipboard and started leafing through it. Tendrils of her hair swung in her face, and she blew them away. "I thought I had everything! We have the food. You've got the gala under control. The art walk is almost done. The muralists are almost done, and I've obsessively checked the weather and lit a few spiritual candles, so it shouldn't rain. I told Ida she was not, in any way, allowed to say anything remotely sexually suggestive, and if she did, I would kick her out of the final exhibition."

"No," I said, laughing. "You need a dress!"

"A dress?" She looked at me blankly.

"For the gala?" I prompted and raised an eyebrow. "Unless you're planning on showing up in yoga pants and a crop top. Not that I would complain, but you know those snooty art-world people."

"I can't afford a dress," she said.

"I'm buying you one," I told her, taking the clipboard out of her hands and guiding her outside.

"There's a nice consignment store a few blocks over," she said once we were in my car. "It's down that street. Oh, wait, you missed it. Turn around!"

"You can't show up in some hand-me-down," I told her as I kept driving. "We're trying to win a huge biennial expo, remember?"

I parked the car in front of a high-end boutique.

"This looks really expensive," Hazel said uncertainly.

I shrugged. "Probably cheaper than New York City."

We walked in. The sales associate greeted us. "Looking for anything in particular?"

"A nice gown for the gala."

The associate nodded. "Floor-length, no train. I think that would be best," she said. "We have several new ones in from one of our exclusive designers. She makes each dress unique so that you're not wearing what someone else has." She pointed to a dress on the floor. "How would you feel about something like that?" she asked Hazel. The dress had a corseted piece with pale-purple lace. It was sparkly and showed a lot of skin. I wanted nothing more than to see Hazel in it.

"Maybe something less risqué," Hazel said.

"Or more," I suggested.

"Let's not."

"You have to be daring, Hazel," I told her. "Be the artist."

"If you're an artist, what about something like this?" the associate recommended and showed us a colorful gown. It was a strapless fit-and-flare.

"It's like watercolor," Hazel said, admiring the fabric. The white silk had artistic blotches and swishes of black accented by tangerine and a deep yellow.

"It will bring out the gold in your eyes," the sales associate said, holding the dress up to Hazel.

"I might need a little more support up top, though," Hazel said in concern.

"You'd be surprised with what a good bra can do," the associate told her.

"It is beautiful," Hazel said, chewing on her lip. "How much is it?"

"Don't worry about it. Just choose what you like," I told her.

The associate ushered Hazel into a dressing room. She came out looking like a princess—a cool, artsy princess. The folded pieces on the bodice showed just enough cleavage to tease. Hazel admired herself in the mirror while the sales associate pulled up her hair into a loose topknot.

"Maybe something like this for your hair?"

"You look stunning," I told Hazel. "She also needs some cocktail dresses," I said, holding out one that had a lace back.

"For what?"

"We have several dinners, not just the gala. Plus you need some clothes for walking around."

When Hazel came out in the formfitting cocktail dress, she looked just as sexy as I thought she would.

"I just want to lick you," I told her seriously.

The sales associate smiled slightly at Hazel. "Gold jewelry with this would be stunning. Pair the outfit with a pointed-toe stiletto."

Hazel also tried on various blouses and skirts.

"I look very French," Hazel said with a laugh as she modeled the outfit. "I really love the pussy bow neck. Don't even say anything," she warned me.

"I would recommend a black strappy sandal," the associate said as she took all of Hazel's clothes to the front counter. "There's a nice shoe shop a few doors down."

I blocked Hazel from trying to read the screen as the associate rang up the clothes. "You've put a lot of work into this bid," I told her. "You deserve something nice."

She made a face.

"I'll have the clothes sent to my hotel," I said, taking the receipt.

"Your hotel?" Hazel exclaimed.

"Surely you aren't getting ready in your studio, are you?" I scoffed.

"I guess not." She was chewing on her lip again, and I leaned in to kiss her mouth.

"Next on the agenda," I said when we walked out of the shop, "shoes, jewelry, and of course, lingerie." I waggled my eyebrows, making her laugh.

"That seems a little excessive," she said. "I probably have some shoes I can wear."

"You're a little on the height-challenged side," I said. "You can't show up in flats. You don't want to be shorter than everyone else."

She shoved me. "Still, maybe I can buy the shoes at a thrift store."

"Maybe," I said. "Except, oh look, we're already conveniently here at this shoe store. We should look around."

"It's expensive," she insisted.

"Let me do something nice for you," I said. "And later I'll do something else nice."

"She needs a sexy black stiletto," I told the sales clerk after she greeted us.

"Just something simple," Hazel pleaded.

"I'll bring out a few options."

We browsed the shoes while we waited.

"These are nice," I said. "Very sexy." The straps crisscrossed over the shoe and tied around the ankle. "You know, Hazel," I said in a low voice, "I might have a latent and surprising foot fetish because I really want to fuck you in these shoes."

"I brought out several," the associate said.

"And these," I added, ignoring Hazel's protests and handing the sales associate the shoes.

Hazel tried on the plain black stilettos. "These are nice, but do you think they go with the dress?" She showed the picture to the associate, who nodded.

"You might try the ones your boyfriend picked out," the clerk suggested. "That's such a cool dress, the way it folds on the bodice. You need cool shoes to match."

"I guess," Hazel said as she laced up the stilettoes. I had to refrain from jumping up from my seat when she paraded around. The shoes were *very* fetish inducing.

"Even if you don't wear those with the dress, we're buying them," I stated.

"I think I will wear them with the dress," she decided. "They're actually not that uncomfortable. They're clearly well-made, and all the straps provide support."

"Try these on for your cocktail dress," the associate said, handing Hazel a pair of red shoes with large bows on the sides. "They're very artsy."

"I love the slight retro feel," Hazel said.

I wanted her to put the black stilettos back on, but no one was asking me, so I kept my mouth shut and handed over my credit card when the clerk rang up the boxes of shoes.

"Don't look at the price," I ordered Hazel as I swiped my credit card.

"Too late," she said. "They're too expensive. Put them back, please."

"I already bought them," I said as the machine spit out a receipt. "And there are no returns. Oh well. Cheer up!" I said, swinging the bags as we left the shop. "We're getting to the best part!"

"You would say that," Hazel said as we walked, arm in arm, down the street.

"Looking for edible underwear?" I whispered when we walked into the lingerie shop.

"I run a café. If there's edible underwear, I'm making it, not buying," she whispered back.

"See if there's anything here to inspire you."

While Hazel tried on bras, I browsed. There were several things that inspired me. There was a practically see-through corset that I longed to see Hazel in. "That would go really nicely with your shoes, wouldn't it?" I asked Hazel, gesturing to the display as I paid for the lingerie that I hadn't yet seen, though I would have her model it for me later.

"I think it's missing a part," she said, wrinkling her nose.

"No, it's supposed to be open right there. You know, for easy access." She shivered slightly. "Now jewelry," I told her when we walked out of the store.

"I think you've already gone above and beyond," she pleaded.

"Hazel, you have to be dripping with diamonds."

"Please, no!"

"I'm just kidding. Surely there's a jewelry store in town you've always wanted to shop at."

"I have jewelry already. I'll wear what I have. You've done enough," she said firmly.

"Okay," I told her. But I was still going to buy her jewelry anyway. "Does that mean you're ready to model your new lingerie?"

"I have a meeting," she replied, raising up on her toes to kiss me. "Someone has to make sure you get your conference center. But maybe I'll have a little treat for you if you stop by tonight!"

CHAPTER 49

Hazel

"Look who had a fairytale afternoon," Olivia said when she came to my café with me after our meeting with the Harrogate Trust. My bags and boxes with the shoes and lingerie from the shopping trip were haphazardly spread on the café tables.

I couldn't stop the goofy grin from spreading over my face.

"This is nuts. You have to show me all the stuff he bought you."

"It wasn't a lot," I said as Olivia opened up the shoe boxes.

"He just gave them to you? He must really like you."

"His mom doesn't seem to think so," I muttered.

"Has she been back to harass you?" Olivia demanded. "You should tell the police."

"I can't call the police on Archer's mom!"

After Olivia left, I wandered around the café, organizing all the boxes for the upcoming judges' visit. I also prepped Archer's surprise. All the talk of edible underwear was enough to inspire me to finish my creation.

I tried them on once I finished the piece. They weren't extremely flattering, but I hoped Archer would think they were funny and sexy at least. After taking them off, I set up my easel for another painting. There was an Etsy order for a kitten in a bushel of carrots. I put on some music as I sketched, in a fine line of acrylic, the outline of where each element would be. Then I started the first layer of color, mixing oranges, yellows, and browns together.

"Back at work, painting?" a man asked. I yelled, and the paintbrush flew out of my hand.

"You ruined my shirt," Archer said, his voice deep and dangerous.

"Sorry," I said sheepishly, reaching for a rag. But he gripped my wrist.

"You want to make it up to me?" he asked. His breath was hot against my mouth.

I immediately felt wet. "I did promise you a surprise."

He pushed down my shirt and sucked at my nipple, his hand gliding under the long shirt. "You're not wearing any panties. I'm going to enjoy this surprise," he growled.

"That wasn't the surprise—I forgot to put them back on."

"Why were they off?" he asked, his hands digging possessively into my hips. I rubbed my nose on the bare chest skin exposed by his unbuttoned dress shirt.

"Sit tight, and I'll show you," I said, pushing him onto the couch. Then I ran into the bed closet and carefully laced up the edible underwear and bra I had made. The bra was made of several strips of the raspberry fruit leather, with little heart pasties to go over my nipples, which were already hard, thinking about him sucking the lingerie off of them. The underwear was high-cut, the front and back triangles held together with another strip of the raspberry fruit leather.

I pranced out of the closet. "What do you think? Or actually, I guess, how does it taste?"

Archer was delightfully rumpled, with his shirt draped on the side of the couch. A slow grin spread across his face. He was hard through his boxer briefs.

"You actually made edible underwear," he said. "You bad little painter." He walked over to me and spun me around. "Nice lingerie. Too bad I'm going to have to rip it off with my teeth."

I laughed as he tore at the little fruity scrap of a bra. He sucked a nipple through the pasties then moved up to kiss me. I tasted the sweetness and the slightly sour punch of raspberry on his mouth.

I leaned over the stool I used to sit on while painting. Archer kissed down my back to the edible panties. He nuzzled them and licked me through them.

"These are actually a bit more of a barrier than they look," he said. "You're trying to block me from my goal." He ripped the edible panties off with his teeth in one motion. Then his fingers stroked me.

"Let me make it up to you," I said, my voice sounding throaty. Archer teased me with his cock, sliding it in my silky wetness. I moaned as he ran his cock along my slit, teasing my clit. I ground back against him. My legs felt shaky. His hand was back, stroking my pussy. I heard him rip a condom open with his teeth. He pulled my head back and kissed me.

"I'm going to make you feel good," he said against my mouth, letting me kiss the sweetness on him.

"I thought you were going to punish me," I whispered. He slapped me lightly on the ass.

"There," he said. "Now for the makeup sex."

I gripped the easel and cried out as he entered me. The thrusts were powerful. He gripped my hips, and I moaned, arching my back.

"You're such a bad little painter," he said, his voice low in my ear as he fucked me.

"Harder!" I begged him. My breath came out in high-pitched moaning gasps as he pounded into me. His pure desire was almost shocking. That I could make a man like Archer come undone was intoxicating. His balls slapped my ass with every thrust. His fingers stroked and teased my clit. I moaned, the feel of his huge cock in my pussy making me gasp and grind back against him.

"You do like it when I fuck that tight little pussy with my cock, don't you?" Archer growled in my ear. All I could offer in response was unintelligible begging for him to make me come. A few more thrusts from him, and I crashed over the edge, pleasure flooding my entire body. I moaned softly as he continued to fuck me, drawing out the orgasm.

Archer came with a curse. His mouth buried in my hair. "That was a nice surprise," he said. "Now I have one of my own."

"Oh yeah?"

"Pack your stuff, Hazel, because we are going to my hotel for the next week to, oh, forever, because once you have Archer Svensson in one of Archer Svensson's hotels, you will not want to come back to this death-trap building with the creepy little bedroom closet."

"I can't move into your hotel!" I protested.

"Too late. I already have the presidential suite booked for us."

I put my hands on my hips.

"Hazel, do it for the good of the conference center. Why won't anyone *please* think of the conference center? Besides, you can't live here while the judges are in town. There're going to be people here cooking, and the judges will come visit for the gallery walk. It looks bad if you're living here."

Archer could tell I was wavering, and he upped the ante. "I'll feed you breakfast in a real bed surrounded by yards of open floor. The bathroom is bigger than Ida's dildo. It has *really hard* water pressure."

"You are so dramatic," I huffed. "Fine. I will stay with you in your hotel *only until* the judges leave."

He dragged me to him, kissing me. "Now we need to celebrate with a snack."

I looked at him askance as Archer picked up the scraps of the edible underwear and took a bite.

"I can make you a sandwich," I said hesitantly.

"It's delicious," Archer said as he helped me pack, and by helped, I meant he started emptying out drawers of stuff into several large Louis Vuitton suitcases he had brought with him and set near the stairs.

"This seems highly unnecessary," I said.

"Says the person who made her own edible underwear," Archer countered, still munching on it.

"I can't believe you're eating that," I said, making a face.

He looked offended. "Of course I'm eating it! That slight hint of pussy really makes it meow!" He pulled me in for another kiss. "Don't make that face, Hazel. It's organic!"

CHAPTER 50

"**C**ome to my hotel so I can make you come in my hotel," I told Hazel as we finished packing the clothes and other accessories she would need for the next week.

I loaded the bags into the car. "Have you ever been to one of my hotels?"

She shook her head. "Nope. I don't think I've ever been to a really nice hotel, period. The nicest place I ever stayed at was a hostel in Berlin. It had a tiny balcony, and I only had to share it with two other people."

"Well, prepare to have your mind blown, and other things as soon as we get to the room." I pulled up in front of the tall, narrow brick building with the ornate detailing that was my first hotel in Harrogate. Actually it was my very first hotel ever.

As the valet unloaded her bags onto a cart, I asked, "Could you take Ms. Loring's stuff to the presidential suite?

She's going to be staying with us over the next week. She's in charge of the Art Zurich Expo bid. Please make sure she has anything she needs."

I greeted the hotel manager and answered a few of his questions. Then I turned back to Hazel.

"Let me give you the grand tour." We started in the bar. "Originally, this building was a hotel in the very late eighteen hundreds. It was the first building in Harrogate to have electricity. It was designed in the elaborate beaux arts style, and we managed to salvage the majority of the original wood and millwork, and," I said, walking into the large atrium, "this chandelier."

"Wow!" Hazel gushed, admiring the sparkling crystals. "It's beautiful!"

"I love hotels—the luxury, the anonymity," I said. "It feels like you can be anyone in a hotel."

"Look at these friezes," she said, gesturing to the colorful paintings on the plaster as I led her up the curved grand staircase.

The elevator pinged at the top of the stairs. "We installed elevators in a look identical to the originals," I explained. "We reused all the paneling and old hardware but brought them up to code. They even have operators. People come here just for this moment," I said, sweeping my hand out. "It's like the staircase scene in *Titanic*."

I chatted with the operator while we rode the elevator up. When we arrived on the twelfth floor, Hazel kept pausing on the way to the presidential suite to admire the paintings.

"I told you I liked art."

"Yes, but these are old masters style paintings," Hazel said, inspecting one. "For some reason, I thought you were more into contemporary art."

"I can't very well put up a Basquiat painting in the Corentin Hotel, can I?"

"Are you worried about people stealing them?"

I shrugged. "That's why I have elevator operators."

The presidential suite was one of my favorite suites in any of my hotels. It had a sitting room, a fireplace, and a balcony that looked over a solarium in the back of the hotel.

Hazel explored while I instructed the valet on where to place her bags. She was texting someone when I walked back into the sitting room after tipping the valet.

"You can't still be working."

"There's always an emergency," she said.

"You're too stressed out," I told her, taking her phone and tipping her head back, kissing her deeply. "You know," I said softly. "There's a really good remedy for stress."

"Oh yeah?" she breathed as my hands slid under her skirt.

"Better to demonstrate, don't you think?"

I leaned her back on the couch. She took off her shirt and undid her bra. I licked and sucked each nipple until it was rock-hard as my hand pushed up under her skirt. "It's called finger painting, and a lot of executives use it as a way to both destress and get into a more creative headspace."

Hazel's eyes were half closed as my fingers played in the slickness between her legs. I slowly pulled down her panties. I leaned over and kissed her, my tongue tracing the inside of her mouth as my fingers made the same pattern in her pussy, hot against my hand.

"I need to fuck you again," I murmured against her mouth as she ground against my hand. I kissed her tits, letting her nipples roll in my mouth.

She had one leg on the ground, the other on the couch. Her legs were splayed, revealing the warm dark-pink flesh. She moaned as I bent down to lick her pussy, lingering on her clit, making her hiss then moan.

"I want you so bad," I told her as she whimpered. "I'm going to fuck you so hard."

I rolled a condom on my aching-hard cock. Hazel was still slick from earlier and tight when I entered her. I let my hand tangle gently in her hair. She gasped as I fucked her. With every thrust, she let out this whimper that drove me crazy. Her nails dug in my back, her legs wrapped around me, coaxing me deeper. I knew she was close, by the way she trembled. She came, sending me over the edge. I came in her, breathing hard.

Smoothing the loose tendrils of hair out of her face, I planted little kisses along Hazel's temple to her jaw then to her mouth.

"You were right," she said after her breathing returned to normal. "It is nicer to be fucked in a luxury hotel."

CHAPTER 51

Hazel

I was up the next morning before the sunrise. The Art Zurich Biennial Expo judges were coming today. My stomach jumped with nerves.

Archer yawned. "Relax," he said, spooning and snuggling me. "They aren't coming until lunchtime."

"There is too much to do," I told him, trying and failing to push the muscular arms off me.

"Just a little bit longer," he said into my hair.

"You need to get up with the sun. Don't waste the daylight."

"It's summer," he grumbled. "The sun rises at five thirty in the freaking morning."

"Suit yourself. I'm going to be in the shower, all by my lonesome."

Yesterday, I was too busy appreciating Archer to fully appreciate the bathroom. It was all white marble, with brass accents and crystal. I stripped off my clothes and turned on the water and almost cried at the amazing water pressure.

I luxuriated in the spray as I let the water flow through my hair. Just because I could, I closed my eyes and did yoga poses in the large, steamy shower enclosure.

I shrieked as strong arms grabbed me, turning me around. Archer's muscled chest glistened under the spray. He had a condom in hand.

"Consider me awake," he said.

"See? It's not so bad getting up early if there's something nice waiting for you," I told him.

"You mean something sexy," he said against my mouth as his hands wandered over my skin, caressing my breasts and cupping my ass.

I leaned against the shower wall as Archer teased my pussy with his fingers. I gasped, the steam making me hot and relaxed. Archer opened the condom packet, rolling it on, then ran his cock along the length of my slit, playing in my opening and teasing my clit.

"I need you," I gasped.

He gripped my hips and entered me in one smooth motion. I moaned as he fucked me slowly, two fingers rubbing my clit while he slid in and out of me.

"Your pussy is so hot," he whispered in my ear, his deep voice rumbling around the shower enclosure.

"*Faster*," I begged.

He planted kisses along my neck. "I think I'll do it nice and slow."

I moaned, my voice echoing around the shower as he fucked me slowly.

"Please, Archer, I need you," I mewled. He turned me so I could plant my hands on the shower bench. My ass arched up as he increased his rhythm, drilling into me. I was slick and wet for him. His fingers worked my clit while he pounded into me. I came with an honest-to-God scream of his name.

"Phew," I said, pushing the wet hair out of my face as the spray washed away our lovemaking. "Maybe that was a bit much this early in the morning."

"I can never have enough of you," he said, kissing my forehead and nose and mouth. "I could just stay here and fuck you all day," Archer murmured, plastered against me. "Isn't this nicer than the bed closet?"

"So much nicer," I agreed.

"I have hotels like this everywhere," Archer said, expression devious. "Hang out with me, and we won't run out of spots to fuck."

"As much as I want to," I told him, "I also want to give the judges a good first impression of Harrogate, and that first impression is lunch."

Chloe was waiting outside the café when Archer and I arrived. A tall platinum-haired man stood with her.

"This is my boyfriend, Jack," she said after giving me a hug.

Another tall, attractive man. Here we go. Hazel, for the love of art, don't blow it.

"Very nice to meet you," I enunciated and extended my hand stiffly.

Jack took it, a little miffed. Archer was biting down a laugh while we shook hands.

"It's not funny!" I shrieked at him. "You know I have a problem. You need to stop having so many egregiously attractive friends and family. It's not right! He's like a walking, talking Dentyne Ice commercial. I mean, look at him!"

"He's a hunk," Chloe quipped.

I snapped my mouth shut. My face burned.

"Don't feel bad, Hazel. Of course you're starry-eyed seeing me, especially if Archer's your standard. I am much more impressive by comparison," Jack joked as he and Archer started unloading Chloe's SUV.

"Please," Archer snorted. "She was tripping over herself when I walked into her café. But then, I do have that effect on women."

"You know," Jack told me, "I have several brothers, if you don't want to deal with Archer."

"Hey, I have brothers too," Archer protested. "Maybe I want to keep it in the family. You don't know."

Chloe and I ignored Archer and Jack while they bickered like brothers.

"I have to make sandwiches for Ida anyway," I told her as we walked into the café, "so I was just planning on making extra for lunch."

"I have the salads prepped, but I need to assemble the rest of the dishes," Chloe said, inspecting the boxes of food. "Baked goods are baked. I have the boxes already at the hotel to place in the judges' rooms. Those cards you made are beautiful, by the way," Chloe said. "Did you see them, Jack?" She pulled up the image on her phone, showing him the hand-painted cards I made, with the sandwiches on one side and scenes of Harrogate on the other.

"You guys are going all out," Jack said, impressed. "I'm glad I put my factory here before this place explodes. You're going to be internationally known."

"That's the plan!" Archer boasted.

Lunch was set out on the upper floor of the Corentin Hotel. It had a great view of the city. The weather was perfect. I was wearing a skirt and sleeveless silk blouse with a funky gold necklace I had gotten as a gift from one of my old friends from art school. She had created one of the sculptures on the art walk.

I fussed with the little cards I had made for the food.

"This looks great," Chloe said, offering me a glass of wine.

Jack and the Svensson brothers had come to the welcome reception. The all went over to greet Meghan and the mayor, my great-uncle, when they arrived. Mayor Barry came slowly over to me. He was a large man and needed a cane.

"This is my great-niece," he boasted, patting me on the shoulder and addressing several judges. "She organized all of this."

"The Svenssons contributed too," I said.

"It's important that business is also on board," Greg added. "We want to see this biennial happen. It would be a boon for Harrogate."

Archer kept me by him as we mingled with the judges.

"Hi, I'm Maxine, president of the Art Zurich board," a middle-aged brunette said, introducing herself. "This is Matt Thomas and Zarah. One name."

Archer kissed Zarah's hand. "Lovely as always to see you." Zarah was an older woman with high cheekbones and a shock of white hair. She also didn't look all that impressed to be in Harrogate.

"It's a bit small," she said. "We just came from Granada, in Spain. It's a historic Moorish town. These official visits are a bit stuffy and fake, but I suppose it's part and parcel of the job. Let's get on with it."

"She's going to be tough to impress," Archer whispered. "Her family's trust donates tens of millions to the biennial expo."

"Chloe!" an older woman exclaimed and rushed over, her husband in tow.

"This is Trudy and Bernard. We're neighbors," Chloe explained to me.

"We're huge fans of Chloe's. The cookies waiting for us in our rooms are exquisite."

Trudy kissed me on each cheek.

"Welcome to Harrogate," I told them.

"We're excited to see what you have planned!"

"Speaking of," Archer said, "I think you're up."

"Thank you all for coming," I said, drawing their attention to the front of the room. "I'm the head of the art committee of the Harrogate Trust. It's a partnership between business, government, and citizens in our small town who want to make sure Harrogate is the best it can be. One of the things that makes our city unique and a good choice for the Art Zurich Biennial is the cooperation of all our stakeholders. Please grab some food from the Grey Dove Bistro. Chloe is bringing a franchise here. It's just one bellwether of the business and interest Harrogate is attracting."

I sat down next to Archer, and he squeezed my leg.

While people ate, we heard several presentations. The mayor gave a talk about the city and its transformation. Then Mace talked about the technology resurgence and new tech industries in Harrogate and the surrounding areas.

Finally Archer stood up to talk about the conference center. The judges seemed impressed as he wove a story of the history of the chocolate factory, its closure, and his vision for it. He ended on the painting I had made.

"How'd we do?" Archer asked after the afternoon session had adjourned. The judges were going to have a couple hours' break, then there was cocktail hour and dinner.

"I'm feeling really good about this," I told him.

"I had a joke about ceramic dildos," he said, "but I decided against it."

"Ceramic what?" Mace asked.

"You mean to tell me you don't have a handmade ceramic dildo?" Archer asked in mock horror. "You're so sheltered."

CHAPTER 52

Archer

After a late night of cocktails, dinner, and after-dinner drinks with the Art Zurich judges, the next day started too early. I chauffeured Hazel back over to her café to prep breakfast with Chloe.

"You don't have to drive me. I can take my bike," Hazel said.

"What would the judges think, Hazel, if they saw you huffing and puffing down Main Street?"

"I don't huff and puff on my bike," Hazel said.

"You do, and it's adorable," I said. "Look at us. We're like Victoria and David Beckham, Bonnie and Clyde."

Jack was in the café already with Chloe. Hazel had given her a key.

"Sorry we're late!"

"Considering that you had to drag Archer behind you like deadweight," Jack said, "I'm surprised you even made it here at all."

"Do you have any inappropriate remarks to get out of your system around Jack?" I asked Hazel.

"No, I'm fine," Hazel insisted.

"See, Jack? Guess you're not that impressively attractive after all."

"You know, I see now why Greg is consistently amazed how you manage to function," Jack shot back. "I had so little faith in you, I even brought Liam here for reinforcements."

"Are you going to help, Archer?" Liam asked. I looked between him and Hazel.

"No inappropriate comments for Liam? Good. He *is* the least attractive Svensson."

"Uh, excuse me?"

"I think I'm inoculated against Svenssons now," Hazel said.

"Geez, I'm a little hurt!" Liam complained.

"I like your dress," Chloe said to Hazel. "It's very nineteen fifties."

"Thanks. It has pockets." The black dress was formfitting in the bodice but flared at the waist to a scalloped edge.

"I picked it out," I said.

"I don't know why you're bragging," Liam sniffed as he carefully sliced tomatoes.

"You hold that really well," Hazel commented.

I laughed.

"There is nothing inappropriate about that statement," she cried. "I meant that he holds the knife very professionally!"

"We all know Archer is a twelve-year-old boy at heart," Liam said.

"While we're grateful for the help," Hazel said, "don't you guys have to work?"

"We're billionaires," I said. "That's one of the perks. We can play hooky in the middle of the day."

"I mean, it's not that middle," Liam countered. "I woke up at three a.m. to come here. Not that I'm trying to guilt-trip anyone. I needed to meet with Mace about the new factory anyway."

Chloe added, "I bribed him with cookies."

"I would make an inappropriate joke about eating your cookies," Liam said, "but then I figured Jack would kill me."

"That is a correct assessment," Jack said.

After preparing all the food, we loaded everything up and took it over to the hotel after dropping Jemma off at Ida's.

During breakfast, Hazel passed out itineraries while I chatted up the judges.

"How is everything?" I asked Zarah, determined to make her like me. I was always very charming, but Zarah looked down her nose at me.

"It's an adequate display," she said, picking at her food.

"I hope you're wearing your walking shoes," Trudy was saying to Maxine.

"Oh, you know me. I can walk a mile in these heels."

There was more than a mile of walking. First, we had to walk for the architecture tour.

Olivia took the judges, Harrogate Trust members, and city representatives to several historic buildings. These included the judicial building, the town hall, and the old mayoral mansion, which was now a museum. Then, we went to one of the shared work spaces in a renovated warehouse. Finally, Olivia announced we would be touring the old

Harrogate estate, aka where my insanely large family now lived.

"I didn't realize this was on the tour," I told Hazel in a low voice as we filed onto the luxury bus.

"The estate is a great example of historic architecture," she whispered back, squeezing my hand.

I braced myself as we drove through the gates. "For the love of God, I hope Remy doesn't insist on showing them the bunker."

Otis, Theo, Peyton, and several of the other boys were waiting, dressed in slacks and shirts, with freshly washed hair, when we walked inside.

"What a gorgeous house," Maxine gushed.

Hunter greeted the judges. "We're very pleased you could stop by. As you can see, our family is committed to art. I believe many of you have visited one of Archer's Manhattan hotels," he said while Otis handed out fruit-infused water and cucumber sandwiches.

"That is so extra," I bent down and whispered to him.

"Shut up, Archer."

Hunter's eyes narrowed almost imperceptibly. Otis gulped.

"While my brother Archer has an impressive collection of contemporary art in his hotels, our family is also committed to historic art. During the renovation process, we restored all of the old paintings left with the house," Hunter explained.

"This house is quite large," Olivia said, "so we're going to see the highlights."

We trooped to the clubroom with the giant antique globe and a random suit of armor then to the library with the mezzanine all packed with books then outside to the grounds.

"We regularly have events for the town here," Hunter said. "One can imagine that during the Art Zurich conference, we would host more intimate art events here." He looked at Meg when he said that.

"This is lovely, just lovely," Trudy said with a sigh.

"This is the cottage Mace and Josie are going to be living in. I'm currently renovating it, up to historical standards of course," Olivia explained.

"There's an extra cottage on the property," I whispered to Hazel. "We could just live there instead of your creepy apartment. I also have a tiny house."

"I'm not living in a tiny house," she hissed.

"Don't knock it 'til you try it!"

After leaving my family's estate, the bus drove up the hill to the Svensson PharmaTech campus for a quick tour of the facility and a walk through the art trail.

"What a beautiful art walk!" Maxine said.

"It's going to extend to the conference center," I explained as I led them down the path, "which is where we're having the gala this evening."

"We'll have the bus bring you all by so you can see it at night. With the lights, it's quite spectacular."

"And you'll have all of this built out by the time the Art Zurich Biennial happens?" Maxine asked. "Presuming Harrogate wins the bid?"

"Of course," I told her. "Already in the works."

Zarah looked dubious. "There's the pressing question of hotel space…"

"There will be hotels," I assured her.

"I sure hope so," McKenna said sweetly. I could tell she was enjoying twisting my arm. There was no way I was going to give her what she wanted in exchange for the land. I hoped Garrett had something devious up his sleeve.

CHAPTER 53

Hazel

"I think they were really impressed," I said to Archer as we began the gallery walk. My Art Café was one of the first stops. Otis and Theo had come with us since their art was the best, and they walked stiffly beside Archer in their formal clothes.

Of course my spirits sank when we filed into my gallery and were greeted by Ida standing proudly in the middle of the room.

"*She is not supposed to be here*," I hissed to Olivia.

"Grandma, we're doing a tour," Olivia said, trying to subtly hint that Ida should remove herself immediately. Ida was, of course, incapable of subtlety in any form.

"I know!" Ida exclaimed. "And I wanted to tell all you judges that these ladies and this fine, and I do mean *fine*, gentleman here have worked very hard to make Harrogate look good. We participants of the art retreat learned so much from Hazel as our teacher. You can see our work on the walls and displayed out."

Please don't bring the dildo. Please don't bring the dildo.

"And this," Ida said, "is what I made." There it was—the dildo in all its glory.

Archer sucked in a breath and covered Otis's and Theo's eyes as Ida walked slowly around the room with her piece of pottery. I had visions of my life, dreams, and ambitions collapsing around me in a fiery inferno.

Then Zarah clapped her hands, laughing. "This is brilliant! I love this! Finally someone who knows how to have fun with art. This is really delightful."

She bent down to smile at Otis and Theo. "And you even have children involved. What a fabulous idea to have children and elderly together, creating. It's so very European. Marvelous, simply marvelous!"

"You should see the edible body paint," Ida continued. "Oh, go on, Hazel. Show the woman."

I wanted to die. Archer, for once, looked stunned.

"Edible body paint?" Matt asked.

"It tastes good," Ida said. "Hazel is a real good cook."

"When did you have it?" I demanded.

"I made Jemma steal it for me," Ida said.

My face burned. The judges all seemed taken aback. Zarah cackled. "Don't get your panties in a bunch over a little creative foreplay. Why, you should have seen me in the seventies. Now *there* was a time for art. I was in an artist commune in Wyoming, and a woman there made edible body paint. I've never been able to replicate it. She took the recipe with her to an early grave unfortunately."

Ida pulled a little glass vial out of her bag. I resisted the urge to snatch it from her.

"This is perfect. Have you used it?" Zarah asked me as she inspected the vial.

I nodded. I didn't dare speak.

"On him, I presume?" Zarah asked craftily, looking at Archer.

"With whipped cream," I said faintly. McKenna had a high flush on her cheeks.

Zarah linked arms with Ida. "It's a pleasure to meet a woman with a true artistic spirit. You're coming to the gala, I'm sure?"

"I'm on the VIP list," Ida bragged.

"I'm drinking beforehand. At my age, you have to do everything and anything to take the edge off. Come have an aperitif with me, Ida. I need to hear all about your creative vision. Can I keep this, and you'll send me more of course?" Zarah demanded, waving the bottle of edible body paint at me.

"Of course," I said, my voice cracking.

"I need to sit down," I muttered to Archer as the judges all went out the door to the next gallery. Archer shoved a bottle of brandy in my hand. I took a swig and coughed.

"Ida to the rescue, I guess," he said as I took another swig.

"Sure. Why not?"

There were a few galleries in Harrogate. McKenna insisted that none of them were as well curated as hers, so she was the last stop on the tour.

I looked around at the paintings hung carefully on the wall in McKenna's gallery.

"This is a Gergiev original," she said, pointing to one painting. I knew that artist; I wrote a paper in school about her artwork. She was big in the seventies, and her paintings still sold well.

I studied the painting while McKenna talked about how prestigious her gallery was. The painting looked—well, it looked off. When McKenna's back was turned, I hung back and took several photos with my phone.

After the tour, Archer and I went back to the suite at the hotel to dress for the gala that evening. We showered, and I opened the closet next to one of the bathrooms. My gown was freshly steamed and hanging in the large closet.

"I always wondered, why do you even need a closet at a hotel?"

Archer shrugged. "To put your gown in. Where else are you going to hang it?"

I watched him. He stood naked in front of the bathroom vanity. The heat and all the brandy earlier were doing weird things to me.

"All that talk of edible body paint making you horny?"

"All that sexy naked man in a stupidly attractive hotel room is making me horny," I replied.

"I thought I was the stupidly attractive one," he said.

"Must be if I'm practically living in your hotel with you."

"This is nothing," he said. "You should see my Manhattan condo." He was tipped upside down, doing that thing to make his hair look half wild. I paused to admire the view.

Archer stood up, his abs flexing, and he grinned. "Hazel! I never took you for the creepy ogling type."

"I'm trying to control myself. I don't want to be late."

Archer sauntered over to me, cupping my breast through the soft bra.

"This fabric is really amazing," I said. "I thought lace was supposed to be itchy."

"It is nice," he said, slowly running his hands over me.

I swallowed. "I wonder what they use. It can't be cotton."

"Whatever it is, it's nicer than the edible underwear."

"I put a lot of work into that!"

"I know," he said, slipping his hand between my legs, "but with these, I can feel how soaking wet you are."

I swallowed again. My throat was dry, and my voice came out more like a croak. "I'm going to have to change."

"Hmm? My apologies," he said, stepping away and walking out of the bathroom.

I almost screamed. I readjusted the bra and panties and fanned myself.

"One more thing," Archer said, coming back in, holding a box. He opened it. Inside was a huge asymmetrical gold necklace studded with amber and emeralds.

"This is insane!"

He shrugged. "It goes with the dress. It was the only piece that would work. I could have had something ordered, but you said not to go to a lot of trouble…"

"Are you going to get dressed or just watch?"

"Watch," he said smugly. "We need to make sure it will work." He helped me put on the large necklace. It sat just over my cleavage.

Archer leaned back against the bed as I admired the jewels in the mirror.

"I love how nice your tits look in that lace," he said, kissing my neck. His cock was hard through the thin fabric of my panties. He kissed down my back. I spread my legs slightly for him. He mouthed me through the panties.

"Fuck!"

"That's what I wanted, but you didn't want to change your panties."

"I have extra," I said, biting my lip to keep from crying out as Archer slowly moved the panties aside and licked me.

He reached up and unhooked my bra. It fell to the floor, and my panties joined shortly after. I shivered as Archer stood up and turned me around, kissing me deeply. Archer placed two hands on my waist and easily lifted me up onto the marble vanity. The Ming vase next to me rattled slightly. Archer rolled on a condom, kissing me as I spread my legs, needing him.

He entered me smoothly then fucked me. My nipples brushed against his muscular chest. He gripped my ass as he fucked me, his cock rubbing against my clit with every thrust.

The counter was shaking slightly, and I grabbed the Ming vase. I didn't want it to fall, but I didn't want Archer to stop either. I came with one hand on the vase, the other tangled in Archer's hair, biting his shoulder.

"Fuck," he said in my ear as he thrust a few more times. "I guess you are going to need new panties, huh?"

I was feeling loose and a little warm when we went downstairs.

"That's a wonderful scent," Zarah said, air-kissing me on each cheek. "Lust mingled with an expensive perfume. Makes a woman irresistible." She winked.

Archer had several limos waiting outside for the judges and one just for us.

"First stop, the art walk," he said as the chauffeurs helped the judges into their limos. "We'll stop by briefly so you all can see it at night."

It was magical at night. The chandeliers sparkled in the trees, framing the entrance to the art walk. We weren't the only people out for a stroll in the warm summer evening. With the sculptures lit up along the path, it felt like a hidden fairy path the way it meandered through the trees. I waved to Josie as we passed her and Mace.

"This is like those old Victorian parks where people would just go out strolling to show off their outfits," I remarked. "I can't wait for it to connect to the conference center."

There was a photographer there taking pictures, and I posed with Archer. He was dashing in his tux. It fit him perfectly, accentuating all the nice bits.

If the art walk was magical, the gala space was otherworldly.

The former factory had been transformed. Sheer drapes hung from the rafters. The freshly cleaned windows sparkled, and strings of lights marked the path to the entrance.

In the entryway were easels with my paintings along with plans and a physical model of the convention center design. The place was packed. Svensson PharmaTech had purchased a number of tickets to give to their employees. There were also a number of people from town attending.

"Let me see your dress!" Jemma squealed. I spun around. The dress flared around my legs.

"Let me see yours! I love the lace and the edging detail," I said, admiring Jemma's black dress and elbow-length gloves.

"We look so good."

"Olivia's dress is cool. It's very architectural." It was made of a stiff white fabric that folded around her elegant frame.

After the mayor made a speech and we posed for pictures, Archer handed me a glass of wine.

"We so have this in the bag," he said, clinking our glasses together.

"I was a little worried there for a second," I told him. "Ida really came through." She and Zarah were laughing like old friends next to the bar. The bartender watched them in bemusement, and the two older women drunkenly flirted with him.

"All's well that ends well," Archer said and shrugged. "Let's dance." A local band was playing vintage versions of popular songs. Archer led me out onto the dance floor and twirled me around. The singer crooned, and the band played a jazzy song. The dress flowed around me like Cinderella's gown. I felt safe and loved in Archer's arms.

A slow song played, and he tenderly stroked my face. "You make me so happy," he whispered to me and kissed me.

When the song ended, he brought me another glass of wine and a plate of cheese and crackers, macaroni and cheese bites, and conch fritters. Then we watched Hunter and Meg studiously ignore each other.

"You think we can convince them to dance?" Archer whispered to me.

"Doubtful." I giggled.

CHAPTER 54

The gala lasted well into the early morning. Ida and Zarah closed down the party. Hazel and I were there until the bitter end because we were organizing the Art Zurich bid, and a good host didn't leave before his guests.

"You guys are too big of hitters for me," I told Ida. She and Zarah were doing shots on the dance floor. The band was packing up, and all the lights in the event space were on. Hazel was nursing a sparkling water and sat slumped on a bench in the corner.

"Getting old there, boyo?" Ida asked.

"Ms. Ida, we need to pack this up," one of the workers said to her, shooing her off the dance floor.

"Come to my room. I have a minibar fully stocked compliments of Mr. Svensson here," Zarah said. She and Ida stumbled to their limo, arm in arm.

"I really don't know what to say," I said, sitting next to Hazel.

"I mean, what can you say?"

Hazel and I rode back to my hotel. Hazel was half asleep slumped against me in the limo. I picked her up easily. The hotel was quiet when I walked in. The chandelier sparkled soft spots of light on the floor. Hazel murmured and snuggled against my chest. I thought my heart would explode. It felt so right being with her. I loved that she had been so happy and delighted with the gala.

When we arrived at our suite, I set Hazel down so I could fish out the key and unlock the door. No keycards for this historic hotel.

"I love how you think of all the details," she said, blinking up at me. Her makeup was slightly smudged, and she was so cute. I kissed her, opened the door, and twirled her inside.

"I don't want to jinx it," I said. "But I think we are going to win the expo." I kissed her, unzipping her dress. It pooled on the floor, and she stepped out of it. I kissed her as she undid my shirt and unzipped my pants.

"Bed," I said, picking her up and taking her into the large bedroom. Finally, I could fuck Hazel on a real bed. On the nightstand was a bottle of champagne in a bucket of ice. There was also another little surprise.

"I hope you saved the body paint recipe," I told her as I planted kisses from her collarbone down her torso. "It could be your new venture—edible body portraits." I popped the cork and poured a glass of champagne.

"I don't need a whole one," Hazel protested. "I'm going to be a wreck tomorrow."

"We can share. Too bad you're all sharing and caring with Ida, though."

"I can't believe her," Hazel said, stealing sips of the champagne.

"I would also say it's too bad Zarah took all of it except"—I pulled a little bottle out of the nightstand—"I stole some the last time I was at your café."

Hazel giggled as I twisted open the little glass jar.

"It's cold!" she shrieked when I painted a picture on her.

"See?" I told her, drawing a stick figure on her chest. "This is me, and I'm licking you." I drew a tongue.

She looked down. "I think you have some sort of disease." Hazel kissed me sloppily. "Yum! You taste like raspberry alcohol." Then she gasped as I licked every inch of it off her breasts.

I took a sip of the champagne, then I kissed down, down. "And you taste even better."

She gasped and cursed as I held her hips down, eating her out.

"I want your cock," she moaned.

I ignored her and continued to slowly lick her, sucking on her clit and slipping two fingers in the hot tight opening. I moved my mouth up to suck her breasts, rolling her pink nipples with my tongue. The slight traces of the raspberry body paint made her taste sweet. She moaned as my fingers moved in and out of her.

"Fuck me."

"That's what I'm doing," I said mildly.

"With your cock," she whispered, her eyes half closed.

I rolled on a condom then straddled her, teasing her clit with my cock. Hazel wriggled under me, her tits brushing my chest. I pushed into her. Her pussy was so hot and tight.

She wrapped her legs around my waist, arching up against me as I fucked her. She came quickly, tightening around me. She bit my shoulder as I came a few thrusts later.

"I should get that tattooed," I murmured against her neck. "Then when people ask, I'll tell them about my sexy-as-hell girlfriend who gets a little feisty in bed."

She slapped me on the hip.

"You're a little bit kinky, Hazel," I said, kissing her jaw. "Between the body paint, the edible underwear, and this strange obsession you have with my nude form."

"You have an obsession with my nude form," she murmured, pressing herself against me.

"That I do," I said, kissing her.

The next morning at breakfast was rough. I was glad to see I wasn't the only one struggling. Zarah and Ida looked fit, though.

"You young people don't know how to hold your alcohol," Zarah sniffed, filling up her plate at the breakfast buffet.

Hazel stood up. She was a little wobbly, so I held out an arm to steady her.

"I would just like to say thank you, everyone, for making the trip out here. We hope you got a sense of the wonderful projects and events Harrogate has planned. We eagerly await your decision. We know Harrogate is the last stop on your tour. We'll see you next in New York City for the announcement ceremony."

We shook hands with the judges, walked them downstairs, and said our goodbyes.

Ida hugged Zarah. "Make the right choice."

I shook my head.

"I'll call you, Ida," Zarah said. "We'll do lunch."

"How do you think it went?" Chloe asked when we went back upstairs to where the breakfast buffet had been set out.

"We're going to win," Ida said emphatically as she went back for seconds and another round of mimosas. "Me and Zarah had a connection."

"And Tracy loves you, Chloe," I added.

"Thankfully I invited them over for coffee and tea a few months ago," Chloe said. "That was before I knew about Art Zurich or that they were even part of the selection committee."

"I didn't want them to come over. They're really over-bearing," Jack said. "But if it wins the expo, then my sacrifice wasn't in vain."

"The expo will be good for your franchise," I told Chloe.

"Definitely. Although I still need to find someone to run it. Neither Nina nor Maria seem like they want to move out here to run it, especially since we have two new ones in New York City they can run."

"I have to go," Hazel said abruptly. "Thank you so much for all your help, Chloe and Jack. I have the art retreat this afternoon to prep for, so I need to run."

"Very nicely done," Josie said to Hazel, hugging her. "I think we made a great impression."

"I'll see you this afternoon," I said, kissing Hazel then letting her go. "Now I only need to wrangle that strip mall site from McKenna," I said to Mace.

"I can't believe you ever became involved with her," my twin said.

"Of my many terrible decisions, McKenna was *the worst*."

CHAPTER 55

Hazel

From the highest high of the successful weekend showing off Harrogate to the judges, my mood was dashed when Archer started talking to Chloe about the Grey Dove Bistro. I couldn't even hate her because she was so darn nice.

I set about cleaning the kitchen. Jemma already had the sandwiches made and had taken them over to Ida's General Store. A stack of mail heralding bad news taunted me from the table. I picked an envelope at random. A boss babe should not just ignore things that would be detrimental to her business. I wasn't going to tackle all of them, though. I didn't have the energy. I slowly took a knife and opened the letter from the bank.

> You are three months behind on your mort-gage payment. Failure to pay will end in foreclosure. Due to the recent law passed

in the State of New York, you can sell back your debt and turn over possession of your house or property, and our bank will forgive the mortgage. Should you wish to seek this option in lieu of continuing your mortgage, please call and schedule an appointment.

I looked around. Could I give up my building? My credit score was already in the toilet. But if I gave up my building and moved back home with my sister, I could probably eke out enough money from selling paintings. I might even still be able to continue making sandwiches for Ida in her general store. She had a small little kitchen there. Maybe I could also find some sort of receptionist's job at Svensson PharmaTech and start paying back my student debt for real.

I sighed. Was this really the end of the artistic road for me?

I took my bike out to clear my head. It was slightly cloudy, so the sun wasn't terrible. I cycled around town, past the fancy shops, to the art walk. It *was* spectacular. The sight helped me shake off the feelings of sadness. Harrogate was awesome. I struck a power pose next to a sculpture that was an abstract version of a female World War I mechanic.

"You are strong. You are a boss," I told myself. "We slayed it this weekend. The judges loved Harrogate, and they loved the art retreat. You will win that grant. Think positive."

Speaking of art, I remembered my thoughts about McKenna and the Gergiev painting. Had McKenna actually plagiarized it? Could it be a fake? I had my suspicions. I didn't have the resources to investigate it, though. I looked over my shoulder. The Svensson PharmaTech building rose behind me, a vision of glass and steel.

I didn't have Garrett's contact info, so I went in and asked the receptionist if I could speak with him, that it was about the hotel project.

Garrett came down to the lobby a few minutes later. "Hazel." He gave a slight nod in greeting.

I bounced on the balls of my feet. "If you're waiting for me to make an inappropriate comment, don't worry, I won't," I joked. Garrett didn't even crack a smile.

"Tough crowd. Okay. So I was wondering if you could look into something for me. I think McKenna forged this painting." I showed him the picture on my phone and explained about the paper I had written analyzing the style and brushstrokes.

"Frankly, I'm skeptical that an art dealer would jeopardize their career and reputation like this," Garrett said after listening to my spiel. "But I'll look into it. It shouldn't be that difficult to figure out. It will take a bit to confirm things, I'm sure. Don't tell Archer. He's terrible at keeping secrets. He'll probably tip her off, and she'll sue us for slander."

"Understood," I said.

After sending Garrett a copy of the paper I had written and the pictures I took, I cycled back to the Art Café with a renewed sense of passion.

Laugher filtered down the stairs when I walked in. I guessed the retreat had started without me. There were leftover mimosas from breakfast that morning, and I took a pitcher and some glasses upstairs. When I walked into the room, I almost dropped the load.

There, in all his nude glory, was Archer, posing on a chair in front of the class. The light from the windows illuminated his tattoos, accentuating the muscles on his chest.

"This is what I came to the art retreat for!" said Dottie, her freshly done white hair permed within an inch of its life.

"What the—*Archer*!"

"I'm not supposed to move, Hazel," he said, trying not to move his lips.

"Hey there, hot cheeks. We're trying to paint. You can't keep wiggling around," Bettina said.

"He can come wiggle around me anytime!" Ida said.

"I think Ida's really in the sauce," Archer said out of the side of his mouth when I walked up to the front of the studio.

"I'm stone-cold sober," Ida insisted.

"You've had two mimosas and a Bloody Mary and a large portion of whatever is in that thermos."

"Oh, thank goodness," I said, taking a peek at him below the waistline. "You're wearing underwear."

"This is an art class, Hazel. Show some decorum. Don't flirt with the models," Archer said, a smile playing around his mouth.

"You're not a model."

"I modeled for you," he stage-whispered. The seniors all cheered.

"Any tips on nude painting?" Ida called out to me.

"Well," I said slowly, thinking back to my art school days. "If you're having trouble concentrating on your nude model, try to think about painting each part of him."

"I know which part *you* want to paint," Archer said.

"I need a drink," I said, rubbing the bridge of my nose.

"I got you covered," Ida said, holding out a thermos.

"You brought your own?"

"Zarah let me empty out the minibar when I stayed in her suite last night," Ida said. "You make a real nice hotel, Archer."

Archer was actually a good model. When he wasn't making lewd comments, he stayed pretty still. I walked around the class and helped with technique.

"That was fun," Archer said when it was over. He grabbed me and kissed me. "I feel like I'm on vacation. It's nice being with you."

"Okay, Mr. Model, put on some clothes."

CHAPTER 56

couldn't convince Hazel to come back and stay at the hotel.

"I can't just take your money," she said.

"Of course you can," I told her, hovering around her while she packed up the clothes I bought her. I'd had everything delivered to her café. Hazel looked longingly at the dress and all the outfits I'd bought her.

"You should return these."

"Already took the tags off."

"Okay, then take them back to your house."

"You don't want them?" I asked her, feeling slightly stung that she didn't want my gifts.

"I don't have anywhere to put them," she said. "You've seen my building. It's crawling with crickets."

"I'll save them for you. Come visit your clothes anytime you want."

I took her garment bags of clothes back to the estate. I didn't really want to deal with the chaos and listen to Hunter's yelling. I thought about staying in the hotel, but I didn't want to stay there without Hazel. I didn't know where to put her clothes, so I took them to my bedroom. I even cleared a space in my closet for them. I lovingly hung everything up, then I buried my face in one of her dresses. It smelled like Hazel.

Hunter was in the home office working.

"Did you solve the McKenna situation?" he asked when he saw me.

"You're not going to solve it for me?"

"I'm busy with this lawsuit," my older brother replied.

"About the popsicles?" I asked, incredulous. "Dude, just pay to get a food permit. They could have had that by now."

"It's the principle of the thing."

"You mean it's the Meghan of the thing."

"Don't you need to figure out your land situation?"

"Not really."

"I'm *sorry*," he said. "This is *your* business."

"I don't know what to do. Garrett's not being helpful. I wasn't even going to worry about it until I knew whether or not we would be getting the conference."

"They make the announcement in a week," Hunter said. "You need to make a decision. We're not paying for that conference center if McKenna isn't going to part with the land. Has she mentioned at all how much she wants for it?"

"Not a how much, but a who," I said. "She wants me."

Hunter sniffed. "That's not going to happen. As much as you annoy me, in no universe would I consider swapping my little brother for an abandoned strip mall."

"Aw, Hunter," I said, flopping on the large chair next to him. "You really like me!"

Hunter grunted. "If you're just going to lie there and suck up oxygen, the kids could use someone to play games with outside."

"*And* there it is."

Though I needed to figure out what I was going to do about the strip mall site, all I really wanted to do was spend time with Hazel. During the day, I stayed in Mace's extra office, periodically moving his stuff around in between conference calls.

"Are you going to come back to Manhattan anytime soon?" Mike asked, annoyance clearly broadcasted over the phone. "And don't use the conference center as an excuse. Hunter told me that you weren't even doing anything about the strip mall site until after the Art Zurich search committee announces their decision."

"Why do you need me when you have all the Mini-Mes over there?"

"You have barely helped train them! And besides, Eli and Tristan are going back to college in the fall. They can't pick up your slack forever."

"Crackle crackle, you're breaking up."

As much as I liked hotels and making money off of hotels, I really liked Hazel. If I was able to build the conference centers and hotels, then I would have an excuse to spend more time in Harrogate. Or maybe I could convince

Hazel to spend some time with me in Manhattan. She did seem to be all in with Harrogate. Maybe I just needed to show her how much fun we could have in Manhattan.

I hung out at Hazel's café in the evenings. She was furiously working on more paintings. She had several canvases up and went from one to the next.

"You're a machine," I told her.

"Just have to send these paintings out before the award ceremony," she said. "I can't stand the waiting."

I turned her around, kissing her hard. "You need something else to take your mind off it. It will be hot, fast, and dirty," I promised. "You've been working hard. You deserve a reward. That's what your painting says."

The lust was clear in her eyes. Hazel reached up and grabbed me by the shirt collar. "You talk too much," she said, returning the favor and kissing me hard.

"Really? I thought you liked it when I talk like this and tell you how much I want to fuck that tight wet pussy with my rock-hard cock." She shrieked as I quickly turned her around then moaned as I stroked her while unzipping my pants.

"Fuck, Hazel, you're so wet."

"I'm ready for your hard cock."

I pushed into her with a curse. "Fuck, you're so tight," I whispered in her ear.

She bent over the little table. I grabbed her breasts, running my fingertips over her rock-hard nipples, pinching and teasing them as I fucked her. I moved one hand down to tease and rub her clit. She was slick and wet, and she bucked into my hand then back against my cock.

Her breath came out in little half cries, half moans that drove me crazy. She trembled and tightened around me and came with a cry, sending me over the edge.

"Did that distract you?" I asked after she caught her breath.

"I think that went beyond distracting and into I'm-not-going-to-get-much-done-the-rest-of-the-day."

Hazel finished her paintings a few days before the awards ceremony. The ceremony was going to be during a Friday luncheon.

"Pack up your stuff," I told her Thursday after she made a whole stack of sandwiches for Ida.

"The presentation's not until tomorrow," she protested. "And I'm busy."

"You need the distraction."

"I thought that was what you've been doing," she said, looking me up and down.

"Oh, there will be plenty of that. I promise you," I said, snaking my arms around her.

CHAPTER 57

was glad that I could spend the day before the big Art Zurich announcement with Archer. He was a good distraction in more ways than one.

"Do you mind stopping at my office?" he asked as we pulled out of the parking deck. "I need to meet with Mike."

Archer pulled up in front of a huge glass-and-steel tower. I gawked at it as Archer handed the valet the keys to his sports car.

"Big, isn't it? Also"—he pointed to the sign—"it has my name on it!"

"Actually," Greg said, coming up behind us, "it has *my* name on it."

He walked with us to the elevators. Archer pushed the button for the sixtieth floor and the one for the ninety-second.

"I talked to Hunter," Greg began, "about your situation."

"*Not now*," Archer said tersely.

"Fine, but there's a portfolio of foreclosed properties one of my bank contacts says is coming up in Harrogate. I'm going to buy the properties. I might consider allowing you to put a small percentage of your hotels in them. *Might consider.*"

Leaving Greg, we stepped off the elevator on the sixtieth floor and walked into the Greyson Hotel Group office.

"This your first time here?" Mike asked me, standing up to shake my hand. Eli and Tristan were at their desks, poring over spreadsheets and data sets.

"Yes. It's a nice office, but I expected a lot more, I don't know, designy stuff."

"It's all in the next room," he said, ushering me into a bright room with material samples and vision boards laid out.

"This is all for a new hotel going up in Brooklyn," Archer explained. "We have to compete with Airbnb. Everyone wants an authentic experience. This hotel has mainly suites with kitchens and living areas. We're targeting families and people in the city on extended stays." He handed me a board with color samples. "Olivia said you're good with colors and design."

"I'm not an interior designer," I said, looking at the swatches. "I just help her out with her projects."

"Maybe you could help me with my projects," Archer offered.

"What, like move to Manhattan with you?" I laughed. "I spent the critical years of my life slaving away in Manhattan."

"Oh," he said under his breath. "Well, that answers that."

I didn't know what Archer was implying. Did he want me to work for him? Or did he want me to be the fun, quirky artist who he went back to when he was bored? It was one thing to hang with him in Harrogate, but in Manhattan, he was in his element, not mine.

After leaving Archer's office, we drove to his condo. When we pulled into the garage, Archer double-parked, straddling two spaces. "I don't want anyone scratching my car."

"Aren't the other tenants going to be mad?" I asked. "The HOA could fine you."

Archer snorted. "The only people who live here are my brothers. This was the first building Svensson Investment developed. The building isn't that big. There are maybe thirty units, one on each floor, like they have in Brazil."

"It's nice that your family is so close," I said.

"It would be an excessive amount of together time, but my brothers are hardly ever here," Archer explained as he carried my bags to the elevator. "The building has some foundation issues, so one of these days, Greg has to have it all fixed up. Then he may kick us out—who knows."

The elevator let us off into a huge foyer. "You could just pitch a tent and rent this space out for a thousand a month," I remarked.

"Who would live here?" he asked with a laugh.

"It has a window and a plant. I've lived in much worse places."

"This is the side of Manhattan you haven't experienced yet," Archer said. He punched a code into the keypad on the huge metal door. "Welcome to my condo. Please wipe your feet. No telling what's on the sidewalks."

I inadvertently gasped when I walked in. "There is so much art. It's like you're living in a museum."

Every wall had artwork displayed. There were also minimalist tables with sculptures artfully lit by downlights.

„Mi casa es tu casa. Feel free to rearrange anything you like. I've been thinking about redecorating," he said, sprawling out on a large couch that let him stretch with room to spare. I think that couch was bigger than the closet I lived in the last time I lived in Manhattan.

"It's so quiet in here," I marveled.

"Double-paned windows with extra-thick glass really makes a difference," Archer said. "Plus this is an old brick building—it was formerly some sort of shirtwaist factory—so the walls are foot-and-a-half-thick brick."

"It's beautiful," I said, walking around. While the building was impressive, more so was the tens of millions of dollars of art on the wall.

Garrett had mentioned that he didn't think McKenna would jeopardize her reputation by selling a counterfeit painting. But as I looked at the expensive paintings on the wall that could buy my building several times over, I sort of understood it.

"You can have any of these you want," Archer murmured against my neck.

"I don't even have anywhere to put it!" I said, flabbergasted. "Besides, you can't just give someone a Gergiev painting as a gift."

"Why not? Art is more personal than flowers." He kissed my neck.

"Is this the nice surprise?" I gasped. "Fucking in front of expensive art?"

"As much as I'd like to," Archer said, stepping back, "we have plans." He let his hand run down the front of my shirt, grazing my nipples through the soft fabric.

"We do?" I asked, blinking.

"I'm going to give you the full Archer Svensson treatment."

"I don't know if I can handle it. I might explode."

CHAPTER 58

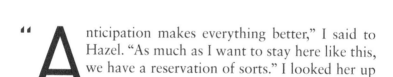

"Anticipation makes everything better," I said to Hazel. "As much as I want to stay here like this, we have a reservation of sorts." I looked her up and down. "You need something nicer to wear."

"I actually put on one of my nicer outfits for the day."

"It's a little business casual for the special celebration evening I have planned."

"What if we lose?"

"That's why we're having the nice evening *before*." I took her hand and led her to the master bedroom.

"I still can't get over how much space you have," Hazel said. "And in Manhattan, no less."

I grinned broadly when she finally noticed the hanging rack with ten-or-so vintage dresses plus shoes and accessories. "One of these should work for the evening."

Hazel slowly flipped through the dresses. "These are nice. Oh, these are really nice. Vintage Max Mara? Where did you find these?"

"Believe it or not, there are companies that source this stuff." I leaned against the back of the couch, my arms crossed, and watched her look through the dresses.

"So did you rent all this?" Hazel asked, picking up a beautiful amber necklace. The silver on it had a nice patina. I could tell it was well-made.

"I bought it."

Hazel looked at me wide-eyed. "Give me a moment to carefully put this necklace down before I drop it—you bought all of this stuff just for me to pick out one outfit to wear?" Hazel sounded a little shrill. She grabbed one of the dresses. "This is vintage Chanel. You don't just buy this."

"There're no refunds, so it's all yours." I smirked.

"All mine?"

I pushed off the couch and rested my hands on Hazel's waist and kissed her. "I also had them pull some vintage lingerie, but the boob cups were weird and pointy."

Hazel laughed. "They didn't quite have that down pat. Plus I don't think I'm quite the size women were back in the fifties."

"I don't know. The buyer seemed to think she found something nice. Maybe later you can model it," I said, kissing her neck. "Which dress are you going to pick?" I asked.

"I don't know," Hazel said. "Can you give me a hint about where we're going?"

"Nope," I said. "Anything here would be appropriate."

After deliberating, she chose a nineteen-thirties gown with feather sleeves in a blush pink. I dressed while Hazel put on the gown.

"I'm so jealous of your bathroom," she called out. "I just want to sit in the huge tub with a book and a cup of tea and some snacks, if we're being honest."

"They don't make gowns like this anymore," she said, coming out and marveling at her reflection in the floor-to-ceiling mirror in the walk-in closet. "If this was the closet I had to live in for years, I wouldn't have had any complaints," I heard her mutter to herself.

I grinned and brought over the box of jewelry.

"Did you seriously buy all this jewelry?" she asked me. "This is a Van Cleef necklace. It's a lot of money."

"It's a gift," I said, draping the long chain of white gold with pearls surrounded by gold beading around her neck.

Hazel looked like an Old Hollywood movie star. The dress accentuated her curves, and the necklace framed her face.

"One more thing," I said when she walked out into the expansive master bedroom. I proudly showed her the final big white box. With a flourish, I pulled the lid off. Hazel carefully picked up the white fur garment, and it unfolded and rippled in the soft light.

"Wow," she breathed. "A vintage white fur cape. It goes perfectly with the dress. This is beautiful. I don't even want to touch it. I want to bury my face in it, but I don't want to get makeup on it."

I wrapped it around her shoulders. "It looks amazing on you," I said. "You are dressed to impress. All the guys' eyes are going to roll out of their heads."

I offered an arm and escorted her downstairs. There was a SUV limousine waiting for us in front of my condo building.

"Overcompensating much?" Hazel teased.

"This is just how I roll," I quipped as I helped her inside.

"Drink?" I offered, popping a bottle of prosecco as the limo pulled out into traffic. She took the bottle from me, took a swig, then grabbed the back of my neck and pulled me to her, kissing me.

I pulled her closer; the cape slid off her shoulders.

"You know, I've never actually gone all the way in a limousine," I said.

"Sounds dangerous," she said as my hand crept under the dress.

CHAPTER 59

Hazel

"We can't do that in front of the driver!" I hissed.

Archer sighed. "Better not. I suppose I can wait. We're almost there." He looked out the window.

"Wait, we're actually going somewhere?" I asked.

"Of course," Archer said, confusion on his face.

"I thought we would, I don't know, ride around in a limo."

"You have so little faith in me. I'm going to blow your mind."

The car stopped, and Archer helped me out. It was dark out, but the trees glowed with lights. Well-dressed couples milled around, taking pictures.

"Welcome to the Museum of Modern Art!" Archer said.

"Is there a party or fundraiser tonight?" I asked him.

He smiled. "There is a new exhibit opening tomorrow. But we're having a sneak preview."

I hoped I looked okay. I fussed with the dress as Archer guided me into the huge atrium. The museum director greeted Archer. They clearly knew each other already.

"Ms. Hazel," he said, kissing my hand. "Always wonderful to meet a fellow artist. And I believe you attended my alma mater?"

"Yes, well, it was a valuable experience."

"Come," he said. "There is an exhibit of Cecile deGama."

"I love her! I attended one of her lectures last year. She has a new series on love."

"I think you will enjoy this."

Archer and I followed the director to the special event space where the exhibition was set up.

I loved Cecile's style. It was somewhat similar to my own though a bit more abstract. Each piece was of a scene about love. A couple kissing, a girl with a little dog, a grandmother with her grandbaby. Archer's arm was around my waist as we slowly walked through the exhibit.

"Her use of color is extraordinary," I told Archer. "I'm glad we came a little early so I could look at these without a lot of people in the way."

Archer chuckled. "We're the only ones here."

I froze for a moment. "*You rented out the whole space?* That seems excessive."

"I don't do things halfway." He led me to an adjoining room with a large window that looked out over the garden. There was a table set for two. Archer helped me into my chair.

"I'm really impressed," I told him as a white-coated server poured me a glass of wine.

Archer beamed. "I plan things really well. I'm the master of grand gestures." He clinked our wine glasses together. "To you, Hazel. We're going to win that Art Zurich Expo, and it's all because of your work and dedication."

I sipped the wine. Compliments always made me feel awkward.

"Once we win the expo," Archer asked, "what are your plans?"

My plans? I couldn't tell Archer how my life was currently falling apart.

"I don't know if I'm going to win the individual grant," I said after a moment. "So it would depend on that."

"What do you have to do if you win?"

"It's open-ended. I promised I was going to continue hosting art retreats and do more public art. So probably more of the same. Though I would be able to hopefully have a nicer space and host better art retreats."

"You should make Ida a resident art-retreat helper," he said slyly.

I almost choked on my wine. "Ida is a treasure, but she does like her alcohol."

"And her dildos," Archer said casually.

"She was happy with the nude modelling session."

The servers set down the first course. We were given crusty bread with an herb butter spread, briny oysters, and a shaved pear and endive salad.

Archer sprinkled some of the vinegary sauce with little bits of onion and pepper on the oysters. I picked one up, and we toasted oysters.

"Cheers! To winning tomorrow."

I ate the oyster in one go.

"That was strangely erotic," Archer said.

"You should see what I can do with a hot dog," I told him with a wink.

"You know," he said. "If your art retreat ever becomes really big, I'm sure we can find some room for you to host it in the exhibition space in the conference center."

"I don't know. I'm sure it's expensive."

"I'm not going to make you pay to use it, Hazel," he scoffed.

"I don't need your charity," I shot at him. Immediately I felt bad. Archer had orchestrated this nice evening. I needed to stop being such a whiny little girl and enjoy it.

I took a sip of wine.

Keep it together, Hazel. This is the nicest date anyone has taken you on and will probably ever take you on. Do not ruin it by being a weird, awkward harpy.

"Hazel, I'm not trying to be dismissive," Archer said. "I like you. I feel like we have a good thing going here. Just enjoy it, and go with the flow."

"Right."

Confidence in one hand, chardonnay in the other.

The tension broke as the server brought out a cold pasta with glassy noodles and tempura fried shrimp, okra, and lotus. I crunched a piece of the fluffy tempura fried vegetables. The batter was slightly sweet, with a finish of salt, and the lotus root was still crunchy.

"This is a really nice summer dish," I said, picking up a forkful of the noodles and dipping them in the small bowl of miso soup.

"Not to be totally uncultured," Archer said after making sure the servers were out of earshot, "but I hope they bring more food than pasta and oysters, or we're going to have to stop at McDonald's after this."

"I thought you might eat me out instead," I said, loving the way his eyes widened slightly in surprise. "I'm sure the servers won't be back for a little bit."

CHAPTER 60

Archer

"You're a terrible tease," I told Hazel in a low voice. "Unless you *do* want me to get under the table right now and eat you out."

"I'm not going to be kicked out before the main course," she said. "And I'm not sure how we would explain that one."

"I could say I lost my cufflink," I suggested.

"I think it would be really hard to lose a cufflink up there."

"Maybe," I said. "Although if you were wearing edible underwear, you could have the excuse that it was just stuck in it or something."

Hazel's foot slipped out of her shoe and slid up my leg. The servers brought out a tray of beef.

"This is Kobe beef imported from the Hyogo Prefecture. Please notice the exquisite marbling," the server stated. "The chef has prepared it three ways. Thinly sliced to dip in this soup—only leave it in for a few seconds—or feel free to eat it raw. Then we have a Chateaubriand cut presented in a sandwich. The beef is breaded with a light egg wash and bread crumbs then put between toasted white bread with a bit of katsu sauce. We have beef lightly seared with grilled vegetables. All of these have very minimal seasoning—the chef only uses salt so you fully experience the flavor of the beef."

"I like my meat raw," Hazel said, picking up a sliver of beef with a pair of chopsticks and slowly sliding it into her mouth.

"I think I really like watching you put all that raw meat in your mouth," I said, my eyes heavily lidded as I watched her chew it.

"It's so good," she said. "I'm not sure if we're going to be able to share. You might need to see if they'll bring you some more of that pasta."

I snagged a bit of the beef before it was all gone though the reality was that I would gladly let Hazel have all of it if she would keep making those sexy noises.

Hazel moaned when she bit into the little bite of sandwich. "It's the texture of a fully toasted marshmallow, except its beef." She held out the other bite to me. "Eat it," she ordered.

I let her feed me, locking eyes. "Delicious. Just like something else at this table."

Hazel visibly shivered.

I picked up a piece of the grilled beef and a slice of eggplant and held it out to Hazel, enjoying the way her lips parted.

"It melts in your mouth, and that's such a cliché thing to say, but it really does. I could totally eat this every day."

"Stick with me, and you can!"

"You're so romantic, offering high-end beef and exquisite works of art instead of flowers and candy. You sure know the way to a girl's heart," Hazel said.

I didn't know why I was so insistent on having Hazel stay in my life. It was starting to come off a little desperate, I thought. But I didn't want to lose her. I would do anything to keep her in my life.

The waiters brought crème brûlée for dessert, and I fed Hazel bites while we looked out over the garden. Someone was having a corporate event, and we watched the people mingle in the space below. Then we strolled through the exhibit again.

"This was the most magical evening ever," Hazel said softly, reaching up to kiss me. "Thank you."

"We should go home so I can give you an even better present," I said as we headed out to the waiting limo. "The evening's not over yet."

She snuggled up against me as the limo pulled away from the curb.

"More meat?" she asked, her hand sliding down under my waistband.

"Better. More dessert," I said, kissing her too, tasting the wine on her mouth. I kissed her slowly as the limo sped to my condo, the colorful night lights sparkling through the windows.

I poured Hazel more wine when we entered my condo. Hazel reminded me of an elegant princess or something as she wandered around.

I brought out the presents I had for her.

"Oooh, what's this?"

"Jewelry? An Ida original dildo? It could be anything! Open it and find out!"

She handed me the wine glass then carefully took off the paper.

"Are you one of those people who saves wrapping paper?"

"You bought a collage from me," she said. "Of course I save wrapping paper, duh."

She opened the box.

"It's not made out of edible anything," I said. "But it's damn sexy."

"I've kind of always wanted a corset," she gushed.

I handed her another box.

"More?" she asked, carefully unwrapping it. Inside were a pair of ridiculously sexy high heels.

"Ready to finish what we were going to start earlier?"

CHAPTER 61

Hazel

"Just give me a second," I said breathlessly. "There are a lot of parts, and I drank a lot of wine. They need to give you directions or something with this lingerie."

There were multiple pieces—the lacy panties and the bra went on first, then the corset. It hooked into the bra, and the straps that came off it also hooked onto the garters on the fishnet tights. At least I could buckle the corset in front. I looked in the mirror, expecting to look strange.

As I studied my reflection, I had to say, I looked freaking hot in the corset. It was one of the less intense kind that ended under my boobs, making my waist narrow and giving me a sexy hourglass shape. It also boosted my boobs up high, and I could see the inner curves of flesh, my nipples barely peeking through the scraps of lace. The bra made a crisscross pattern over my chest to my neck. I turned around to look at my back in the mirror. The panties were high-cut. The straps from the corset lay softly over them.

I strutted out and posed for Archer. "Do I look like a sensual baroque painting?"

"You look hot," he said, his deep voice washing over me.

"That's not very eloquent!" I teased as he approached me, dangerous and beautiful as a panther.

Archer ran his fingertip lightly down the corset then knelt in front of me, pressing his face between my legs and making me gasp. I dragged him back up, kissing his mouth. His slightly stubbly jaw was rough against my skin, and his mouth was hot. He took my mouth with his tongue like I wanted him to take me. Archer moved his head down to lick and nip my breasts through the sheer lacy bra, his fingers pushing their way into my panties, stroking me.

"You are dripping wet," Archer purred, moving up to kiss my neck. "I love it."

He kissed me again, and I bit his lip when his fingers found my clit.

"I want to see you," I said, tugging at his belt.

Archer kissed me and pushed me back against the bed. I watched as he slowly unfastened the leather belt. It rasped as he drew it out of the belt hooks and clunked as the buckle hit the polished concrete floor. Archer undid his zipper, and his hard bulge was outlined under his boxer briefs.

He pushed me back farther onto the bed. I cupped his face, pressing greedy kisses along his jaw as his fingers stroked me through the skimpy lace panties. There was a slight tug at my hips, and I opened my eyes. Archer held up the ripped, barely there lace panties. He tossed them aside then kissed down the corset to my bare skin. Archer pressed his face between my legs, licking slowly, his tongue making twisting motions on my clit.

I let out a stream of curse words as his tongue traced lines of pleasure more intense than his fingers had been able to coax from me. Fingers tangled in his hair, I came quickly as Archer coaxed every shudder from me.

I reached down, feeling the hard bulge in Archer's boxer briefs.

He took them off, throwing them to the floor. "Your tits look so good in that bra," he said, kissing me hungrily. Then he tore it off.

"You shouldn't just rip things like that," I said with a whimper.

Archer pushed me back into the bed. "But I want to give you an honest-to-goodness bodice-ripping evening." He sucked and rolled my nipple in his mouth as he rolled on a condom.

Archer rubbed his cock in the wetness between my legs, then he was in me. I moaned deep in my throat as each thrust rocked me. I wrapped my arms around his neck, forcing my mouth to his. My legs spread wide, begging him to go deeper. Archer's rock-hard cock rubbed against my clit as he thrust inside of me. I let my fingernails rake up his back, catching on every ridge of muscle that rippled under the smooth skin.

Archer stopped.

"What are you doing?" I groaned as he flipped me around.

"I wanted to see a different angle, you know, like how in painting you have to try different viewpoints?"

"That's a real stretch of the metaphor…"

"Really? Because you look positively edible from this angle." He pressed his mouth to my pussy, teasing me with his tongue.

"I want your cock," I moaned.

"So demanding," he said. He stood up. I was on my hands and knees on the bed, Archer standing behind me. He teased my opening with his cock. I arched my back, begging him to take me.

"You want me to come in your hot tight pussy?" he whispered in my ear.

I whimpered, my hips making little circles. Then he was in me again. He had one hand cupping my breast, two fingers pinching and rubbing the nipple. The other hand held my hip tightly as he lazily thrust into me.

"*Faster*," I gasped. "I need you to make me come." The last word was cut off by a moan from the sensation of him. I panted as he fucked me. I felt so hot and charged. I tipped forward on my forearms as he fucked me. His thrusts increased, and his rhythm grew slightly erratic. I came with an honest-to-God scream of his name.

Archer flopped down beside me, hands tracing up and down my body as he kissed me sloppily. "You know," he murmured, "there were several ancient tribes that thought sex rituals were good luck. They would have orgies before a big event like a battle or a hunt."

"Sounds like lies and fan theories," I said, my eyes half closed.

"It's true; I read it on the internet," he said, tenderly kissing my collarbone. "After the session we just had, I know the competition gods are totally smiling down on us." After a beat, he added, "And they're probably really horny."

"What if we lose?" I asked, panic creeping in around the corners of my mind. I barely registered what he said next.

"I'm in love with you, Hazel," Archer said, sounding already half asleep. "Even if we don't win, we'll go to Boston. You'll wear that corset. I'll fuck you in one of my hotels. We'll drown our sorrows in sex and alcohol."

CHAPTER 62

woke up too early when Hazel sat straight up in bed.

"Today is the day!" she said.

I pulled her back down. Her bra and panties were off. The corset was still around her waist. It was so erotic, I couldn't help but kiss her bare skin.

"We have several hours," I said. "And as I promised, I am here to distract you." I kissed her on the mouth. She moaned softly as I moved her legs aside slightly and kissed down her skin, licking her tits and kissing her through the soft lacy corset down to the slit between her legs. She was still wet and warm from our lovemaking last night.

"I don't know if I can," she whimpered as I licked her.

"Oh, I think you can," I said. I raised her up slightly. Her breathing became more erratic, and I rolled on a condom and positioned myself over her then pushed inside of her with a groan.

I ran my fingers over the corset, catching on all the ridges and buckles. I pushed her back into the bed and spread her legs to fuck her, making sure my cock rubbed her clit in all the right ways. I was rewarded with a loud moan, and Hazel tangled her fingers in my hair, pulling our mouths together.

I fucked her faster into the bed, loving the little high-pitched pleading noises she made every time I thrust into her. Her panting got faster and higher pitched as I fucked her, her legs wrapping around me, begging me to go deeper. She tightened around me, and I knew she was close. I sped up, her tits heaving against my bare chest.

Her nails dug into my scalp when she came. I came in a few more thrusts.

"Look who's awake," she murmured as I kissed her nose. "I need a shower."

"But you smell so good."

She scooted out of the bed.

"Maybe we should just skip the lunch," I suggested, admiring the way the corset accentuated her hourglass shape. "Mace can tell us what happened."

"We cannot skip the ceremony," Hazel said.

"Don't be nervous. We're going to win. I know it."

After breakfast, Hazel sat next to me in the car, twisting the strands of her necklace. I grabbed her hand.

"I don't want to lose," she said with a sigh.

"We won't," I promised. "We have a very good chance. Even if we don't win, I think I can still make the conference center work. It might be on a smaller scale and may include more office space. Did you know my brothers Weston and Blade are thinking about moving their company headquarters out to Harrogate? The mayor is offering them tons of tax breaks. If I'm not using the entire complex for exhibition halls, some of it can be a hotel. Also, you heard Greg say he's going to buy more land out there anyway. Don't worry, Hazel. It will be fine."

"Uh-huh."

She was still a ball of nerves when we walked into one of my larger hotels. It had large event space for weddings, charity luncheons, and other events. It was a former luxury hotel from the roaring twenties. Then it had been used as apartments until I purchased and restored it to a luxury establishment. Art Zurich held their annual charity luncheon there.

We filed into the high-ceilinged event space. Hundreds of round tables were set for lunch. Before taking our seats, Hazel and I walked around the room, greeting the judges, representatives from competing cities, and several reporters there to cover the announcement.

Chloe and Jack were seated at our table.

"I'm so nervous!" Chloe said, hugging Hazel. "I hate losing. I want a win!"

"You and me both."

The Art Zurich board filed in and welcomed everyone. Hazel picked at her food through the speeches.

"Not as good as the meat you ate last night, huh?" I whispered.

She rewarded me with a small smile.

"If you do go ahead with the conference center," Chloe said, "what are you going to do about catering? You need a whole business exclusive to the conference center."

"You're not catering?" I teased her.

"I can't even find someone to run my *own* franchise. I might have to move to Harrogate."

"You can stay at my family's house."

Jack looked at me askance. "As much as I like you guys, no."

"We have a tiny house."

"Double no."

I held Hazel's hand through the announcements. Finally after lots of bland speeches, Zarah stepped up to the lectern.

"This is it!" Chloe exclaimed, clapping.

"We're going to win. I know it!" I assured Hazel.

"As you know, the Art Zurich Biennial Expo is committed to bringing art to all places, not just the same few large cities. There is a sense of adventure with good art, of exploration and boundary pushing. The search committee visited many cities around the globe on our quest to find the next Art Zurich host. All the places gave an outstanding show. However, one place went above and beyond. This small but plucky city has everyone on board with living the spirit of art, from the smallest child to the industry scions to the elderly. Everyone in the community is involved to create a true culture of art that is for everyone, not just a few art snobs. This town is Harrogate. Congratulations, and we look forward to the biennial in the next two years. We know we will see great things from you."

Hazel and I jumped up and cheered.

"Conference center, here I come!"

"Oh my God, we did it! This is amazing!"

"Sit down," Greg hissed at me. Everyone else at the luncheon applauded politely.

"See, that's the spirit I like to see!" Zarah shouted out.

"She referenced your art retreat," Jemma whispered to Hazel. "You're sure to win the grant now!"

"As long as it's not McKenna," Hazel whispered.

"Yes, lord, please," I muttered.

Maxine stepped up to the podium, putting on her glasses. "As is tradition, we also award a grant to an artistic resident from the host city. This young woman has done great things in her town from highlighting historic elements to being involved in the committee that organized the winning bid for the biennial. Olivia. Congratulations!"

Hazel looked momentarily crushed. Then she rallied and hugged her friend.

"Nicely done, Olivia," I said, hugging her before she walked up to the stage, beaming.

"All of the entrants represent what this foundation is about—bringing art and creativity to your local communities. Not aiming for international recognition so that you can escape but rather to bring eyes and influence to help raise up your local communities. We think that Olivia has exemplified this spirit the most. Her approach to architecture gives a blueprint for other small towns and designers in those locales to make a lot out of very little. She represents the sprit that has historically made Western New York a unique place. Congratulations, Olivia."

Hazel's friend was teary-eyed as she shook the judges' hands.

We took pictures after the luncheon was over. Hazel smiled, but I could tell she was sad. I whispered dirty jokes in her ear, but she didn't even acknowledge me.

CHAPTER 63

Hazel

couldn't believe it; Harrogate had actually won. But I lost. I was standing outside of the large event hall in a little out-of-the way alcove. A Fang Fei painting above me mocked me as I struggled not to cry. We had just finished taking pictures. Olivia, Josie, Archer, and the rest of the Svenssons were still inside basking in the congratulations.

I hastily wiped at the tears when Olivia hurried through the heavy double doors.

"Hazel, I'm so sorry," Olivia said, running to me, arms outstretched. I hugged my friend.

"You deserved it," I told her, my voice cracking.

"Don't cry," Olivia said, starting to tear up. I felt terrible that I was acting like a little girl instead of being supportive of my friend.

"I'm not," I told her, dabbing at my eyes. "I just haven't had enough sleep."

"I'm so sorry, Hazel," she repeated, grabbing my hands. "We'll split the money."

"It's too late. I'm so far behind on my debt, it would go to waste. Do something awesome with the prize money. It was a long-shot Hail Mary for me anyway."

"Why don't you ask Archer for help?" she asked, petting my hair.

"No way. I had to beg my uncle for money a few years ago, and I'm done with begging for handouts. I'll figure something out."

"What's wrong?" Archer asked, concerned, as he drove us home. "We won. You should be ecstatic."

"I wanted"—*needed,* my mind countered—"to win the grant. Like Chloe said, losing sucks."

"But you still have your business," Archer reminded me. "I know you don't want a handout, but if you do want to branch into catering, once the conference center is up and running, there will be a ton of work."

"So," I said, "you're definitely going to build your conference center."

Archer grinned. "Looks like it. I called in to the city and put it under contract. Money is floating away in cyberspace from Greg's bank account as we drive."

"You have enough hotel space? Greg didn't make it sound like it was going to be enough. What about McKenna?"

"I have something in the works," he assured me. He was being awfully cagey.

"So Mike's just going to let you do the conference center without knowing if you have enough keys?" I pressed.

"Hazel, we won," Archer said. His eyes flicked to me and back to the road. "Not doing the conference center is not an option. I will do anything to make sure this goes off without a hitch."

"Right."

"You want to get a drink?"

I mumbled, "I should do some work." *Slash, pack up my life, wallow, wonder where it all went wrong,* my brain reminded me.

"Are you sure?" Archer asked, pulling up in front of my café. "We should go celebrate. My brother is throwing an impromptu party. Ida might be there covered in nothing but body paint."

"I'm tired," I said.

Archer pulled me into a hug and kissed me. "I'll stay with you."

"No, go to the party. I know your family wants to see you."

Archer gave me a long look. "All right. I'll come back later to check on you."

After he left, I looked around the café. It had been my home and my business for the last year. Now it was slipping out of my fingers.

What am I going to do?

I started with sorting through my mail. There were bills, angry threatening postcards, and another letter from the bank reminding me I could sell back my mortgage under the new law.

I flicked on the lights. Nothing happened I cursed. The power was out. Right, because I hadn't paid the bill. Using my phone as a flashlight, I went upstairs to start packing. Was this really my life? I was moving back to my childhood home—almost thirty and a complete failure. At least I had Archer. But would he want to be with me when he realized how poorly I had run my business?

My phone dinged, making the flashlight flicker.

Melvin: *Hey Hazel! Long time no text!*
Hazel: *Oh my God, hi Melvin! How's Seattle?*
Melvin: *Have a nice house. It's bigger than a closet. I saw you on Instagram! I follow Chloe and she posted a picture you. I've been meaning to tell you congrats on opening your own business.*

I started crying. I could barely text him back.

Hazel: *Thanks, but actually it's about to fail. Packing up now.*
Melvin: *I'm so sorry to hear that! Don't feel bad! Restaurants are hard. There's one down the street from me that's changed owners three different times in the last two years. Just regroup and start another one. You're awesome. You can do it!*
Hazel: *I don't know. I need a change of pace.*
Melvin: *If you want change, you could come out West. I'm sure we could clean out a closet for you to sleep in *grin**
Hazel: *Ha ha.*
Melvin: *No I'm serious. I know for me just escaping New York made me feel like a different person. I always knew you were going to do great things Hazel. Come out to the*

West Coast for a few months and clear your
mind.

Hazel: *I'll seriously consider it.*

Melvin: *Just come! Don't overthink it! YOLO!*

I looked around in the dim light from my phone. Leave Harrogate? Leave New York? It was tempting. But what about Archer? Also what about my debt? With my bags packed on my bike trailer, I wheeled my bike out of the café and locked up for the last time. The letter from the bank about selling back my property to get out of my mortgage was tucked in my bag as I slowly pedaled down the street to the bank.

Terrence, a guy who went to my high school, greeted me when I walked inside, one of my sandwiches in his hand. "Hey, Hazel, we were about to close, but I'll stay late for you!" Terrence said, ushering me to his office. "I owe you especially since you're keeping my grandma out of my hair and convincing her to do something other than yell at the TV. That art retreat was a bang-up idea. Also your sandwiches are great!"

"I'm actually done with the café business," I said, trying to swallow the lump of sadness in my throat.

Businesses fail all the time, I told myself. *You'll start over. It will be fine.*

"I am behind on my payments, and I received this letter." I shoved it at him. Terrence set down the sandwich and took the letter.

"I'm sorry to hear that." He looked sadly at the sandwich.

"There might be a possibility for me to still make sandwiches for Ida," I told him.

"Good! This is the high point of my day. Banking isn't all that exciting, I'm afraid." He pulled up my account on the computer. "Are you sure you want to do this? We might be able to look at some other options."

"Yes," I said. "Hopefully the building will go to a good home."

"Property turns over fast in Harrogate now with the Svenssons," Terrence said, typing on the keyboard. "They snap up anything as soon as it's on the market. I'm putting your building in a package of properties that they're going to buy from our bank."

"Are you really supposed to tell me that?"

He shrugged. "It's all a matter of public record. The system will update tomorrow, and everyone will know who the new owners are. Besides, I'm hoping to stay on your good side! I need more sandwiches. You have to promise me this isn't the last Art Café sandwich I ever eat." He grabbed my hand.

"All right, all right! I'll call Ida tomorrow."

Somehow it did give me a little comfort to know that maybe Archer would turn my building into a very chic, very exclusive boutique hotel. I just wanted the building to go to someone who cared about historic architecture, and Archer clearly did.

Terrence had me fill out several forms. I was there for a half hour after closing while he inputted all the information in the system. Then he printed out the forms and had a coworker come in and notarize it.

"There you are. All set," he said, handing me my copies. "You are officially no longer the owner of the Art Café."

CHAPTER 64

Archer

H azel wasn't returning my calls. It was dark when I snuck out of the party my brothers were throwing at the estate house to go by Hazel's café. It didn't look like anyone was there. All the lights were off, and the door was locked.

Where was she?

"Just give her some space," Mace said when I went back to the estate house. "She was under a lot of stress with the competition. She probably needs to rest. I'm sure you kept her up all night too."

"Mace, there are children present," Hunter warned.

"Holy smokes, I didn't mean like that. I just meant because he's a night owl!"

I went back by the café the next day. It was still locked. I peered through the windows. I didn't see any sign of sandwich making.

Archer: *Where are you?*
Hazel: *Sorry! Went to my sister's house.*
Archer: *Okay… I'll come see you later?*

She didn't answer. I paced around outside her café in frustration. I looked up to see a familiar woman approach.

"There you are!" McKenna said. "I thought you might come by here. Have you thought about my offer?"

"I told you, McKenna," I said in irritation, "I'm not going to date you. I don't want anything to do with you. And don't stand there and insult Hazel."

A car pulled up. The door opened, and my mother stepped out. Why were the two women I despised the most here and the one I loved wasn't?

"Mom, I warned you—"

"I'm not here for money!" she cried. "We're here to help you."

"We?" I asked, eyes narrowing.

"It's an intervention," Merla Vee said.

"I do not want to deal with this," I announced. "I'm leaving."

"But we have information about Hazel," McKenna said. I stopped in my tracks. McKenna had a smug look on her face.

"*What about Hazel?*"

"Dear, sweet little Hazel has been playing you this whole time," Merla Vee said.

"No, she hasn't," I growled. "Stop spreading lies."

"It's not a lie," my mother insisted. She held out several pieces of paper. "I found this in her mail."

"You stole Hazel's mail?" I shouted, snatching it from her.

"It was for a good reason. I'm trying to protect you. Isn't that what mothers do?"

"Read it, Archer," McKenna said.

I looked over the papers.

"This says she was in debt," I said, confused.

"And behind on her utilities, her student loan payments, *her mortgage payments*," McKenna added. "She saw you as a meal ticket."

"That's not true!" I shot back. "Hazel always says she doesn't want a handout, unlike *some people*."

"Don't be naïve, Archer. Everyone wants a handout," McKenna sneered. "Hazel played you. She told you exactly what you wanted to hear."

"This is just speculation. You don't have any proof."

My mother and McKenna looked at each other. Then McKenna pulled out her phone and navigated to a page.

"Look," she said.

"What am I looking at?" I asked tersely.

"The property record for this building," she said, pointing with a French manicured fingernail. Hazel's fingernails were always covered with paint... I shook off the ache and read the web page.

Former Owner: Hazel Loring.
Current Owner: Pending sale to Svensson Investment.

"How?"

"She slipped her building into some property you and your brother were buying," my mother said. "She tricked you into buying it. Now watch, you're going to go confront her, and she'll make it sound like it's a really grand idea, that she can play girl boss and you can foot the bill."

"That's not true. None of this is true," I said, refusing to believe it for a second. "Hazel loves that building; she would never sell it."

After driving around for several hours and trying and failing to call Hazel, I went back to the estate that afternoon and called Greg.

"The property you bought," I said in a rush as soon as he answered.

"You are not going to build hotels on all of it, Archer," my older brother said. "I hear you still haven't figured out how you're going to secure that land from McKenna."

"Look, can you just shut up for once!" I shouted. "Did you buy Hazel's property, yes or no?"

"No, of course not," my older brother said, an undercurrent of anger in his voice. I would probably pay later for yelling at him, but I didn't care. I needed to know the truth.

I breathed a sigh of relief.

"Why?"

"Nothing."

"You better have a good reason for your outburst," he said in a clipped tone. "I will not—oh."

"What?" I yelled.

"Calm down. I will not have you shouting and carrying on. The bank sent me an updated list of properties. Her property was not on the original list, but I'll check this one."

"It's on Main Street," I urged.

"There are two Main Street properties, 506 and 1080."

"Hers is 1080," I said, defeated. "There must be some mistake."

"We didn't seek out and buy these properties. These were all various foreclosures," Greg said carefully. "The only way her property would be in this bundle is if she defaulted on her mortgage and the bank took the parcel back."

I felt sick. "I have to go," I mumbled and hung up on Greg.

Normally that would be a death sentence, but I ignored the angry rings and drove over to Hazel's sister's house.

CHAPTER 65

Hazel

"If you're here for good," my sister Meg said when I was in the kitchen making breakfast the next morning, "I'm going to gain a dress size because of your cooking."

I had spent last night wallowing, watching movies, and eating junk food with my sisters. Now I was determined to face my failure and fix my life—even if all I really wanted to do was curl up in my childhood bed and sob.

"I can find you a job in the city," Meg offered.

"I don't know. I'm not sure what I want to do. Maybe I'll move to Seattle."

"Seattle?" Meghan gasped.

After fielding my sister's questions about why I would move to Seattle, I headed over to Ida's to talk to her about moving the sandwich operation to her store.

"I'm so sorry, lass," she said, giving me a big hug when she saw me.

"If you still want to sell sandwiches, I will need to make them in your kitchen."

"Of course!" Ida said. "I'm offended you would think otherwise! I already had the ingredients dropped off here."

"I can't believe you walked away from your business," Jemma said as we set up in the general store's small back kitchen.

"I just couldn't make it work," I said, trying to sound like a professional woman who had only experienced a minor setback and not a little girl who failed at everything she tried.

"What about Archer?"

"Seems to me," Ida said, "if you're sleeping with a billionaire and his ego, you should be entitled to some perks."

"Archer doesn't have an ego—okay, not *that* big of an ego. But I don't want any handouts. I'm going to figure out what I want. It will just take some time."

"You can have a couple shifts at the store," Ida offered. "Zarah invited me to go on a fancy yacht with her. There's going to be hot crew members and expensive liquor and everything. The timing works out perfectly."

"What about Bert?" Jemma asked.

"What Bert doesn't know can't hurt him. This is a girls' trip."

I felt a little better after making the sandwiches and arranging them in the display case.

"Change is good," I told myself as I stood at the register while Jemma went to pull inventory out of the back storage room. "Change makes you stronger. Adversity is an opportunity to grow."

But sometimes, I decided as the door to the general store opened and McKenna and Archer's mom waltzed in, you could have too much of a good thing.

"Hmm," McKenna said, looking at me thoughtfully and tapping her designer shoe. "So you couldn't hack it as a business owner. Why am I not surprised?"

"If you aren't buying anything, then stop scaring away the customers," I retorted.

McKenna scowled. "You need to be nicer to me. I'm the future Mrs. Svensson."

"Shut up. No you aren't." My stomach clenched.

"Oh, but she is," Archer's mother announced. "Archer and McKenna are back together."

"It's because he wants the strip mall site. I expect a proposal soon."

"That's not true," I said meekly. Archer wouldn't, would he?

"You two were sleeping together for a few weeks," McKenna hissed. "But Archer and I have a history."

"Unfortunately, my son was using you," Archer's mother said, her face a mask of sympathy.

"No, he wasn't."

"*Of course* he was," McKenna sneered. "I mean *look* at you. You have nothing, no business, no career. You're not even that pretty. You think someone like Archer would want someone like you?"

I chewed on my lip, repeating to myself that McKenna was only trying to psych me out.

"That's what happens when you play at our level," she continued. "It's all transactional. Archer needed Harrogate to win the Art Zurich Expo, so he used you. Now he wants the hotel site, so I'm more valuable to him."

"It's true," Archer's mother insisted. "He's just like his father. Those types of men take whatever they want. He didn't become a billionaire by being nice."

McKenna smirked then turned to leave. Over her shoulder, she launched one more parting shot. "Just watch. He's going to dump you over some stupid, silly thing, tell you it's all your fault so he doesn't have to feel bad."

I slumped at the counter.

"I have to go," I said when Jemma returned.

"Oh, uh, okay, what happened?"

But I was already out the door.

A storm was forming as I pedaled home. I just wanted to sit up in my room with some candles, a good book, snacks, and hot chocolate.

Surely McKenna was lying. *I mean, come on!* Archer already said he didn't like her. But he had been cagey in the car. Maybe his mom was right. *Maybe Meg was right.* How well did I really know Archer Svensson?

To clear my head, I set about making creamy macaroni and cheese with spicy chorizo sausage, sharp cheddar, and cavatappi noodles.

The doorbell rang just as I slid the casserole dish into the oven.

"Archer!" I exclaimed when I saw him standing there on the porch. He gave me a tight smile. His shirt was slightly damp from the rain. "Do you want to come in?"

He ignored the invitation. "I need to ask you something." He shoved a wad of papers at me. "Why didn't you tell me?"

I unfolded the papers. My heart sank when I realized they were overdue bills and late notices. "What are you doing with these?" I screamed at him. "Were you snooping in my mail? This is my private business."

He glared at me. "Why didn't you tell me?"

"It's not any of your business," I said flatly, crossing my arms.

"Okay," he said, nodding. "Okay, well, why didn't you tell me about your building?"

"What?"

"You sold your building," he pressed. This was not the easygoing and friendly Archer. He was abrupt and mean.

I was flustered and on edge. "Again, *none of your business.*"

"Oh, except it is my business because you tricked me into buying your building."

Right, what Terrence had said—he was selling my former building to the Svenssons.

"It wasn't a trick," I stammered. "I just—there was this thing at the bank."

Archer was staring at me, his gray eyes flat.

I was getting tongue-tied. "I just, you know." I waved my hands, flailing. "I'm not sure how it works. There was a law passed, and I wanted the building to go to a good home. It seemed like it might be for the best. Maybe I could come by if you put a hotel in it. You know, for old times' sake. I could run a restaurant or something or, I don't know, do the room service thing. Sorry, I'm not making any sense. Do you want some pasta?" I offered hopefully. I needed to start over. I sounded like a lunatic.

"No, thank you. I understand perfectly well," Archer said, his voice a low snarl. "McKenna was right. Apparently, you just wanted me to buy your building and let you play entrepreneur."

"I wasn't playing restaurant!" I snapped at him. "How dare you? You saw how hard I worked!"

"I saw what you wanted me to see."

"Get off my property!" I screeched at him and ran inside. I watched through the window as he walked angrily to his car, slamming the door after he sat inside. I watched in horror and confusion as he drove off. What had happened? I spent the next half hour staring at a wall until the smoke alarm went off.

Meg came home as I was pulling the pasta out of the oven. It was a little burnt. I set it on the counter and stared at it. Then I remembered what McKenna had said—that Archer had been using me and would find some dumb excuse to dump me and make it all my fault. I wiped tears away angrily with the oven mitt. *Screw him.*

"Hazel, what happened?" Meg cried, dropping her purse and running to me.

"That stupid Svensson," I choked out, pushing her away and running upstairs. "Dinner is on the table. I'm not hungry."

I was looking at flight tickets to Seattle when Meg came upstairs, followed by Minnie and Rose.

"I had Minnie buy you some donuts to cheer you up," Meghan said, opening up the box to show me.

"I love donuts," I said and started sobbing. "I'm moving to Seattle. I'm going to live with Melvin."

"I can't believe you're leaving!" Minnie yelled. "How can you do this to us?"

"It's just for a little bit. You can come visit me," I said, feeling guilty.

"I'm never coming to visit you!" Minnie declared, crossing her arms and not looking at me.

"This is why I told you two to stay away from the Svenssons," Meg said to Minnie and Rose.

"Yeah, I see that now," Rose said. "Screw Archer. Screw Hunter. Screw all of them."

"I told you, you can't trust the Svenssons. They only care about themselves," Meg said.

"I guess I should have listened to you," I said, my voice rough with tears. "I just thought..."

"You thought he would be the answer to all your problems and that he would be there for you? Yeah. I know that feeling," Meg said, rubbing my back.

"But I didn't want a handout," I told her. "But the whole time he was treating me like a child, like someone he could buy off when I became inconvenient."

"He used you and tossed you away. Sounds really familiar," my sister said angrily. "So you're just going to turn tail and run?"

"I guess I am."

"No," Meg said. "You have to fight."

"I'm not like you," I sniffed.

"What happened to all your boss babe quotes, hmm?" Meg retorted. "I have one of your inspirational paintings in my office. When I'm feeling down, it gives me a pep talk."

"There is no force more powerful than a woman wearing heels, determined to rise!" Minnie quoted.

"You need to go have the last word. He can't treat you like this," Rose insisted.

"You know what? You're right! Bring the donuts," I told Rose. "We're going to the Svensson estate."

CHAPTER 66

Archer

"**S**o that's it," I said when I told my brothers what had happened. We were sitting in the kitchen. Mike brought liquor, and we locked the kids out. Greg had driven to Harrogate and was now sitting across from me.

"You acted very uncharacteristic over the phone," he had explained. "I thought you were going to do something rash."

"I don't understand," I said, staring at my drink. "I'm good with women, like *very good*. How did I screw this up?"

"How *did* you screw this up?" Mace asked.

"Maybe we should ask our resident expert at screwing over women," Garrett said tersely.

Hunter ignored him and continued eating his sandwich. He did not seem as concerned about the situation as I was.

"You made your bed," he said around the sandwich. "Now you have to bear the consequences."

"You're eating Hazel's sandwich!" I yelled at him. "You think you're going to eat another one of those? No. You're bearing the consequences, too, so maybe try to be a little more helpful and brotherly."

He looked down at the sandwich. "Fuck."

"Now you know how I feel!" Garrett yelled at him. "Your idiocy has cost me business calls and several tickets. Enjoy that sandwich because that is the last one you'll ever eat."

Hunter glared at me. "I can't believe you would inconvenience me like this, Archer," he said, his voice full of reproach.

I gestured at him with my drink. "You? What about me? I just lost the love of my life. And apparently she was just using me to buy real estate."

The doorbell rang. There was a mad dash of yelling and pounding feet as all the kids ran to be the first to open the front door. We could hear them chattering through the walls.

"I thought you were going to break them of that habit," Greg said.

"There are other people in this house who could do something. I don't know why you all expect me—"

The kitchen doors swung open. They revealed Hazel wearing a black apron covered in flakes of sugary glaze, holding a box of donuts, and sporting lemon custard filling and chocolate sauce on her cheek.

"You," she spat, gesturing with the half-eaten donut in her hand, "Are a piece of shit. You don't get to use me for your stupid little backhanded dealings."

"Holy smokes," Mace said, looking concerned. "I think she's here to kill you, Archer."

"I'm not here to kill him. However, I am here to tell you that from this day forward, I will be making your life a *living hell*. In no universe are you allowed to use me to secure your convention center and then try and dump me by feeding me some bullshit excuse about how it was my fault. You are a sociopathic billionaire playboy, and I hope you and McKenna are miserable together!" She stuffed the entire rest of the donut in her mouth and chewed, looking like an angry chipmunk.

I looked blankly at her. "First of all, we've been over this. I'm not getting back with McKenna. I don't care what she's offering. I don't want it."

Hazel looked stunned. I set my glass down and stood up to take the donut box out of her hand before she dropped it.

"I didn't use you. I love you, Hazel."

"No, you don't," she said abruptly.

"Of course I do. And it's not infatuation." I reached out and wiped the donut filling off her cheek. "Did I ever tell you how awful my father was?"

"A little bit," she said in a small voice.

"He would take wife after wife, most of them teenagers. He would promise them the world, then once they were at the compound, his wives would be forced to live in abject poverty. My father would only show up to impregnate them or yell at the kids they would pop out every year. I hate my father. I will never be like that," I said, needing her to see. "I will never use you. I will never hurt you."

"Oh. I'm sorry." She looked down at her apron.

I tilted her chin up. "There is only one woman for me, and that's you, Hazel. I want to marry you and live with you for the rest of my life in a ridiculously nice house, then die and be buried together. I have some grave plots already picked out."

She rolled her eyes.

"You don't like the fancy house? Fine. We can fix up your café and live there. Although if we stay in that building, it's probably going to cave in around us, so we might be doing the dying-together bit before everything else."

"That was creepy and weird, Archer," Greg said.

"Yeah, maybe you should have a do-over," Mike suggested.

"But McKenna said—" Hazel protested.

"Don't believe anything McKenna says," I snapped, then I thought about it. "And I should probably take my own advice."

"You came over to my house and accused me of tricking you into buying my café," Hazel said, arms crossed. "Is that why? Because of something she said?"

"We just didn't understand why you would sell it," I told her. "I thought there was no way you would ever part with that building. You love your café and your studio. But then my mother showed me the bills and the late notices…"

Hazel looked angry. She snatched a donut out of the nearby box, and I flinched as she raised her arm… and took a bite.

"Sorry," she mumbled around the pastry. "I'm getting sugar on your suit."

I let out a breath and took one of the donuts for myself. "I thought you were going to throw that at me."

"I wouldn't waste good donuts!" Hazel said in horror.

"We don't want to waste donuts!" I heard Chloe call out.

Hazel immediately grabbed onto me and starting sobbing.

CHAPTER 67

Hazel

"Why are you crying?" Archer asked, wiping at my face. The tears were smearing with the donut filling and sugar. I was a freaking wreck.

"It looks like a bakery war zone in here," Chloe said, walking into the kitchen with Josie.

"What did you do, Archer?" Josie warned. "Mace told me you screwed up."

"I didn't do anything!" he protested. "I'm trying to make her explain why she had us buy her business."

"You sold your café?" Chloe asked me. I could only nod. "Why? I thought you were doing great."

"No," I said, wiping my face on my apron. I smeared a splotch of cheese sauce on my face for my trouble. Archer wiped it off and licked it.

"Hmm, that's tasty."

"Archer, you can't just eat stuff you randomly see on someone," Hunter reprimanded.

"Sure I can. It shows a baker that everything on, and in, her is great tasting." He petted my hair. "I'll just give you your building back, Hazel. Problem solved!"

I shook my head. "I don't want a handout. Besides, I don't have a viable business plan."

"You make really good sandwiches," Mace said.

I shrugged unhappily. "It doesn't matter. I can't compete with the Grey Dove Bistro. Chloe's restaurant was going to take away any customers I had. It sucks because you're so nice, Chloe."

Chloe ran to me, hugging me.

"I didn't realize! I thought you had other things going on. You seemed so confident!"

"I'm not," I admitted. "I'm a mess."

Chloe and Josie guided me to a stool at the long kitchen island.

"Liam said you were on the ledge, so I brought cupcakes," Chloe said, shoving the box in front of me. "Though I see you already have donuts."

"We also brought mac 'n' cheese," Minnie offered as Meg ushered her and Rose into the kitchen, scowl firmly planted on her face. Minnie had brought the casserole with us in the car. It was wrapped in a towel and secured in an old, empty Amazon box.

"We can just hire you here to make sandwiches," Hunter said. "There, problem solved. Honestly, you can just have a hobby bakery if you'll make me this sandwich every day."

Meg peered around me and looked at Hunter. Her eyes flicked between him and the sandwich.

"Oh shit," he mumbled.

"Is that my sandwich?" Meg screeched. "I knew something smelled familiar. I had to spend the last five minutes prying my sisters away from your stupid little brothers after we just had a talk about how shiftless Svenssons are." She glared at Minnie and Rose then turned her ire back on Hunter. "And now you're eating my sandwich. That might be the last one in Harrogate."

Hunter shoved the rest of it in his mouth and chewed furiously. "She's going to make more," he said.

"No, she isn't," Meg said primly. "Hazel is moving to Seattle to live in a closet."

"Seattle?" Archer and all his brothers chorused.

"No, you can't go to Seattle."

"The traitors are in Seattle."

"Frank isn't worthy of your sandwiches," Hunter said with a scowl.

"That comment is totally inappropriate, Hunter," Archer said. "Also, Hazel, your sandwiches are mine."

"You really do make innuendoes out of everything," I said.

"We'll pay you to stay here and make sandwiches every day," Hunter insisted.

"We even have an extra tiny house you can stay in," Remy said cheerfully, dragging Isaac and Bruno Svensson into the kitchen with him by their collars. "Might even get some goats."

"No!" Mace and Hunter said.

Remy shook the two teens he had corralled. "I think there're some crumbs that need to be swept up. If you have energy to flirt, you have energy to clean. Hop to it." He handed each of them a broom. My sisters giggled over the dish of mac 'n' cheese they were sharing.

"Are you going to let the whole table have some?" I asked them.

"We're not sharing food," they said.

"Oh yes, you are. Also, I can't take the restaurant," I told Archer, grabbing plates out of the cabinets then fighting my little sisters for the serving spoon.

"You're not going to Seattle," Josie insisted. "We just won that huge art expo. Between all my marketing work and the Harrogate Trust, I have no time to organize it. I thought you were leading the charge."

"See reason, Hazel," Archer begged. "Think of my conference center and my starving siblings!"

Chloe whistled, and we all shut up. "Hazel is not wasting her time making sandwiches as your personal chef, Hunter, or making you feel good about yourself, Archer, or cooking for a bunch of hungry-bellied men who, though they have billions of dollars and too many degrees, can't figure out how to make a basic casserole between them. No *I* am the one who needs Hazel's skills and business expertise." Chloe turned to me.

"How would you like to be the proud new owner of a Grey Dove Bistro franchise?"

I stared at her blankly.

Striking a cheerleader pose, Chloe stretched her arms, making spirit fingers. "Ta-da! Please help me out because Maria and Nina, who are supposed to be my friends, do not want to move out here, and I'm freaking out about this franchise failing!"

"Are you serious?" I asked, a glob of mac 'n' cheese falling off the serving spoon to the counter. I wanted to cry, but I needed to act like a professional even if I was covered in sugar, cheese, and raspberry donut filling. I swallowed.

"I would like to discuss that. Maybe we could schedule a meeting to figure out the terms. I think this could be a great partnership." I held out my hand.

Chloe shook it.

I cringed when I realized it was covered in donut bits. "Sorry," I said, trying to wipe off her hand.

"What's a few crumbs between bakers? Besides, you saved me!" Chloe said, wrapping her arms around me. "This is going to be so awesome!" She jumped up and down.

"I guess I'll have to learn your recipes."

"Some of them, yes," Chloe said, waving a hand. "But the vision is for each franchise to have unique Instagram-worthy foods. Each franchise should be a destination so people will be compelled to visit all of them, not just the closest one. So think of some unique foods. People already like your sandwiches on Instagram. I posted pictures from the luncheons and breakfasts from two weeks ago. Hope you don't mind."

She took out her phone and snapped a picture of us. "This is going in the history books."

"This is such a wholesome train wreck," Archer said.

"Train wreck?" Chloe snorted. "Do you know how much dough I make, son?"

"Dayum, that's puny!"

Chloe smirked.

"I can't believe you believed McKenna over me," I said, going back to dishing up the pasta.

"I can't believe *you* believed McKenna over me," Archer countered, swiping the dropped cheesy glob off the counter. "You don't even have any idea what she did to me."

"Oh, here we go," Mace said.

"She's manipulative. She—" Archer looked angry. "I wasn't born a billionaire, obviously."

"Of course," I said.

"McKenna thought I wasn't moving up the Forbes richest men list fast enough. Instead of going into hotels, McKenna wanted me to stay in investment. I wanted to start Greyson Hotel Group with Mike. McKenna tried to manipulate me and come between me and Mike and break up our company. Then when that didn't work, she tried to seduce Greg."

"Goodness gracious." Archer's brothers seemed to barely contain their anger as Archer told the story.

"And when that didn't work—because if anyone is immune to crazy manipulative women, it's Greg—she lied to me and said Greg tried to force himself on her. You know what the worst part was? I believed her," Archer spat.

"You were trying to be the advocate," I said. "You are a good man and came from a bad situation. You wanted to give her the benefit of the doubt."

"All my brothers sided with Greg. I didn't speak to any of them for months. The only reason I found out was because McKenna bragged about it on a group text message with her sorority sisters."

"That is really crazy," I said.

"Yeah, I'm an idiot," Archer said.

"You're not," I said, putting a hand on his arm.

"Now she's trying to ruin my convention center," Archer said unhappily.

"She can try," Garrett said, tapping on his tablet. "I think I have a solution to our McKenna problem."

"Tell me!" Archer demanded. Garrett ignored him.

"Deputy Mayor," Garrett said, a triumphant smirk on his face. "Why don't you call a meeting with McKenna? I think we should discuss some property acquisition."

CHAPTER 68

We walked into one of the conference rooms in the town hall the next day. McKenna was already there. She seemed unhappy to see me walking in with Hazel and my brothers.

"You didn't bring Merla Vee with you? Pity," I said. "I was looking forward to telling her to get lost."

"She's out of town," McKenna said, nose in the air.

"Good. She better stay out."

McKenna flipped her hair. "You know my terms," she said. "I tried to make this easy for you and give you an out. I really did. If you think I'm selling my land to you, you're sorely mistaken. Not only that, I'm going to fight your development every step of the way. As a neighboring property owner, I have rights. Our properties share a boundary line. I will not make this easy for you."

Garrett smirked. "But we're going to make it easy for you." Garrett sat down in front of McKenna and slid three pieces of paper across the table. "This is a painting you have in your gallery. Hazel, as our resident art expert, could you tell us what these paintings are?"

"This is a Gergiev painting that is hanging in the Museum of Modern Art," Hazel said. "This is a painting you have hanging in your gallery. The card says it's a Gergiev. This is a Gergiev you sold a year ago for eight hundred thousand dollars."

McKenna crossed her arms.

"You know I studied her paintings in college," Hazel continued. "I am very familiar with her style. The brush-strokes, the use of color—they don't match. See here? These brushstrokes are dissimilar. She would also never use yellow in this manner."

"You can't prove anything," McKenna said. "And if you go around spreading vicious rumors, I'll sue."

"Oh, but I do have proof," Garrett said. "I did some digging into the history of this painting. The previous owner you bought it from? Died a full month before you claim to have bought the painting. He did have an extensive art collection, yes. However, his estate has no record of the painting."

McKenna's nostrils flared.

"Now," Garrett said, writing a number on one of the printouts that seemed far too generous for what McKenna had put us through. "I'm not an art person. If Hazel hadn't brought this to my attention, I don't think anyone would have noticed. And I certainly don't begrudge you the sale. You sold it to one of the Holbrooks, and we here don't particularly care for them. We're willing to offer you a more-than-fair price for the strip mall. Additionally, what we discussed about the paintings stays here with us." McKenna took a few quick breaths. She looked from the number to Garrett's stony expression.

"Fine," she snapped. "Fine. I accept."

Greg handed her a stack of paperwork, and she signed where Greg pointed.

"Man!" I said as we all walked out into the sunshine. "My life is awesome! I have my girl. I have my convention center, my car, my good looks—"

"What about your family, your health?" Hazel asked.

"Right, those are important too."

"Now all we need to do is win the lawsuit," Hunter stated.

"Lawsuit?" I asked. "Are you seriously still suing?"

"Of course I'm still suing," Hunter said. "We have to go in front of the judge in two hours."

"Don't think I'm going easy on you during the hearing," Meg warned. Hazel and I looked between them.

"You know," I whispered to him, "I'm starting to wonder if they don't both actively enjoy this."

CHAPTER 69

That afternoon in the courtroom, Judge Edna perched on her chair, peering over the bench at us. Ida was there with Dottie. They were carrying signs for support for children in Harrogate.

"No protesting inside my courtroom!" Edna said, banging her hammer. "Remember, this is a preliminary hearing in the case of Svensson versus the city of Harrogate. I have drinks tonight with an old college friend. Lawyers, do not waste my time. Now, Mr. Svensson, come tell me why I shouldn't just toss this lawsuit out."

"Your Honor," Hunter said, standing up and buttoning his suit. "Meghan has a vendetta against my family."

Edna glared icily at him. "Actually, I think she has a vendetta against you personally, but go on."

"Objection!" Ida shouted.

"Ida, do you want to be in here or not?" Edna shouted. "I will throw you out even if you are my sister." She turned back to Meg and Hunter.

"There is a system to secure a permit," Meg interjected. "The Svenssons refused to follow the procedures."

"I know there's a system," Edna said, "but Harrogate just won the Art Zurich Biennial Expo. The news media has their gaze on our city. Harrogate cannot be known as the town that wouldn't let children sell popsicles."

"It's a public health risk," Meg insisted. "The Svenssons need an inspection in a kitchen that meets city health department standards."

"Can we come to some sort of agreement so that, God forbid, this doesn't end up in front of the Supreme Court and shame the Harrogate name forever?" Edna asked them.

"*Please, for the love of God,*" Mace said more loudly than he probably intended. Josie shushed him and giggled.

I raised my hand.

"Yes, Hazel? Speak up! This isn't a classroom or a real court session. It's a preliminary hearing," Judge Edna said.

"I think I have a solution," I said. "Nate and Peyton can run their popsicle business out of the Art Café kitchen this summer. It's already passed the health inspection. If they want to keep up with it next year, which is doubtful because food service is a heck of a lot of work, they can work out something more permanent."

"Great. Sounds like a plan," Edna said. "Can you accept that, Mr. Svensson?"

"I have to ask my clients," he replied and turned to Peyton and Nate. They trotted up to the bench. "Can you accept making your popsicles at Hazel's restaurant?"

They nodded. "My clients are fine with this solution. We withdraw the lawsuit."

"Great. File it. I need a drink," Edna said. "It's too hot for all this drama."

"Who won?" Ida asked as we left the courtroom.

"I won," Meg said.

"No, you didn't," Hunter countered. "I withdrew the lawsuit, and my brothers are able to sell popsicles. I won."

"Let's take a vote," Ida said.

"Would you rubber-stamp my conference designs if I give you my vote and"—Archer gestured loosely to the group of Svenssons—"all of my brothers' votes minus Hunter?"

"Not rubber-stamp but, let's say, grease the wheels," Meg said.

"Fair enough. All right men, all in favor of Meg?" Archer's brothers all raised their hands.

"Traitors," Hunter said.

Meg did a happy, wiggly little dance. Hunter almost combusted. Archer and I snickered.

"Since we're downtown," Archer said to me when we were in his car with the AC cranked up, "there's the little matter of keeping my promise to you." He pointed to his hotel building down the street. "My office is free. I have a couch."

Though Archer was the vision of confidence, I felt the sweating start as soon as we walked into the hotel.

"Just act like we're here on business," Archer whispered and pulled me into his office, locking the door. "Which technically we are. In exchange for winning me the convention center," he said, kissing me, "you, Hazel, are entitled to have me eat you out until my jaw locks."

He pushed me back onto the couch, pulling down my pants and burying his face in the wet pink flesh. I cursed as he licked me slowly. He sucked on my clit then back to my opening, trailing his tongue between the two.

"Stop teasing," I whimpered.

He slipped two fingers in my opening. I was slick and hot for his cock.

"I want to enjoy this," Archer said. "I have to make up for lost time."

"I was barely gone for two days."

"Two days too long," he said, his voice slightly muffled. I spread my legs wider and arched up into his mouth.

"I need you to fuck me, Archer," I begged. He moved back, his fingers still stroking me. I heard a condom pack rip open.

Thank fucking God.

"Fuck, I love you, Hazel," he said, pushing into me. I groaned when his large cock filled me.

"You feel so good," he said in my ear. I couldn't speak. My words came out in little garbles of curse words and moans. His fingers worked my clit as he fucked me, his large cock feeling so good as he slid in and out.

"Harder," I gasped. Archer flipped me around and put one hand on my hip. The other tangled in my hair. Then he rabbit fucked me, his balls slapping my ass. Archer slapped a hand over my mouth to muffle the scream as I came.

"I swear," Archer said, "forbidden office sex is the best sex."

We held each other for a moment.

"Okay," Archer said, "now we have to go to Ida's."

"Why?"

"I promised you I would eat you out until my jaw locked then make you pizza rolls."

"The dream team is back," Ida said when we walked in. Archer waved and went to the frozen-food section.

"People are very upset to hear that there won't be any more sandwiches," Ida informed me. "You should rethink your move to Seattle."

"Oh I—"

Archer came over with sandwiches and a bag of frozen pizza rolls.

"What's with the pizza rolls?"

"They're part of her reward," Archer said, "for winning."

"Your reward was pizza rolls?" Ida asked me. "You'd better get something better from that man."

"I mean that was a partial reward…"

Ida gave me a knowing smile. "You get it, girl!" she hollered, giving me a fist bump.

CHAPTER 70

Hazel couldn't still be thinking about moving to Seattle, could she? But that was what Ida had said. I was silent on the drive back to my family's estate.

"Is something wrong?" Hazel asked.

"I meant what I said," I told her when I parked the car in the roundabout.

"Said what?"

"That I love you."

"I love you too," Hazel said, taking my hand.

"And I will eat you out every day," I told her. "I can even do it again right now."

"I might need to work up to that."

"So…"

"So, what?" Hazel asked.

"Are you going to Seattle?"

"No, of course I'm not going to Seattle!" she said.

"Phew!" I said, feeling light as we walked into the estate house. "That's good. We couldn't have you go to the dark side."

"The dark side?"

"My traitorous brothers live in Seattle. I was going to have to move over there with you. I would have been disowned, I would have to grow a beard and become a vegan."

"More likely you would be homeless under a bridge," Greg said. He and Garrett were at the dining room table going over some charts and graphs.

"I think I could open hotels over there," I boasted.

"You're going to compete with Salinger?"

"I might."

"Good freaking luck," Garrett said with a snort.

"You guys and your feuds," Hazel said as several of my little brothers ran into the room. "I can't even keep up with it."

"Help make popsicles!" they yelled, jumping on her. I wrestled them off. "I guess I did just promise we were going to make them."

"What do you have in your kitchen?"

"You can't make popsicles in the kitchen," I reminded her. "We don't have a health permit." I took a set of keys out of my pocket and jingled them. "Who has a health-food-permitted café?"

Hazel was momentarily taken aback. "I can't just take it. I meant you guys could use it since it's permitted."

"Technically it's yours again since you're the new owner of the Grey Dove Bistro franchise in Harrogate, or it will be once the title finishes transferring to Chloe."

"I hope you didn't charge her for it," she admonished.

"Of course I did. I get free meals."

"Excuse me? We're not running a food pantry."

I put the keys in her hand. "Who wants to make popsicles?"

Hazel was giddy when we drove up to her café. "I can't believe this is really happening!"

When we parked behind Josie's car, I pulled out a sign that said, GREY DOVE BISTRO.

"What is that?" Josie asked, pointing to the hand-painted sign.

"This is Hazel's new temporary sign. I painted it myself."

"It looks like something died on it."

"I thought you were in art class, Archer," Mace commented.

"He spent most of the time drinking and loafing around," Hazel said, unlocking the door.

"Why am I not surprised?" Mace asked.

I grabbed Hazel and kissed her, tipping her over like we were in an old Hollywood film.

She yelped in surprise then kissed me back.

"Welcome to your new old restaurant," I said, picking her up and carrying her over the threshold.

"So you all just poured fruit juice and candy into molds?" Hazel asked uncertainly as Peyton laid out the popsicle molds. "I think we need to up the wow factor, don't you?"

I was making popcorn. "Don't mind me. I'm over here slaving away."

"Don't let it burn. Spin it a little faster," Hazel said, holding my hand.

"Aww, Hazel, if you wanted to hold hands, you should have just said." I thought for a moment. "I should have snuck a ring in this thing of popcorn."

"If you propose to me with an expensive ring covered in oil, we're going to have a problem."

"Can you make boozy popsicles for the adults?" Josie asked. Her bare feet were up on Mace's lap, and she was tapping away on her laptop. For once I didn't feel the pangs of longing—I had Hazel right behind me. I bumped her hip.

She jumped up and kissed me on the neck.

"This is so cozy."

"Hurry up with that popcorn!" Josie said to me, snapping her fingers.

"You corrupted her," I said to Mace.

"All right," Hazel said, "let's try something a little more upscale than fruit juice."

She placed various ingredients on the counter.

"Since you're there at the stove already," she told me, "stir these raspberries."

"Aww, Hazel, are these our love berries?" I asked.

"Yes, though let's not ever call them that again, shall we? They are on their very, *very* last leg, so they'll be good for popsicles. We're going to make raspberry lemonade popsicles with a hint of mint."

Peyton was tasked with squeezing lemons, while Nate carefully cut up the mint. Hazel mixed up a batch of bright-yellow lemonade and a batch of pink raspberry lemonade.

"Were going to freeze them in batches so we get a nice swirl."

"These came out beautifully!" she crowed several hours later.

"I love how the yellow and pink mix and that you can still see the bits of raspberry," Josie said.

"There's a splash of vodka in these here," Hazel said.

"The booze makes them a little glossy," Josie said, holding one up and marveling at it. "Looks like a work of art. This is going on Instagram. I'm helping Chloe with some of her marketing. As much as I like Mace's brothers, it's a little dry doing engineering marketing. Bakeries are so much more fun!"

She found a large white plate and arranged sprigs of mint and slices of lemon on it along with the popsicles. Then she snapped several pictures. "Posted!"

"Now that you have a bit of leisure time," I said to Hazel, "while you and Chloe figure out the restaurant—" I stuffed a Popsicle in my mouth and kissed her. "What are you going to do?"

"I don't know. Hang out. Do some art committee work. Make sandwiches. Maybe next week Chloe will have some time to meet."

"I don't know," Josie said, holding out her phone. "I think you're about to be busy."

CHAPTER 71

Hazel

"I'm so sorry, but we sold out of the popsicles already," I told the Instagram influencer who was pouting in front of my shop. The past week the popsicles went viral. It was suddenly the new It food.

Chloe immediately told me I couldn't waste the moment. I had spent the rest of that evening developing several new flavors. The next morning, there was a line of people. The popsicles sold out by that afternoon.

"It's like a pop-up shop," Chloe said a few days later. "We'll just tell people you're open for a limited number of popsicles."

They sold out in a few hours the next day. Though they were supposed to be limited edition, visitors were saying they were coming in from states away. It wasn't in my nature not to feed people, especially if they had been traveling. The crowd waited around while I made several more batches of popsicles. They were sold as soon as they were done.

The next morning, people began standing in line at three a.m.

"This is nuts," I said to Chloe.

"Did Archer's little brothers even help you?" she asked.

"They did a little bit, but Peyton says he's tired of popsicles and he's going to start a bike repair business. Thankfully Jemma's helping!" I bumped hips with my friend.

"Between the popsicles and the art walk, Harrogate is trending on Instagram," Jemma said. "It will probably die down in a couple weeks. That's the nature of these things."

"We need to sell other viral foods," Chloe said. "So think of some other good ones."

"I'll have a brainstorming session later, but I can't think right now. I'm cooking!" I was frazzled. I wanted to go to sleep, Archer's strong arms wrapped around me, but we had the final show for the art retreat that evening.

I finally closed up after lunch.

"That's the last popsicle," I said to the crowd.

Ida knocked on the door after they dispersed. She was wearing an elaborate painter's costume. "I'm ready for my big moment! I want the hulk to have a special place, front and center."

"We'll have to see about that, Ida." I did not want the dildo to have the star spot in the gallery, even if it did help us win the Art Zurich conference.

Archer showed up shortly after with a bag of tools and supplies. He kissed me, and Ida whistled.

"You've hooked a fine male, Hazel!" she said.

Archer smirked and started to hang up the paintings. "I love how all of them are of me."

"This dildo was inspired by you," Ida said, lovingly stroking the sparkly green-and-purple monstrosity.

"I don't know, Hazel," Archer said thoughtfully. "Do you think I should bedazzle my junk and coat it in glitter?"

"Edible glitter body paints!" Ida exclaimed as she stuck price tags on the paintings. "That's your next viral food."

"I'm not sure Chloe is going to go for that," I said as I made the snacks.

After several hours of work, we finally had everything ready for the gallery showing. Remy had come over and laid some old stones out on the little courtyard between my building and the one Chloe already had next door. Then he and Archer strung up lights.

Terrence, from the bank, was the first to arrive with his grandmother, Bettina.

"Wow, that is a nude," he said, looking at the paintings and artwork displayed around the café. "Is that you?" he asked Archer. "I see why my grandmother really liked this place."

"The men and the booze," she said, raising her glass.

More people arrived. The Svenssons all packed in to see Theo's and Otis's paintings. Melvin had even flown in with his husband, kids, and their guinea pigs.

"This is so cozy!" Chloe said. "This is going to be a great partnership. You already did so well!"

Greg, Mace, and Hunter were staring in shock at all the Archer-inspired paintings.

"Geez, Archer, you modeled for them?"

"Yeah, I look great too. Look at that!" he said, pointing to the painting Ida did.

"Why are you yellow?" Mace asked.

"It's abstract," Garrett said, coming up next to them.

"I should have all of these up in my house," Archer decided.

"Please don't," Hunter said.

"Too late," Archer said with a grin. "Hey, Ida!"

"Hey, hotcakes!"

"I'm going to make you famous like Fang Fei!"

"You will?" Ida asked, shaking Olivia. "Did you hear that? I'm going to be just like that grandmother who became a famous painter in her nineties."

"God help us," Olivia muttered to me. Meg wordlessly refilled Olivia's glass.

"You boys ever think about modelling?" Dottie asked, tottering by on her cane, alcohol sloshing out of her glass.

"I can't say that I ever considered it," Greg said slowly. I hurried over to rescue him.

"Honestly, Greg," Archer drawled, throwing an arm around his older brother while I directed Dottie to the snack table to hopefully soak up some of the alcohol. "It's very freeing to pose nude for a dozen admiring eyes."

"I hope you didn't do it in front of Otis and Theo," Mace said with a frown.

"You better not have," Greg snarled.

Archer jerked his hand away. "Please. They were safely tucked away upstairs, painting T-shirt designs."

Greg scowled.

"Also, Greg, might I add that I am very proud of you for sticking it out this long. I know you detest parties."

Greg's scowl grew deeper. "I don't detest parties."

"You constantly complain about them," Mace added.

I hopped up on a table and whistled. Everyone turned to look at me.

"Thank you so much for coming and celebrating a successful art retreat," I announced. "Please enjoy the alcohol and snacks. Hopefully we'll do it again soon."

Archer extended a hand and helped me off the table. Then he got down on one knee.

"You better not be proposing," I warned him.

"Please, Hazel, I know you too well to know you don't want a whirlwind marriage that ends in a messy, high-profile divorce to rival Brangelina. No, this is way better than a ring and a party where you invite a bunch of family members you hate."

"Wedding! Wedding!" Ida chanted.

"Hazel, from the moment I first saw you, I told you I wasn't going to have sex in that closet."

"That's a little ironic," Melvin drunk-whispered to his husband.

"I know you lusted me, but now I know you love me."

"I do love you." I bent down and kissed him.

"You saw me and begged for my paintbrush. And now here it is!"

"What is this?" I asked, taking the box.

"It's a key to one of the cottages on the estate property. Also, there's the key-code number to the Manhattan condo, but I already texted that to you, so it's a little anticlimactic. Yeah I called dibs, assholes. I'm moving out!" he yelled over his shoulder to his brothers.

"Maybe we should split the cottages," Josie suggested. "They're so big. We could do like what the queen does at Windsor Castle."

"I'm not sharing with him," Mace said flatly.

"We're going to be neighbors!" Archer exclaimed.

"Hazel didn't say yes," Greg reminded Archer.

Archer looked at me expectantly.

"Uh, yes?" I was feeling a little overwhelmed, but in a good way.

Archer picked me up and swung me around. "Did you hear that, everyone? Hazel wants my paintbrush!"

"You are too much!"

"But you're going to move in with me anyway, and we'll make paintings all night long." He handed me a glass then opened a bottle of champagne Ida handed him. When he poured it, some spilled over my hand.

"I will remove that forthwith," Archer said. He grabbed my hand and licked it… and kept licking it.

"What am I painting with my tongue?" he asked. "Come on, Hazel!"

I concentrated. It was hard with the slow, steady motion. "I-L-U-V-U."

Archer smiled. "Hazel, I love you too!"

The End

Paint Him

"Really, Hazel," I said, stepping into her café after the lunch rush. "This is a bit much. I feel like you have an almost unhealthy obsession with my phallic symbol."

"If you're going to be here distracting me," Hazel warned as she packaged a batch of green tea popsicles, "you are no longer welcome in my shop."

"I thought Josie said the popsicle phenomenon was going to die down?"

"That's what I thought too," Hazel replied. I snagged a chocolate and sea salt popsicle out of the large freezer that was in the café then stole a kiss from Hazel.

"I love you," I whispered just because I could.

"I love you too," she said as I kissed her again, getting chocolate on her mouth.

I licked it up. "I can't believe you're not making these anymore."

"I wasn't going to sell popsicles this long, but it's been so warm, even though it's after Labor Day, that people still want them. But I swear, this Friday is the last popsicle day until next summer." She sighed. "Now I need to come up with a new dessert." She looked around the small café.

"At least you'll have a brand-new space," I reminded her.

"I'll miss this place," she said. "The contractor is starting demolition next week after we move all the equipment into the new Grey Dove Bistro space next door."

"I won't miss it," I declared.

"Really?" Hazel teased, lightly dragging her fingertips down the bare skin showing through my unbuttoned collar. "No more sex with you behind and me bending over a rickety table?"

"I'm going to bend you over something else," I growled, kissing her.

Hazel laughed. "Keep your popsicle in your pants for now! I have customers!"

It had taken a little getting used to, that the Art Café, now the Grey Dove Bistro, was busy all the time. I missed having the place to ourselves, but then I was glad Hazel was successful. I always knew she would be. Still, I didn't want to lose her to the café. I wanted her to be mine forever.

My twin brother, Mace, grunted when I explained this to him in elaborated detail. He sighed as I described how amazing the popsicle was I had just eaten.

"Why don't you explain to me again why you are still in my office? You have the conference center under construction. Eli said you have internet. You could put a desk in there, a mini fridge…"

"I can't believe I got roped into giving Eli a co-op position," I complained half-heartedly.

Mace looked smug. "You like having an intern. You're more domesticated than you let on."

"Ha!" The reality was that I *was* more domesticated than I let on. That billionaire playboy life? Done. I'd hung up my clubbing clothes and traded them in for an apron. Or rather, Hazel in an apron and nothing else.

Was I still impulsive though? Of course. My latest quest? Make Hazel my wife.

CHAPTER 2

Hazel

I n the months since the popsicles had gone viral, I had
been busy—busier than I had ever hoped to be. It was
awesome, but it was a little tiring. I also felt bad because
I was never able to spend enough time with Archer.

I wanted to just have a night alone, the two of us. But
between the Grey Dove Bistro, his little brothers, my sisters,
Archer's business, the conference center, and the Harrogate
art committee prep for the Art Zurich Expo, it seemed like
we were never together. All I wanted to do was curl up next
to him.

I wished I had someone to come in and give me a
breather. Ever since Minnie and Rose went back to school, it
was a little touch-and-go. Over the summer, I'd been paying
my little sisters to help in the bistro, and I'd really come to
rely on them.

Now, when I wasn't working, I split time between my
sisters' house and the Svenssons' house. The cottage Archer

promised me was on Olivia's to-do list. She grimaced that afternoon when I asked her about it.

"I'm really busy," Olivia said. She was overseeing the decorating of the Grey Dove Bistro next door and had stopped by to go over the plans for the former Art Café building. It desperately needed a makeover.

"I'm so tired of sneaking around the Svennsons' estate," I said. I was packing up boxes of supplies to move next door.

"One last night before you move out of this café," Olivia reminded. "Make sure everything is out by next week. We're going to start demo so that I can see what's going on behind these walls."

She showed me her sketchbook.

"I think we should put an apartment on the top floor of this building," Olivia said. "You can live there slash have your little sexcapade pad."

"It's so small."

"I can work with it," she assured me. "Plus, then, when this space becomes the cool bar slash café while the next-door building is the cool bakery slash café, you can host visiting artists and have retreats. They can stay in the apartment when the cottage is done."

"That would be nice."

"How are the popsicles?" Olivia asked, taking one of the last ones out of the freezer.

"I am so ready to be done. But I need to come up with a new viral dish. Chloe's coming into town for the grand opening tomorrow."

"What are you going to make?" Olivia asked.

"It needs to feel like fall," I mused.

"Pumpkin spice?"

I made a confused face. "Pumpkin spice what?"

"Uh, everything," Olivia said. "I just ordered like ten pumpkin spice candles, and I'm going to have a bath with a bunch of candles burning like that scene from *Elizabeth: The Golden Age*."

CHAPTER 3

Archer

Propose to Hazel—that was my obsession. I needed a proposal plan. There was one video online where a guy pretended to fail to catch a ring and instead fell off a roof, but he had a big inflatable pillow below to catch him. While funny, that might be a practical joke too far—better to keep it classic. All our friends and family would be at the official Grey Dove Bistro opening on Friday. I decided to do it then.

But first, I needed a ring.

Harrogate, while a small town, was able to support some high-end shops, thanks to the high wages Svensson PharmaTech paid their workers. With the Art Zurich announcement, Harrogate also had several artists move into the area to complete work for the art walk and other art pieces around town.

Over the summer, there was a pop-up stand in the town square. The artists would move into booths in the conference center once it was up and running.

I wasn't sure what kind of ring Hazel would want. It had to be diamond but couldn't be something basic. I didn't want to buy her anything McKenna would like.

I decided to impulse buy and sort it all out later. The first place I went had nice rings. I found two minimalist rings Hazel might like. They were thin gold bands—one had a diamond shaped in a triangle, and the other one had a round stone. Both seemed like something she would like. I walked out of the shop feeling good about my purchase. Then I thought, wait, what if she *did* want a huge diamond? I hurried to another store and found the biggest diamond while making sure the settings didn't look tacky. Then I thought, maybe I should buy her something in the middle, like a happy medium.

"You might try a ring with a stone other than a diamond," the salesperson suggested. "We have a nice sapphire ring similar to Princess Diana's engagement ring."

"Better add that to my tab," I told her.

I walked out of the shop. "She has to like one of these. But wait, Hazel likes vintage stuff. Crap." There was another jewelry store that sold vintage rings. I rushed inside before they closed.

"We have a ring from the nineteen twenties that is in an art deco style," the jeweler informed me.

"I'll take it," I said.

By the time I was done, I had a shopping bag full of rings. Did I go overboard? Could you have too many engagement rings?

I drove home to the estate house, the bag of engagement rings in my car. I needed to secure them. I didn't want Hazel to find out and ruin the surprise.

"What are you up to?" Hunter demanded when I walked into the large home office where the safe was.

"Nothing!"

"He's been spending money," Garrett said, not looking up from his computer.

"It's my money. I can spend it how I want!"

"The credit card company called me and said they thought someone had stolen your card," Garrett continued. "You bought *fourteen* engagement rings."

"Archer, what the hell?" Hunter asked.

"You're turning into Dad," Remy said. He was sitting opposite Hunter at Hunter's desk with a big folder filled with pictures and information on goats. "I'm just saying, Hunter, Halloween is coming up. We should have a party and offer hayrides."

"Remy, I cannot deal with this right now. Archer is going off the rails."

"I'm proposing to Hazel," I said.

"Excuse me?" Hunter asked.

"Don't tell Mace. He'll freak out," Garrett said with a slight smirk.

"I thought she wanted to wait," Remy said.

"You really are acting like Dad," Hunter interjected, a pinched look on his face.

"You need to cool it with the comparisons," I snarled. "I am nothing like him."

"You're head over heels in love with a girl you just met," Garrett said in a flat tone.

"Yes, because I am a feeling human being, not some robot like you," I shot back at my younger brother.

"Don't you think you might be taking this too fast?" Hunter asked.

"No, see I love Hazel. I already have our future planned out," I said.

"What happened to waiting?" Remy asked. "If you do this, she may think you don't respect her feelings."

"See, Hazel said she didn't want to pull a Britney Spears and get married on a whim. But I think I found a loophole—we'll have a very long engagement. So she can be my fiancée for three years, and we'll leisurely plan the wedding. Then when we actually are officially married, we'll also have several years under our belt."

"You think you want to slow down?" Remy asked.

"Not really. Our six-month anniversary is coming up."

"From when you started dating officially?" Garrett asked. "Because that is not six months. You need to learn how to count."

"No, stupid, from when I walked into her café and she gave me the best popcorn ever. I feel like it's time."

CHAPTER 4

Hazel

That evening, I looked around. I needed to finish packing and sorting. The walls were bare; my favorite cooking items were in a box to be carted next door. The new Grey Dove Bistro had all new stainless-steel commercial-grade appliances. There were two bright-yellow gas ranges that I would periodically sneak over and hug. Anything not going next door was going to be donated or repurposed.

Chloe: *Any thoughts on a new viral dessert?*
Hazel: *Working on it! I promise I will have something spectacular!*
Chloe: **Smiles**

I felt the familiar churning in my stomach. Chloe was a true boss babe. When it came to running her businesses, she was nice, but she wasn't messing around. I dug through the remaining items in the café that hadn't yet been moved next door. I found the remains of the popsicle ingredients. I had canisters of matcha. Could I make green tea pancakes? But those had already been done.

I sat down to sketch. Though I still made art, mainly to finish up any lingering commissions from Etsy, my creative outlet was now cooking. Hopefully art would help me think up a viral dessert. I had just started the franchise, and I didn't want to fail.

Baking gods, give me inspiration! Who was the goddess of baking? Hestia?

But instead of a visit from a baking goddess, a different kind of god appeared in my café.

"Hazel!" Archer called out. "I'm here to distract you unless you're working on something important."

"It's fine," I said. "I can't really think."

"About what?" Archer wrapped his arms around me, rubbing my back.

"I need a viral dessert."

"Let me be your inspiration," he said, jumping up on the counter and striking a pose in one motion. I laughed, the tension leaving my forehead. Archer swung his long legs over the counter to land lightly on his feet right in front of me.

"You work too hard."

"It will be easier once I'm in the new location. Depending on their schedules, my sisters may come in and work before or after school. It will be fine," I assured him. "We'll see more of each other. I promise."

"You could always live the socialite life as the wife of a billionaire," he offered. I punched him lightly in the chest. He didn't even budge.

"Ow," I said.

"I have very hard muscles," Archer said, taking my hand and kissing it. "And hard other things."

I shivered a little bit. "All that talk of bending over and sex this morning really stuck with me."

"It was very inspirational," Archer whispered, bending down and tipping my head back and kissing me.

"People can see through the windows," I said breathlessly after he released me. He reached out and flicked off the lights. I blinked at him in the darkness as his face came into sharp relief.

"Don't you want to have one more celebratory dirty romp, you know, to really send the place off? For old times' sake?" Archer asked, teeth white in the dark. He kissed down my neck, slowly unbuttoning my blouse.

"I'm covered in sugar, and I think I have chocolate in my hair," I said, biting my lip as Archer freed my breasts of the lace bra and kissed them then licked each nipple.

"It just makes you taste even better," he whispered, his hands sliding under my skirt. He moved his lips down my thigh, maddeningly close to the wet heat between my legs.

"I want—" I gasped, unable to form a coherent sentence. I grabbed blindly for his head, grabbing his hair. Archer chuckled then licked my pussy, teasing my clit. He moved deliberately, his tongue flicking out and hitting all the right notes. Two of his fingers slipped in my opening, and he stroked me while his tongue licked my clit. I was sweaty and moaning when Archer abruptly stood up.

"What the—" He turned me around, stroking me. I heard a condom packet rip. Then he was in me. I still felt raw from his expert mouth, but it was a good kind of sensory overload. The feel of Archer's powerful, muscular body pressing against me and inside of me, his eyelashes fluttering slightly against my cheek, Archer was everything I had always wanted. I felt desired and cherished.

I arched my back, groaning as his cock slid into me. It was hard and fast, just what I wanted. I needed the release. Two of his fingers made fast little circles on my clit, and I came a few moments later. I felt him still moving in me, and I let out little panting noises as his cock ignited aftershocks of my orgasm. When his movements became erratic and more forceful, I knew he was close.

After Archer came, he turned me around, holding me, the *thump thump* of his heart vibrating against my jaw.

I kissed his bare chest. "You're all mine," I said.

Archer kissed my neck. "Always." After a moment, he said, "That was a good send-off. Come to the hotel with me, and we can repeat this. I'll get a room."

"I have to work," I said reluctantly. "Chloe is going to ask me about the new viral dessert tomorrow."

Archer caressed my hips. "I'll stay with you."

"You're a distraction."

"I'm inspiring."

Archer left after pressing me against the wall and kissing me until I was about to beg him to take me to his bed and fuck me. I leaned against the counter and grabbed my sketchbook.

I need a viral dessert. I sketched something that looked like a scoop of ice cream with an STD.

"That's not going to work."

I ripped the page out, then I sketched a corgi cream puff. That might work, but it seemed a little too cute for fall. I filed it away to revise as a Christmas Corgi dessert.

Maybe something Halloween themed? What about a Jack Skellington cookie? I started sketching a man in a suit. It didn't look like Jack Skellington; it looked like Archer.

I looked around the café and remembered when we'd first met and how flustered I was. And then the way he'd pranked me. What was that name he'd used? Donut Danish.

"Oh my God, I'm making a donut Danish!" I clapped my hands. Now I really felt bad about shooing Archer away. I wanted to do something nice for my boyfriend to let him know I appreciated having him in my life. Maybe something nice at the opening party? He did seem to like public displays of affection, if the last hour was any indication.

I wanted to call him and take him up on the offer of meeting in his hotel. But I had to go back to my sisters' house and cook dinner. It was my turn—actually it seemed like every night was my turn. But it was nice to see my sisters more often. I knew Meg needed the help.

Minnie and Rose were at the kitchen table finishing their homework.

"I'm making quiche and a nice salad," I told them.

"I want to come work with you," Rose whined.

"You need to show that you can handle your school-work," I told them. "Remember? Meg doesn't want your grades to suffer."

"What is the next dessert you're going to make for Instagram?" Minnie asked as I chopped up the onions.

"A donut Danish."

"What is that? Like a crème-filled donut?" Rose asked.

"I'm not sure," I admitted. I put the onions in a pan with butter, a little salt, and a pinch of sugar to caramelize. I had pie crust from the café that I brought home and rolled it out.

The quiche was done when my sister Meg returned home.

"Uncle Barry's not coming," she said. "He's out for a dinner with one of the Svenssons."

"Is it Hazel's boyfriend?" Rose asked, giggling.

"You should make Archer buy you a really big house, and we can come live there," Minnie insisted, "so we don't have to stay here with Uncle Barry."

"You're not living on the Svensson estate?" Meg asked brusquely as I served the quiche and salad.

"You could live there too, Meg," Rose said cheekily. "Maybe you and Hunter could get back together!"

I was planning on working on the donut Danishes the next morning. But then there were all the hundreds of sandwiches to make, and because this was the last day, so help me God, that I was serving popsicles, there was a rush of people at my shop. FOMO, or fear of missing out, was hitting hard.

There were still a few people lingering in the café when I was finally able to work on the donut Danishes.

They had to be donuts, and they had to be Danishes. A donut was a donut. A Danish usually has some nice fruit or sweet cheese filling. Since it was almost fall, I decided to try a cheese version first.

I made the donut batter then started a sweet cheesy custard in the double boiler. I set aside several batches to flavor differently. The first donuts I decided to just fill. They didn't look that pretty, though they were tasty. They were just custardy crème cheese filled donuts. Tasty, but not Instagram worthy.

"That's not it," I mumbled. "Danishes are dough with something yummy in the middle. Let's try that."

Unfortunately, the donuts looked like they had a disease when I fried a round donut with no hole and dabbed the cream on top of it in the middle.

For the next version, I fried a regular donut with a hole. Then I filled the hole with custard, using the piper. It looked like a nice pretty Danish, but the custard leaked out the other side.

I looked out the small window to the little courtyard between my building and the brand-new Grey Dove Bistro next door. Chloe was directing while Jack and the Svenssons carted in food that Chloe must have made at the Manhattan restaurant. Several reporters and photographers were already there to take pictures of the grand opening. I needed to change and go over.

I didn't want to leave the donut Danish problem unsolved. I felt like I almost had it.

"I need something to keep the cream from falling out." But I was out of time. I needed to go home and change. I packed up the donuts and custard in a box and put it on my bike. I didn't want it to be accidentally thrown away.

As I biked home, I had another stroke of inspiration— crème brûlée.

"Of course, brain, you had to deliver at the last possible moment. But better late than never," I said, glancing anxiously at my phone clock. I hurried to the kitchen when I arrived home. I grabbed sugar and a small blowtorch from the cabinet. I carefully sprinkled a layer of sugar on the custard in the middle of the donut. It melted and caramelized beautifully. While it cooled, I did the same to several more donuts. Then I flipped them over, smoothed out the filling, and brûléed the other side.

They looked really cool. I bit into one. It crackled nicely under my teeth, and the vanilla-flavored cream was smooth and rich but not too heavy, so it was a nice counterpoint to the donut.

"Perfection!" I crowed. My phone rang.

"Where are you?" Jemma asked. "The party started half an hour ago! Are you coming?"

The sounds of music and conversation blared through the phone.

"I'm coming!" I yelled and hung up. I was covered in sugar. I needed to change, but I didn't have time.

I picked up the plate of donut Danishes, wrapped them up, grabbed some things out of my craft box on my way out the door as a surprise for Archer, tied everything to the bike, and pedaled furiously to the Grey Dove Bistro.

CHAPTER 5

It took a herculean effort to bring my entire family anywhere. Fortunately, we were not bringing the entire clan.

"This is a nice bistro opening," Mace said as Henry clung to his leg and howled. "You can't come. You'll have fun here with Remy."

I was admittedly a little anxious about my big proposal.

"Stop it!" Hunter snapped as my leg bounced in the car as we drove over to the bistro.

Chloe was already there along with her boyfriend, Jack, and several of his brothers. His brother Owen and my brother Liam were setting up the sound system.

"Where's Hazel?" I asked Chloe.

"Don't start yelling at me about where Hazel is," Chloe warned, wagging the sharp-looking knife she was using to cut the Saran Wrap off of various platters of food. I was so nervous, I wasn't even hungry.

Get it together, Archer.

"You're missing two-thirds of your family," Chloe continued. I looked around. I didn't see anyone missing. Even Greg and Carl were here.

"Uh—"

"Where are your little brothers?" Jack asked.

"You seriously want them here, running around?" Mace asked, eyebrow raised.

"I made all this food," Chloe said, puffing up like a cat, "because I thought you were bringing your giant freaking family. Jack, I literally cannot right now. Where is Hazel?" she asked, hurrying over to Meg, who had just arrived at the party with Minnie, Rose, and Mayor Barry.

Jack patted me on the back. "Why don't you go round your little brothers up?"

"They have homework," Mace started to say. Chloe glared at us from across the room.

"I'll go grab them," I said hastily. "It's Friday, Mace. It will be fine."

I wanted to go find Hazel, but Chloe was giving me the evil eye.

I drove back to the estate as fast as I dared. Remy was in the sitting room with my little brothers, promising them a tour in the bunker when I came home.

"Table that terrible idea, Remy. You have all been invited to the grand opening!" My little brothers cheered. "First though, I need some volunteers. I have a special plan for Hazel."

As I made sure the kids were appropriately dressed, I explained their parts to play in the proposal.

"Yeah, but what if she doesn't like rings?" Nate asked. "Maybe she likes something else."

I froze.

"Like a proposal necklace?"

"Or a proposal pony?" Henry said.

"I really wish you had said something earlier," I grumbled. "But it's too late."

"Maybe you could do something more personal, like a card," Otis said.

"Hazel's not going to go for some last-minute macaroni concoction. But…" A dangerous and most likely highly effective idea formed in my brain. "Maybe there's something else we can do for just a little extra assurance."

The green school bus pulled up in front of the new Grey Dove Bistro twenty minutes later.

"Is Hazel here?" I asked aloud after shooing the kids inside.

"No, but everyone else is," Mace said. "I think half the town showed up." There was spillover space in the courtyard and the back patio. People were crammed out on the sidewalk too.

"Anyone seen Hazel?" I asked Olivia.

"Good question," Jemma said, pushing through the crowd. "She said she was on her way, but she should have been here by now."

I rubbed my hands together and snatched up Arlo before he could bump into Greg. My older brother looked down then up at me.

"For shame, Archer. I can't believe you weren't going to include everyone in your proposal attempt."

"It's not misguided! She'll say yes," I said confidently. "I have a plan and a backup plan and a backup to the backup."

"I never said it was misguided," Greg said. "You're my little brother, and I want you to be happy. Besides, she's probably the best you'll ever be able to do, and you should nail that down before Hazel comes to her senses and realizes how obnoxious you are."

"We're having a brotherly moment," I sighed happily, resting my head on his shoulder.

Greg glared down at me, and I scooted away. "Don't push your luck."

Chloe tapped the microphone. "Thank you all for coming. Our baker of honor, Hazel, is on her way. But feel free to eat and grab a drink."

"I'm here!" Hazel yelled, pushing in through the crowd. She was still in her apron, had custard on her cheek, and was covered in sugar. She was beautiful. "I'm here! Sorry I'm late! I had to make these." She held up the platter of baked goods festooned with sparklers and candles. "Where's Archer?"

Chloe pointed, and Hazel turned around and grinned. "Happy six-month anniversary!"

"Hazel, you remembered!" I picked her up.

"Do not squish these! I worked all day on them," she said.

"What are they?" Mace asked.

"Archer?" Hazel prompted, holding a baked good out to me. "What is this?"

I looked at it.

It looked like a normal donut except the round hole was filled with what looked like a mini crème brûlée.

"Is this..." A grin spread across my face. "A donut Danish? Hazel, you *are* the perfect woman for me." I plucked the platter out of her hands and handed it to my little brother Nate.

Then I kissed Hazel properly, to a chorus of cheers and whistles, mainly led by Ida and Zarah, who was in town.

"You taste sweet," she said against my mouth.

"So do you," I whispered, making her blush. "And I have something for you." I decided to just keep it simple. I took off my shirt and got down on one knee.

CHAPTER 6

Hazel

"Why are you taking off your shirt?"

"Holy smokes, Archer!" Mace yelled.

"Put your shirt back on," Greg ordered.

"No!" Ida hollered. "Take it off! *Take! It! Off!*"

There were pink smudges on Archer's shirt as he balled it up and threw it in the crowd. "Hazel, my love." Archer spread his arms wide.

"Is that some sort of art project?" I asked him.

"This is the tattoo that I'm going to get!"

"No!" Greg and Hunter shouted at him.

I giggled.

"You seriously can't read it? Crap. I used hairspray to set it and everything," Archer said, looking down at the pink smudges on his chest.

"Um, I don't think it works that way." I studied the writing. Did it say what I think it did?

"Don't act like you can't read that, missy," Ida yelled out. "He wants you to marry him."

"Aww!"

"Say yes! Say yes!" Minnie and Rose chanted.

"Don't worry," Archer said. "I'm not dragging you to the courthouse tomorrow. We'll have an egregiously long engagement. Henry, the rings!"

His youngest brother scampered over with a plastic grocery sack.

"Dude," he whispered, "I told you to put them in a nice box and you and everyone do a dance like in *Chorus Line*. Honestly, why does Hunter even feed you?"

Otis came running over with a papier-mâché box.

"This is not what I asked for—"

"We all signed it!"

"Why?" Archer asked. "Seriously, it's my proposal. Hazel doesn't want to deal with all of you."

"It's adorable," I said, hugging Otis and Henry.

"We forged Hunter's signature," Theo said matter-of-factly.

"You what?" Hunter yelled.

"Archer, that's so sweet," I told him, getting teary-eyed. "I love how giving and open you are. I love how much you care about your family and this town. And I love that you eat my food."

"And you eat—"

"Ida," Olivia hissed to her grandmother.

"Show us the rock!" Zarah hollered, and she and Ida fist-bumped.

"I'm honestly regretting introducing the two of them," Archer stage-whispered to me.

Henry handed him a box… then another box and then another box.

"How many engagement rings did you buy?" I asked as Archer presented me with a handful of rings.

"Enough to ask you every day for the next two weeks to marry me. Also these are not refundable."

"Oh my word."

"Pick one at random; we're going to let chance sort it out. Let's see what fate has in store for us. Henry." His little brother solemnly selected a small mahogany box and handed it to me.

"No, Henry, geez. Just a moment, Hazel," Archer said. "Honestly, you get what you pay for, and I'm working with free child labor here."

He dumped all the rings in his little brother's arms, took the box from me, and opened it with a flourish.

"Hazel," Archer said seriously, "will you marry me?"

"Yes," I said, smiling a stupid smile, tears rolling down my face as Archer slid the ring on my finger. It was a vintage art-deco-style ring.

"It's beautiful!" I said, admiring it. I bent down and kissed him. "I would be honored to marry you, Archer."

Archer jumped up and swung me around, kissing me. Everyone cheered. Ida opened a bottle of champagne with a sword that she got from who knew where.

"Learned that from Zarah!"

"We are going to have the best engagement ever, Hazel," Archer said, still kissing me and spinning me around. "And you can have a giant wedding of your dreams!"

"With your family, isn't everything giant? That's sort of a given!"

"I have other giant things," he whispered in my ear. I swatted him, then we fielded congratulations.

"Put your shirt back on," Greg said, giving me a one-armed hug as Jack's brother Owen handed Archer his shirt.

"I want to give you a hug," Chloe said, bouncing on her toes, "but you're covered in some sort of sticky fluid."

"Now who's making inappropriately sexual comments?" Jack teased.

"The only thing inappropriately sexual are these donut Danishes," Chloe said, taking one off the platter Archer's brother Nate still carried and taking a bite. "This is insane!"

"I'm still tweaking the recipe," I said as Archer tucked me under his arm.

Henry, Peyton, and several of Archer's other brothers were handing me ring box after ring box.

"Stop it," Archer said, batting at them playfully.

"Archer bought them all for you," Henry insisted. "You should wear them all!"

"A woman can't have too much bling," Zarah said, coming over and hugging me.

"Sorry," I said. "I'm covered in sugar, custard, and—"

"Edible body paint!" Ida finished, giving me a big hug.

"It's good to see two people have fun with sex," Zarah said. "It's liberating to have a healthy sexual attitude."

"So why don't I try some of those rings?" I said loudly to Henry. He and his brothers happily chattered about the rings I should wear.

"This is what being part of their large family is!" Josie said, hugging me. "Welcome officially to the chaos!"

"Will someone at least get me a trash bag so I don't keep feeling bad getting food all over everyone—oh, thank you, Garrett." He handed me a large white trash bag.

"It's antimicrobial and pineapple scented," Garrett said.

"It smells like death," Archer said cheerfully as I put it on over my clothes.

"You have one too," Garrett told him. He waited until we put them on then hugged each of us carefully.

"Welcome to the family, Hazel. I can take the rings you're not using. The kids are going to lose them."

"One's missing," Henry announced.

"Too late," Archer said.

Hunter ordered the little Svenssons to find the missing ring.

Archer pulled me close.

"What did you call this?" I asked, resting my chin on his chest. "A wholesome train wreck?"

"Thinking about backing out?" he asked, touching our foreheads together.

"Hell no! I'm looking forward to it," I said with a big grin. "Nothing better than spending the rest of my life with you, Archer, the love of my life."

He smiled down at me, wrapping his arms around me and kissing me. "You were the love of my life first."

The End

Acknowledgements

A big thank you to Red Adept Editing for editing and proofreading.

And finally a big thank you to all the readers! I had a great time writing this hilarious book! Please try not to choke on your wine while reading!!!

About the Author

If you like steamy romantic comedy novels with a creative streak, then I'm your girl!

Architect by day, writer by night, I love matcha green tea, chocolate, and books! So many books...

Sign up for my mailing list to get special bonus content, free books, giveaways, and more!

http://alinajacobs.com/mailinglist.html